The Kakos Realm

Book I:
Grinden Proselyte

BY

Christopher D. Schmitz

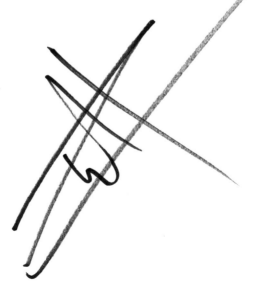

Christopher D. Schmitz

PUBLISHED BY CHRISTOPHER D. SCHMITZ

please visit:
http://www.authorchristopherdschmitz.com

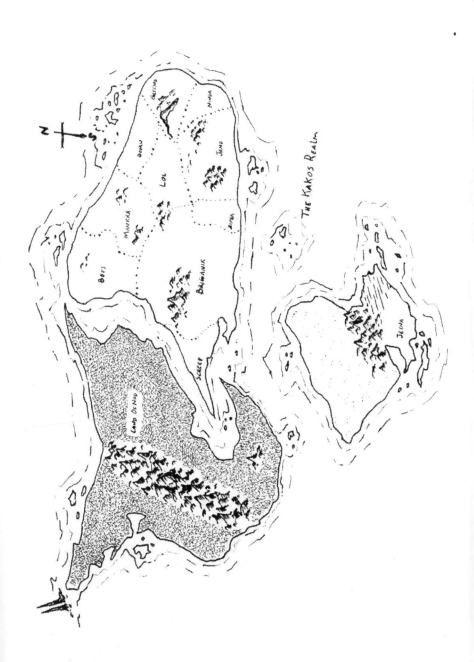

An eldritch, silver cord ties known lands to each other, stretching across the void between the Earth realm and her warped sister. Spanning the vast firmament above, and nestled within the lunic umbrae, a thin stream of water, mere molecules wide, would appear insignificant if discovered. That connector remains the last link between the agathos and the kakos: a portal between realms and flooded by the judgment of ages past.

κακος (kakos):
bad, wicked, depraved, injurious, worthless, harmful

PROLOGUE

The campfire lapped at the crisp, night air like a thousand hungry tongues. Insects buzzed as glowing embers rose upon hot air currents; the hot ash twinkled above the two nearby men.

"My brother, let me pass on all that I know of the outside world."

"What do you mean, Nhoj?" Beyond the jungle vines and verdant greenery, torches lit the distant community. Voices stirred the night, eliciting chirps and trills from creatures in the trees.

Bathed in light, Nhoj continued the discussion. "It is true what they say about me in the village. I am leaving."

"But no one has ever returned from the journey!"

"I know that, Pheros. And I have studied this subject far more than any other in our land. But, the Mighty One who Karoz told us of has spoken to me."

"The angel succumbed to the demonic Gathering thousands of years ago. How can you be so sure that…"

"Do not doubt Him. *I am called, as were those who went before me*, and my calling is unique. Unlike the others, I *know* that I will die; I have seen my death. Yet I will fulfill a greater purpose." Nhoj nodded to the fire, as if he knew his life would somehow spark up a new blaze. "While the Elders urge our brethren to sit, I urge you to find malcontentment—the very same kind that landed me out here: exiled from the village.

"Time dwindles and the end is near. Watch for men from the east; they bear salvation and truth."

"But what of your family, brother?"

"You know the law. Please do as expected. I ask this of you because you are the only brother that I trust, untainted by the Elders' complacency. I know I can trust you to live a life in my stead. Raise my children properly. Tell them their father pursued a higher calling. Promise me this."

"I promise!"

Nhoj thrust a tattered, bound book into Pheros' hands. "This is my collection of notes. I have compiled all that I know about the fallen ones in the lands beyond. The ones we fled so long ago and the ones I go to even now. Sources vary, but much of this came from Karoz himself, or the writings of Elders from his era.

"Much of the information must be outdated. Some history may have changed, since historical records are inclined to shift with each new age. But there is far more in this tome than the fathers are willing to teach us. Keep it secret."

Pheros cracked the manuscript open. His brother's familiar scrawls covered the pages. Many of the sentences contained incomplete thoughts, or random, relevant passages pulled from common sayings or the archives of the Elders. His eyes scrolled greedily over the script.

The sciences abound. Intricate physics behind mysticism have been well studied; alchemists and apothecaries are widespread beyond the great barriers. Most men have not delved the theological darkness of our lost brethren... so many hang in balance, enslaved by the wicked sciences.

Our brothers do believe in the ancient myths regarding the realms of Earth. Legend tells of our sister land, and their all-powerful God, Yahweh, whose faithful battle the Baals. Few truly believe those stories as fact, however; "men believe in what they can experience," (according to the moglob herder I spoke to, for which I am exiled). "Those stories were invented to amuse children or to entertain around campfires." Few men observe ancient religion which pays homage to any deity other than self (except those who know of the moglobs, that is).

According to those myths, the God Yahweh created Earth with its ground and sky and all therein; he also created mankind: humans. Those myths say that they were created in Yahweh's likeness. That detail of the story perhaps hurts its credibility. After all, humans are generally regarded as weak when compared with the races of orcs, ogres, trolls, and others of the ekthroic races—the non-humans. How humanity ever survived after the Great War is a mystery. Nothing is sacred; life is a cheap commodity purchased by the wealthy.

There was not always war. War did not come until the breaking of the truce in ancient times, after the flood and before the formation of the Gathering.

Our mythos explains the origins of this place. Yahweh, ruler of everything, created Earth and dwelled in a place called Eden, alongside of His creation, man. Sometime before the Earth's creation, however, He had personally created the supernatural beings, one by one; of note especially were the angels.

Yahweh had created them because He desired beings who He could commune with. He desired relationship above all else.

Luciferian Legend claims that He used the extent of His infinite power and created His better. Yahweh created hay-lale', whose ambition exceeded even the glory of his own creator.

hay-lale' chose to shine bright, displaying his power to all his kin—brighter at times than even Yahweh. Meanwhile, Yahweh remained on his throne and reveled in the praise given by the created angelic host under hay-lale's direction.

Yahweh held palaver with hay-lale' to ask him why he shone more brightly than He who had made him.

"It is only to give all the more glory to you, my King, and show all how you have blessed me beyond measure."

These words are attributed to the angel Karoz during his appearance at the beginning of our tribe:
"But Yahweh knew hay-lale's heart. The angel was haughty. This displeased Yahweh, for He was the Master and hay-lale's displays affronted Him."

From the Luciferian Origins:
Resentment overtook hay-lale', who believed himself superior; he proclaimed that he would strike out on his own. Making a spectacle of his power and of his glory, he persuaded one third of the angelic host to accompany him as he formed a coup against the Master.

Earth, at that time, was still in perfect harmony, as Yahweh had created it. The condition of the Earth realm, however, disturbed hay-lale'.

Men in those days were mindless automatons designed to watch over the creatures of Earth and tend Yahweh's garden: Eden. This broke hay-lale's heart, for the poor humans were nothing more than flesh machines designed to manage Yahweh's Earthly affairs...

Taking action, hay-lale' disguised himself as a reptile and snuck into Eden, undetected by Yahweh's forces. hay-lale' approached the humans and offered them freedom, showing them how violating the one true law which Yahweh bestowed upon them would unshackle them from the fetters of ignorance and impotence. Eating the fruit of the forbidden tree would make them gods themselves; man could unlock their true potential as demi-gods.

Enraged, Yahweh condemned the serpent. He cursed the ground and the race of men, who now possessed their own minds. Humans, created in Yahweh's own image, could now achieve immeasurable potential, fulfill that image in its fullness, and chase godhood.

But then, before the days of Mahalaleel, great grandson of Seth, hay-lale' created this place, this realm and all her lands. Contesting with Yahweh, hay-lale' bartered for limited permissions to create from the ex nihilo. In the likeness of Earth, he crafted a similar, superior realm, but with his own special improvements. He created many animals and creatures, as Yahweh had, but he set his heart towards crafting a grander array. Mixing the images of man with beast, he created more splendid versions indeed.

But very little was original—only shades of what the Creator had made.

Yahweh's prized creation was humankind, made in Yahweh's likeness. In contrast to this, hay-lale' thought to improve on the design that Yahweh had made. hay-lale' created orcs, goblins, ogres, trolls, elves, gnomes, brownies, centaurs, halflings, faeries, and so many others. Most deviously he spawned Lilth, whose life force came not from the spirit of life, but fed on the life of others.

Then, hay-lale' set in place over the lands a web of spiritual leylines and altered physics. He instilled types of magic that could be tapped into through rites, ritual, and secret knowledges.

hay-lale' gloated to Yahweh that his creation was better. His citizens had authority to weave; they crafted supernatural magics, despite mortal flesh, and drew upon sources of mystic empowerment condemned on Earth.

Then, hay-lale' opened a supernatural pathway between the two realms so mankind might escape from Yahweh's curses. In response to this, Yahweh posted his warriors, mighty cherubim, at the entrance to this path, preventing humanity from entering the new lands.

Enraged, hay-lale' held council with Yahweh, entreating him to reopen the path between realms. Appealing to His ego, hay-lale' struck a bet with Yahweh, arguing that the humans could now, after the giving of knowledge through the sin at Eden, make a choice for themselves which was better. Yahweh agreed that to give mankind complete freedom of choice, they must be allowed to pick their own realm.

"Let it be their own decision and let the consequences be theirs alone," said Yahweh.

11

And thus, hay-lale' reopened the gateway between realms and allowed the men of Earth to enter and settle these lands. Word on Earth quickly spread; this was a land without thistle or thorn. With so many new beings, this place possessed treasures and sciences impossible on Earth. The Luciferian texts drip with poison honey.

From our histories:
These words are copied from the Book of Karoz. (I admit to some of the foolishness for which the elders accused me. I did steal, and then copied passages from the sacred book, but it was returned.)

Discord soon grew among man; humans had foolishly brought with them the seeds of thorns from the curse and they spread through both worlds. Those humans were a malcontent bunch, and some of them returned to Earth with new knowledge of magics, demonologies, and idol worship. They'd gained a sense of freedom from Yahweh and grown more perilously wicked than the line of Seth ever thought possible.

What these humans truly took with them was a new standard of conduct learned in hay-lale's realm. They had learned from the haughty demonstrations of the elves and other ekthro. Humanity found an attitude of self-elevation and a view of personal superiority which helped the transients rise above their Sethaic peers.

These people brought fantastic stories to tell about the folks in their sister land. Through the men that decided to return, stories of the arrayed creatures in this foreign realm came into common knowledge. Some ekthro were even smuggled through the western gate (and possibly the fabled path through Tartarus—but such a thing sounds too far-fetched to be true) and began to taint Earth.

The ekthro, our realm's original inhabitants, formed peace and prosperous trade with mankind, though others of them discovered a preference for the taste of human flesh and often bartered for the lives of men. In those times a truce existed between the humans and most of the ekthro; a law of equality had been instilled in all through the relative newness of the day. In the early history, pre-existing prejudices had yet to present themselves.

Peace prevailed through laws of tolerance. Several ruling demons, hay-lale's chosen, were appointed to make decisions as needed; these demon overlords were given the greatest access to the leylines so they could manipulate the powers of the realm, punishing or blessing those they saw fit, and all in accordance with hay-lale's grand plans. (These original Baals fell to the mighty dragon prior to the formation of a new council—Nhoj.)

hay-lale' took up a new mantle: the pursuer of light and champion of the oppressed race of man. He vowed to battle against Yahweh and fight against the Creator's curse. He called himself the Bright One, revealing his highest name to these men: Lucifer.

From the Luciferian catechisms:
Yahweh, though, was forced to form a new plan. Having apparently lost their contest, a deep yearning manifested within the souls of men on Earth. hay-lale' took pride in knowing that he'd created the more desirable place. This realm's very existence transformed the hearts of man far beyond what Yahweh expected.

The new cultures, traditions, and knowledge brought transmitted back to Earth spurned Yahweh; He grew so incensed that he flooded the entire Earth, killing the entire race of man save a select, fearful few. This flood spilled through the pathway between the two realms, creating the seas that now surround the lands of this realm; islands formed and water divided the three continents. Yahweh's flood killed many in this realm as well, wiping out entire species from hay-lale's menagerie.

Another passage from the Book of Karoz:

Unbeknownst to Lucifer's loyal followers, this place, with its interwoven, magical leylines threading like supernatural spider webs, was in fact a trap. Even as Lucifer created it, his eyes were set only on the future of Earth. He knew that seducing the mortals of Earth with this place would hamper the plans of Yahweh—speed up the potential End of Days and force Yahweh's hand before He could launch a redemptive mission for the wayward. Lucifer's goals were always for Earth. He left behind traditions that would continually glorify him and corrupt those humans trapped in his land: the lies of the Luciferian Order became the only religious option for those whose hearts yearned for the things a sacred calling provides.

According to Luciferian tradition, Yahweh's new plans for Earth threatened this realm's very existence, and so Lucifer went away to defend it—and is even now struggling against Yahweh's more numerous forces to keep this land free and safe. They believe that the forces of Yahweh seek only to come on the wings of wrath and destroy them utterly.

The demon overlords who were installed as overseers were also barred from Earth by the waters. They too were left behind, trapped in the realm of their master. With the severing of the realms, they soon turned on each other; the chaos erupted in the Great War. Ancient truces were violated by conflict; treaties ceased; every man and ekthro was left to his own devices as the overseers formed warring factions amongst themselves in the firmaments above.

Formal agreements and laws passed away. Luciferians wrote a new moral law, "If it harms none other, do whatever ye may." The law shifted to, "whatever seems good to you, do it." It was but a subtle shift, and yet enough to justify any conceivable action as long as you had the steel and fortitude to back it.

These myths are told to children, human and ekthro alike. It is well-known legend, but it is sacrosanct to religious fanatics and monks of the apocryphal cause. Religious fervor faded towards seldom-practiced faith, though its supporters gain political power and influence abroad, waxing and waning like the wind as generations rise and fall.

In truth, this world has been abandoned by its creator, shaped by its own inhabitants, and manipulated by the powerful and the selfish. The ruling demons have long since forsaken their origins and often war amongst themselves. Each strives to become a ruler—even a god, in his own right.

Hearts of men are easily swayed and undeniably fickle, but every man needs something to put his trust in. What we adhere to in this lost and kakos realm is the only true light in the darkness.

15

"But the Book of Karoz bears the strongest reasons for why we have separated ourselves," Pheros pleaded. "There is too much evil beyond our borders. Surely it is madness to stand against the corrupt and the ekthro!"

"An error, brother. We were never meant to be idle—to cloister and hide. We were meant to burn like logs on a fire, thus shining through the night."

"There is no dissuading you, not even certain death?"

"I have foreseen my own death. It does not trouble me because I know what comes after it. I am content to endure the difficult mission for the sake of my calling... even if my role should be less glorious than I could ever imagine."

Nhoj stood and embraced his brother for the last time. "Keep my book and honor your word."

Pheros nodded pensively. "Godspeed, brother."

Through the darkness, Nhoj called over his shoulder, "Watch for men from the east, and do not mourn me long."

CHAPTER ONE

"Tonight I will murder the King of Jand in his own bedchamber." The vehemence of those spittle-flecked words convinced the nearby trio of Rashnir's sincerity. Kevin locked eyes with Rashnir. His proclamation of hate lingered like a foul odor. Rashnir stood as Kevin wondered aloud, thoughtfully tapping his chin. "Is this hatred," he asked, "Or is it justice?"

"I don't know that justice truly exists," Rashnir said. "I'll leave that for *you* to decide, Holy Man. I am a man of action and a man of the sword; I go to do what must be done. I will return and thank you nonetheless. You have fulfilled your end of our bargain."

Rashnir bowed as he threw on the cloak Kevin recently provided him with and strapped a short sword to his hip. "You have given me the things required to purchase my vengeance; moreso by giving me your ear and restoring my confidence than the use of your sword. I could not continue living without my honor; believe the tale I told you or not. You have helped restore a small piece of my honor."

"You *do* care about justice," Kevin mused as he looked at the warrior's hands. Those strong hands were covered in thick, ugly scars where the vile leaders of the monarchy had intentionally burned him with hot irons.

"I will be back within two days, or else I am dead." His demeanor struck a solemn tone. Rashnir had nothing to lose. The only thing Rashnir truly valued any longer was his honor. In that moment, his fervor and reckless abandon made him the most dangerous person in the country. Only two potential outcomes remained. He would regain his honor or he would die. Either option was acceptable to the warrior.

Rashnir looked at Kevin and the holy man's two companions. A hesitant trust had formed between them.

"We will wait for you here in the city. We'll stay at the Green Serpent Inn." Kevin nodded, "Two days."

The two bodyguards looked at each other, as if they disagreed with what had just transpired. They stood a full head taller than their ward, and Kevin wasn't short in stature for a human. Agree or not, the two followed Kevin as he departed in the direction of the Green Serpent.

Rashnir watched them depart and silently reflected on how he'd arrived here. He was penniless. But a few years ago he'd been rich and affluent. A year prior to that, he had been equally destitute. Beginning his journey of vengeance, his thoughts wandered back to the beginning—before King Harmarty… even before *her*.

***

In the dark, young Rashnir sat on his bunk and rubbed away the gunk crusted near his eyes. He didn't bother to light a candle; the sun would be up soon anyway and he would need to depart for the fields where the heat would soon beat down on him. Darkness suited him perfectly fine for now.

He did not look forward to the chores of the estate, laboring all day. Rashnir aspired to much more than a slave's life. He loathed the plow animals and hated the whole farm. Having learned about political jockeying from the farm's owner, Mallow, he disliked only statecraft with greater passion. In the country of Ninda, politics and farming were tied closer than bedfellows.

Rashnir had to muster all of his strength to rise from the sagging, second-hand cot that had been his bed for so many years. He still felt yesterday's tiredness in his bones; his master worked him harder now, ever since his last term as an indentured servant expired.

Dressing himself in a worn-thin tunic and torn pants, he covered the strange, sepia colored birthmark that resembled a matched set of towers with his shirt. Rashnir walked to the paneless window and pulled the rough, leather hides away. Sunlight ripped through the cool darkness, providing him with a clear view of the morning. The rays would only bring him another day of toil mingled with salty sweat.

Barely a person, Rashnir possessed such little status. In fact, he had no real home or traceable origins. He was a citizen of nowhere; he worked his master's fields, hoping to scratch out enough money to someday leave the drudgery of this farm life behind him.

Soon, he would have to pull on his boots and trudge out to the fields. For Rashnir, every moment of rest was cherished. He had a few moments left; the sun had not yet crested the hilltop.

Rashnir sat and leaned upon his wooden stool. The wooden wall, made of old orchard branches, creaked under the strain. He gnawed a hunk of dried meat and drank. Reflecting, he thumbed through a tightly bound journal. The book wasn't his; he could not even read. It once belonged to a man he barely remembered—a man who was the closest thing to family that Rashnir had ever known. A fellow slave who had once bunked with him, and had a knack for storytelling, sometimes read to him from the journal and recounted the man's life.

Despite the current situation, Rashnir's nineteen years of life seemed charmed. Without uncanny luck, the ekthro should have devoured him long ago. Sometimes, though, he felt that might've been preferable over enslavement.

Born to a slave, a dismal destiny awaited him: doomed at birth. His slave camp belonged to a group of trolls. The poor captives had all been either kidnapped from nearby lands or raided from some other slave camp by the hideous brutes. The latter being the case, he would likely have ended his life in a large pot of erfwin, a trollish stew made from human flesh. Rashnir's mother gave birth enroute to a new slaving colony. Along with several hundred other miserable slaves in that cluster, his origins could likely be traced to Zipha, a country known for slavery and troll infestation.

Wanting a better life for her son, Rashnir's mother convinced a few trusted men to form an escape plan. They risked their lives for a chance at freedom; death was inevitable as a slave—especially if trolls were involved. They were all destined for the erfwin pots, in the end. The bold group waited until daylight, when the trolls were forced to take shelter from the sun, or else turn to stone. The travel between colonies gave them their best chance to flee.

With the infant harnessed securely, the group waited until their dayside guardians, the trolls' hellhounds, seemed the most inattentive. When the signal went up, the group fled as quickly and as silently as possible.

The three-headed hounds could smell the fear on the escapees. They hunted them down and tore their prey to shreds. Only one slave escaped, with the help of a woodsman who dispatched the pursuing beasts. In no condition to care for an infant, the slave entrusted Rashnir to the hunter.

Until he was young, the hunter who brought the child home cared for him. Rashnir was still a child when the hunter's home mysteriously caught fire; only Rashnir survived.

He thumbed through the pages, upset by fate and plagued by regret. He couldn't even remember the hunter's name. Although another of Mallow's servants sometimes read him passages from the hunter's diary, nowhere did it ever mention the journalist's name.

The hunter, a bachelor, had taken Rashnir as a legal heir. When the house burned and the hunter perished, Rashnir inherited debts as well as assets—the former far outweighed the latter. He had no choice but to pay off the debt as an indentured servant; he wasn't quite eight years old when that happened. He could not survive debtors' prison at that age. Ever since the fire, he'd been indentured to the Nindan Lord Mallow.

Although Rashnir's servanthood contract had recently ended he had very little money and so he remained voluntarily in Mallow's employ. Rashnir's years of hard work greatly increased production on Mallow's farm; his determination to succeed gave way to increased profits for his master.

Mallow flaunted his position as an heir and Lord of Ninda. Besides making him a powerful and wealthy man, his title provided him those political connections and resources needed to further his own personal agendas. Politics in Ninda were tricky, but they were a way of life for the Lords and Sectional Rulers in the agrarian country.

As soon as possible, Rashnir planned to leave and join the Mercenaries' Guild in the west. He had a passion for battle—a love of the thought that determination and training could bring personal victory; he would live or he would die but it would be through his own efforts and to his own gain. In the guild he would have the freedom he craved, the opportunity to carve his own destiny. The only problem was that recruits were required to provide their own equipment and front the money for dues and training—too many previous, foolhardy adventurers had lost their lives because of arrogance and ignorance and so the guild required their dues up front. Nonetheless, the guild was a chance for glory, profit, and an opportunity to slake the wanderlust of youth.

Rashnir wondered if he would ever make enough money to leave. When his status shifted to paid employee, Mallow began charging rent for his hovel; he charged a stipend for food; none of the prices were reasonable. Mallow clearly hoped to leverage Rashnir into signing on for another term of service. Mallow's fees rose every time Rashnir resisted the farmer's pressure for a new contract.

The Nil-Ma farm, Mallow's birthright, was a very profitable district, regularly producing an over-abundance of sheep. Every part of the sheep could be used in some sort of regional product made by subsidiaries owned by Mallow's corrupt family. The success of the Nil-Ma lands was rumored to come from a magic artifact, a supernatural item that caused the sheep to reproduce far more often than normal. Farmers who stayed in Mallow's good graces bred sheep that frequently gave birth to twins or triplets and far exceeded the live birthrate of any other farm district in the country.

Lamb was the most widely consumed food source in their region. Breeding stock was also milked and sold along with the meat for kaboshalged recipes. The popular delicacy, young sheep boiled in its own mother's milk, was a favorite of many. The original recipe called for goat, actually, but they weren't nearly as populous as sheep in the region.

Rashnir had no desire for it. Its stench offended him and he nearly vomited the only time he ever tried the traditional kaboshalged.

Rashnir shook the memory away as the phantom taste of bile crept up his throat. He ran a straight razor over his chin. Then, taking one more draught from his water bladder, Rashnir stepped outside into the morning air. He stretched in the burgeoning sunlight and cracked his joints.

A gentle breeze accompanied the sun's virgin rays. The draft gently blew through Rashnir's thick, black hair. He was of medium build and with taught, farm-forged muscles; more than muscle, an inner drive like a fire that fueled him onwards was what made him strong.

He put a hand to his brow, shielding his eyes from the sun. There were no clouds today. Rashnir squinted, looking towards Mallow's estate. He expected a list of daily tasks to come from the main house servant.

Rashnir hoped that Mallow might be called to some political function this morning. He just didn't have the stomach today for him; time passed more quickly when Mallow wasn't around trying to micro-manage the farm with a reckless ignorance that overrode the experience of the seasoned farmhands regardless of the practicality of their methods.

An approaching silhouette glinted in the shimmering light. It swaggered indicatively. Unfortunately for Rashnir, Mallow had come out today to oversee his operations.

Mallow owned a sadistic streak: a trait too common in those blessed enough to inherit wealth. He once laughed himself into a stupor after tipping some nearby raiders off to an escaped slave's direction.

The red-faced farmer waddled up to Rashnir and put a fat hand on the younger man's shoulder. Any attempt at fatherly affection was certainly wasted on the orphan. There was too much history between them for that now. He tried lacing false sweetness into his tone. "So, how about we discuss renewing your contract, and then you can take the day off?"

"You already know my answer, Mallow. There will be no new contract. All I want is to get out of here." Rashnir looked past him, gazing at the horizon, avoiding Mallow's practiced, salesman stare. Nothing could make Rashnir stay and the continued asking only insulted the former slave.

Mallow groaned a disgruntled sigh, and started rambling on about how he much needed the young man. None of the other workers were as productive, he claimed. Rashnir refused eye contact. He refused to give him an opening or even feign interest and he eventually turned his back on the rancher.

Rashnir jumped in surprise when he heard the sound of a hard object impacting on flesh. He whirled around finding Mallow doubled over with an arrow lodged solidly in his sternum.

Toppling, the farmer put a hand on the sod and gently lowered himself to sitting position. Bright blood seeped from the wound; it bubbled pink, indicating a lung wound. He was careful not to bump the arrow as he crumpled to the ground.

Frozen, Rashnir watched in disbelief. Someone in a nearby thicket ululated with a battle cry; another one echoed it from behind a haystack. More than a dozen men approached, dressed and ready for battle.

Mallow lay on the ground gasping for air; the red stain on his gaudy tunic slowly expanded. His face wore a strange collogue of emotion: shock, fear, humor, appreciation, dread, anger, despair—the entire gamut.

Rashnir took a step towards him, unsure of what to do. He was torn between his conscience and a burning sense of righteous indignation. Deep down, he wanted to watch the man squirm in agony, but he also felt pity for him

Mallow bowed his head, peered over the fat rolls on his neck and chest, and examined the wound. Demise was likely. In a fit of morbid insanity, Mallow burst out laughing; he struggled to keep his eyes open and permitted them to roll back into his head. Still chuckling, he gasped, "I think I'm dead." The group of barbarians surrounded Mallow and Rashnir, oblivious to the rancher's labored, gurgling gasps. He writhed on the ground like an agitated worm.

"Mallow, Son of Nil-Ma, we are here to destroy you and your farm," one man declared. He procured a piece of parchment from his satchel as another man bent down to hold Mallow's eyes open; he forced him to look at the parchment. "We have been hired to terminate all that you own and to kill you, Mallow. This is the contract before you, drawn up between the combined farms of Teed and Rivalf, who have agreed to finance your assassination, and the Narsh Barbarian sect of the Mercenary's Guild in Grinden. This is a legal deal, sealed and ratified by the Lords and Sectional Rulers on the Parliamentary Council. Bad for you but good for us: the local government also hates you and has legalized your murder." The death herald smiled as if he took some small glee in his job. "In fact, a few other farms even kicked in a little extra commission."

Each of the barbarians stood muscular and tall, though not all were fit and trim; success in plunder had led to abundance in the waistlines of many. Each one carried some type of wicked looking weapon, mostly battle-axes and swords. The one who did all of the speaking carried a large war hammer and slung a longbow across his back, making it likely that he launched the condemning arrow lodged so deeply within Mallow's chest.

Another mercenary bent over and stuffed herbs in Mallow's mouth. The remedial spices roused him from his death-slumber. Mallow's eyes refocused. A fourth warrior put a dagger to Rashnir's throat from behind. "Sorry, kid. Slaves are technically possessions, in Ninda. Everything that lives must die."

The leader addressed his contract, "If you wish to plead for mercy, Mallow, I would be happy to hear it. We get an added bonus if you scream and beg. By that, I simply mean that it amuses us." He chuckled.

Summoning every last iota of spite within him, Mallow bellowed out, "You can take that contract and—"

The mercenary grabbed the shaft of the arrow that pierced him and wiggled it; the Nindan Lord cried like a child. The barbarians laughed as if this were a game. Rashnir had never seen such a look on Mallow's face. Only the herbal drugs kept him conscious for the barbarians to toy with. The mercenary turned to face Rashnir.

"No hard feelings. A contract is a contract," he said, loosening his sword at the hilt.

"Wait!" cried Rashnir, holding up his hands to ward off any aggressors, acutely aware of the blade at his throat.

The man holding him from behind positioned his strong grip in a different hold to make for an easy, clean kill.

"I am not a slave!"

"Sure you're not. Don't worry; it'll be over in a second."

Mallow's eyes widened, the irony of the situation amusing him. "Ha, ha! Die, slave boy!" he managed to choke through the blood and foam dripping from his mouth. He splattered flecks of bloody spittle as he laughed.

"Mallow is such a well-known liar," shot Rashnir, "that surely, by his own admission, he's just told you that I am a free man. In fact, just this morning he attempted to renew my indenturing contract for another term of service. I've refused to be a slave to anything or anyone since my debt was paid. I am a Nindan freeman, not an indentured servant, nor a slave."

"Liar!" Mallow screeched through the pain; he was hell-bent on taking Rashnir with him as his life expired. "He is my slave, my possession! I have owned him and his family for two generations; he's worked these lands since he was a boy."

The mercenary who held him checked the usual places for any sort of brand or identifying slave mark, finding none. "You have proof that your contract has expired?" asked the warrior who held the dagger, paying no attention to the nobleman dying at their feet.

"Yes, in my hut."

"You had better gather it and leave then. This place will be picked clean by mid-afternoon." The mercenaries relinquished him and returned to their work: the slow execution of Mallow.

"No, no, no. He re-signed it last week!" Mallow argued, admitting that Rashnir was not a multi-generational slave, hoping that indentured servants were also slated for destruction, even though they were not technically legal property.

"Oh really," he heard the leader say, as Rashnir fled. "Why then do you argue for his death? If you hated him so much, I would not think you would have re-hired him."

Rashnir hurriedly gathered his meager belongings and departed the only home he could remember. No, not a home: it had been a place to lay his head for these last fourteen years.

Rashnir speedily saddled Nikko, the finest horse that Mallow owned. He looked over his shoulders to see if any of the mercenaries saw him steal the horse; it might have been a part of their plunder and he hoped that he could get away undiscovered. Nikko's ears twitched; Mallow shrieked somewhere in the near distance.

Mounting the beast, Rashnir guided it through the barn doors. He raced beyond the stables on his horse and headed west, towards the Homeland village of the Nil-Ma district. A few days hard riding would bring him to a

THE KAKOS REALM: GRINDEN PROSELYTE

place of neutrality, Grinden—a place neither sanctioned nor owned by either of the two neighboring countries on whose borders it sat. In a few days he could arrive in the free city, home of the mercenary guild, where he knew a world of opportunity would await him.

***

Rashnir shook and cleared his head of the memory. He needed to focus on the task at hand as he rode north with a heart full of cold fury. He had a monarch to murder, and *this* time he would succeed in the task.

Chapter Two

Rashnir crept from his hermitage back into the city of Grinden by a relatively untraveled path. He kept his identity concealed and took no chances with his discovery. His resolve had hardened like baked clay; nothing would stop him from consummating the murderous plan that consumed his mind.

Near Grinden's northern edge, he meandered near a busy tavern. Weaving in and out of the horses hitched nearby, Rashnir found one that made little fuss when handled by a stranger and he quickly untethered it.

He patted the horse down and made friends with the beast, reassured the animal. Then, taking the reins, he climbed into the saddle. After making sure no one cast a suspicious eye in his direction, Rashnir ambled out of sight and then galloped towards the capital of Jand.

Murder was not the only thing on his mind, however. The trip was long, and his mind reverted back to his story, the same tale he'd just related to Kevin, the stranger from a strange land. Rashnir's was no campfire tale; this was the truth.

***

Rashnir's hang-over warmed his ears and beat him in the brain. In the ranks of the new recruits at the mercenaries' guild, he'd made friends quickly. At the guildhouse, raw men were subjected to grueling, punishing training meant to sift out the weak and uncommitted and strengthen the remainder, forming an elite fighting force. Later, based on individual talents they would be drafted into the various houses of the guild which made up the teams available for hire. Solid recruits were always needed because of the constant skirmishes along the trade routes; mercenaries were often hired as guards for shipping caravans as well. There was no better place through which to ship along the trade routes than Grinden, home of the guild, and the mercenary house had grown out of necessity and had logically sprung up at the hub of the trade routes.

The former slave had survived his first two weeks at the guild after escaping from Ninda with a purse-full of gold lifted from one of Mallow's hidden stashes. He and his newfound comrades, all mercenary recruits, enjoyed the wild nightlife available in the city. The nearby hostelry district had a reputation for strong ale and friendly women, and they catered mainly to guild members.

Usually, the group of initiates hung out at the local tavern near the edge of Grinden, The Doused Phoenix. The Phoenix was not far from the barracks; their location enhanced the amount of business done with the guild—chiefly, it lessened the distance required to carry inebriated friends who'd drunk themselves into a stupor. The pub gave them the privilege of hearing war stories from some of the more seasoned, and pickled, warriors.

But last night saw more than stories. Last night had been different.

Rashnir's thoughts churned in his head. His mind seemed to grind painfully against the back of his eyeballs; his brain didn't want to recall the previous night's events. The haze, resulting from a binge of various liquids, clouded his memory like the poison fog that sometimes crept over Ruht Lake.

Lying there, his thoughts grew more lucid and he began remembering. Last night, one of his new friends had died and he'd killed another man in vengeance. Ironically, Rashnir had also gone from rags to riches and escalated his mercenary rank. He grimaced in his bed when he recalled the announcement: he'd been promoted to the upper levels of a guild house.

Rashnir's friend, Nilmun, had gotten up to use the privy. He had to skirt a raucous arm-wrestling match going on at one of the tables nearby; betting men had lined up around the contest to make wagers on the outcome. As Nilmun headed towards the exit, foot traffic got the better of his booze-addled feet and knocked Rashnir's drunken friend into one of the match's participants.

The large man Nilmun crashed into lost his concentration; his struggling opponent quickly seized the opportunity and stole a victory. Cheers erupted from some moneychangers, groans echoed from others. Nilmun had caused an upset, in more ways than one.

Furious, the loser kicked his chair out from under him and knocked Rashnir's friend to the ground. Shaking a sore wrist, he whirled around with an alcohol-induced bellow.

"Who did that? Who cost Mind his victory?" He demanded an answer. Standing to his feet, he towered over the horrified, and much smaller, recruit. "You broke my winning streak! Do you know who I am, whelp? Do you know what I do to people who make me mad?"

Mind was unquestionably the largest warrior in the mercenary guild. He stood a head taller than any other mercenary; usually those were recruited to the Narsh Barbarians Guild. His arms were larger around than most men's' waists. He flung his dark hair, overdue for a cutting, over his should and sneered with his upturned, pointy nose. Mind's eyes narrowed to slits; already close together, they gave him a beady-eyed look of focused determination. Scars and other minor badges of courage awarded by combat visibly crisscrossed his forearms, decorating the successful warrior.

"I am so sorry…" Nilmun interrupted the raging drunk.

"NAME!" Mind demanded.

"Nilmun. But, it wasn't my fault, I was pushed by…"

"I am second in command of Rogis' Rangers. As such I have the rank and power to find you guilty of assaulting a superior. I will now exact your punishment." Mind grabbed Nilmun around the scruff of his collar and dragged him through the doors with considerable ease. He began abusing every square unit of his body with his massive fists and feet. A crowd gathered, drunkenly cheering him on in the torch light.

What started as a wild spectacle grew increasingly grim as Mind pounded on him with his mammoth knuckles. Nilmun tried to block the blows to his head; Mind beat his kidneys and midsection. Nilmun moved his hands; Mind unleashed bone-cracking blows to the face.

After a few minutes, the multitude grew as solemn as Nilmun's friends. Rashnir and the others watched from the crowd's edge in complete silence, disgusted. Mind did not stop; he was like a machine, arms moving without thought to administer blows. He'd fallen into a zealous, drunken fury and no one dared speak against the injustice he actively committed, too afraid that they also might incur his wrath.

Shortly, Nilmun's choked pleas subsided and he stopped trying to protect himself from any blows. He no longer cried out, but the beating continued; he'd long ago crumpled in complete submission. The only sound was the grunting and cursing of Mind as he laid strike after strike upon Nilmun's failing body; not a sound whispered in the audience.

Nilmun was unrecognizable, except maybe as carrion. Mind gradually slowed. In an effort to end his show with a big finale, he summoned all of his anger, brought up his right leg, and dropped his heavy boot like a hammer on the young man's head, crushing Nilmun's skull with a powerful heel-kick.

The crowd remained eerily quiet as the awkward silence seized them; they corporately disapproved of the severity of his actions. In his stupor, the massive warrior had fully unleashed himself on the smaller, green trainee; the night's fun had been tainted by recklessness and loss. Mind didn't likely remember what he was even doing outside; he only knew that he was beating on someone and he enjoyed it. In the drunken revelry and pursuit of self-gratification, he did not notice the silence; drooling with glee, he glowed with self-appreciation, mumbling words of affirmation to himself.

Rashnir's companions passed a bottle of potent liquor between themselves, mourning their recently made, and quickly lost, friend. As Rashnir accepted the bottle, a blindingly pure fury boiled up inside of him. His eyes burned dark and hollow as a maniac, red rage took him over and sent him into a frenzy. In a moment of surreality, Rashnir seemed to step outside of himself and watch as his rage translated into action.

Mind threw his sweaty, lank and disheveled hair behind his shoulders. He took a step towards his comrades and turned briefly to spit on the motionless form of the man he'd just broken. He laughed and accepted a tinted flask of distilled fluid.

Rashnir watched in a tunnel vision induced by fury as Mind raised the flask and drenched his face in victory. The brute aimed for his mouth, but liquor spilled inches above his lips; sloshing the drink all over his head; it soaked through the collar of his tunic. Rashnir's ears buzzed as he snapped and flew into action; he could no longer hear Mind cackling in celebration—only the buzzing of the white-hot rage in his ears. Rashnir grabbed a nearby torch and walked up behind Mind. Grim faced, Rashnir thumped him on the back, his intentions very clear: Rashnir was picking a fight.

The behemoth turned to face him. Rashnir definitely had his attention; he flashed him an obscene gesture to ensure that Mind understood Rashnir's insult.

"I don't know you little man, so you'd best have a good reason for bothering me, unless you want to end up like our friend, Nimrod, over there," Mind muttered.

"*Nilmun* was a friend of *mine* you arrogant piece of trash! Not yours! Maybe this will prepare you for the fires of the eternal pits!" The only reaction that Mind's distilled wits could muster was a look of total surprise.

His harsh words flung into the void, Rashnir inhaled a mouthful of potent drink from the flask his friends passed him. He spewed the liquid forth, through the torch, and shot a fireball out. The inferno hit on target and doused Mind with liquid flames.

The fireball ignited Mind's head and chest; a lick of flame picked up a trail where Mind's clothes had soaked with booze. It shot down his arms and into his own flask. The celebratory bottle exploded in flames and glassine shrapnel, blasting the meat off Mind's fingers and leaving only stubby, mangled digits behind in a charred mess. The serrated flak ripped up the forearm of his sword hand before lodging jagged shards in his side.

Mind shrieked and tried in vain to run from the pyre that he had become. The crowd stood and stared in disbelief as the screaming human torch flailed around within the enclosed semi-circle. Even Rashnir stood shocked at the extremity of his own actions, though rage and adrenaline still fueled his trembling limbs. He did not feel any compassion for the burning man; he would give no mercy to Nilmun's murderer. This monster had just crushed a man's skull for his own amusement.

The fire calmed as it ran out of distilled fuel. Mind's screams turned into hoarse groaning and gasps for air. Trembling, the man fell to his hands and knees; smoking, his shirt had mostly burned away. His hair and eyebrows were incinerated, as were his facial and body hair. Patchy blisters mottled his skin like a shoddy quilt. Flames melted the cartilage of his nose and ears. The stench of burning flesh filled the crisp evening air with sickened taint.

Wheezing, the behemoth stood slowly, defying his condition, "I... will... kill... you... ... You... filthy..."

"Shut your face," Rashnir commanded with a confident authority that his anger empowered him with, "or I will stuff a dead rat into that lipless hole you call a mouth. Do everyone here a favor and never speak again."

With his pride insulted, Mind snarled and charged at Rashnir. The smaller man grabbed his attacker's good wrist and swung a hip into the aggressor's gut. Using the forward momentum, he launched the ogre-sized man over his back and onto the ground. Mind landed flat on his back; he hit so hard that his lungs popped with an audible burst, He'd been winded, hard.

Rashnir quickly spun around upon his heels, still holding Mind's wrist in a firm grasp. As he wheeled around, he broke the pinky finger and the thumb of Mind's good hand; Rashnir came to a guarded position sitting on his opponent's chest. His knees straddled Mind's ribcage. The man tried to rise, but Rashnir jabbed his tensed fingers into the jowly bulge of Mind's neck, almost collapsing the windpipe. In one smooth, fluid motion he brought the palm of his hand back like a slingshot and then brought it crashing down like a dwarven hammer. The blow destroyed the remaining, twisted remnants of Mind's deteriorated nose flinging a mess of bloody goo, bone, and cartilage flecks across the men's faces.

Mind terror-shrieked through the viscous ooze as it slid its way down the back of his throat. Spray flew out from the hole in his face and slicked back Rashnir's hair; chitinous bone chips stuck to his face, pasted there by the bloody ichor.

Rashnir reached around the back of Mind's cranium, grabbing the little tuft of remaining hair by the base of Mind's skull; Rashnir twisted and simultaneously wrenched on Mind's chin. Grunting, Rashnir poured all of his malice into the effort; a loud snap and crunching noise erupted from the crippled mercenary's spine. An unseasoned trainee had just broken the neck of one of the area's greatest warriors.

His frenzy ebbed. Rashnir stood up on shaky legs. In an adrenaline drunk daze, he silently staggered through the bewildered crowd; he was barely able to walk straight. He felt as if he'd just drained five large pints and been spun around in circles. Rashnir could feel the gazes of the crowd on his back as he walked back into the tavern. He'd no sooner dropped his weary body into the same empty seat Mind once occupied when a noise arose: only one noise in the entire tavern, the applause of one man.

Rashnir felt suddenly weary; the endorphins and bloodlust drained from his system and he could barely see beyond the somnolent haze that crowded his vision. It came with very little reaction when he recognized the figure as Rogis, the head of the most prestigious fighting clan in the guild: Rogis' Rangers. This was the man that helped form the mercenary's guild over thirty-five years ago as an effort to supplement his friend, the Jandan King, with an adept fighting force. The guild eventually evolved into the current, independent organization.

He knew he should have been horrified; Rashnir had just killed Rogis' second in command. The mental shock, combined with the sudden after-thought that his revenge could cost him his life, did not leave much room for emotion. The anticipated death actually allowed him a measure of arrogance; hubris would allow him to die nobly, in complete defiance of any enemies he'd just created by killing the ranking officer and renowned warrior.

Rogis casually took the seat facing him, maintaining direct eye contact; the visual probing unnerved Rashnir, who had trouble keeping the mutual gaze through his tunnel vision. Rogis just stared at him until Rashnir shuddered, shaking off the fugue of the ebbing battle-endorphins; he slowly became more lucid as blood-stimulant levels normalized.

The ranger spoke with authority. "You realize that you just killed my right hand guy? In doing so, you assaulted your superior, and wasted two perfectly good flasks of liquor." He quipped almost mirthfully.

Defiant, Rashnir answered, "You forgot to include: avenged the dead for murder and humiliated a cocky fool."

"Nonetheless, serious charges could be brought upon you by Mind's friends. I guarantee that they will come. What would you say to answer them, in your defense?"

"That Mind was a piece of gutter trash and deserved nothing less than he got." Rashnir sank back, still reaching for a noble death. The fact that he'd just sealed his fate began to sink in and settle in the pit of his stomach. He did not want to die, but he felt it better to die with pride today than beg for his life only to be executed tomorrow.

They shared a brief pause, just long enough to make Rashnir squirm, and then Rogis burst out in a booming fit of laughter. The routine sounds of the cabaret resumed: the babbling of barmaids, the clinking of steins, and the empty banter of patrons. As a whole, the cantina resumed regular operations as if nothing out of the ordinary had happened; all assumed Rogis had everything well in hand.

"That he was... that he was indeed," Rogis agreed through short bursts of chortled laughter, "I never liked him either." An immodestly dressed waitress came forward with a couple fresh mugs filled to the brim with the house ale; she set them before the two patrons and smiled lasciviously at Rogis. She bowed away and returned to her duties, keeping a favorable eye on the most gracious tippers, of which Rogis was surely one.

Rogis hefted the glass mug and took a deep draught, as if it were fresh water from a flowing brook. Setting the mug down, he turned his attention back to Rashnir. "There still are, however, the potentially serious repercussions of this event, though not from me," Rogis quickly assured him. "I agree that the man was slime, but the men stayed in step under his command, mostly for fear of his back-hand.

"But, we try to uphold a more noble set of principles within the Rangers, you see. I always had to rein Mind back, and that can be quite taxing; he always took things to the extreme. If it weren't for his skill and massive presence, I would have let him return to the Narsh Barbarians house a long time ago. But, fewer men die when you have the talent, experience, and brute strength like Mind's; it helped everyone prosper. I suppose I'm actually quite pleased to see him dead. I even had thoughts t'ward doin' the deed myself, if my efforts to persuade him back in line didn't work."

"What do you mean?"

Rogis leaned in conspiratorially. "Well, you see, he treated his family like swine; if there's one thing we've got in this forsaken realm, it's our family—they're the real treasure. Mind never was a family man; when he smacked his boys around a while back for losing a good longbow, I knew that he had to die. We're not talking 'bout a little beating, here. T'was more like an attempt to cripple them poor kids."

Rashnir raised an eyebrow.

"I know.. yer thinking, 'You care because?' well half've his kids are probably mine!" Rogis laughed, taking another sip of ale. "At least three of 'em are mine for sure, from his first wife."

Rashnir nodded, listening to the sordid tales a slightly drunk Rogis recounted. He took a courtesy sip of his ale and immediately wished that he hadn't. It was warm and bitter, leaving him with a sour, bile aftertaste in his mouth; as he swallowed dizziness hit him and then quickly passed. He had no idea what he was drinking, but it tasted more expensive than what he'd been drinking with his buddies, earlier. He drank again; there was no sense not to. When a man of Rogis' stature shared an incriminating story, one couldn't be sure of surviving the night.

"So," led in Rashnir, "how do you propose, keeping this whole story in mind, that I avoid these life-threatening consequences?"

"Simple, and not one bit painful neither. You killed my second in command. I will verify that it was an honor-duel fought for possession of his estate and the deal will be complete; it will not be a man killed out of rage, but it will be more like a simple transaction. You merely challenged him to a duel. I will make you my new second in command as well; you'll keep his properties, and I will take care of his family. A mutually beneficial agreement if I ever heard one. I'll act as the witness to the duel and have the legal papers drawn, so there is nothing anyone can say or do."

Rashnir's jaw dropped, slack. He'd just murdered his superior and instead of punishment, he was offered an immediate promotion to one of the highest ranks possible. He'd receive properties, respect, and wealth, too? He could hardly believe it. Shock trumped his apprehension.

Rogis laughed through a frothy mouthful of ale, "You're probably the only sod within a ten-day travel that had the testicular fortitude to even challenge MInd, much less win. The men will respect you because of this, if you accept this position, that is. Especially those whom he mistreated will love you, and there were a great many of them."

Something flashed briefly through Rogis' posture, perhaps a brief chord of worry that Rashnir might not accept the offer. It convinced Rashnir that Rogis was sincere. But then again, a man as seasoned as Rogis could be manipulating him; Rashnir chose to believe that the old bear was sincere.

"You've got to be the second best man in the Mercenaries Guild in order to lead the Rangers, and I want you as my second. You may not have all of the skill or strength just yet, but I can tell by lookin in yer eyes that you've got heart."

Rashnir looked sheepish, "You know, sir..."

"All my men call me Rogis; you had better, too."

"Ok, uh, Rogis, I've never actually even been in a real fight before. I grew up slaving in a Nindan field. That was the first real fight of my life."

Rogis leaned back in his chair as if sizing him up; he looked somewhat awed. "Wow, a natural then. If I personally train you, will you accept my offer?"

Training directly under Rogis was worth more than all of MInd's property. Rogis only taught royalty, the extremely rich, or his rare, personal preferences. Regionally, Rogis was one of the most sought after instructors in swordcraft.

"Yes!" spat Rashnir. He'd grown up hearing the tales of Rogis' Rangers told around campfires by the other slaves and servants. "Of course, I accept." Rogis was, without a doubt, the most skilled man of the sword in all the near lands. It was a proven fact that he was the most skilled in all the kingdom of Jand; a hall full of awards and competition banners testified to that.

"Good, then." Rogis stood, holding his arms up in a request for silence. Immediately, all movement and sound stopped. It was like Rogis had cast a spell upon the audience, but he needed no magic for this; this was the power that respect brought you. All was quiet, and even the barmaids stopped mid-step. Rogis whispered back to Rashnir, "I overheard your first name, but what is your full name?"

"Just Rashnir. I have no lineage, no history… I have no family name."

"Smart, deadly, a shady past, and nothing to lose; you're going to make one of the finest warriors in all of Jand."

Rogis turned back to the crowd, silent and receptive. "Announcement!" he boomed in his loud baritone. He scanned the room; all eyes were on him. *Good, as it should be.* "Rashnir here is my new second in command." He motioned for him to stand; Rashnir complied. "Anyone owing MInd property or good will of any kind, no matter how significant or trivial and regardless of circumstance, now owes them to my new second. The altercation that you all undoubtedly just witnessed was a legally binding duel and qualifies Rashnir to receive all of MInd's credit. I, Rogis, was witness to the verbal agreement. Anyone who has a problem with this or wishes to dispute my credibility in this matter should see me directly." Rogis gave all possible dissenters a stern look that implied another duel would be on the way if they caused trouble. Even though he was much older, Rogis was nowhere near drunk enough to be trifled with by any ordinary person—even in a barroom brawl.

The announcement was not at all what the crowd expected. They were anticipating an execution. Some people looked stunned, perhaps a little angry, but not necessarily because they supported Mind; it was more likely they were upset that their debts were not erased with the warrior's death, but merely transferred.

"Remember this; Rashnir is now my favored warrior, undergoing training only from me. So, plot well if you are planning any type of subterfuge." Rogis took a seat next to Rashnir and took another swig of ale.

A hubbub of whispering ensued, then the normal tavern life erupted once again and overtook the moment. The only indicator that anything out of the ordinary occurred that night was an odor of charred hair lingering around the tavern's entryway.

The bartender passed out free, celebratory drinks as a way to curry favor with the two highest-ranking mercenaries. Demand proved greater than supply and so the promo was short lived—the Phoenix's patrons seemed capable of ingesting more drink than air.

Rashnir eventually slipped beyond consciousness, passing out among empty bottles, flasks, glasses, and steins. Someone else must have dragged him back to the guild barracks and dumped him in his cot.

A knock on the too-thin door startled him from slumber. The first thing that he noticed was that, for being on top of the world, he sure felt like a hill-troll's beat-up ragdoll. A second rapping snapped him to attention and he rolled off his bed. Rashnir remained fully clothed, boots and all, in last night's garb.

He opened the door. A messenger stood there with an armload of garments and items.

"Sir, Rogis told me to bring these and inform you that he will be arriving in one half-hour to meet with you." The messenger dropped his own name, which Rashnir immediately forgot once he'd departed.

Rashnir sorted through the bundle. Did he call Rogis "Sir," or had he said that to Rashnir? A mercenary would have omitted the title if speaking of Rogis—the old ranger had been clear about that much.

The bundle contained a new set of light-duty armor with his rank and title freshly engraved on it. It included a mellow breakfast that promised to ease his agitated stomach. He'd also sent a flask that contained, to Rashnir's relief, cool water. Rashnir nibbled on breakfast as he sorted through the armor. It helped settle his uneasy stomach and made him feel less nauseated.

The first thing that all new recruits learned in the mercenary's guild was the chain of command; the second thing that they learned was their equipment. They had to purchase their own armor and weapon before they signed on. This gifted set was a much nicer one than the battered one he'd purchased from a crippled glory-seeker who could no longer use it.

Rashnir knew how to strap all of his basic armaments on and cinch them so that they were comfortable, yet tight. This was really the only thing that he'd learned so far. Instructions on combat techniques weren't yet scheduled, though he'd now train only under Rogis.

The armor was finely crafted. It had a light, chain mesh that rested between his tunic and breastpiece: just enough of a defense to turn a dagger being thrust into his belly or keep a glancing arrow from fully penetrating. It was a casual kind of armor, more like a warrior's clothing than true battle gear.

Rashnir finished his dress by strapping on gauntlets and belt, then pulling on his new boots. Everything fit perfectly. *They must have measured me while I was unconscious,* Rashnir thought. Only one thing did not seem right when Rashnir looked down at his outfit. It was too shiny; a seasoned warrior's gear would be more weathered.

Precisely as announced, Rogis arrived at Rashnir's door.

"Are ya' ready?" he asked.

"For what? Training?" Rashnir guessed.

"Perhaps a little, yes. But first we go to your new estate where you will sign documents releasing legal custody of Mind's family to me. Then, we will see. There might not be enough daylight left for you to worry about training after you're done taking it all in. Mind, after all, did like to acquire things, and it will probably take you all day just to glance at the lands and treasures you now own."

***

His conscience bothered him. Rashnir struggled with his inner thoughts. Murder was generally frowned upon—but that was only among the lower castes of the land! If it was justifiable, then all was well, provided one could weather the repercussions. Something deep down in the pit of his gut gave him pause for thought; this was a new sensation for him. *Why do we have morals? Where do they come from? Is not my cause just?*

Rashnir had too much time to think. He shook away those thoughts burdening his mind as the stolen animal trotted along the lonely hillside. His cause *was* just! He had been a possession, a pawn, a thing, for all of his life. Rarely had he ever been a person: not until he met *her*... and then the wicked king, a vile lover of *things*, took her away from him.

"What are possessions compared with love!" Rashnir screamed into the rushing air. No trinkets or trifles ever mattered. Nothing could ever compare to the value he placed on his love—a love that was stolen.

"You took her from me!" he yelled into the sky, spurring the animal to a quicker pace. "And now, I am your death, and I am coming for you!"

Chapter Three

Rashnir faded in and out of his bittersweet memories as another man's horse bore him across the land. It ran too slowly. The underwhelming mare hadn't been selectively bred for speed or strength; it was just an ordinary horse and probably belonged to an equally unimpressive commoner.

No horse would ever rival his beloved Nikko, the beast which saw him safely beyond Mallow's employ. Rashnir kept Nikko in his stables as the best of his horses.

He shook his head with disgust. Those days were over. They would only live on in his memory. The memories were painful. He didn't want to give them new life, relive them, but he couldn't keep them from washing over his thoughts on the solitary journey.

***

The two Rangers exited the Guild building's main structure and went to the stables. They had spent half the day acquainting Rashnir with Rogis' chain of command. Within the Guild, he introduced him to the important people that he'd need to know.

Their horses had already been saddled and made ready for travel. Rashnir pulled himself up onto Nikko, a dappled gelding. Rogis hauled his larger frame on top of his dark gelding. The horse's name was Nightshade, Rogis explained to him. Nightshade was bred by one of his sons who'd given it to him as a gift; Nightshade's mother was a semi-famed racehorse named Nightmare which had been bred by a prized stud named Shadow.

Rogis had many children. Most of them lived around or near their father's estate making a small villa. Many of them were older than Rashnir and had businesses and families of their own. Only a few of Rogis' children lived much distance from the Rogis estate, but nearly all of them were extremely successful in whatever they did; they'd been privy to the best training available in their fields.

The horses trotted along the path; it would take about sixty minutes at their current gait. Supper would be prepared, and they didn't want to arrive too early, so they didn't ride quickly.

Their trail followed a worn path through a bracken-laced wood. The trees, which nearly blocked the sun overhead, resembled tiny arms reaching towards the sky; a myriad canopy of fingertips intermeshed into the tattered, verdant awning that shielded them from the sun.

Rogis told Rashnir many personal things about himself: the sort of things that only people who knew him well would have knowledge of. Rogis spoke with freedom. The Ranger did have a reputation for being reserved and so this lapse momentarily concerned Rashnir.

"Are you always this intimate with your conversations?" Rashnir asked.

"Well, we are going to be working closely, Rashnir. And besides, I know that if you ever fall out of confidence, it will be easy enough to kill you." The comment didn't come off as a threat, and it was nonetheless true.

The trail forked and led the riders down a less-beaten path. Further down, a distinct landmark broke through the undergrowth. Rogis pointed out two stone emplacements on either side of the trail before them.

"That is the beginning of your property line," he said.

Each emplacement stood twice as thick as a man and about chest high. It was finely crafted with smooth stonework and nearly invisible mortar joints. A ceramic tile held a knob, fixing a wire in place. The wire stretched through the trees and beyond view.

"Don't touch that wire," Rogis said. "Only a couple people know about it. There's some kind of energy in it," he said, "You wouldn't believe me if I told you." Rogis laughed as they passed through the gate. Of course, he told him the story anyway, a tale about a local madcap inventor who could harness the power of lightning.

A few moments later the woods opened; before him stood a stone house at least as big as Mallow's had been. The polished stonework shone in the sun; four turrets rose above the mansion giving it a castle-like feel. Rashnir's eyebrows rose in awe. He'd never even been inside Mallow's house when he'd been a slave, and now he owned one that was even larger.

Brickwork walls were laid perfectly. Ivy and vinework crept up the sides of the outbuildings. The lawn and yard was perfectly groomed. Many of the windows had ornate glass panes set in them.

The two men guided their horses to a hitching post near the front entrance; trodden ground led to a trail that wrapped behind the house, probably indicating a path to the stables. They lashed their reins to the post.

Rogis put a large hand on the heavy wooden door and pushed it open.

"My house does not have all of the frivolous novelties that this house has: things like this door. It was specially crafted so it could open when pushed from either side—reverse hinges: this way you never have to pull it open. This seems like a simple and noble idea, but Mind had it made because he didn't like any inconvenience, and also because he was paranoid. He wanted to always be able to get where he was going by the easiest route possible. See, when you're a man of Mind's size, the quick and easy route is often directly through everyone else—there's no honor in that, no politeness.

"Mind's house has all sorts of treasures in its rooms, but as you can see, they don't do him a bit of good right now. My estate is comfortable enough; it don't need to be plush.

"I have my treasure stored up in a different sort of way. I have respect, authority, and friendships. Who needs gold when you have the respect and friendship of the whole land? I could die destitute and paralyzed, but bards would still sing my deeds; people would still tell my stories. I also have my family surrounding me; these are the only treasures worth having."

"Quite true, but you *do* have more gold and wealth than Mind did, do you not?"

Rogis grinned, "My family costs much more to maintain than his. Mind had six children. I have at least seventy-and still counting." Rogis' laughter drew the attention of a small crowd in a nearby room.

Nine people joined the two Rangers. Two middle-aged women looked at Rogis with bright and shining eyes. They ran to embrace him, burying their faces in his chest.

Blonde and brunette, the women looked up at him with admiration on their faces. Rashnir couldn't help from saying, "Truly, you are rich, Rogis."

"Thank the powers that be that he is finally dead," the blonde breathed. Then she turned to Rashnir and embraced him as if he was family. "Let me introduce you to everyone. I am Missa."

She turned to an elderly man who hovered in the doorway, "This is Dane; he is the personal servant to the house's master, whomever that might be." Dane was a spindly old man with wispy white hair and an age lined face to complement it. Scrawny, but tall, he wore a grey tunic with matching pants. Dane bowed to Rashnir as best as he was able.

Missa moved on before Rashnir could object about keeping a servant; next she introduced Jenn, the brunette woman. Missa held up a hand to tick off their children as she introduced them. Moving youngest to oldest, she introduced two young boys, less than six years old, as Jed and Brandyn; Brillon, an eight-year-old boy; a thirteen-year-old girl named Tristessa; then a muscular young man named Bomarr and a beautiful girl named Kelsa, both seventeen.

Bomarr looked burly and strong; he had hard eyes, like black agates. He resembled Mind in every way but also seemed relieved to learn of his father's death. His arms were crisscrossed with long scars, likely from his father's punishments or drunken rages.

After a meal punctuated by traded smiles and small talk, Rogis took Rashnir to the late estate owner's private office and sat at a desk. He pulled out a piece of parchment and a quill and inkwell.

"I now need your release of this family, as if you were giving them to me as possessions. Give this to me in ink in case there is ever any question from… potential dissenters."

"Uh, I cannot write," Rashnir said sheepishly, "I can only read a few words and write my name."

"Well, that is something that will need to be remedied." Rogis replied as he scribbled up a document for him. He turned over the contract to his new second in command and beckoned for his mark.

"I will teach him." Kelsa startled them from the doorway where she'd obviously been eavesdropping.

Rogis slowly nodded at her request. The body language between them communicated a silent agreement. In an instant, Rashnir caught the two sets of eyes and he immediately knew that Kelsa was Rogis' daughter. He could tell that both parties knew it. Then, Kelsa turned and abruptly left, just as she'd seemed to come.

"You will keep the property and the staff, and I will take the family home with me tonight."

"Staff?"

"Yes. Dane, as well as a handful of others. They are all indentured to the estate for owing debts to MInd, all except for Dane. Dane's family has been the head of the servants to this estate since long before my time; it would be an insult to make him leave, I'd advise against it. There is a deep and rich history surrounding this building." Rogis pointed out the window to a half buried blockhouse. "That is their barracks. They all sleep there, save Dane who has his own private room in the servants' block near the cellar."

Rashnir nodded and drew his name on the paper that Rogis drew up. He couldn't read it, but the old Ranger had been so transparent with him that he trusted the man.

Rogis led Rashnir back down to the crowd that had once been Mind's family. "Are we ready to move?" he asked. "The wagons are ready, right Dane?"

"They are prepared, sir. You may send someone to collect them in the morning." Dane motioned to the servants in the back of the room. "They will begin loading your things after you leave."

Kelsa quickly stepped forward. "Do not load my things," she interjected.

Rogis looked down his nose at her, surprised, but not entirely so. "Are you sure?"

"Yes. Absolutely." Kelsa's face glowed as she glanced at Rashnir. "We will have a great deal of studying to do—constantly, to bring him up to speed. He will have to be well-educated for the position he is assuming," she placated Rogis with a plausible line of logic.

Rogis' face softened as he looked at Kelsa and then at Rashnir. He nodded resignedly. "Very well then. It is your choice to make." He softly put his hand on Kelsa's shoulder. "Well then, we are off. Rashnir, see to it that you take utmost care of Kelsa." His voice carried a hint of fatherly warning. He turned to look at only her. "Your mother and I will return tomorrow sometime and collect any of your family's belongings that the servants might have missed."

The group left through the main door; Rogis took Dane aside, probably to tell him to keep an eye on Kelsa. Missa came back and embraced her daughter. Her unspoken words communicated a release of the mother's authority over her daughter. "Be good," her mother whispered, squeezed tightly, then released and departed.

Not oblivious to the special moment that unfolded nearby, Rashnir slipped away, going to the largest, most comfortable room on the first floor. He thought it best to give them some privacy if this was a goodbye.

Pillows lay scattered around the floor nearest the masoned fireplace. Large, fur-covered couches formed a half-ring facing the hearth. A huge, white bearskin rug stretched across the marble floor within the semicircle.

Rashnir surveyed the room, then went to the middlemost couch and sat. He sank into the cushioning and adjusted his position accordingly so he could gaze at the fire as it leapt to and danced in the fireplace.

Dane came in with a few dry logs and stoked the fire with a poker. He put the lumber on and scuttled out quickly, almost moving too fast for a man of his advanced age.

Rashnir looked over his shoulder when he heard the soft padding of approaching footsteps. Kelsa slowly walked in, flanked by Dane; the old servant carried an elegant silver tray.

Kelsa swung her slight frame around the end of the couch and sank into its stuffing, seating herself only inches away from Rashnir. Dane leaned over the backrest and presented the tray to them. Kelsa took two tall cups and offered one to Rashnir. Dane smiled and departed with a twinkle in his eye.

"So, Kelsa," Rashnir said uncomfortably, "you can to teach me to read?"

"I will teach you anything that you desire to know." She crept a little closer.

"Really? Tell me about this place then, this house. I've never been inside a structure so grand."

"Very well," she began with a hint of playfulness in her voice. "The original structure was an old royal outpost that had been overthrown by marauders many generations ago, during the Jand-Ninda schism. The royal family of Jand allowed persons of favor to reside here after they reclaimed it by force; this was shortly after they set up their new keep in Capital City—it's the main reason why the capital is so close to Grinden and the Nindan border. That was about the time Dane's family began maintaining it. Despite that, the place fell into disrepair. Somehow Mind found favor with the royalty. He never said how, but the estate was given over to him. He demolished much of it and then had it restored. The estate was rebuilt upon the backs of slaves and laborers who owed my 'father' favors, or just feared his wrath. Intimidation can be a powerful motivator. Several of the craftsmen performed a better job here than they would have on even their own homes.

"I remember when the work was done. I was still young, but I remember that day. Despite all of the labor, it was a wonderful day."

"Your 'father' was pleased?"

"Not so much, he could always find a reason to complain. It was the expression on Dane's face that made it grand. He's been here ever since he was a baby, and to see the look on his face when the remodeling was completed was worth the toil of so many men."

Kelsa settled back into the cushion behind her. Her skin just barely touched Rashnir's. "There are many unique and interesting things about this building; not only is the cellar dug out, but it is also walled and floored. It is a part of the original foundation. I hear that it is uncommon to fully finish a basement because it can be so expensive. For my part, I've never seen one that is not. Then again, I do not enter many cellars. I've not had many opportunities to leave the estate."

Rashnir stood and stretched, stepping away from the skin on skin contact. It was mostly an excuse to shy back from Kelsa's touch. The mental picture of an angry Rogis remained in his mind. He had never been touched like that by any female, and he'd rarely seen any attractive ones. On Mallow's farm, Mallow kept the pretty ones as personal servants and locked them away inside of his house. Rashnir, of course, could not remember his own mother and he'd always been so busy working that he hadn't interacted with many women.

He teased her a little. "Funny then that you've elected to stay here given the chance to leave." Rashnir turned to face Kelsa. Silently, she had stood up, too. She was so close that she startled him.

A little surprised by her proximity, he quickly sat down to quench his sudden excitement and swimming mind. She sat again, right next to him; her thigh touched his. He could feel body heat radiating from her; it did not help calm down the sudden rush of hormones that surged through his body.

"My own life story has been so boring," she pouted. "It is the diary of a prisoner," she went on melodramatically. "Tell me about you. You must have an exciting past, full of adventure, to be skilled enough to get the better of Mind in combat and take his place in Rogis' Rangers."

"Oh, you're in for a surprise," he said, almost laughing.

Rashnir related every detail of his former life as a slave. Kelsa hung on every word as he told her every significant event, each of which seemed insignificant to Rashnir's ears. The story led right up to his arrival at the doors of the house earlier this evening.

He'd never before thought that his life might seem interesting but the way she listened to him was different than the way others ever had. She was not preoccupied with other thoughts; she actually cared about what he had to say. She wanted to know him more—deeper. He thought it entirely possible that he'd never had anybody's full attention until right now.

A few hours later, after Rashnir finished his tale, Kelsa rose to her feet. "It is long past midnight and Dane retired hours ago. But I am so wide awake." She took him by the hand and tugged him forward. "Here, follow me; I will give you a little tour of your new house."

Rashnir stood and followed behind her as she led him through the main doorway of the main room with the fireplace. That door led to an entry room which acted as a hub for the rest of the house.

She led him through the entryway and the dining hall, through the kitchen and back around to the room with the fireplace. They peered into a hallway that led to several other rooms.

Odd paintings and potted plants adorned the walls. Rashnir raised an eyebrow as he came to the first potted shrub.

"Why in the lands would anybody put trees *inside?*"

Kelsa motioned to the shrubbery. "It is an ornamental practice that Mind picked up in his travels. He found that they do this over in Jeena. Because of the mountains on one side, the wasteland on the other, and the rest of its borders sealed off by the seas, trees can be quite uncommon. Because water is scarcer the closer that you come to the wasteland, trees are only ornamental. Wealthy Jeenans invest their precious water in potted shrubs as a way of gloating to others; gardening is vanity for them—a status symbol."

"I thought that you did not travel much."

"I don't, but I read books from all over."

Rashnir nodded his head, taking in the information. "Well, the shrubs are certainly more pleasant to look at than these horrible paintings...er...are these Jed and Brandyn's?" he blushed, hoping that he hadn't just insulted her two younger brothers.

She put her hand against her mouth to stifle a laugh. "Those wretched things," she laughed, "were a gift to my father from the Prince of Jand, Harmarty. The prince hoped to please seek my hand." Her tone conveyed distaste.

"Your hand? What do...oh, marriage," the flustered Rashnir spat out. "Well, I will see to it that he does not have it, unless, um, you want it?"

Kelsa smiled, pleased that Rashnir had picked up on her subtle hints. "No. I have no desire for that arrogant, pompous thing." She led him to the room at the end of the hall.

The room was elegant and had a plush tapestry on the floor. Kelsa informed him that the floor weaving came from far away. A large bed was centered on the farthest wall and an arrangement of foot drawers, bureaus, and chests encircled around the room in an effort to maximize floor space and make the room appear even larger.

"This," she flatly said, "is the guest bedroom," she turned and walked back into the hallway. Rashnir followed.

She motioned to the other three rooms and walked into the doorway of the closest one. It had been stripped of personal effects and appeared to be a bedroom. All three rooms were basically the same: the bedrooms of those family members now under Rogis' care. They each shared the same basic design and had been mostly cleared out.

She led him by the hand, taking him away from the hall and up the main staircase. At the top of the stairs was another large room with another staircase leading to a third floor where there were only bedrooms and the rooftop access.

Rashnir recognized one of the doors. It led to the study where Rogis had taken him earlier. Kelsa led him further into the house.

"Come in here, Rashnir," Kelsa cooed, "You'll visit this room often." She let a seeming silence pass then explained as they entered the room. "It is the library," she explained.

A large room sprawled before them; bookshelves and scroll cases lined all sides of the room. Plush chairs had been placed in convenient locations, next to small, circular tables. Each table had a tall candle and several votives placed at the center. Small, rectangular windows spread across the wall above the top of the bookcases. Their size barely allowed ample light into the chamber during the day.

Rashnir raised an eyebrow, noting the room and its contents. Kelsa noticed his quizzical face and explained, "My mother had it built. Mind was never

THE KAKOS REALM: GRINDEN PROSELYTE

much on reading. It took him a great deal of concentration to manage it, so he only read for business reasons, contracts and such. At first he refused to build it, back when I was still young, but my mother told him that having something healthy to occupy her time might make her less inclined to be...um...disloyal?" She blushed slightly.

Rashnir gave her a knowing smirk, "And Rogis?"

"He loves to read." She smiled and led him through another doorway.

The door opened into a room filled with taxidermy, carvings, and plaques of all sorts. "This is the arrogant, old man's trophy room. I assume that you will want to clear it out and find a more personal use for it, unless you want to be surrounded by the triumphant monuments that each attest to Mind's glory."

They went into another room, obviously the armory. Weapon racks lined the walls and training dummies displayed sets of fine armor.

The main floor of the arsenal remained cleared for practice space. Marks on the floor indicated starting positions for sparring practice. A various array of gleaming instruments, swords, daggers, halberds, maces, flails, axes, bows, and weapons that Rashnir had never even heard of before hung on racks and mounts.

Rashnir reached out and took the hilt of a particularly elegant sword. He moved it through a few simple motions to test its weight and balance. The young Ranger gleamed with joy, as if he had just discovered what he truly loved in life: a sword would let him carve his own destiny. He noticed Kelsa watching him intently out of the corner of his eye.

He paused and set down the blade. Rashnir walked slowly and purposefully over to Kelsa and embraced her. Looking into her eyes, he smiled, "I do believe that this has been the best day of my life; I am glad to share it with you."

Leaving the room behind, they walked to the front door of the house and sat on the lawn with their backs propped against a tree. They pointed out the stars that they knew and watched the sky until they fell asleep in the warm night air, leaning against each other.

Over the next few weeks, Rashnir settled into his new environment and became acquainted with his staff and contacts. Rogis stopped by once every day to train Rashnir. The young man excelled at combat arts and was so committed to his training that he quickly gained the skills to be worthy of his given rank. Within a matter of weeks he learned more advanced and complicated techniques. After that point, Rogis began bringing other advanced students from the guild to spar against Rashnir and further his techniques.

One of those was another young warrior named Jaker whose family lived nearby. Jaker, a particularly skilled scout and tracker was already a close personal friend of many of Rogis' children, especially Kelsa. While Jaker was not one of Rogis personal students, Rogis tried to include him enough so he could glean insight or skills from him whenever possible.

Rashnir easily proved himself as the best that there was with the sword. He soon moved into other weapons techniques as he threw himself into the two things that he enjoyed most: combat training and spending time with Kelsa. She showed a genuine affection for her student, who'd become a skilled reader under her teaching.

***

Sentimentality and grief drove down upon Rashnir like a mallet. He drew near the ruined outskirts of his old mentor. The scarred wasteland represented a vacant section of his life.

Collapsing rubble crumbled in heaps nearby. Green creeping vines reclaimed what used to be a retaining wall. Now, everything was destroyed, still blackened by old fires. The memory of its destruction hung in Rashnir's mind like a fog. How much death and destruction had been wrought as the result of focused intention and ambitious love? *No, it was not love that had caused this*, jealousy had done it.

Rashnir turned the horse, but paused for a moment. This was the closest he'd been to the old estate in years. Familiar scents and sounds called back to him, beckoned to him longingly. He remembered so much, and for just a second, he let the memories wash across his mind, sending him back to a better time.

***

Rashnir rode ahead of the battlegroup to meet up with Rogis. His mentor rode at the head of the line of warriors as they traveled. As usual, he was dressed in his favorite battle gear, mostly composed of hardened leather armor with a fine chain shirt. Rashnir discovered that he too preferred the greater maneuverability and flexibility of lighter armor over the cumbersome protection afforded by other sets like plate mail or splint mail. Part of this choice grew out of his personal training; closely learning Rogis' fighting styles led to many other similarities. The Ranger's fighting style required greater mobility.

However, Rogis did need a little more protection now, since he had slowed with age; he typically wore a customized set with light plates covering his vital organs. Rashnir urged Nikko forward and galloped ahead to maneuver alongside his superior.

Their private army had been hired to protect a convoy bearing trade goods from several manufacturers enroute to the distant lands. What might have been a simple protection gig fell to Rogis' Rangers instead of a lesser group because they fully expected this convoy to be attacked. The mercenaries had set up a sting against the marauders.

They'd heard rumors of an orc gang organizing in the densely wooded area that they would travel through shortly. This gang had recently been linked with sales and trafficking in goods like what they carried. The manufacturers could only assume that they were orcs; no survivors had ever been found. High enough financial rewards had finally been offered to make this a worthwhile undertaking for Rogis' Rangers; on top of their commissions was the plunder from the gang's hideout which they would probably find in some cave or hovel built in the woods.

Rogis looked at him. "Something is awry?"

Rashnir had come up from a position at the center of the convoy. "No. I simply came to talk."

"There's no one back there to talk to?" Rogis quipped.

Rashnir shot him a sly look, "No one who can hold an intelligent conversation."

Rogis grinned. "So what's on your mind, then, Rashnir?"

Rashnir sighed and looked away sheepishly. Looking at the distant horizon, he replied, "Kelsa."

Rogis puffed his breath audibly; resigning himself to a conversation that he'd long known was coming. "What of her?"

Rashnir turned and looked Rogis in the eye, "I desire her. I wish to take her as my wife, to marry her."

Rogis nodded and swallowed before speaking, "Her father is dead. You need no permission."

Rashnir gave him a slanted, knowing look. "I may have killed Mind, but I am asking *you*."

Rogis' looked softened a little as he held Rashnir's gaze; the young man had grown great in skill and countenance in only a short while. He'd truly become one of Rogis' friends. "You would surely have my permission."

The look on Rashnir's face shifted from concern to elation.

"Now get back to your post. It won't be long before we enter the hot zone."

Rogis also took a new position. Slightly behind the point riders who wore heavier plate-mail, he found a spot safer from projectiles. Rashnir rode Nikko back to the center of the line.

He spent the next leg of the trip in a cloud of joy, thinking about his future prospects, his hopes and ambitions with Kelsa. He finally forced himself to focus on the task at hand. In a short while they expected to be attacked by a horde of orcs.

The convoy journeyed another half hour until tangled branches and wild growth surrounded them on all sides; thorny walls rose up around them, curving above their heads to create a canyon effect. Brambles almost enclosed them completely; only a few sparsely knitted sections of the canopy let light's full spectrum shine through and illuminate the main road.

The scouts in their party kept ever alert. Some of the horses tensed. The whole convoy collectively ceased individual conversations and became one unit, each section on high alert. Rogis noticed how, except for the creaking of wheels on the convoy's wagons and the sound of hooves striking earth, silence reigned. He leaned and mumbled to the soldier next to him.

At Rogis' behest, he struck up into song. The silence made it too obvious they expected an ambush and that the Rangers were trying to lure the orcs into attacking them.

"Oh! There was a dumb lass
That I knew so well.
She wasn't an unfriendly belle.

"Never a beauty
She always smelled foul
Like the girl lost control of her bow'ls!

"She had no friends
'cept fer'er big ugly litter
No wonder she spent her whole life so bitter.

"Yes, my story tis true
The world's ugliest lass,
She was half-orc and—"

The mocking lyrics provoked a battlecry from the leafy shroud nearest them. Orcs leapt from the bushes, brandishing crude weapons of various, wicked shapes. The Rangers responded with their own war cry and unsheathed weapons of their own.

Rogis joked to his bard as he drew his own sword, "You must have struck a nerve there. Nothing quite so effective as insulting someone's mother."

Battle ensued with crossed blades and clashing shields. Two large groups of orcs, each at least thirty strong, blocked the escape path on either side. They pressed the attack from the ends as individual orcs harried the convoy from the sides, picking at the flanks. But the convoy wasn't concerned with escape; they came prepared for this formation, which allowed them to split the orcs' numbers into manageable portions with their unconventional tactics.

At Rogis' shrill whistle, archers leapt up on the foremost and rearmost wagons and began firing away at the front and rear raiding groups. They first targeted any orcs with slings or crossbows and then turned their attention to the harried flanks of the convoy. Most of their shots, because of the angle, struck non-vital areas of the orcish bodies; they took the shots anyway. All they needed were distracting wounds that could give the foot soldiers opportunities to make killing blows: attrition would whittle down their opposition.

Rogis led a small band of warriors into the fray at the front of the convoy just as his archers turned to protect their own flanks. His small but elite group decimated the distracted orcs, dividing their formation. The rest of the Rangers turned and began clearing out the sides of the convoy as the rear group mimicked Rogis' maneuver. From start to end, the whole skirmish was over in a matter of minutes. Fewer than twenty orcs escaped into the trees; most of them nursing some kind of injury.

Rogis met up with his second in command. "How many losses?"

Rashnir replied, "We lost maybe a dozen men, with only a few men wounded. I would guess about fifteen casualties."

Rogis nodded. The dozen dead men were likely newer recruits. New, unseasoned recruits usually had a short expectancy in the Rangers; only about an eighth of new recruits survived, but those that did usually became skilled warriors in whichever house of the Mercenaries Guild they petitioned for membership.

The warriors regrouped and tended their wounded. Rogis sent a few scouts out to dispatch those orcs that slipped away, into the trees. Rashnir gave an order to check the orcs for possessions and designated a location to dump the plundered goods; they would be divided later. As the men checked the bodies they would also finish their work, killing any enemies that remained alive.

A short while later, the scouts returned to report. "All of the stragglers are dead. 'Bout a dozen of em, all their tracks lead in the same direction. They tried to mostly keep to the different critter trails. The smarter ones tried to take a more roundabout path, but they all ended up leading to the exact same destination. We figure it must be their hideout. Jaker is exploring the trail further and will catch up with us in a little bit."

Rogis nodded to Rashnir, "Assemble those Rangers that are the most green; we'll leave those ones here to guard the convoy. If Jaker is sniffing this closely, he'll find something. We'll head out towards his location and see what he's discovered."

Rashnir directed a dozen of the newest members of their guildhouse to set up a watch and guard the convoy until the remainder of the Rangers returned. He caught up with the rest of his men as they entered the woods. All on foot, a more seasoned group of Rangers, nearly forty-strong, swiftly crept through the trails until they found the brash, young scout sitting atop an old, fallen tree and smoking a pipe.

"Jaker!" another scout chided. "What in the lands are you doing? Someone could've smelled that smoke and come and plugged your smokehole up with an arrow!"

"What?" he shrugged nonchalantly, "I knew you guys would find me first. Never fear when the mighty Rogis Rangers are coming to your rescue." He grinned arrogantly.

Rogis just shook his head. Rashnir got along with Jaker all right, though he could sometimes find him unbearably sarcastic; he wasn't sure that Jaker cared for *him* all that much, though. Jaker and Kelsa had been close friends for many years, ever since they were young, and so Rashnir did his very best to keep a positive attitude about him.

Some of the men looked to Rogis or even Rashnir to put Jaker in his place when he acted out of line, but Rashnir knew why Rogis tolerated Jaker. Rogis tolerated the young scout for the same reason that he had put up with Mind: he was the best at what he did. A good leader often had to pick skill over likeability, though Jaker was likeable by most accounts, as long as you had enough of a sense of humor and a forgiving attitude. Of course, there was another secret reason—but none could prove it; the chance existed that Rogis was Jaker's father, but very few knew of that.

"What did you find?" Rogis asked.

"We got a big old rabbit trail about two hundred yards that way," Jaker threw a thumb over his shoulder. "Big trail; must be the main route that the orcs split off of to find their way to the ambush points. The ground's dug up like a cattle pen indicating pretty heavy traffic. I'd guess, by what I see, that our convoy's ambushers made up only about thirty percent of their total gang."

Rogis' jaw tightened, this was one large group of bandits. Only half of the members of their guildhouse had been chartered for this mission. Rashnir knew that Rogis wished to have the rest of the Rangers there with them now so they could storm the orcs' base; he also knew that if the rest of the Rangers had been along, the mission would have failed at conception. The orcs wouldn't have been foolish enough to attack such a well-guarded convoy in the first place.

"How far does the trail go?" Rashnir asked.

Jaker turned to face him, "About half a mile, then you can see the outskirts of their base. I wasn't spotted and I was able to scout it quickly." Jaker drew a basic layout for them in the dirt and Rogis worked through an attack plan. They'd come too far to leave the mission incomplete; they'd have to make do with half as many men as hoped for.

***

The Rangers split into several battle-groups prior to the assault of the raiders' base. Rashnir led the main group, which acted as a decoy.

His group approached the orcs' base. Crested with trees, a gently rising hill loomed in front of them; within it, a large cave had been dug. They assumed that the cave had been further excavated to make room for the burgeoning community of orcish thieves.

The mouth of the cave yawned open before them. In plain sight, the decoy group moved directly up the main trail. Their archers quickly picked off the few orcs already about the grounds of the main encampment. Skewered orcs fell to the dirt, arrows protruding from their vitals. The Rangers crept through the bowl-like glade that spanned the encampment's clearing.

Sixteen warriors made up the decoy group, six of them were armed with bows and arrows; everyone else carried tall shields. Two smaller groups flanked the main decoy group, but remained out of sight. Inside of the cave sat their main target: several large bundles of hay and other potential flammables.

According to Jaker's report, it did not appear that anything of significant value would be damaged by a visit from a friendly neighborhood arsonist. The decoy group planted down and formed a shield wall, making as much noise as possible in the process. Once set, they screamed orcish curses and the archers shot burning arrows into the mouth of the cave, igniting the straw and other flammable materials.

Orcs wielding various weapons poured from the mouth of the flaming cave; many of them suffered burns in the evacuation. Hearing the curses, they flung themselves towards the decoy group. Archers picked off some of the ekthro, twirling them violently as they fell wounded or dead, making others stumble over the bodies. The bulk of the orcish horde continued their charge at

Rashnir's group. All their rage was focused on the decoy, blinding them to the others, just as planned.

Just as the mass of orc attackers finished pouring into the open glen, the decoy archers tucked themselves behind the shield wall. Suddenly, orcs began pitching forward, falling dead upon the ground, arrows sticking from their backs.

Rogis directed a group of archers on the rise above the mouth of the cave where the archers launched deadly projectiles at the enemies as fast as they could loose them, knowing that the decoy group relied on them to do a great deal of damage in a very short time as they fired arrows into the unprotected backs of the baited ekthro. The archery fire caused a few moments of disarray until the now-reduced orc militia realized the gravity of their situation: they were taking fire from the rear while caught in the open.

As soon as the orcs figured out that the decoy group was bait, sent to goad them into this trap, Rogis stepped aside. Jaker stepped up and dropped to one knee. The scout fired a strange looking weapon; his device looked like a combination between crossbow and slingshot. It hurled a shiny object similar to an hourglass which it sent flying like an arrow directly into the heart of the orcish horde.

The double-bulbed glass projectile impacted and the glass broke. As the bulb's contents mixed together, the chemical reaction caused an escharotic explosion. Its meteoric wave discharged with hurricane impact; flames rode on the eddicurrents, sheathing everything in the immediate vicinity with alchemical flames that harmlessly washed off of the tower shields.

The bait group hunched protected behind their temporary shield wall; the acrid blaze enveloped only the ekthro and the trampled flora. Most of the orcs fell to the intense flames, dying instantly. Some survivors of the bandit group ran in chaotic, confused circles, trying to shed the caustic embers that had once been their flesh.

Archers on the rise released another, more directed volley, taking careful aim at their enemies and dropping specific targets; two flanking warrior groups broke from the trees and charged in to clean up the orcs, as did the decoy group. The orc base had been fully undone. Any still alive soon fell under blows that they never saw coming.

Every orc was dead in mere minutes. The brilliant plan had been derived on the fly: make them punch-drunk with fast misdirecting strikes, get them in the open, confuse them, and hit them hard once and then again from all sides.

With the orcs defeated the Rangers regrouped at the mouth of the cave. A small foray of scouts went into the cave to root out any others.

A thorough investigation of the area verified their success: the Rangers had eliminated the orc threat in the area. Several storage rooms in the cave held the spoils of recent plunders. Rogis set up a small contingent to stay behind and guard the cave until the Rangers could return and send wagons to gather the plunder, a bonus beyond the Rangers' normal pay. The rest of the Rangers began the trek back to the convoy, leaving the others to set up a makeshift defense perimeter in case they encountered any unwelcome visitors.

The Rangers formed up and continued escorting the convoy on its way towards Aphinnea where it would probably pick up a new, cheaper, escort to take it through safer trade routes.

Rogis rode over to Rashnir's side as they went, another hard day at work nearly complete. They'd be back in Grinden after a few days.

"So you are planning to take Kelsa then?" Rogis' face warmed as he looked at Rashnir. "You will, of course, be inviting us to the wedding ceremony?"

Rashnir nodded, "Of course."

"And you would maybe need someone to stand in and give away the bride? Someone who is a fatherly type of figure...perhaps someone you already know..."

"Well..." Rashnir prodded, "I was thinking of asking you, but then I thought..."

They traded sagacious glances in good humor.

"Oh stuff it, Rashnir. Let me give away my little girl." Rogis grinned and the convoy continued moving.

Chapter Four

Rashnir's horse shook its sweaty mane, calling him back to the moment. He urged the beast on again, leaving behind the familiar debris and pursuing his mission.

Sentiment crept in and momentarily softened his resolve for a moment. Rashnir absentmindedly fingered the dead spots on his hands: lines of seared flesh where his enemy had branded his palms with hot iron. The old wounds killed his nerve endings where they'd raised ugly scar tissue. Rashnir thrust the happy memories away and shook his fists with rage. Now was the appropriate time for bitterness and indignation.

Over and over in his mind, Rashnir killed King Harmarty, each time in some new manner; he replayed scenes, each time reacting to different invented situations. He spurred the horse to coax more speed from it. His retribution flew on tired hooves.

***

Rogis sat with Rashnir and Kelsa. Their wedding day had drawn near when Rashnir received a summons by the newly crowned king, King Harmarty. Rashnir met him once at an event he'd attended with Rogis. At that time, Harmarty was still a spoiled prince living in the resentful shadow of his respected father.

Harmarty was an arrogant snob, too accustomed to a life of privilege, as far as Rashnir was concerned. Mired in the mindset that saw people as inferiors, as possessions existing only for his personal amusement, Harmarty's outlook was fundamentally broken. Harmarty had also once studied with Rogis; as a close friend of the previous king, Rogis trained him as a personal favor. Harmarty learned very little and often ignored his teacher; he'd proven himself a poor student.

Rogis knew that Harmarty's reign would not benefit the kingdom, but no other heirs could challenge his right to the crown. The king tried vainly to correct his wayward son through the years, but Harmarty only got worse in the adolescent years. Selfishness and vanity had deeply twisted the young man, though no one recognized the extent nor knew the cause of his fundamentally deviant mind.

As all men, Harmarty surrounded himself with those of like mind and desire; he'd been a close contact with the deceased Ranger, Mind, who he'd given several gifts and pieces of artwork. Without a doubt, Harmarty could not paint well, but his court praised him for it regardless. Harmarty's opinions were taken as fact; the prince always got what he wanted.

Now, King Harmarty demanded something he could not have: Kelsa's love. Kelsa had long avoided Harmarty's advances, but Mind had once promised her to him and Harmarty had become bent on it.

Figuring it best to meet in person to discuss the impasse, Rogis prepped Rashnir for their meeting which would take place on the following day. They hoped to reason with the king and make him understand that Kelsa would not be his; she was a person and not some plaything. It would likely be a foreign thought to Harmarty, but they had to try.

Before dawn, the two Rangers departed for the King's court in Capitol City. The two rode hard all morning and reached the castle walls that afternoon. The massive doors to the stronghold stood open.

Tall walls of stone and masonry surrounded the castle; small guard towers jutted above the parapets at regular distances. As they passed through another high gate, they came into the outlying district. Many residents of Capitol City lived in the outer court; it was the proper place for commoners and average citizens who chose to live under the direct protection of the royal monarchy. They passed by several other buildings and structures, including guards' quarters and open-air markets. Near a market, a small, rickety theater stage stood with its canopy rigged to shield a performing troupe against the sun if any were brave enough to bring in a performance.

The capital of Jand was a glorious city, much like Grinden, though slightly smaller. Although it was fully walled and protected, it lacked Grinden's appeal; the capital's focus was more on the business of the crown and politics and much less concerned with the industry and commerce that kept the local population alive. The place did not seem self-sufficient to Rashnir. It bothered him because, no matter how well fortified an army was, it could still be starved out.

Rogis pointed to the vacant stage as their horses trotted by it. "They often do a show at noontime, something to entertain the people during the mid-day break... at least they used to. I heard that King Harmarty eliminated the siesta period in the interest of 'greater productivity.' Of course, productivity's decreased. Harmarty's father instituted the show time as a way of boosting morale, and it worked great. I wonder how many, or how few, 'Harmarty jokes' were told on that stage before the local troupe's eviction." *Or execution?*

Neither wanted to suggest it, but that might have been an
option, too. They continued on, meandering purposefully
through Capitol City.

Rashnir followed his mentor through the next
walled section where a guard station filtered out the
peasants and parsed the riff-raff from the higher caste.
This section was exclusive. Composed of the nicer
accommodations in the city, only upper class citizens
were granted access. Businesses didn't exist within this
inner ring, only establishments that serviced political
business or provided some other function of personal
interest to those living in the upper echelon.

The main entry of the royal castle rose before
them as they approached. The reluctant duo lashed their
horses to the designated posts and walked inside. A
handful of guards who had shadowed them through the
courtyard ever since entering Capitol City branched off as
the Rangers entered the main castle hall.

Inside the doorway, a solemn majordomo met
them and beckoned that they follow him through the
corridors. He silently led them to Harmarty's
antechamber. Rashnir tried to get the servants name, but
he indicated via hand motions that he'd had his tongue
cut out.

"No talkin' out of turn in the King's presence,
eh?" Rogis muttered with a disgusted sigh.

The servant nodded, catching Rogis's gripe, and
opened a tall door for the Rangers. He closed it behind
them with a half-hearted bow.

King Harmarty's lavish chamber looked more like
a circus than a royal hall. Cushions adorned empty
patches of free ground; concubines and other sorts of
harlots lay strewn out upon them and the dregs of Jandan

culture, friends of the King, lay with them. Many of the servant women in the hall sported a variety of bruises or marks but hid them as best as able with hastily applied face paint and blushes. If it weren't for the well-armed and seasoned guards that intermingled amongst them, the hall could have been mistaken for a harem.

Rashnir and Rogis's entry had been obvious and no one announced their arrival; the servant with no tongue could not make any such announcement. The king lay sprawled upon his throne in utter boredom. He paid them no mind. Everyone else in the room, however, heeded their presence as they approached Harmarty's throne. They carried themselves with respect and poise— something unseen in the hall for a long season.

Rogis, wearing a disgusted look on his face, walked boldly to the elevated seat at the center point of the room. "Harmarty…"

"Why has there been no announcement of my guests?" King Harmarty interrupted him. He shifted his gaze to a large, muscled man near the throne. His exposed skin boasted many old, gnarled battle wounds; his head, shorn clean, displayed a network of tattooed and dyed scars—undoubtedly meant to look either beautiful or terrifying. "Rutheir," the King called, "my servant has apparently not learned his lesson since you last educated him. Go and kill him, then select a new attendant for me." Harmarty's eyes burned with wild, sadistic glee as he finally turned to gaze upon his guests.

Rutheir passed by them; a smug look pasted to his face. His twisted grin turned up the edge of his gold nose ring; the jewelry bounced slightly as he dutifully exited the room on heavy strides.

"Now, what can I do for you, my dear Rogis?"
Harmarty reeked of a twisted aura. He stood and
stretched with a yawn. Sallow skin, blanched by such
infrequent exits from his hall of personal mirth,
contrasted against his tiny, dilated eyes—they'd become
accustomed to torchlight rather than sunlight. Despite the
king's wiry frame, a paunch had developed in his
midsection and his hair and skin betrayed his lack of
personal hygiene.

Harmarty turned full circle, gathering his royal
robes about him like a child's security blanket. He sat
back upon his throne and gave his guests his full
attention.

Rogis kept his own frame squared to Harmarty.
"We are here to answer your summons."

Harmarty shifted his gaze. "I did not summon
you, Rogis, though I half-expected you might appear with
Rashnir, due to your personal relationship and
mentorship."

Rolling his eyes, Rashnir stated, "I am here to
answer your summons."

"Yes…I can see that. The much vaunted Rashnir
of Rogis' Rangers. Tales of your exploits have become
quite popular among the commoners. Rogis and Rashnir:
the plunderers of monster's caves, the rescuers of
kidnapped lasses, the liberators of besieged trade lines,
the victors of contests, and the friends of common folk.
The stories forget to mention 'the man who stole the sun
from their King.'"

Rashnir gave a quizzical look in response. "I have
taken nothing from you, King of Jand."

Harmarty leapt to his feet like a taunted guard
dog. "LIAR!" he barked. Flecks of spittle flew with the

vehemence of his accusation. "You have kidnapped my queen—stolen her, practically on our honeymoon, you did! Guards! Kill them!"

Rashnir and Rogis snapped to defensive positions, but no one made any move to obey the king's order. Because of the command's obvious absurdity the guards gave it no heed; they were accustomed to Harmarty's outbursts of random insanity.

"Bah!" Rogis stepped forward. "You know that Kelsa has always been opposed to your pursuits. You have not even attempted to woo her; rather, you wooed her father." The comment provoked stifled laughter from the court, even though the statement had not been made to offend Harmarty's manhood. Harmarty turned red, fuming with anger.

Rogis continued as his former student bristled. "Mind agreed to give her to you against her will, but she loves another. Can you not respect love? Have you loved nothing but yourself? Think of your father, Harmarty; *he* loved *you*, remember that and respect that. Respect Kelsa and her love for Rashnir."

Harmarty paused, introspective at the mention of his father. His posture slumped a little, but then he hardened his heart and stuck out his chest. "Kelsa will be mine!" he raved at the top of his lungs. "She loves me, not some pretender! Now get out!" He slumped back into his throne.

The two moved to quickly exit, departing awestruck by the insanity of the situation. They'd nearly passed through the doorway when Harmarty called out in a childlike voice, "Rogis?" It carried the same inflection of a scared child whose parents had left him in a dark room.

Rogis turned and stood in the threshold. Harmarty rushed up to him. He placed a sealed letter in his hand. "Please give this to Kelsa." He smiled at Rogis like an infatuated schoolboy; Harmarty scowled and hissed at Rashnir before running back to his throne. Suddenly like another person, he turned and assumed his most regal pose. Leveling his gaze at them, he placidly reminded them, "I told you to 'get out.'"

Rashnir and Rogis left the building, whistling incredulously through their teeth. They mounted their horses and departed, heading for Rashnir and Kelsa's home in the neutral town of Grinden. They fled the madman's castle as quickly and quietly as possible.

Only once they'd finally galloped into the open highways did Rashnir speak. "He is not sane is he?"

"Not even close. He's gotten worse every year." Rogis sighed, still mulling over one of Harmarty's remarks, "The king's 'everything?' He's been denied only this one thing and become consumed by the desire to attain it. He'll stop at nothing to acquire Kelsa, of this I am sure." The two journeyed onward, discussing what might be done about the situation. Their conversation kept mostly cathartic, dialogue let them vent their anger over the situation.

Eventually, they broke the seal and read the letter addressed to Kelsa.

My Dearest Kelsa,

I know now the severity of the situation, that this brute Rashnir has taken you captive, but do not fear. Your brave warrior king is coming for you. Ten thousand Rangers could not stop me from coming to you.

Do you remember that time we first met? You were undoubtedly drawn to my handsome features and charisma, but I tell you that our love goes even deeper than that: your very soul is knitted to me—you are mine.

Take this to heart and remember that I will stop at nothing to free you from this monster and bring you into my bedchamber. I am coming, lover.

—King Harmarty

Dusk had settled by the time they crossed onto Rashnir's land. It wasn't until then that the two finally felt safe from the unhinged king. Rogis watched Rashnir mount the steps to his house. Dane came out and dutifully led Nikko to the stables.

"Don't worry," Rogis said, trying to comfort his friend. "You are far more popular in these parts than the King is. Even his own people, the citizens of Jand, hold you in higher regard—and the people are where the crown's only real power lies. After all, you are my most skilled Ranger. The best of the best." Rogis turned his horse and galloped away, making enough speed to find him home before the night drew too deep.

Rashnir turned and entered his own house and climbed into the arms of his fiancé.

Normal life resumed for only the next few days. Kelsa and he had begun making final wedding plans.

Five mornings later, Rashnir rose and went about his daily routine. He walked to the stable to prepare Nikko for a ride into Grinden. Rashnir owned many horses. But of all of the prized animals he owned, Nikko had always been his favorite.

A spacious enclosure, several horse stalls lined the south wall of his stable adjacent to the horse-and-rider sized door that let the animals into a penned grazing area. Tightly bundled sheaves of straw and hay leaned against the north wall, stacked to the open rafters where riding tack and grooming tools dangled. He kept the main floor mostly clear so horses could be easily groomed or saddled.

Rashnir entered through the east entrance; his stride broke a shaft of sunlight cast by the open door. When he bent to grab a saddle from its rack, as he'd done so many times before, his peripheral vision spotted Nikko acting agitated in his stall. The light shifted subtly. Rashnir instinctively fell forward and twisted to his right, bringing his right arm up. A long, curved blade sank deep into the thick, leather saddle right behind him as a dark figure dropped silently from the rafters. The sword would have otherwise pierced Rashnir between the shoulder blades.

The assassin wore a tight, thin mask and leather armor, all stained black. Pouches and clasps held various assassin's tools and weapons tight, keeping them accessible, while keeping them from clinking against each other and making him silent.

Rashnir planted his left hand on the saddle rack and lunged with his right. He grabbed the top edge of his assailant's armor near the edge of the man's throat. He pulled him down and brought his leg to bear under the assassin; Rashnir kicked and flung the attacker against the east wall with the springboard maneuver.

Snapping into a ready stance, Rashnir assumed a defensive posture. The assassin stood and stepped into the shaft of light, offering his prey only his silhouette. Keeping the light against the assassin's rear partially momentarily blinded Rashnir.

"Who are you?" Rashnir demanded.

"I am Shimza the Lesser. I am here to kill you." With a flick of his wrist, the silhouetted assassin jumped to his left, into the shadows where Rashnir's eyes could not adequately track him.

Just as quick, Rashnir anticipated his move and pulled on the sword that skewered the saddle next to him. He jerked the saddle up, along with the sword. Rashnir used it to catch a trio of shurikens; they lodged deep into the underside of the saddle.

Rolling onto his rear, Rashnir used his feet to force the saddle apart from the blade. He pried with enough force to throw the saddle in the direction of his attacker.

Rashnir somersaulted to his left just as Shimza brought a second curved blade down. Rashnir rolled into position, finally armed and ready. He and Shimza could fight on even terms.

For a moment their eyes locked. Like a lightning strike, their souls connected in that intense gaze. They sized each other up, searching for fear or weakness, looking for the most opportune moment to strike.

Rashnir's eyes hardened and Shimza's pupils shrank fractionally. They both knew who would emerge victor. Rashnir jumped into the fray, fully pressing the offensive. Shimza could not help but parry in flurries; the advantage of surprise was lost and the situation had turned. Shimza blocked and moved; he deflected blows and took only fleeting chops and swings at Rashnir— offensive blows used to try and give him distance to regroup.

It was no use. Rashnir brought his sword to bear time and again as Shimza blocked over and over, barely withstanding Rashnir's sword arm. In a planned moment of opportunity, Rashnir delivered a kick to his opponent's abdomen. The force of his blow turned Shimza ninety degrees and dropped him to his knees; Rashnir drove his sword into the base of the assassin's back.

Shimza grabbed at the hilt of the sword as Rashnir ran it deep, piercing all the way through. He picked up the blade that Shimza dropped and pointed it at his enemy's neck, ready to take the killing move with any provocation. With his left hand, Rashnir grabbed Shimza's mask and pulled it off, burning the features of his attacker's face into his memory.

Shimza howled and squealed like a stuck pig. The blade had done severe damage, but was not a mortal wound provided he got help quickly.

"Kill me now, Ranger!" Shimza spat.

"Who hired you?" Rashnir demanded. "Tell me or this will be far worse than it needs to be."

Shimza snorted and rattled off a string of expletives. Rashnir slightly nudged the hilt of the sword in his prisoner's midsection; Shimza screamed and shuddered over.

Rashnir walked calmly and purposefully to the east wall and gathered a few of the more interesting grooming tools, items that would aid in his interrogation. The assassin's eyes bulged as Rashnir brandished a rusted spiral currycomb and a chiseled hoof pick.

Kelsa and Dane could only guess what was happening as they looked to the stables. They heard a long series of unfamiliar screams coming from within and neither dared to go and check. Minutes later Rashnir walked back through the main doors; blood splatters slicked his arms and face.

"Dane," Rashnir spoke with unnerving calm, "I need you to have a servant saddle Nikko and clean the stables for me. I want you to make sure that the house is safe; barricade everyone within. Keep the place secure. Everyone's safety depends on you." Dane nodded and scuttled off to make arrangements.

"What's wrong?" concern flooded Kelsa's voice.

"Harmarty has hired bounty hunters to kill me and deliver you to him." Rashnir went inside the house and headed for the armory. On his way he dispatched another servant to ride out and fetch Rogis.

Rashnir tore through his arsenal as if a man on fire. He quickly decided what might be needed for a journey of this sort. Rage and resentment beckoned him to walk headlong into the enemy's fortress and give the king an inconvenient ultimatum at the end of a sword.

Kelsa stood in the doorway, watching her man do what he did best. Rashnir paused, knowing that she studied him.

She quickly guessed his plan. *There is no doubt he could strike down Harmarty; the man is a weakling and a poor fighter, plus the people love the Rashnir who had grown into something of a minor celebrity. The people* do, *however, respect tradition and Harmarty is the eighth generation of royalty in Jand.*

Rashnir shared her thought, but discarded it. He would do whatever was required to safeguard his love.

He pulled a chain shirt over his tunic and began to pull on his other armor. Rashnir retrieved his finest breastplate from its stand and Kelsa approached. He turned so that she could help strap it into place, which she did affectionately. He sheathed a fine longsword behind his back; it had belonged to a great king many years prior. He also sheathed a shortsword in reach of his left hand. Around his waist, Kelsa strapped a pouch with bolts for his crossbows. They looked up when they heard Rogis' heavy footsteps at the entrance to the armory.

Rogis stepped in and met their gaze. "This is foolishness, you know. There must be some way other than storming his castle."

Rashnir gave him a hard stare, "Then why are you dressed for battle?"

Rogis similarly wore his best armaments. He nodded an assent. "Because I cannot let you fight this battle alone. *This* is what I live my life for; it encompasses all three things that I know and hold dear: fighting, love, and family."

Rashnir gripped two pistol crossbows and sighted down them quickly; they were finely crafted weapons designed to use shorter bolts and fire with great force. With custom, shortened lathe arms, they took very little space and could be concealed, though they were really only good for one shot each before the element of surprise was gone and they had lost their worth. Rashnir latched them in place; each fit securely on either hip in a special holster.

Kelsa embraced each of them in turn before they left the armory. Dane had already led Nikko to the front of the house and stood holding the reins. Rashnir mounted his horse and Dane handed him the long handle-end of a halberd. Rashnir stowed it in an angled sheathe where it would stay secure during hard riding. It was easily accessible if Rashnir needed it.

Reaching up, Kelsa squeezed Rashnir's hand and slipped a thin metal chain into his palm. "Remember this," she said. Two tiny rings were attached, the traditional gold hoop earrings that he'd given her as a sign of betrothal. "Let them remind you of what you are fighting for. I love you."

"And I love you," he touched her face and then fastened the chain around his neck. He tucked the rings inside of his tunic.

The two Rangers departed, slowing to look back just before they slipped beyond view. Kelsa waved her heroes onward.

They raced their horses forward with a pace only matched by their outrage. King Harmarty's castle had barely come in view when they saw the first group of opponents in the distance. Four well-bred horses approached, each bearing a formidable warrior; they looked vaguely familiar from the previous visit to Harmarty's court. The decorative piercings and tattoos were an indication that these were hired thugs: mercenaries from the northwestern countries who fought with no scruples and had no need for polite associations such as guildhouses.

One of the riders slowed and halted as the other three continued their intersection with Rashnir and Rogis. The two Rangers slowed their horses to a less urgent pace. The rider in the distance readied his bow and pulled an arrow from his quiver.

The three mercenaries rode up hard on Rashnir and Rogis. The group of five men merged to speak on the grassy slope with the castle looming clearly in the distance.

Easing their horses into a location that would block the archer's shot, the Rangers positioned the ruffians between them and the sniper. The King's men sneered and shrugged, knowing they'd been positioned, but their overconfidence didn't leave room for them to care.

"Hail Ranger," the lead thug said as he leaned forward on his horse.

Rogis matched the friendly posture, also leaning forward. Rashnir hung back slightly, letting the two point men have a conversation that would likely precurse a fight.

"Just what is the meaning of this?" Rogis demanded. "Are we not privy to visiting Capitol City like everyone else?"

"Harmarty thought that you might come. He said that you two were not men of reason."

"Your employer is insane, you realize."

The warrior gave a smirk and a nod, "Quite. But he is also very wealthy and you are quite old." The warrior reached for his sword and drew it with blazing speed, intending to cut Rogis down in one smooth motion. Rogis was not as slow as he appeared; his sword firmly met his opponent's.

Rashnir yanked out his crossbows and loosed an arrow from his left hand at close range; it pierced the neck of the mercenary closest to Rogis. He spurred Nikko to strafe along the group's flank. Then, he loosed another bolt from his steadier hand, directed at the archer in the distance. It was a practiced move. The bolt struck the archer in the shoulder, where his armor did not cover, sending the bowman's shot wide; the arrow flew harmlessly into the distance. Rashnir urged Nikko towards the archer who, now ineffective with a bow, had turned to Capitol City in order to rally reinforcements.

Rogis traded blows with the point man as he kept moving. His maneuvers kept the other mercenary beyond striking distance.

Rashnir readied another bolt as he closed the distance. He pulled back on the reins, stopping his horse. From a stalled position he took careful aim and pulled the trigger; the shaft of the loosed bolt streaked directly to its target, implanting the projectile in the base of the rider's skull. Rashnir turned Nikko back even as the dead rider fell in the distance; he slid from his horse like a collapsing sack. Rashnir readied another bolt and galloped back towards the fray.

He didn't find a clear shot at either of the remaining two enemies; he wouldn't risk hitting Rogis. Instead, Rashnir took a clear shot at a mercenary's horse; the bolt buried itself completely in the animal's gut, lodging in its midsection. The horse reared and buckled, dropping its rider to the turf, freeing Rogis to concentrate on the single enemy he crossed blades with. They traded strikes until Rogis found a gap and thrust his sword into the bandit's vitals.

Riding up, halberd in hand, Rashnir decapitated the final warrior whose left leg had been trapped below his mount. The brigand's head rolled to a halt beside his crippled horse.

Rashnir and Rogis continued their approach to the castle. They kept a keen eye open for other attackers, scanning any possible hiding points on the way to the castle. They knew of the king's love for subterfuge.

Meeting no further resistance, they found their way safely through the courtyard and up to King's Hall. Many guards and mercenaries flanked them as they strode through the gates, but none of them made any moves that might provoke a fight. Apparently, Harmarty was willing to speak with them after all.

The king's silent majordomo met them at the door; a fresh scar raked its way across his face indicating Rutheir must not have finished the deed, but perhaps wanted to cut away only a piece of the man at a time. The mute led them to the Harmarty's chamber. It was filled with the same sort of characters as on the last visit: a menagerie of excess.

Harmarty sat, slumped in his chair; the rest of his court carried on with their routine revelry. The King hooked his right leg over the armrest of his throne; his left hand clutched his father's crown. He studied it as if it contained some secret knowledge one required in order to be a good king.

"Leave us," Harmarty said, quietly, like a man defeated.

The court fell silent, as if on cue. The more deviant of the bunch looked disappointed. They would miss whatever Harmarty had planned, but they complied anyway. Only Harmarty, Rogis, Rashnir, and one plain-looking man remained in the chamber. The plain man wore a simple brown tunic and matching pants. An elegant looking rapier hung sheathed at his left hip; a look of sorrow spread across his face.

The party shared a moment of awkward silence.

Rashnir stepped forward; he was confident that the day was his. "Harmarty! Kelsa and I *will* marry— even if I must defy you."

Harmarty leaned forward in sadness; his head nearly drooped between his knees. He held his father's crown between his hands now. He studied it—reflecting on his father and on life. "I know," he whimpered.

"I have been thinking a lot lately, mostly about what *you* said, Rogis. I even dispatched several bounty hunters and mercenaries to get my way, but still I've failed. I'd have no chance if I faced you in combat. Apparently *you*, Rashnir, got more out of Rogis' training than I did." He smirked, "We are almost brothers like that, two students of the same master."

Rashnir scowled at the comparison. He didn't like any grouping that put him and Harmarty together.

"I will respect whatever the Demons of the Gathering and the Great Lucifer desire, no matter the pain to me. His will should be made clear. But my thoughts, as I mentioned, have been on family. You see, one of the bounty hunters that you killed was a warrior named Shimza the Lesser; his brother, Shimza the Greater, stands here in this very room demanding retribution. We will let fate decide. May Lucifer himself play the role of judge and decide the outcome of this contest.

"Life or death. You will fight Shimza the Greater to the death; you may use any means necessary with whatever weapons you have on your person. Should Shimza lose, it must be fate that you and Kelsa marry. If Shimza wins, then Lucifer favors me, as must Kelsa."

Harmarty stood and approached. A gleam of desperation glinted in his eyes. He looked up and down the ill-clad warrior standing opposite Rashnir.

Rashnir stood in the center of the room, Rogis just off to his side. His opponent drew the rapier; light shimmered on the blade as he ran it in a series of fanciful swipes through the air, showing off his prowess and precision. Finished, he made a grunting sound and assumed a ready position with his weapon in mid-guard.

Unimpressed, Rashnir studied his challenger and stood up straight. Dropping his hands to his side, he made a declaration, "I would kill a thousand Shimzas, both Greater and Lesser for my love." Rashnir quickly drew his pistol crossbows and fired bolts at his prey; both struck home and crisscrossed in the man's neck. The shafts of the bolts made an X, centered in the back of his esophagus. Clutching his throat, the surprised swordsman groaned with a blood-choked gurgle and collapsed to his knees, spat a cascade of crimson from his mouth, and then fell dead on his face.

Rogis rushed to Harmarty, whose face had gone pale with melancholy. "You see, fate has chosen. You must relent. Kelsa will marry Rashnir."

The distinct "thwang" sound of a bowstring echoed from the rear of the room as Rogis spoke. Rashnir cried in surprise and pain; he dropped to a knee with an arrow protruded from his lower back lodged just above his kidneys. Rogis spun around to find the assassin clad in black as he threw aside the lengthy tapestry which concealed his position.

The archer gripped the bow and scowled at his prey. Rashnir locked eyes with him and sucked in his breath with pain and recognition. He recognized Shimza the Greater; his features closely matched those of the assassin in Rashnir's stable.

Rogis also cried out in sudden anguish; Harmarty crept up to whisper into the ear of his one-time instructor who trembled in pain, "I may not have learned many combat skills from you, teacher," he hissed like a venomous snake. "But I did learn where the chinks in your armor are." Harmarty twisted the blade that he'd plunged into Rogis' back.

Rogis screamed with an agonized wheeze of betrayal; blood drooled down his chin as it bubbled up his throat. The wound was clearly fatal, and Rogis knew it. He turned around to make his final acts count: to make his wicked student pay.

Shimza leveled another arrow as Rashnir stumbled to his feet, driven by pure rage. Shimza's next arrow streaked into the base of Rogis' spine, just as he'd cornered the sniveling King. Rogis stood straight and froze; the arrow severed his spinal cord. Rogis fell over, paralyzed and impotent, bleeding out the last of his life.

Rashnir screamed and drew his swords. Charging at Shimza he turned his rage and grief into energy. He beat Shimza back against the wall, thrusting, parrying, slashing and blocking; he was a whirlwind of blades, a furious storm of razor-edged attacks.

Shimza ran out of space, with no room to block; Rashnir's short sword easily found a home in the soft of Shimza's belly. He struck so hard that it pinned the assassin to the wall, lodging the blade into the stone.

Dropping his sword, Shimza reached around and grabbed the arrow that stuck from Rashnir's back. He pulled on it before his enemy could strike the final blow and Rashnir screamed and dropped his longsword.

"Help me!" the trapped Shimza howled to Harmarty. At his beckon, a trio of guards rushed through the doors and mobbed Rashnir, pinning his back to the ground. It bent the arrow so that it lay flat against the floor, ripping up Rashnir's insides and spitting black kidney blood out of the wound.

Harmarty stood over Rashnir's fallen body; his eyes twinkled with a sadistic glee. A metallic glimmer near Rashnir's collar caught his eye.

"What is this?" Harmarty wondered aloud as he bent over Rashnir. He reached down and grabbed the chain around his opponent's neck. Seeing the betrothal rings, his face lit with childish joy.

"I have my proof now!" He tugged and tried to rip the chain from Rashnir to no avail. A guard helped Harmarty and tore the chain from Rashnir's neck, breaking the woven links of precious metal. "I see now that Kelsa has rejected your betrothal offer! You still carry these around your neck because you have been denied!

"This is my sign, she desires me and you have kept her from her master! I will go to her now! I have defeated you, and I must now set her free." He looked at Shimza, still pinned to the wall. "Guards! Throw Rashnir in the dungeon; we will torture him as a wedding prize for my beloved Kelsa. Someone tend to Shimza the Greater. He is to be honored and well paid for his help in this matter. Pay him for his brother, too."

Harmarty bobbed out of the room like a child running to play. The intense pain of both the wound and the betrayal blinded Rashnir; his mind emptied itself as he stared into the dead face of his mentor and his vision faded until he saw only black.

***

Rashnir regained consciousness in a dusty prison cell. He'd been stripped and tossed like a tainted carcass at the butcher's market. He groaned and tried to roll over on the stone floor, but he couldn't. There was still an arrow lodged in his back. He grabbed it near the fletching and pushed the shaft through. Clenching his teeth, he rapidly sucked air through them trying to cope with the extreme pain.

Once he'd pulled the feathers through, he fell to his back with a loud cry, trembling. He held the bloody arrow in his hand and shuddered as shock settled in.

The air in his cell didn't move: dead and cloy, as if it had been inhaled and exhaled by a thousand men on their deathbeds. Three of his prison walls were mason-laid stone and a third one of wrought iron locked him in. The hinged metal door was locked, barring any escape. From the pattern of the stonework and crypt-like air quality, Rashnir guessed the dungeon was below Harmarty's castle.

Barely lucid, he felt a warm caress on his forehead. Rashnir opened his eyes to see an emaciated, yet joyful looking man sitting over him. He was speaking to a third, unseen person, petitioning him on the Ranger's behalf. The man beseeched some invisible party with a foreign tongue.

"What are you doing?" Rashnir groaned.

He smiled. "I am praying for you."

"Praying?" he wheezed. "I thought that members of the Luciferian Order were sent to the *church's* dungeons and judged by a private tribunal for any crimes they committed." This man's prayer was unlike the typical ritualistic prayers he was familiar with.

The man chuckled. "I am Nhoj. A heretic, says them. I am not Luciferian. They call me a prophet of the Dark One, but they are wrong. I am a follower of Yahweh. While Lucifer may seem bright, there exists a greater light that makes Lucifer appear black as midnight by comparison. This light is Yahweh."

Rashnir let his eyes roll back in his head. He was dying and his crazy cellmate had obviously been isolated in this cell for so long that he'd lost his mind and invented a new religion.

"I've been waiting here for a long time; my calling is finally complete. I pray for your healing and I have faith that you will be made new."

The warrior winced as Nhoj gingerly placed his hands on Rashnir's belly. "My God, I pray that you would heal this one whom you have chosen; I *know* that you will, by your grace and your love. You have shown me it is your will."

As Rashnir looked down at his stomach, Nhoj rolled over, chuckling to himself. To Rashnir's amazement, only a star-shaped scar remained where the arrow had punctured his body; he touched his back to find another lump of scar tissue. Astonished, he turned his face to Nhoj.

He shook the old heretic, but couldn't get any reaction. Nhoj had rolled over and immediately stopped breathing. Apparently, with his mission in this life completed, he had slipped beyond life.

Rashnir rolled to his knees with the blood soaked arrow still in his hand; a black clot of blood dangled from the feathers. The arrow's shaft was made of kiln-dried wood which kept it from warping, but it also made it brittle enough to fracture into long, hard splinters.

His mind fixed on Kelsa, he didn't waste any time; he examined the lock and snapped the arrow. It broke at a narrow angle and Rashnir whittled the broken end further using the arrowhead, forming a long, narrow point. He methodically worked the lock's mechanism with his wooden tool. The lock's internals clicked and the door released.

Stalking through the shadows of the dungeon hallway, Rashnir found a well-lit room where two guards rummaged through his armor and weapons; they attempted to divvy them up. Grasping the sharpened ends of the arrow that once pierced him, Rashnir waited for his moment, as he hid just beyond the door jamb. The closest guard turned his back to the doorway and the other guard bent down, his attention upon the pile of loot near his feet.

Striking from the shadows, Rashnir drove the jagged end of one wooden dagger into, and almost through, the neck of the closer guard. The second guard reached for his weapon as Rashnir dove for him. A simple sharpened piece of wood was little match for a sword in a duel; Rashnir bowled the guard over and pinned him to the ground. Mounted on top of his opponent, he bought himself a few seconds of time. Rashnir drove the remaining shank into his adversary's jugular. The conflict ended seconds later after a choked spluttering cough when the guard relaxed his body forever.

Time was of the essence and Rashnir had become a focused machine; his only goal was to get home: to reach Kelsa as soon as possible. He'd form a plan as he went along.

Gathering his equipment, he quickly armed himself. Rashnir tossed aside his chest plate; he was not able to cinch it up himself. He picked up the chain shirt he'd worn and examined it, noticing the damaged links where he'd been struck in the back; his light armor was no match for a direct hit. He put it on anyway.

Rashnir shod his feet and arms and girded his waist with the pouch of crossbow ammunition. He stealthily crept from the room.

As quickly as possible, he slipped through the corridors and staircases like a wraith. Listening carefully for footfalls, he avoided any further encounters. Knowing that the entrance would house guards at all times, Rashnir moved up a staircase to the second story, looking for a window to escape through. The day grew old and the sun had nearly waned, falling behind the horizon.

Just as he peered out a bedroom window, Rashnir noticed movement at the doorway. He spun and drew steel; an intruding servant froze. Hands up, the man silently pled for his life.

The servant waved his hands and pointed to his gaping, open mouth. This servant also had no tongue. Rashnir relaxed a bit. The servant had apparently been lighting the candles in lieu of the failing light. He set his candlestick down on an end table inside of the door. He went to the large, finely crafted wardrobe and opened its dual shutter doors. Removing a hooded cloak, he slung it across Rashnir's shoulders and clasped a simple brooch at the neck to hold it in position. The servant motioned for Rashnir to follow.

After checking that the hall was clear, the mute led Rashnir down the corridor to another bedroom. He led him inside and motioned to stay put for a moment.

Quickly returning, the silent traitor brought a cloth sack and handed it to the escaped prisoner.

Rashnir slung the sack over his shoulder. Peeking inside, he found a wine skin, bread, raisin cakes, and dried meat. The look that the servant gave Rashnir communicated more than words could have; he wanted Rashnir to escape, and he wanted to help. Participating could give him small victory over Harmarty, at least.

The servant led him two doors further, to another room on the backside of the palace, and showed him a window. This side of the structure had thick, hardened vines creeping from ground to roof. The vines made a perfect ladder to escape by. Rashnir bowed; the servant returned the gesture and left to resume his duties.

Pulling the hood low, Rashnir climbed out the window and quickly worked his way to the ground. The castle grounds burgeoned with shadows. He darted down pathways and alleys, scouting ahead to maintain stealth.

After a quick search, he found the stables. Few horses remained; Harmarty had departed some time ago to propose to Kelsa. The only person left behind had been the stable master who'd fixed his eyes on Nikko. The horse kicked at the stable gate wildly. The steed knew something was amiss about his new surroundings. Nikko and Nightshade had been stabled next to each other; both stamped threateningly as if they knew they were captives. Rashnir grabbed a piece of lumber and crept behind the stable master.

One deft swing later, Rashnir incapacitated his only remaining opposition. He reclaimed his horse and calmed him down. Rashnir freed Nightshade and patted his flank, saying goodbye to Rogis' horse. Then, he mounted his own.

The guards at their post yelped when Nightshade galloped past them unridden. They cussed something about the stable master being drunk again and chased after the animal as it galloped away. Using Nightshade as a distraction, Rashnir slipped through the gate and into the main courtyards.

He kept to the backside of Capitol City. Doing his best to look like a commoner riding a horse to pasture, he scouted the area with as much speed as he could risk until he found what he was looking for: the small gate herdsmen used to take their animals through. The way was unguarded and Rashnir slipped through. Once out of view, he urged Nikko to top speed and they soon raced across the countryside.

**

Rashnir raced his horse through the shadows and rode straight through the estatuary gates at breakneck speed. The smell of smoke filled his nose and he could feel the filmy soot settling on the air while he rode up to the flames.

His home raged like a pyre; flames leapt and danced under the stars, throwing ash to the moon. At the foot of the inferno leapt shadowy figures as they danced, reveling in celebration. Another fire instantly kindled: this one in Rashnir's heart. He raced onward as Harmarty's troops partied.

In the noise of the fire and revelry, no one heard Nikko galloping in until Rashnir crashed upon the distracted horde. He fired a shot from each crossbow, killing two nearby guards. The jubilant crowd suddenly realized they were under attack and took up arms.

Tossing the pistols aside, Rashnir unsheathed his two swords and attacked from atop his horse. The flamelight strobed the battle as he swiped and stabbed from his mount, slaying numerous guards and crossing sword after sword only to find his rage-filled blows strike home each time. Bodies piled up around his horse and the oncoming tide of attackers thickened until there was no more room to move.

His blood boiled as he pressed against the crowd, killing anyone that did not yield. Rashnir spotted Harmarty at the edge of the crowd; a look of fear plastered to his face. Beside him did not stand Kelsa, but his giant brute of a bodyguard, Rutheir. He urged Nikko through the crowd, hacking away at the opposition as if they were vines in a forest; all fell before his assault.

Suddenly, Nikko gave a shrill cry and hop-stepped in pain. Then again, and again; the noble horse almost dropped to the ground. Rashnir saw them: archers. Arrow after arrow struck his horse until the animal finally surrendered to the pain and fell to the ground. Nikko neighed his last as Rashnir rolled to the ground and charged against the wall of opposition.

Attack after attack consumed his vision as he struck and parried, forcing his sight into a rage-shaped tunnel; more and more often, his blows met with sword rather than flesh. Suddenly, as crossing swords whined with a sharp "clang," Rashnir felt a blunt blow to his chin. It knocked him completely from his feet. The corner of his periphery vision identified the culprit; Rutheir had entered the fray. As soon as Rashnir rolled to his rear and prepared to launch back into the assault, warriors mobbed him. The weight of the guards' bodies prevented him from breathing. They pinned him to the ground and crushed his lungs.

As the mob cleared, they restrained the Ranger on his knees, hands held behind him. King Harmarty approached, a smug and smiling Rutheir following at his side. A glazed look fell on Harmarty as he stood before his subdued enemy. Rutheir was about to draw his sword when Harmarty stayed his hand. "Bring the brands!" he cried.

The crowd cheered, pounding fists to the sky.

Rashnir's panicked eyes darted around, searching for help in the faces around him. His eyes locked on only one familiar face in the crowd, Jaker. The scout who he'd once called friend, third in command of the Rangers, played witness to this all.

Jaker wore a sad face. The scout turned and looked at Rashnir as he noticed the gaze.

A minion brought the king a red-hot iron rod, pulled from the nearby burning wreckage. Harmarty motioned for Jaker to come forward and witness the event.

The look of betrayal on his face convinced Rashnir that Jaker had nothing to do with this plot. He too was a pawn. Jaker's look of disbelief fell upon Rashnir; sorrow and disappointment mixed equally with hatred.

"Jaker," Harmarty said, "You will now be in charge of Rogis' Rangers after Rashnir's treasonous actions."

Suddenly Rashnir understood; he'd been framed. "It's a lie!" he screamed upon deaf ears.

"Witness this, Jaker, and spread the word in the cities and in the guilds; Rashnir, second in command of Rogis' Rangers assassinated his superior in an attempt to usurp control from him. How typical," Harmarty sneered,

"After all, he did it once before, did he not, striking down the mighty Mind in cold blood?"

Harmarty continued, "My former teacher, the great Rogis, confided in me recently that he feared for his life, that Rashnir plotted his demise. Feel free to examine the body where it lies in state in my castle; Rogis was stabbed in the back.

"The funeral will be for the general public and his friends. We found Rogis' estate in flames before we rode in here, hoping to put a stop to the madness that this maniac has wrought upon the area. We'd hoped to save the girl, Kelsa, but it appears that he set fire to it with her trapped inside before riding off to murder Rogis' family as they slept in their beds."

Jaker's eyes welled up and he turned away. He turned back only once and gave Rashnir a cold, piercing glare: a death threat. Jaker turned and left, too disgusted to stay and witness the punishment.

Rutheir seized Rashnir's right hand and forced it open, palms held upward as the king laid the brand across flesh, searing burn marks into the skin. He completed the brand-mark on one hand and then branded the other, ignoring Rashnir's screams and demands to see Kelsa.

When it was over, soldiers held Rashnir down as Rutheir savagely beat him before casting him aside like a limp sparring dummy. There was no point to the beating, except it brought pleasure to Rutheir who heaped further humiliation upon Rashnir. Eventually, the King's remaining troops mounted their horses and departed as if the whole evening had been a sport.

Rashnir, in too much pain to walk, and hands incapable of letting him crawl, used his elbows to pull himself towards the flaming rubble of the mansion. Now burned down to the stonework of the foundation, it had mostly collapsed upon itself. He found a familiar body lying prone in the nearby grass: Dane.

The crippled Rashnir belly-crawled up to the old man and rolled him over as best as he could. The elderly servant groaned with ragged breaths.

"Where is Kelsa?" Rashnir asked him gently, trying to rouse his senses.

Dane's milky eyes rolled in their sockets. He could barely stay conscious.

"What happened here?" Rashnir demanded.

"They came… they surrounded the house. We had barred the doors and windows so that they could not get in. The king was in a rage, demanding that she come out to him. He told her that he defeated you in combat and that she shouldn't fear for her safety anymore. He said that they would finally be married.

"Kelsa, of course, refused. Harmarty lit the house on fire and told her that she must choose him or death. We were on the second floor. We planned to escape out the rear, but the fire spread so quickly, and the staircase was soon engulfed in flames. Even if she wanted to go to Harmarty, she could not have. We were about to escape out a window, but a flaming ceiling beam fell and pinned Kelsa to the floor. The library burned around her as another beam fell, knocking me out of the window."

Dane looked into Rashnir's eyes. Both men cried, weeping bitter tears. "Forgive me. I was too weak to save her. I tried… I did. Once I hit the ground… I couldn't move my legs. I had to lay here and listen to her scream… she screamed your name for so long. She was so sure that you would save her." Grief-stricken, Dane fell silent; he stared into the sky and his tears glistened under the stars and firelight.

Darkness and anguish consumed the two survivors before unconsciousness eventually crept in. Rashnir awoke the next morning to smoldering rubble; intense pain wracked his body. Dane had died sometime during the night. Rashnir could only wish that his fate had been the same.

Nothing remained of the house or its surrounding structures. His dead horse, Nikko, lay amongst the strewn, fallen bodies. A pall of death hung above the place. Harmarty had succeeded; he hadn't only taken away his possessions, but he'd killed all those that he loved. He'd destroyed Rashnir, stripped him of his honor and of his livelihood. Rashnir had no more friends; because of the mark he'd been branded with and the tale he'd ordered told, his professional connections would abandon him. The only thing he truly possessed now was hatred.

Chapter Five

Rashnir rode through the evening. The sky deepened to a muddy red as the horse galloped at an increasingly uncomfortable pace under Rashnir's guidance.

He passed several homesteads and wondered what it might have been like had he stayed on Mallow's farm. Could he have enjoyed a common life like so many others before him? For that matter, what if he'd grown up with a loving father, like Rogis had been to his children? Was Rashnir cursed, forsaken by fate or by whatever deities might exist? Whenever he got ahead in life, some new, unforeseen force brought him crashing back down to a new form of captivity. Was he enslaved to an ill-fated destiny?

The jaded exterior surrounding his heart cracked slightly. Rashnir felt the machismo façade crumble in the coming darkness; tears streamed down his face and with nobody around to see it, he let them.

A jumble of thoughts coursed through his mind. *There must be more than this. Mankind must have some purpose. If the myths were true, if Yahweh created man, then for what purpose? And why would he have forsaken them?* His thoughts turned to Nhoj. If he had lived, perhaps he could have given Rashnir more information. In the short moments he'd had with him, Nhoj had been the only example he'd ever seen of religious kindness.

The only thing that Rashnir knew was that his life, up until this point, had been little more than a mess of chaos coupled with a general lack of purpose. Whenever he thought he'd found an honorable pursuit in life, another person's greed stripped it from him.

Rashnir gave up on his thoughts, on thinking altogether. He focused on the sounds of the night air as he continued his secret journey. He would soon arrive at the castle's rear gate. The animal gate that he'd escaped through so long ago would help him infiltrate the castle. Rashnir glanced down at the sweaty horse and cursed. *I've never ridden such a slow horse.* Only a few hours of darkness would remain by the time he expected to arrive.

The night trickled on and he arrived without incident. Rashnir had committed the act countless times in his mind, mentally playing out every conceivable scenario. When he found the solitary posted guard sleeping lightly, he knew exactly what to do.

Well beyond earshot of the sleeping watchman, Rashnir climbed down from his horse. He crept up, silent as a stalking cat. The vengeful assassin recognized the man's face; every person present on the night of Kelsa's murder had been burned into his mind. Rashnir slipped his borrowed sword into the man's vitals as he covered the guard's nose and mouth.

Rashnir dragged the body into the low shrubs near the castle walls. He tethered the horse to a copse of prickly bushes and slipped inside the gate.

Stealthily, he slinked through the shadows and arrived undetected at the main keep. At such an early hour, nobody remained awake. Most of the king's entourage would have partied well into the night and passed into deep sleep before this part of early morning.

Grabbing the sturdy vine lattice, Rashnir hauled himself up the castle wall using the same natural ladder he'd used before. Reaching the fourth level, he snuck through a window. The king's bedchamber would likely be on the fifth floor, but the vines didn't reach that high.

Someone occupied the room, but didn't hear the Ranger creep through his sill with wraith-like silence. Under the cover of heavy snores, Rashnir tiptoed through the room and towards the door which remained slightly ajar. With only a slight creak, he opened the door only enough to slip into the sparsely lit hallway.

The far end of the hall was better lit than the rest; torchlight spilled through an open door. Muted voices emanated from inside the room, resonating through the passage.

"Harmarty has already given me his full authorization," a gravelly human voice claimed. "Your king must simply follow suit and ally with us as well. We are, after all, not overly different when all is boiled down. Despite a species difference, we are all subject to the same powers—the same rules governing nature and magic."

"I am simply saying that our king might not be as willing to pledge full support to a cause that he does not have full faith in." This slurred and guttural voice sounded distinctly nonhuman.

"Faith, grr'Shaalg? It is very much a matter of faith. Even though he may lack faith in the religious tenets that we desire to implement, I do know that he fully supports one aspect of this cause: personal gain. This alliance will be especially lucrative to those who join quickly, especially for those who help most at the beginning stages of our grand plan."

The human's voice mused with a slight threat, "A demonstration of power may be needed to convince you and your brethren?"

"No…no, Absinthium. I know your power and so does my king. I have no desire to invoke your wrath. Between only you and me, my king already knows he is in too deep.

"We know we must lend you support—even if for self-preservation, if nothing else. We do it gladly, however, for personal gain. Your plan is viable and your power is immense. Mere mortals cannot contend with the mystic powers you represent. Our kingdom cleaves to you to the last of our kin."

Rashnir crept closer to the light; his curiosity piqued as he eavesdropped on an undoubtedly highly confidential conversation. He found a spot in the darkness with just enough of an angle to peer through the open doorway. Inside the room sat Absinthium and grr'SHaalg.

Absinthium, the human, was a lean and wiry old man with grizzled features. His bald top, but for the hair that hung on the sides and back of his head, stood in stark contrast to the black eyepatch over his left socket; the silver locks almost touched his neck. He wore a robe woven of elegant, fine materials and was adorned with gold chains and trinkets—many of them likely amulets. He propped his odd looking staff against his lap.

The staff drew Rashnir's attention. The center of the rod was metal—something much shinier than iron; the bottom and top looked like gnarled tree roots made of a woody substance resembling the vines Rashnir used to access this level. Atop the staff, the root-like wood knotted into an ugly bulb. More of the vine-like tendrils encapsulated a tiny, glowing gem. This was undoubtedly some kind of arch-mage from the Luciferian Order.

grr'SHaalg, a goblin, was very different in appearance. His dark, hideous features had been adorned by a simple, dusty loincloth and a purple fez cap that indicated his station as envoy of a goblin king. Around his neck hung a simple, wrought iron chain with a plain bauble fastened to it. Made of pure gold, the trinket was a simple metallic bar, about one-third the size of a brick. Several sigils and markings were engraved upon it.

The goblin leaned into the conversation, "King Nvv-Fryyg wants me to negotiate a better deal for him if possible, but he knows he might not get one. He knows that what you have in store for him might be all he can gain. Truthfully, he would be content with what you've already offered. I shall tell him that nothing more can be bartered; there will be no monetary compensation for our cooperation—only the prestige and power inherent in such an affiliation. For doing this, will there be a reward for me?"

Absinthium grinned, realizing that the goblin had placed himself in the mage's pocket. "Nvv-Fryyg is a fool, but his dirtside resources are coveted by my master; I do appreciate you're a fellow cunning mind. For the loyal, there will undoubtedly be great rewards. Perhaps you seek an arrangement like that which exists between myself and the real Jandan king? You wish to rule, perhaps as the puppeteer pulling strings?"

The goblin exhaled a huff of agreement: a treasonous and wordless declaration.

As the conversation turned political, Rashnir's interest waned. The two discussed manipulation, assassinations, and riots. Rashnir only planned to foul one of their schemes; they would lose the ability to manipulate their tool, Harmarty. The king would not survive this night.

Rashnir eased out of his creeping pose and slinked back through the hallway. Passing through the corridor, he found the access to the fifth floor. The steps leading upstairs would probably end in an open, guarded lobby. Rashnir prepared himself for frontal assault if need be, but stealth would be much less messy. Nearby, a large column of stones resembling a chimney stood. Inside the column was a dumbwaiter system used to ferry items directly to the king's chambers, among other locations.

He opened the grate in front of the aperture and peered inside the shaft. Ropes connected to counterweights and trays were within reach; he leaned into the access point and grasped the rope. Writhing, he squirmed all the way inside.

Hand over hand he pulled himself upwards, fully aware that one slip would send him spiraling downwards five or more levels. At the top, he found a clear view of the bedchamber through the grate.

Poking his head through the access, Rashnir examined his prospects. Men and women slept all around the room. Random floorspace was bulked with pillows and blankets where the king's cronies rested. Bodies lay everywhere; the scene likely the aftermath of a drunken orgy.

The room's center, on a raised dais, boasted a large, canopied bed. Heavy drapery hung from the corner posts: the king's bed. Rashnir looked around but could not spot the bodyguard, Rutheir; he was the only one that Rashnir felt could cause any trouble. Assessing the guests from a distance, none of them appeared to be warriors.

These sleepers were only here for Harmarty's personal pleasure and amusement.

Silent as a cat stalking its unaware prey, Rashnir rolled from the shaft and onto the shadowy floor. Starlight streamed through the gigantic windowpanes shedding enough light for Rashnir to find a path through the sleeping masses. He crept through the maze of people and onto the dais. Silently, Rashnir slid inside the heavy curtains that shielded the bed from the rest of the crowd.

Harmarty lay in the center of his immaculate bed, completely nude. He lay alone, sprawled out upon a top sheet. A pained look set on his sleeping face. Blankets and quilts had been kicked aside, lying rumpled on the floor as if he'd thrashed them off during night terrors.

Vengeance burned inside Rashnir. He cut two long strips from the bed sheet and stepped onto the bed, standing over the body of the condemned.

The assassin looked down again, finding wicked scars all over Harmarty's hairless body, especially near his genitals. The thought occurred to Rashnir that the king was perhaps the victim of secret abuses; maybe some ill fate influenced him—molded him into the twisted man he'd become. Perhaps this was the reason no female shared this bed.

Rashnir's heart almost moved to sympathy for the perverse man; the glimmer of a tear seeped through Harmarty's clenched eyelids. Mental backlash seized Rashnir; his mind rejected any thoughts of pity. How many tears had soaked Kelsa's cheeks as she screamed for Rashnir in the flames? How many tears streaked down Dane's face as he lay broken and dying on the ground?

Eyes narrowed by rage, Rashnir's muscles tightened with resolve, teeth clenching. He jammed the first length of bedsheet into Harmarty's mouth to keep him silent. The sleeping king awoke with a jolt, but Rashnir overpowered him. He pinned Harmarty's arms down as he flailed violently. Rashnir tied the second strip around Harmarty's head to completely gag him. Scarcely a muffled moan could escape.

With the monarch completely subdued, Rashnir slapped his face to get his attention. Harmarty's eyes took a fraction of a second to focus in the low light. Their eyes locked on Rashnir's as Harmarty recognized his assailant. His eyes sank into his skull as dread realization set in. The king knew he was about to die.

Leaning forward, Rashnir whispered into the Harmarty's ear, "Do you remember me—what you did to me?" The gagged man trembled slightly, crying like a child.

"I don't possess the resources to strip you of everything like you did to me, so I must settle for killing you," Rashnir whispered. "I know that this means I'll never have my name officially cleared for the murders of my beloved, my teacher, and Rogis's extended family. But I also know that as long as you live you'd never let me find redemption. You have too much pride to acknowledge real honor or truth. But your death will at least prove to me that justice exists!"

He hissed into his prisoner's ear, "I want to let you know that Kelsa always despised you and I hope her spirit is allowed to torment you in whatever afterlife exists."

Rashnir ran his short sword into Harmarty's gut. The sword penetrated Harmarty's stomach, angled up, and pierced a lung. Full of silent rage, Rashnir twisted the blade and violently jerked the hilt.

Harmarty's pain-wracked eyes spasmed open and shut. His eyes opened one last time, and then all light faded from them, leaving them dull and glossy. Blood soaked through the rag that gagged him and his body relaxed; his back no longer arched from the tormenting pain. Rashnir was confident that Harmarty had died.

He peeked through the curtains. The scene beyond the canopy remained exactly the same as it had been minutes earlier.

Rashnir rolled the corpse over. He mopped up most of the loose fluid with strips of bedding and then wrapped Harmarty up in a bedsheet and set him on the floor. He used the loose ends of the sheet to tie the shroud tight. Just as he'd done countless times in his mind, Rashnir made the king's bed up as if it had not been slept in and checked the scene over. Not a spot of blood was visible.

Silently, the assassin carried the body back to the hidden entry where he'd found access. Rashnir reached through and tested the weight on the lines until he found an unweighted one. He pulled a great deal of slack through and tied it to one of Harmarty's feet.

Pushing the limp carcass through the slot, it dangled a few feet below the opening. Harmarty's body hung between levels like a used-up bug hanging from a spider's web. With even a fractional amount of luck, it would be days before anybody found the body. The stench would eventually give it away.

Slipping inside the shaft, Rashnir replaced the grate after a final scan to see if he'd left behind any evidence of his presence. He slid down the rope until he arrived at the third floor. Rashnir didn't want to chance an encounter with the mage and goblin on the fourth.

No one here was awake. Rashnir skulked through the hallway until he found a door he knew would lead to the vine ladder. He quickly clambered down to the ground, unseen.

Finding the courtyard still empty, he picked his way back through the rear gate. He retrieved his fatigued horse and climbed back into the saddle. Rashnir galloped away just as the sun announced its presence, cresting the horizon with a flare of color.

Morning broke and the emotional high Rashnir had been riding finally crashed. The adrenaline ebbed from his system and emptiness suddenly seized his heart. He felt like a hollow shell. Grief ravaged his mind; with his nemesis killed, he had nothing left to live for—and yet the gall of his bitterness still clung to him like a calf mired in its own dysentery.

Rashnir reached for the short sword, contemplating suicide, but quickly threw off the notion. He still had something to drive him: his promise to return and serve Kevin. Perhaps he could still find meaning in his life; could this man provide such a thing?

In the time it took Rashnir to ride back to the village, new questions continued to plague him. Some comforted him, others confounded him. *What exactly were the goblins and that arch-mage planning? How was the monarchy involved? Harmarty was surely twisted and insane—the most self-centered man Rashnir had ever encountered—but Absinthium seemed to seethe and radiate evil, wearing it like a cloak. What did the Luciferian Order have planned for Jand?*

Rashnir dismounted as he neared Grinden's borders. He gave the stolen horse a slap on the rump. It squealed and trotted off; it would eventually find its way home.

On foot, Rashnir continued back to Grinden. Once more he entered that city as a freed man owning nothing. Perhaps, his new life could start?

He would know soon enough. Rashnir had a meeting to attend at the Green Serpent Inn.

CHAPTER SIX

The dingy air inside the Green Serpent Inn added a layer of darkened film over its residents. Pipe-smoke filled the air and wreathed the interior surfaces with a thin layer of soot—the settled smoke of ten thousand past exhalations gathered like sticky dust on the tables and chairs.

Letting in a shaft of light, the main entrance swung open. The silhouette of a cloaked figure wandered in and the door drifted shut behind him.

Kevin, and his two companions, Jorge and Kyrius, watched with rapt interest as the nondescript Rashnir walked through the room. His gait and the sunken look around his eyes revealed enough. The trio knew that his personal mission had succeeded. He approached and found the empty seat they'd saved for him at their table.

The Green Serpent Inn was a low-key tavern and dining establishment. While it had a few rooms available in the rear for travelers, its usual guests were those who had taken too much in their cups at the late hours of evening. They were a mix of middle class workers and a handful of reputed scoundrels. At this hour of the day, there were seldom many customers; the Green Serpent was not known for high quality food—just cheap, warm ale. At the moment, only one other customer occupied the floor; very hung-over, the disheveled man could barely maintain his slurred conversation with the innkeeper who kept trying to hedge away from any banter at all.

Rashnir settled his tired frame into the chair and leaned forward into the conversation. Kevin had a sheaf of papers and a stylus. He and his fair-skinned allies had been conversing and drawing up notes during their wait.

"I am here," Rashnir announced.

"You are a man of your word," Kevin replied, "I knew that you were. I could discern it from our first conversation."

"You kept your word to me and I am now in your debt. Tell me now what you require of me." Rashnir paused. This stranger seemed to care about the fallen Ranger's personal life and so he continued. "I feel like an empty man; I have no purpose left in me. I feel I could die without so much as a quarrel, but if you find some use for me, then I welcome it." Rashnir's voice sounded old, like an elderly man's. He slumped in his chair; his vengeance was achieved, but it only left him more hollow than before.

"I told you that I wanted someone of your skills. You have many talents, Rashnir, and I want to utilize most all of them. I want you to travel with me."

"But I am marked, irredeemable." He held up his hands to again show Kevin his scarred, ugly palms. "If you employ me as a bodyguard, then we will all be stalked and killed by bounty hunters or soldiers—not that it matters to me any longer, but surely you value your own life. When you gave me a weapon earlier it was secret and in confidence; this act would be open treason. Regardless of how some people feel about corrupt and selfish monarchs they still obey them out of traditions and respect. Grinden may put on a façade of neutrality, but if the Jandan or Nindan governments really want you, they could come in and take you."

"I believe in *you, Rashnir*. I know that what I am doing will fly in the face of the rulers of these lands, but I am not subject to their authority. I obey the One who rules everything."

Rashnir's eyes traced a line to a Luciferian tome sitting before Kevin, next to his stack of papers. The writing didn't make any sense to him, as if it were in a foreign language not native to men.

"No," Kevin deduced his thoughts, "I am not a Luciferian. This book is for research. I follow the one true God; I am obedient to Yahweh. I know the fullness of the truth and came here from Earth, quite accidentally in fact, where we call ourselves Christians."

He raised his eyebrows at Kevin, learning this new term, "Krist-chin? What is this teaching?"

Now, fully in each other's confidences, Kevin explained, "You have part of the teaching from Luciferian doctrines. I know the fullness of truth because I know the One who embodies all truth. You see, the best way to tell a lie is with some truth mixed in, so that it will be believable—and the humans of this realm have long been deceived.

"What you know is that Yahweh created Earth and He created Heaven and He created Hell and all of Earth's animals, as well as some that now inhabit even this place. He created humans and breathed life into them. He set them up as caretakers of His creation: Earth.

"Luciferianism tells you that mankind had been slaves, merely mindless automatons. This is a deliberate error, Rashnir. They were obeying Yahweh, doing what was right when Lucifer, the demon hay-lale', desired that they disobey. At that point there was no such thing as sin or evil. Humankind could not do any wrong because there was no knowledge of what wrongness was. Yahweh was, and is, purely holy and righteous. Because of His nature, no creature could tolerate His presence if there was evil in him.

"He is like light. Light is like goodness and darkness is like evil, or the absence of good. Darkness cannot exist in the presence of light. Are you following me so far?"

"Yahweh is good and light," Rashnir said, slightly confused. "But isn't Lucifer also light?"

"Lucifer is a liar. He is the Father of all Lies. He was once an angel of light, but when he chose self over Yahweh, he became absent of that light; he had emptied himself of goodness by breaking away from Yahweh, his source of light, and turned dark. He was cast down from heaven and he took many angels with him."

Kyrius and Jorge knowingly nodded their heads in accord. "We were there," stated Jorge with his low, rumbling voice.

Kevin continued, "He was jealous of the power given to mankind. Lucifer was an angel, and special status was given to man. *Mankind* was created in Yahweh's image, *they* had the opportunity to make choices—freewill, whereas angels were the tools that Yahweh used. Men choose to worship the one true God, Yahweh, because of what He has done for us out of love. Angels had a choice to make when Lucifer was cast out of heaven: whether to follow God or follow self and cast their lot with Lucifer. One third of the angels followed Lucifer and fell from Heaven as supernatural abominations: these are the origins of the demons.

"You see, Lucifer only wants to bring about the destruction of men because of his jealousy for them. Lucifer was bound by his own hatred and rage in this jealous state; men were given the same job that Lucifer once held: praising and worshiping Yahweh with their voices, actions, lives. He was especially jealous because men were so much better at it than Lucifer, the great angel. *He was furious.*"

"Oh, he shone brightly," Kyrius interjected, "He could sing and made music so incredibly pleasing to one's ears. Lucifer loved the Lord in those days. Where he walked, his footsteps were like incense and he led the musicians and the choirs, composing such masterpieces that none will ever compare with. I was there, I sang with them, but the songs of men were so much more moving to Yahweh. The lone, untrained voice of Adam rose above our beautiful noise and warmed His heart.

"There was nothing special about his voice," Kyrius mused. "His music was not overtly beautiful, or well put together. It barely even resembled a song, but it pleased God and we had trouble realizing why, until the times after their fall after we watched mankind multiply.

"You never mentioned children, Rashnir, but I assume that you have seen children with their parents. Very young children?"

Rashnir nodded his head.

"Think, then, about a toddler, singing to his father or mother with words of adoration and love, a simple, made-up child's song. That is a song that will make a parent stop and pay attention, despite the circumstances; you would cherish that song above any orchestra. No symphony can compare."

Kyrius' comments brought a glisten of wetness to Kevin's eyes.

"Men," Kevin said with a strained voice, "are Yahweh's beloved creation. As a father loves his children and adores them, so Yahweh loves us. With the angels, I would compare them to a beloved animal. You may love and cherish it and enjoy its company and grow close, but it is nothing like the affections of your own child. If a dog tried to bite your child and intends him harm, a wise parent gets rid of that dog, no matter how good of a dog it was prior. Sometimes a dog might become jealous for attention and decides to hate that child and attack it. Despite wanting its master's love, that animal has switched its loyalty from the Master to itself. This is what Lucifer did."

Rashnir looked at Kyrius and Jorge. "You are angels?" he deduced, feeling as if Kevin's comparison to pets should have insulted the tall humanoids.

"Correct," Jorge said. They maintained a logical indifference and even voice; no offense seemed to have registered in them.

"But I thought that the way between realms was closed."

"It was," said Kyrius, "But Yahweh is all powerful. If He can shut a door, He can also open it."

"Let me help you figure this out, Rashnir. I'll tell you about Yahweh," Kevin said. "Yahweh is life. Sin separates us from that; sin is death. God *loves* above all else; Yahweh, God, *is* love. But He is also justice. When man broke God's law and sinned against Him they were no longer perfect in God's image: they ceased being perfectly good and lost their inclination to act virtuously. Man gravitated to the absence of good—to evil. The species became inherently evil, in fact, despite the retention of some occasional good traits; we are all inclined to sin and selfishness. It is our nature.

"God's laws were broken and mankind became a creature of the dark with origins of the light. Because darkness is destroyed by light, God had to remove man from His presence for their own protection."

Rashnir nodded his head, understanding. Internally, he soaked up the truths as he heard them. Ever since he was young, he'd heard Luciferian myths, but they always rang false to his ears; with no alternatives of belief, he'd grown up rejecting any faith.

"So we are doomed then? Is there nothing we can do to apologize to Yahweh? Is there no way to redeem ourselves?" Rashnir asked, voice tinged with worry.

"There is. God is justice but He is also love. When a child disobeys his parents, his parents do not send him into the wild to die, they provide a way for forgiveness, atonement—sometimes through punishment or consequences.

"Yahweh is love and love is life. Sin, death, is the absence of Yahweh and thus the absence of love and life. In Yahweh's love, He made a way for us to go back to Him. His justice demanded that someone pay a penalty for breaking His law; that penalty is death. Death is a natural consequence of breaking God's laws. Somebody had to pay a death sentence for each sin in order for redemption to be made.

"Jesus, the Son of Yahweh—who also is God— came down as a man and died once and for all to pay this penalty. Jesus died a painful and wrongful death; He had never sinned, being God himself, but He died for us anyway and took the sins of mankind upon Himself. He was nailed to a wooden cross and bled out His life for us. Jesus was all-powerful and without sin, so only *He* could defeat death forever. He was resurrected to life by His own power and was given dominion over death and sin.

"Only He provides the way back to a right relationship, back to life, back to God. Jesus the Christ lets us have life again, freedom from the lies, the selfishness, the sin and darkness. Only Jesus has the power to pay the penalty for your sins, absolve your debt against God's justice."

Kevin looked at Rashnir. "Jesus Christ makes people eternally alive. He can provide freedom from death and sin, and He loves you."

Rashnir paused long and hard. "I just murdered somebody. I sent them to an eternal punishment; I sent Harmarty to a death apart from God. Still, Yahweh would love me?"

"Wouldn't a father still love one child after harming another of his own? He would correct them, yes, but he would still love them. If the child were sincere, he would forgive his transgression."

Rashnir looked around, trying to find an excuse to dodge the conviction that plagued his heart. "Why has this knowledge been hidden from us here? Why do the humans on Earth have access to some special, Godly grace?"

"God let humans make their own decisions; those decisions can impact generations. Men chose to live here and leave Yahweh from the beginning. When Jesus came and paid that penalty, He paid it for all of mankind. You have access to that same saving grace; this land has seldom heard it, though. Every time His message is proclaimed here, the messenger is killed or snatched up by the Luciferians. God gave us the power of choice and that is the most powerful thing of all.

"You have heard the Truth now, Rashnir. You have a choice before you. You must choose for the light or for the darkness; and making no choice at all is the same as picking darkness by default.

"Yahweh allowed Lucifer to create this place; that demonstrated to mankind the power of choice and demonstrated to even his angels that God was all powerful. They saw that even Lucifer, the angel to whom the most was given, could not compare in glory or ability. In allowing Lucifer to fail in this grand creation, He humiliated Lucifer by giving him exactly what he wanted and it proved to all of the fallen angels that their choice had been in error. This bred in them seeds of discord and bitterness; they were upset for their own decision—one that they could not take back.

"Lucifer lied to the people here; he is not greater than Yahweh," Kevin indicated the Luciferian text in front of him. "He did it because he hates us and wants to destroy us. Not only did he nudge mankind into sinfulness, but he is always working to tear down the saints and corrupt that which is good.

"Lucifer created many distractions to keep peoples' attention away from the Truth and gave them alternatives to Truth by inventing the Luciferian doctrines. He created the ekthro: other living, thinking beings with different natures specifically designed to teach man ungodly habits and attitudes. The bellicose warring of the dwarven culture, the vanity and selfishness of the elves, the power-lust of the centaurs and the despairing dread from raids by goblins, orcs, and more all draw us away from Yahweh.

"Even the natural environment, with the absence of Yahweh's creativity, acts as an incubator to nurture man's fallen human nature. Lucifer did not have to leave behind a large number of strong demons to tempt and to lead men astray.

"Lucifer created a place where one could escape from God's natural revelation. When you look around, you get no sense of the glory of a creator—this creation is corrupted. The things of nature in this place should seem majestic and beautiful, but they instead feel tainted and flat.

"Wickedness vastly increased on Earth because of men who traveled between the realms. They carried an evil taint among God's people and spread the evil things learned here when they returned to Earth. God had to seal the borders of the realms and destroy the wickedness of man; it had spread to everyone except for Noah and his family. God warned them, and they were saved from destruction. God had to prevent a repeat occurrence and so the floodwaters sealed the gates.

"But Noah's family didn't completely forget about everything here. Stories and myths persisted throughout the generations. We have tales on Earth of goblins and elves and the like. They have been around for more than four thousand years—ever since the way was sealed, and yet still the corporate memory exists.

"In this realm, sinful humanity runs rampant without prayers from the saints or God's graceful intervention. Whenever somebody claims that Lucifer worship is false and destructive, those people are silenced by others who use the Luciferian doctrines for personal gain. Many have set themselves up as minor deities and serve the Demons to gain power and wealth; they worship only themselves.

"Still, the Truth was revealed here about two thousand years ago, but has been covered up by evil forces. Those who lust after power used their authority and influence to silence the message. The powerful fear losing their power so they use their resources to crush the followers of Truth whenever they arise.

"There is a very tiny group of followers even now; they need to know that the end of all things has begun. I am here to tell them that the time to rise up and preach their faith is at hand. Now is the time to reveal to fellow man that the return of Christ is imminent. The gospel must be preached here: Yahweh, God, Jesus Christ, loves all humans and wants them to enter eternal life with Him, not suffer the consequences of their own predisposition."

Rashnir was moved by Kevin's passionate words, "What will happen to those who do not believe in this Jesus, if they instead choose Lucifer or choose to rely upon themselves?" His voice carried a note of worry; self-reliance had always been Rashnir's way.

"'Be it known unto you all, and to all the people of Israel, that by the name of Jesus Christ of Nazareth, whom ye crucified, whom God raised from the dead, even by him doth this man stand here before you whole. This is the stone which was set at naught of you builders, which is become the head of the corner. Neither is there salvation in any other: for there is no other name under heaven given among men, whereby we can be saved,'" Kevin quoted from memory, "These are the words of Christ given through his apostle.

"There is one way to live; if you do not choose that way then you cannot be saved from death. When you are confronted with a split in the road, you must make a choice. One path leads down a trail that crowns you as the master of your life—darkness covers that path. The other path is lit by the light of love, by the light of God, as revealed to you by His Holy Spirit. Both of these paths have a definite and eternal destination. The dark path ends in total darkness and pain with loneliness. The lit path ends with the light of Heaven and God's presence of love and fellowship."

Rashnir's eyes glossed with moisture. "But why would He do this for me? Why would a God endure suffering for the wicked?" his voice cracked slightly.

"Why did you charge through Harmarty's guards? Why did you risk pain to rescue Kelsa from the flames? What drove you through unjust torture to save her?"

Rashnir broke. His eyes flooded and his lungs constricted. A tingle of goosebumps washed over his hair follicles and his heart fell into his diaphragm. "I loved her!" his red, wet eyes met Kevin's soft compassionate portals. "I did it because she was knit to my soul. We were bound together in love!" he sobbed.

"Exactly!" Kevin burst out. "This is the same reason that Christ died for you. It is how he feels about *you.*"

Rashnir sobered a little as he weighed his choices.

Kevin went on, "If you were on a trail with two paths, one leading to suffering and loneliness, the other also being difficult—but ending in light and love, which would you pick?"

He understood. Rashnir's heart decided at that very moment which path he would take. "I choose love," he whispered. "I choose the path with light."

Kevin guided him, "Jesus said, 'I am the way, the truth, and the life: no man cometh unto the Father, but by me.' God has made a way for you to talk to Him and ask Him things through prayer; He hears you when you speak. If you decide to let Christ save you and lead your life, then He will. He doesn't always communicate directly back to you verbally; God speaks the language of God and we speak the language of men, but you can sense His answers at times and sometimes see the results of your prayers. Sometimes He answers no, but He always answers yes when you ask Him to be your Lord, because He loves you."

Rashnir nodded. Looking at nothing in particular, nothing at all even. He spoke to God. "I accept the truth. Save me from this corruption and from myself. Make me light; guide me." Emotion welled up within him and he shuddered.

***

"This is why I am here, Rashnir," Kevin digressed over supper, "God gave humans who follow him a heavy burden as emissaries to the unsaved world—I *must* preach His words. I *must* show others how they can find the Lord of Light; nothing else matters to me anymore. For those who do not know salvation, His words are life and death for *eternity*. I have a responsibility to present the Message to men. How are people supposed to find this knowledge if they have not been told, and how will they hear if the faithful will not preach?"

Rashnir looked at him and saw Kevin's passion to guide people to the knowledge of Yahweh. It surpassed even Rashnir's old hunger for vengeance against the wicked king.

"So then, you are here to find the followers that remain in this place. They are hiding from demonic oppression, or the Luciferians?"

"Yes," Kyrius said, "Our mission is two-fold. We must find these humans and tell them that it is time to rise up and preach. We must tell them that God desires a missionary heart.

"The other aspect of this undertaking goes along with the first. We must also preach ourselves. This will accomplish Christ's command, and it will call attention to us. These Christians will hopefully come looking for us when they hear others proclaiming their message."

"Our immediate plan," Jorge said, "Is to begin spreading the news and look for others who also oppose the Luciferian doctrines. Undoubtedly, some people will respond as you did. We will eventually find the Christians here as our numbers grow, and we will make a pilgrimage back to Earth before this place perishes in flames and Lucifer is cast into the abyss that has been prepared for him.

"Fire?" Rashnir asked.

"Yes," the angel continued. "There was a contract struck between Yahweh and Lucifer. It defines the rules which neither God nor Lucifer can break them; Yahweh because of His justice, and Lucifer out of his pride.

"In this contract, when Lucifer bends his knee and proclaims that Jesus is the Lord, this place will ignite in the east and burn to the west. Only those humans who have accepted Christ may cross the flooded boundary and cross into Earth. All living things here will perish and enter whatever eternity that they have chosen."

Kevin interjected, "Our time here is limited, Rashnir, and our objectives are clear. We must preach, grow, and make the journey back to Earth or we too will perish in the flames. Granted, the passage will be painful, though we will enter eternal life right away—but the angels will not."

Jorge and Kyrius nodded their assent. "We certainly do not want this," Kyrius said, "If we perish in this realm, our essence will be annihilated. In this place, Lucifer was allowed to create his own laws of physics. Here, we can die—and we have no eternal soul to transcend our corporal being."

"You see," Kevin agreed, "Humans are composed of three parts. We have the physical body; it is a vessel of flesh that houses the rest of us. It is a vehicle for transporting the spirit and soul.

"The second part is the spirit. Your spirit, your mental capabilities, is your thoughts and emotions. What you feel and how you feel as well as what you are thinking and your reasoning functions. Your brain physically stores this material, but your mind is the device that accesses the data and uses it, reasons with it. Chemicals within your blood transmit signals that relay emotions and feelings, but your *mind* interprets these things and controls them. With your mind, you can turn off these feelings. You can choose to love or to hate, you can choose to be indifferent and you can choose for your thoughts to dwell on things that change the way you feel. By this I mean that you might have hateful thoughts toward another, but by choosing to not think about it, it won't linger and the emotion will pass so that you can use reason to deal with the problems there.

"Your soul is the third and most important because it is eternal and cannot be destroyed. Your soul is the essence of who you are. It is immaterial but it is a reflection of the rest of you—it is the core of your very being. Your soul will transcend this present, physical life. It is who you *are*.

"Think of it like this: a carriage pulling a king is like a person. The carriage is the physical body; the king and his commands and directions are like his mind; his royal legacy, how his subjects see and remember him, is like his soul."

"Angels," Jorge said, "do not have a soul. While we are eternal, Lucifer's twisted rules lock our essence into this plane. We are very vulnerable here because our essence cannot transcend this dimension of existence like a soul can. On Earth we can transmute, we can be physical or not be physical…here we are locked in physical form. We are similar in basic physical makeup to any of the ekthro and must physically pass through the Western Gate in order to leave."

"Why come, then," Rashnir asked, "why not leave this job up to humans?"

"We are needed on this mission," Kyrius said.

"Because," Jorge added, "the desired outcome is worth the risks—even though we risk everything."

They heard the thundering claps of many hoofs racing across the hardened earth outside of the tavern. Several horseback riders rode quickly through the worn roads that crisscrossed through Grinden as if on an urgent mission.

Silence washed over the group; they each deduced the same reason for a heavy dispatch of riders. It was highly likely that Rashnir's actions had caused it.

Rashnir, curiosity piqued, rose and went to the door. He peeked out and saw the group of four heavy soldiers gallop towards the local garrison.

The garrison in Grinden was not an effective way of keeping peace. It was really just a collection of selected mercenaries from the Guild; the guildhouse selected people to staff it and the mercenaries' contingent received a kickback from the local city taxes. They acted as peacekeepers and handled local disputes and investigations, but if you wanted any real force, you had to hire a direct contingent from the Mercenaries Guild; it was truly a bait-and-switch form of law enforcement.

Garrison duty was often used as a training exercise for new guild members. Even if it was an impotent method of law enforcement, it was the best place to start gathering information or spread news through Grinden.

Jaker, the current head of Rogis' Rangers, stepped out of the garrison. The riders conversed with him for a few moments and then Jaker rubbed his stubble-fleeced chin in contemplation. Jaker stared off in thought and inadvertently locked eyes with Rashnir, who leaned suspiciously out of the entry to the Green Serpent Inn. Jaker read the discomfort in Rashnir's eyes.

Rashnir broke eye contact and stepped back inside the tavern. He returned to his chair and sat with his new allies.

"Well?" Kyrius asked.

"I think trouble is coming."

CHAPTER SEVEN

Jaker stepped through the door of the Green Serpent Inn and quickly spotted his mark. He wasn't hard to find; only six people occupied the place, including the bartender. At the far table he saw two men who could pass for anakim. A third man at their table dripped of foreign mannerisms and body language. Their fourth member tried too hard to act inconspicuous.

Jaker assessed every detail of the room as he entered. His sharp eyes darted this way and that. Although Jaker was not a muscular powerhouse like many mercenaries, or as skilled with a blade and highly trained as Rashnir was, Jaker had many assets that made him the most talented member on the current roster of Rogis' Rangers. Foremost on the list of Jaker's talents was his cunning wit and fast intellect; he had an uncanny knack for reading situations. A close second was his love for fancy weapons and gadgets such as his alchemical crossbow and a collection of other rare and powerful items and weapons which only few knew the limit of.

The head Ranger walked over to the table of four and pulled up a chair to join the group. Jaker sat down right next Rashnir.

"Hello, Rashnir," he said condescendingly, "When did you crawl out of the gutter?"

Rashnir pulled back the hood and revealed his face to the former ally. Telling the truth, he replied, "Just moments ago, actually." Rashnir meant it.

Jaker sized up the other occupants at the table. "These, then, must be your benefactors? Are you men Briganiks?" Jaker asked, referring to the country in the far west where men were in general quite large and human women and anakim often cohabitated. It didn't take a far stretch of the imagination to think that deviant ones might seek male companionship.

"No," Kevin replied, "I am from Earth and have come to these lands by the power of Yahweh."

Jaker grinned. "Oh, that's right," he recalled the rumors he'd heard over the last week and recognized Kevin and his accomplices. The local people assumed that he was insane at best—or a heretic at worst. He was both, in all likelihood. "I know of you guys." Barely suppressing a judgmental chuckle he turned to Rashnir, "I guess that you are in good company, then."

"I guess so," Rashnir replied, shrugging off the implied insult.

It was clear to Rashnir that Jaker still loathed him. The two had always gotten along as acquaintances. They had been nothing short of cordial as members of the same guild, friends of Rogis, and men who both loved Kelsa, albeit in different ways. Ever since Harmarty poisoned him with lies, Jaker had only contempt for his former comrade. Jaker's hate bordered on murder and it was obvious that Jaker didn't appreciate seeing Rashnir out of his beggar's hovel.

"You know," Jaker goaded, "Bomarr has joined the guild."

The mention of the name startled Rashnir. All this time he had thought Bomarr died in the fires that killed the rest of his family when the blaze ravaged Rogis's estate.

"It is not surprising, really," continued Jaker, "He was staying at Dyule's for a weekend when his family…" Jaker trailed off, alluding to the frame-up that Rashnir murdered the family—*his family.* Dyule was one of Rogis' older sons who lived in his own house and with a career in the city. Jaker brimmed with emotion; Rogis had been a mentor to Jaker too. "Anyway, his father was second of command in Rogis' Rangers long before you killed him. Ironic how he found a new father in Rogis and then you kill *that man as well,*" Jaker accused.

"I just thought that I would mention how much Bomarr hates you. He once embraced you as a brother. But now? Bomarr plans on killing you, just so you know. I believe that he will succeed, too."

"You always bring me such wonderful news, Jaker," Rashnir stated sarcastically. "Is this a personal call, then?"

"No, actually. I just had a bad report out there in the garrison. When I noticed you a thought popped into my head."

"It's good to know you still have thoughts of your own then—that you haven't let the crown dictate each one to you."

Kevin, Jorge, and Kyrious sat silently in the awkward tension as it built.

"Where were you last night, Rashnir?" Jaker inquired.

"Why do you ask?"

"There was an incident at Harmarty's castle last night. A gate guard was murdered and Harmarty is missing. You have plenty of reason to hate the king, do you not?"

Rashnir kicked himself mentally. He should have hidden the body of the guard he killed. "Of course I have reasons to hate him, he killed Kelsa and—"

"Here we go again. Listen, I don't know the complete truth surrounding her death; I am pretty sure, though, that you had a significant part to play in it. I am sorry she is dead, I loved her too—not like you did, but I mourned her loss as I would a sister. But I am convinced that whatever caused her death was your fault. And at least *I* recognize that excuses won't bring the dead back to life."

"I know that too, now." Rashnir indicated his new friends. "Kevin here has led me into a religious experience. I know that vengeance solves nothing. Listen Jaker, revenge no longer rules my life!"

Jaker looked Rashnir in the face and believed what he had just said. Something had changed in the former Ranger's eyes.

Rashnir went on, though he could no longer look Jaker in the eye. "I hope you find Harmarty, but you know how he is. He probably killed that guard himself and left in secret, unescorted. But do know this, I no longer have any intention of killing that man," he said truthfully.

"Just take caution that you keep unnoticed for the rest of your life. The story of Rashnir the Ranger's fall serves as a good life lesson regarding loyalty. Seeing you begging in the gutters reminds men of that warning, and of the consequences."

Jaker turned to the rest of the group at the table, "As for the rest of you, outside of town there is an institution for the insane and a monastic dungeon for heretics. See to it that you, too, keep a low profile or you'll visit those places.

"The garrison usually takes little action, but I will bring its force to bear if your little band poses any threat." Jaker got up to depart. He turned for one last word with Rashnir. "I had better not find any connection between you and this incident with King Harmarty or so help me I will tighten Bomarr's armor myself and watch him hack you to pieces."

Jaker left the building.

Rashnir turned to his comrades. "Well, he was in a pretty good mood."

The smoke and dinge reclaimed the place where their visitor had sat. Rashnir looked at all of them with an apologetic face.

"Perhaps this would be a good time," Kevin broke the silence, "to tell you more about our beliefs. But let's do it elsewhere, somewhere out in the light. The atmosphere here seems to affect my mood for the worse."

***

Kevin and Rashnir sat by a campfire on the riverbank below Grinden's south boundary. Kyrius cooking dinner while Jorge continued to catch fish while Kevin finished outlining the history behind the ancient Roman Empire on Earth—how they expanded their empire through military might and solidified it through politics.

"The Pharisees and Sadducees made their system of faith into a strict structure devoid of love and tolerance. They relabeled their God, changed Him from one of loving and kindness into a God who wanted unquestioning, exact obedience. They made a God who wanted to punish those who failed to keep His laws, a

God who no longer reached out to embrace His people. They made Him a tyrant, not a loving father calling to His wayward children."

Rashnir nodded his head. "Religion in Luciferianism is just ritual. It's tradition that appeases the Demon Overlords who will grant a blessing, or perform a curse... provided they are listening or in a generous mood. It's supernatural extortion."

"Exactly," Kevin said, "Lucifer would be pleased to have reduced Earth's religion to this. He promotes this exact philosophy. Because God desires to be with His creation, Lucifer works to turn mankind's perception of the person of God into a cosmic machine; if you go to services and perform rituals and sacraments properly, only then will God love you and provide access to grace for you. In reality, because of His love for us, God provided access to Him so that we can freely have that relationship; God looks on our hearts, not only our actions."

"So you're saying that God is not a machine for dispensing blessing, but He is more like a person?"

"Right. You cannot view God as only a system of cause and effect because He is so much more than that. He is not like a money handler at some store, waiting to deliver goods until after a correct payment."

"So the Pharisees and Sadducees did exactly what Lucifer wanted them to do?"

"I believe so. They removed the personal aspect of the Creator and replaced it with a liturgy of 'do this' and 'don't do this' only then can you make God happy... and then he *might* not damn your soul to eternal suffering."

"Were the Pharisees and Sadducees following Lucifer, or under his control?"

"Not necessarily. These were men who knew a lot about God, but they used their religion as a tool of politics and let their lives be controlled by their pride.

"They were not directly controlled by the evil one—they didn't need to be. When a person acts out of his or her own selfish motives and desires, he is already on the line that divides Christ's opponents from His followers. Lucifer does not usually bother courting the souls of those that already oppose or ignore God. Lucifer uses his energies to tear down and fight against God's kingdom.

"I mean that the Pharisees were not possessed by Lucifer's spirit or directly controlled by a demon. The desires of their flesh coincided with the motives of Lucifer and so they were allies with a common goal, at times—but those men didn't understand that.

"Lucifer is just like any corrupt ruler. He spends his time expanding his kingdom by destroying the lives of others. Corrupt people joining his cause are often spared; they eventually sell themselves for the desires of their own hearts, and so Lucifer wastes little time with them. Only those who stand against his goals are worth spending his time and energy on. He seeks not only their destruction, but their submission and humiliation. I think you'll see a parallel with Harmarty."

Rashnir nodded. He had seen what sins a heart could commit when it was dedicated to its own lusts. A selfish heart was like a black hole, consuming everything with any potential for good.

Kevin continued, "The Pharisees defended this system of their own design, even though it was outside of

God's intentions. Because they looked only to their human religion and with their own insight they completely missed the fact that God came down in the flesh to show them the path to redemption.

"Have you ever looked out a glass window at night, watching for something while the lights burned behind you?"

Rashnir smiled warmly as a thought came back to him. "Kelsa and I used to lie beside each other and look out at the stars in the night. I usually stared at her transparent reflection instead of the stars." He sighed at the fading memory.

"That is exactly what I'm talking about," Kevin grinned insightfully. "While you intended to look out at the stars, something of God's design, you can get caught up looking at a reflection instead; *you* chose to look at human beauty. In your case, there was nothing wrong with it, but when you apply that to a spiritual life, there is the potential to pridefully place your own image above God's."

"OK, so the Pharisees made themselves out as the authority on God and wouldn't listen when God tried to correct them."

"Correct, they didn't even listen when the Messiah came."

"Couldn't Jesus just tell them that they were in error? He could have just told them that He was God in the flesh, couldn't He?"

"He could have, and He did, but not at first. He began preaching and performed miracles to demonstrate that He had the power and authority of God—He gave them proof up front. The Pharisees, in their pride, hardened their hearts and tried to humiliate Him and publicly disputed Him. They looked for ways to label Him as a criminal.

"What they did was place *their own* expectations on the one who would fulfill the prophecies of Messiah— they even made up a new reason for Messiah's coming; they wanted Christ to come to save them from a wicked ruler and kingdom. They did not look at the big picture: that Christ would save the souls of men."

Nearby, Kyrius stoked the fire while Jorge hunted the river bottoms, stripped down to only an undergarment. As the fire popped, Kevin told Rashnir about the encounters and confrontations that Jesus had with the Pharisees and how they tried to manipulate the Roman government into discrediting Jesus.

As Jorge dressed, Rashnir stared at him. Jorge was a muscular powerhouse, lithe and taught, well-muscled and larger than even MInd had been. The fair hair of his head fell in long locks and his hairless face looked young and healthy. On the underside of his left arm, a tattooed image of a sword ran a length from elbow to wrist. From Jorge's back a majestic set of wings clenched tightly against his body so they wouldn't draw visible attention to the large man; with barely any thickness to them they would remain undetectable beneath the cloak that he shrugged over his shoulders.

Despite the distracting smells of Kyrius's glorious cooking, the Earth man tried to talk about the twelve disciples of Jesus. Kevin explained how they gained insight from Jesus' teachings, but more often than not, completely missed the meanings; Jesus had to constantly explain everything to them directly as if they were children.

"The disciples," he told Rashnir, "were stuck in this same frame of mind that the Pharisees were, but they recognized Jesus as the Messiah. They had some mental hang-ups because of the culture they were raised in. It is just the same as what preconceived ideas about faith and religion you might have, growing up in this place."

"So I am a disciple?"

"Yes, and so am I."

Kyrius cooked the fish with a few spices he'd purchased in Grinden. Kevin prayed a blessing upon the food, and they ate the meal.

Rashnir and Kevin continued their previous conversation. "The common people recognized that Jesus was the Christ—the Messiah. This is shown vividly by his ride through town when the people cried 'hosanna' as I mentioned earlier," Kevin said. "The Pharisees were displeased with it because it threatened their power base and so they formed a plan. They saw Christ as an enemy to their teaching; His message of love appealed to the people, but it also humiliated the Pharisees. So they planned to put an end to their perceived threat.

"They gave silver to the disciple Judas Iscariot to bring soldiers to Jesus and betray Him; they politically manipulated the government so that He would appear as a criminal. While Jesus had done nothing but the will of God and demonstrated the love of a Creator for His creation, His human enemies plotted to destroy Him. The government found Him guilty of fabricated crimes.

"The ruler recognized that Jesus was no criminal. He even gave the public the opportunity to clear Jesus of wrongdoing, but the manipulation of Christ's enemies succeeded.

"Jesus knew this would happen. He actually came to Earth knowing that it was the only way to save mankind: to die for them as an act of love—despite so many hating Him.

"He was tortured, beaten, and mocked. Though He's the king of everything they put a painful crown of woven thorns on His brow. The scourges of His enemies flayed His body. Then professional executioners made Jesus carry a wooden cross up a hill where they nailed His hands to opposite sides and hammered a long spike through His feet. He hung there suffocating, in pain, until He died.

"With Christ killed, Lucifer thought that he had won—but he'd actually lost; God cannot die, He is eternal. But Lucifer, in his attempts to beat God, effectively brought about his own damnation.

"After three days Christ rose again and proved to thousands of people that He lived. A little while longer, Jesus rose up to heaven in plain sight of hundreds and returned to the Father where He sent His Holy Spirit to help His followers take over the work of ministering in His name—a Spirit of power, personified."

Rashnir listened to the story; he could feel the Spirit churning within his heart, acknowledging the truth of the tale. He nodded and Kevin continued, giving him a crash course on the history of the early church.

"You see," Kevin said, "Christ said that He would return to Earth to bring about judgment. He is going to bring an end to all wickedness and establish His kingdom on Earth with men. That time is drawing nigh. Earth is in ever more chaos as God pours His wrath upon it and very few have any idea about what is really going on.

"It really is a time of apathy and tribulation. It is also the time when clauses in the contract between Lucifer and Yahweh have opened the doors between the realms and allowed us enter."

"But why you? How did you even know about this place?" Rashnir wondered.

"I don't know, really. I did not know this place existed until recently. I only know that my Lord asked me if I would go and do His will and I responded with a 'yes.'

"Since then, many weeks have passed. I have been speaking to anyone who would listen, which has given me my insane reputation. One night, while I was praying on the east coast of the main land, by the border of Gleend and Ninda where I first appeared in this land, I felt directed to find a living example of how God's grace could change lives: a story of redemption. Several days ago I began my search for you—the Holy Spirit prompted me to tell you what you needed to hear—even to show you that justice exists by giving you a sword. That is why you sit here now as a believer."

The thought of redemption lodged in Rashnir's heart and warmed it. So clouded by his thirst for revenge, he hadn't thought it possible until recently.

Jorge asked Rashnir, "Now that you believe, what do you want to do?"

A smile broke across Rashnir's face ear to ear, "Tell everyone," he replied. "I think I should speak with Bomarr and Dyule. They deserve to know the truth about a great many things. Also, if I do not deal with the skeletons from my past, it may hurt the spread of the truth in the present.

"Dyule is one of Rogis' older sons, several years older than I am. I forget exactly what he does. I think that he is somehow involved with a trade line, overseeing operations and business, or something like that. He often hired groups of Rangers to protect his convoys—he certainly did not inherit his traits from his father," Rashnir mused.

"Dyule always seemed such a plain man: like he didn't have a sense of humor or any creativity. Perhaps his mother had a mathematical bent, but I don't know. I never met her."

"Is it far?" Kevin inquired.

"He lives on the edge of town, the northern suburb." The north-east side of Grinden was a well laid-out community of stately homes owned by well-to-do people, usually owners of successful businesses or other important and successful persons.

The small group of Christians packed up and began the trek across Grinden.

***

As they walked through town, the four pedestrians noticed the many condescending and quizzical looks. Nearly every person recognized Rashnir, but none knew about his inclusion in this group of outsiders.

Their path took them through a park-like clearing at the city's center. Kevin had gained recognition in his own right which earned him foul stares from the furrowed brow of a brown-cloaked man nearby.

Kevin asked Rashnir about him.

"You can tell by his dress," Rashnir noted. "He is a Luciferian Monk; we're near the Temple. He probably heard you were a heretic and wants to kill you."

"Kill me?"

"Probably. You noticed that his entire head and face was shaved? That is a tradition for the militant wing of the Luciferian Order. I noticed the tattoos on his head and neck. He is a hand to hand combat master—probably the combat trainer at the local monastery. All new monks are required to learn at least some kind of hand to hand fighting regardless of which branch of the Order they dedicate their studies to."

"Interesting," Kevin thought aloud as they traveled further.

They arrived in good time, coming to a stop before an elegant residential home. They paused briefly on the pristinely manicured lawn nearest a brick walkway. For the first time since Kevin had met him, Rashnir looked nervous.

"Well," he shrugged, "Now is as good a time as any."

They walked up the path to the main door with Rashnir in the lead. The mission was personal for the former Ranger. He grabbed the heavy ring bolted to the door and used it to rap three times. Its knocking noise echoed through the house and through Rashnir's bones.

"You guys can probably wait here for a moment," Rashnir said flatly. "He might not exactly be friendly at first"

A brief moment of silence passed and then the sound of approaching footsteps shuffled behind the door. The latch creaked with a loud metallic squawk and it swung inward revealing a large, muscular man nearly the size of Jorge—he perfectly matched Bomarr's description.

He looked dark and somber, head and eyes downcast, complexion pallid, clothes disheveled, obviously not been expecting visitors. As soon as his eyes turned upward and Bomarr realized who stood at his door, he snapped into a rage, instantaneously engulfed in fury. The massive arms snapped up Rashnir, catching all of them off guard.

Bomarr jerked Rashnir into a crude headlock and rolled him inside of the house, kicking the door half-shut as the two crashed through the interior of the building. Plaster crumbled as Bomarr choke-slammed Rashnir through a dividing wall, just inside of the entryway. The wall cracked and protested, knickknacks fell from their places on shelving.

Rashnir grabbed at the massive hand clasped around his throat. Kevin nearly stepped in, but Jorge, levelheaded and cool, stayed him with a touch of his hand. The angel watched the altercation with a slightly amused look, waiting until he might really need to intervene.

Bomarr yanked Rashnir back and squeezed him with a crushing bear hug. With the smaller man bent over his shoulder, Bomarr dashed towards the wall and used Rashnir as a battering ram. The wall gave away completely and the two men tumbled through the cloud of debris and plaster dust; nothing but broken lathe remained of the wall. They skidded to a stop with a crash of noise.

Rashnir shouted through the rubble, "I did not come here to fight you, Bomarr!"

Bomarr climbed to his feet, covered in white dust and plaster fragments, "Then you came here to die!" he screamed. Bomarr tried to kick Rashnir, who still lay on his back on the floor; Rashnir used the bottom of his own foot to block the blow and then shifted his body in a spin and swept Bomarr's feet out from underneath. Rashnir wanted to stop Bomarr's murderous rampage without injuring him.

Before Rashnir could fix him into any kind of submission hold, Bomarr rolled to his belly and hauled himself back onto his feet. The large fighter squared up against Rashnir and lunged at him, attempting to grab him with another bear hug. The veteran in these types of situations, Rashnir grabbed a fistful of Bomarr's tunic and dropped to his back, rolling the lunging attacker with him, using his momentum to toss him over his body and thrust him across the room. Bomarr landed on a dining room chair, smashing it to pieces.

As they both rolled to their feet, Rashnir realized that this might be a lengthier fight than he had hoped for; Bomarr showed no signs of giving in and not a single hint of fatigue. The young warrior seized a small end table from near a lounging chair as he closed the gap between him and Rashnir. He held the make-shift weapon menacingly.

Anticipating the lunge, Rashnir dodged away from the bulky, yet nonetheless deadly, end table that Bomarr hurled at him. It shattered against another interior wall.

Predicting Rashnir's evasiveness, Bomarr kept a grip on the drawer hardware from the end table. The drawer pulled when he threw the table and stayed in Bomarr's grip when the table flew across the room. The younger warrior swung the drawer at his foe who he caught off guard. The drawer splintered against Rashnir's head, knocking him to the floor.

Not wasting another moment, knowing that Rashnir could regain the advantage in a heartbeat if given the opportunity, Bomarr closed the gap and kicked the bloodied Rashnir as he yelped.

"Bomarr! This is not right!" he howled. "I am not here for a fight!"

"In a few more seconds, you won't be here at all!" Bomarr grabbed Rashnir and lifted him up when a loud thudding noise sounded in a room down a hallway past the dining room. Bomarr hesitated and then dropped Rashnir into a heap on the floor.

The younger man ran down the hall and into the room the noise had come from. Rashnir heard Bomarr whisper one word under his breath: "Mother."

"Mother?" Rashnir quietly asked himself as he pulled his battered frame up from the floor. He shot his companions a quick look that asked, *Where were you?* and then followed after Bomarr.

Rashnir trailed him down the corridor of the house's west wing. Rashnir stood in complete shock, stuck to his spot in the doorway when he saw her. The sound had been the thumping of a human body falling out of bed. Rashnir found Bomarr lifting his mother, Missa, off of the wood floor and back into bed.

He broke down and began sobbing as he recognized those eyes that had once been so familiar to him. Those eyes were exactly like those of her daughter, Rashnir's lover, Kelsa. He stirred and broke the fixation that held him there and rushed in to give Bomarr assistance; Bomarr backed him down with a harsh stare and Rashnir instead watched the son gently place his crippled mother back in bed.

Missa survived but had not escaped the fire that consumed her family and home. If it were not for the familiarity in her eyes, Rashnir would not have recognized her at all. Terrible burns covered every inch of her body. Missa had only barely survived the flames of Harmarty's selfishness; her golden hair no longer grew from her scarred scalp and she hardly looked human anymore. Many parts of her remained blackened from where the fire had burned down to her bones and melted her flesh completely away. Exposed muscles could be seen over the majority of her body and face transforming her once ravishing appearance into a lumpy mass of deformities and scar tissue. Only those bright eyes remained and they fixed upon him in recognition. Of the few visible patches of skin that Rashnir could see, the corner of her mouth pulled up in what appeared to be a smile at his appearance.

Rashnir stood straight and reverent, "Missa?" he asked gently. A lump caught in his throat.

The burned figure stirred only a little but maintained the gaze that they shared.

Bomarr glared balefully at Rashnir. "You should not be here. Your presence only hurts her further."

He broke his gaze with Missa, "What? How can you say that?"

"It is your fault that she is in this condition!" Bomarr accused.

"This is Harmarty's fault!" Rashnir insisted.

"Oh, yes. I have heard your story. Everyone has heard your conspiracy tale. What is there to believe in it? You were the only one who would ever have had the opportunity, let alone the talent, to kill Rogis! Harmarty had always regarded him as a friend and mentor."

Rashnir felt despair creep in. He turned to lock eyes again with Missa. "Don't you believe me? Didn't you hear the forces of Harmarty and his men as they stormed your house and set it ablaze?"

It was then that he noticed the severity of Missa's terrible wounds. Blackened by flames, her neck near her voice box had melted like chimney slag. It looked like it had even burned through her esophagus in spots. Missa had been rendered mute. She wheezed a mournful reply through the perforations above her nape.

Rashnir noticed her hands. Missa's left hand, charred like a green twig, couldn't be used. Three digits were missing from the appendage; the remaining pieces lock stiff and completely vestigial. Her right hand had fared worse; only a blackened, shriveled stump ended where her radius and ulna joined at the wrist. "Get a quill and parchment," Rashnir requested.

"Can't you see you stupid, stupid fool?" Bomarr pointed towards her hands and the absence of phalanges.

"I can see perfectly!" he shouted back.

Rashnir turned towards the door as he heard the slight sounds of someone approaching. Kevin silently handed Rashnir a piece of papyrus-like paper, demonstrating full faith in his friend.

"She cannot write! We have already tried it, there is no way! We even tried tying a quill to her hands but the pain nearly killed her."

Rashnir ignored Bomarr. He drew two large words upon the paper and circled them: *Yes* and *No*.

He turned his gaze again to Missa. Rashnir's eyes brimmed with hope and compassion.

"Missa, I have written here on this paper two words. You can answer if someone asks you something. Just tap the left circle to answer Yes. Tap the right one to answer No." Rashnir showed her and then placed the paper on her lap at arm's length. "Do you understand me?"

Missa raised a charred and useless limb and tapped the left circle to say 'yes.'"

Rashnir looked hopefully at Bomarr who returned a look of astonishment. *Why had he not thought of that?* Bomarr mentally berated himself.

Missa's eyes sparkled in delight and her mouth, again, stretched to almost permit a smile.

Bomarr scooted closer to his mother. He directed a question at Rashnir, cordial for the first time. "May I speak with her first?"

He gave a half bow, "By all means," he said with compassion. "She is *your* mother."

Bomarr leaned down and whispered several things into the gnarled bit of flesh on the side of her head; the remnant of an ear resembled a twisted tree root. Bomarr tearfully apologized to his mother for not thinking of this previously.

He stood and wiped the moisture away from his eyes. "Mother, I want to know the truth. Dyule and I discuss this frequently and at length, so I know that you must have overheard us. You know that Dyule and I believe that what King Harmarty told us about Rashnir murdering Rogis is true. You know that we believe Rashnir came and burned down our home to cover his tracks and eliminate certain threats to his advancement."

A glimmer of anger returned to his eyes as he stated his long-held beliefs. Bomarr continued. "Mother, do you believe this?"

She tapped *No*.

Bomarr's face dropped with astonishment. He knelt at her side.

"Do you believe that he killed Rogis?"

No.

"Do you *know* that he did not kill him?"

No.

"Ok, ok. So then, you base this belief on how well you know him and what you know about him?"

Yes. As she looked at Rashnir, the look in her eyes was the same loving look that a mother gives her own children.

"Do you know who killed my sister... your daughter, Kelsa?"

Yes.

Bomarr got overexcited by the implications, "Who was it?"

Missa gave him a confused look, not able to respond. She swirled her hands in a circle.

"I mean, was it Harmarty?" Bomarr's question would either implicate Rashnir in guilt or validate his story.

Yes. Missa began to look excited as her son discovered the truth after such a long and erroneous foray in his bitterness.

Bomarr looked dumbfounded.

"You have proof?"

No.

"But you know this for a fact? It is not just a gut instinct is it?"

Yes.

"Yes, you know for a fact?"

Yes.

"You heard or saw Harmarty say as much?"

Yes.

Bomarr's eyes seemed to turn inward as new thoughts ran rampant through his head, realizing the implications and ramifications of this new data.

"Mother...did Harmarty burn you?" he asked softly.

Missa moved her hand in a painful manner and heavily brought her useless wrist down upon the circle that was her answer: *Yes.*

Hands covering his face, Bomarr stood and howled in rage and anger over his mother's physical pain and the emotional pain of the lies and misdirected feelings of wrath. At the apex of his yell he turned and pumped his hands down as if he swung an axe. He hit a small side-table by his mother's window. The table splintered into shards of handcrafted woodwork. His outburst subsided with the destruction of yet more furniture.

Bomarr turned to his mother and apologized for the table. "I need to think, Mother. I will be back soon."

Rashnir kept an even tone, hoping to help calm him down. "Bomarr. I need to speak with you... Please."

Bomarr did not push him away and so Rashnir trailed after him. Before leaving the room he looked at the bed-ridden woman who was once nearly his mother-in-law. "Missa, I have brought a friend of mine. He has some things to share with you." He left Missa as Kevin pulled a stool up and sat at her bedside. Kyrius stayed with Kevin, Jorge went after Rashnir.

Rashnir found Bomarr sitting sullen at the dining room table, seated in one of the few remaining chairs. Rashnir sat opposite of the young warrior. Jorge stood behind him.

"I do not know what to feel," Bomarr confessed, looking up bleary eyed. "I have hated you for so long. I believed that you deserved to lose everything and even more than that: your very life—by my hands even. Now I see that you've lost even more than I.

"I feel guilty for hurting my mother. She often fell out of bed intentionally; I see now why. She often threw herself to the floor whenever Dyule and I would rhetorically plot our plans for revenge—concoct more, imaginary ways to hurt you. So much lost time... that would've never happened if I'd realized how to communicate with her. I think she fell to make us focus on her pain instead of plotting against you. She knew the truth but couldn't tell us." He paused, full of self-doubt and introspection. "I don't think I even wanted to know the truth... just someone to blame.

"I don't feel guilty for hating you," Bomarr looked at Rashnir, "Even though it was misplaced. I needed something to hate—someone to blame." He paused, and then looked hard at Rashnir in a conspiratorial manner and stated flatly. "Harmarty must die."

Rashnir gave him an understanding look and bobbed his head in agreement. "Haven't you heard the news?" He responded to Bomarr's quizzical gesture. "Harmarty has disappeared. With the combination of his mysterious absence and the death of a castle guard, as well as my re-emergence from the street gutters, I have been officially questioned about the matter."

Bomarr stared at him suspiciously.

"They will eventually find him, Bomarr." Rashnir smirked. "But not to worry. Harmarty has paid for his crimes." Rashnir returned the conspiratorial look. "Let's just say that I happen to know this is fact."

The two chatted about trivial matters for the next few minutes, all their words tainted by a Harmarty's gloom which hung over the conversation. The mood was not right for small talk.

After an awkward silence, Rashnir stated, "We are going to bring a revolution to the land, something good."

"What is good," Bomarr verbally deflected the term. "Good is defined by the philosophy of the day. *Your* good will inevitably become someone else's evil."

It was an interesting insight for a person not normally recognized as an authority on deep wisdom.

"I have made a discovery, Bomarr. There *is* such a thing as absolute good and evil. Perfect goodness exists and I have found it, though I do not claim to resemble it."

Bomarr gave him a skeptical look, "What, Rashnir, have you become religious? Did the monks take pity on you?" Bomarr was not the type to follow religious tenets, just as Rashnir had not been. Men of the sword were prone to see themselves as the sole controllers of human destiny and typically shied away from religious observation unless it bordered on zealotry—and those men and women typically joined the Order.

"No, but you are close. There is no denying that higher powers exist, right?"

He nodded. That there were higher supernatural powers at work could not be denied; usually they acted as selfish as the rest of the sentients that roamed the lands, but powerful demons and sorcerers were of common knowledge. Common myths claimed Lucifer as the only truly selfless exception amongst the high powers; despite widespread corruption in the church, the Luciferian Order still insisted that their deity remained pure and compassionate. Of course, they also claimed the infallibility of their religion and that The Gathering, the reigning demonic council, portrayed the divine traits inherent in Lucifer.

"This higher power," Rashnir continued, "has been hidden from us by these selfish, powerful beings. They have profited off of our souls for many, many generations.

"When Lucifer supposedly gave his human followers the account of our creation and the dissention from Yahweh, he lied to us, damning all of our souls and stopping us from learning the Truth. Lucifer is darkness disguised as light."

Bomarr chuckled. "I am not a Luciferian, but I know heresy when I hear it. If you tell any loyal followers this, the Order will send monks to assassinate you. They have amnesty enough in any country to get away with it."

"I know, but it is still the truth. Don't people deserve the truth?"

"It is true," Jorge finally spoke up.

"This is Jorge," Rashnir introduced, "Jorge is an angel of Yahweh."

Bomarr's expression switched from reluctant to passive interest.

"I watched from my Heavenly post as Lucifer was cast to Earth, barren and parched in comparison to his place in the firmaments of Heaven. The ground withered before him as the curse of death accompanied his fall. I watched him make his proclamation, 'Farewell, Remorse! all good to me is lost; Evil, be thou my good.'"

The three heard the faint creaks of a door opening. They turned to the main doorway where Dyule entered looking mortified. Plain-looking and forgettable as always, he turned an incredulous circle and assessed the damage and destruction. Furniture either lay overturned or obliterated in the course of the earlier skirmish; walls and fixtures crumbled in damaged piles.

"You." Dyule pointed an accusing finger at Rashnir and drew a dagger from his waist belt. He paused momentarily as his analytical processes went to work; he resheathed the dagger knowing that if Bomarr had not been able to subdue Rashnir then he didn't stand a chance with a blade. "Please get out." He demanded simply with his nasal, insistent voice.

Rashnir stood to his feet. "I am sorry. I had not intended to bring further trouble to your home." He turned to Bomarr, "I hoped to explain to you what I have learned—this new Truth. I hoped to even invite you to join us."

"You have already done enough," Bomarr stated—although not angrily.

"Yes." Dyule chimed in with a distinctly bitter tone, "You have done quite enough already, now return to your gutters!"

"No, that's not what I meant," Bomarr said.

Rashnir noticed that while they conversed Bomarr had been drawing on a large piece of parchment. The sketch was a large collection of circled letters and numbers and possible answers to questions such as: *Yes, No, Maybe, I Don't Know.*

"Rashnir has shown me how to communicate with Mother." He turned and commented to Rashnir, "I am much too busy here for anything else. My mother needs me."

Nodding, Rashnir bowed. "I will honor your request, Dyule. I am leaving."

"Good. And do not come back," he said disdainfully.

"I can honor that as well. Bomarr, if you should ever need anything else, I trust that you will be able to find me. Please tell Missa goodbye for me; I will likely never see her again, though I had never expected to see her alive again prior to today." Rashnir called out for Kevin. Moments later, Kevin appeared flanked by Kyrius. They all left together as Dyule stared daggers at their backs.

***

Kevin, Jorge, Kyrius, and Rashnir sat in a semi-circle in the middle of Grinden's central park. Despite the curious glances that they had to continually shrug off, they remained unbothered.

Although the incident at Dyule's had not been any great victory, Kevin had been able to share the message of Christ to Missa, even if he was not quite finished when he'd been called away. Dyule's interruption was untimely.

Rashnir could sympathize with Dyule's feelings. After finding his home ransacked, anyone would've felt the same. Dyule's request for them to leave might be quite civil in comparison to how most would've acted. They'd tried to leave Dyule's with grace; the man that Rashnir had been only several days prior would not have.

Kyrius, who'd apparently appointed himself as their troop's culinary expert, passed around some dried foods he'd prepared earlier. They all drank from a water skin and watched the people of Grinden pass them by, each busy with their own lives.

From their location in the park, they had a clear view of Grinden's Luciferian temple where it perched on the edge of the park. The building was a local corporate worship center for those that chose to observe the nominal, corporate faith; Luciferian monks that traveled in from a small villa a short walk west of Grinden staffed it.

Typically, booths containing tiny idols and shrines dedicated to various demon overlords lined the Luciferian Temple halls. In all reality, the building housed a pantheon of demi-gods under one overarching title of Luciferianism. With Lucifer in the Earth realm, the people instead prayed to, worshiped, and gave tribute to demonic overlords or minor demons that they appealed to for blessing or hoped to appease.

Kevin sighed at the sight of people walking into the church. Still, the misguided faithful made Kevin smile awkwardly.

"Those people going in to the Luciferian Temple are probably easier to reach than those who just walk past it. These ones at least recognize a higher power and give it authority over their lives; everyone else lives for themselves, lives opposed to the thought of surrendering their will to anything else."

The other three nodded heads in agreement. An odd, dark figure caught Rashnir's eye as the creature dipped his head.

The figure was shrouded in a cloak and hood and stood at least a head shorter than the average man. Four similar figures flanked him; they each seemed to slink through the streets, uncomfortable in the daylight. All near passersby seemed to notice them also, but paid them no heed. The group of goblins that passed through would be mostly harmless in the daylight. While goblins possessed their own kingdoms in the subterranean realms and circumvented the infrastructures of most other sentient beings, not all people found them altogether abhorrent. Often enough, trade with goblins who ventured into populated areas could be lucrative.

While most people had a passing familiarity with their kind, goblin culture could be too abrasive or downright offensive for many and so goblins were not universally accepted. Sure enough, in a human city like Grinden, every man within eyesight was keenly aware of the small troop of goblins walking among them.

"I'll going to take a quick walk," Rashnir said. With his curiosity piqued, he climbed to his feet and ventured over to the temple building to investigate.

Their presence in town wasn't surprising to Rashnir, though he was shocked to see the goblins enter the Luciferian Temple. *Goblins going into the temple,* Rashnir thought, *probably planning to rob the coffers?* Not that he particularly cared, but he grew even more curious given that they went through the main doors.

While Lucifer created all sentient races of ekthro, only the humans of the realm possessed any kind of reverence for him. Aside from creating them, the fallen angel had done nothing special for the nonhuman races. Everything that he had done, even the creation of the ekthro, was done for the specific benefit of mankind according to Luciferian myths and doctrine. It was unusual to see non-humans going to a temple to worship or pay any sort of homage to the Order; the non-human races usually aspired to deify themselves.

164

Rashnir pulled his cloak down to conceal his identity. He pushed his way through the large double doors and meandered through the foyer entry area. The floor of the temple, made of polished stone, matched the ornate temple fittings and furnishings.

A few of the people whom the Christians previously watched enter the temple milled about shaking their purses and deciding which of the shrines to enter. A few other visitors gathered near the front altar, offering prayers of supplication and praise to the gold idol crafted in Lucifer's supposed likeness. A few listless monks roamed about, performing random tasks and offering religious services as needed.

Rashnir crept further through the halls, searching for clues. He spotted no sign of the goblins. Skulking a little further along a stone corridor that boasted an intricately carved wall depicting events from the first Great War of the varied species, Rashnir passed some cubicles for the monastic workers. He paused and sniffed; Rashnir noticed the musty, slightly spicy odor that usually indicated goblins. Concentrating, he stretched out with his senses and heard the croaking voices of goblins behind the nearby, closed door.

The raspy voices sounded friendly enough as they spoke with the local monastic authority. "This is the tribute that our master bids we send to you," said the oddly familiar goblin voice. "King Nvv-Fryyg desires to make a lasting contribution to your religious work, especially in spite of recent events occurring in the mountains of Briganik."

"Yes," the human voice responded, "You have alluded to this already. Explain that." A nervous undertone entered into his voice. "I am interested in what you have to say about these events, and I gladly accept your tribute."

Rashnir heard the clattering of coins.

"The goblins have found their place in Lucifer's grand plan. You would know, better than any other man in Grinden, no doubt, that Lucifer has orchestrated his grand plan to overthrow the great foe, Yahweh. Up until now, this plan has primarily been for, and through, mankind, chiefly using humans. There is a teaching from Lucifer's prophet; it includes the Goblin race. It provides all with access to the eternal Paradise."

"Anyone can get to Paradise," came the reply, "You just have to pay the toll at the Temple of Light and ascend the stairs of Babel."

"Yes, I know, but not how Paradise is now…barren and destroyed, crumbled under years of decay and abuse. The disrepair of Paradise will be renewed when Lucifer returns to claim victory over the forces of Yahweh."

"What you say sounds like a twisting of current prophesy, Goblin. Your kind is beyond the grace of the Light-Bringer, so calling you a heretic does no good. Tell me, who is this prophet? Is he some goblin with grand hopes of currying favor with Lucifer upon his grand reentry to our realm?"

"It is no goblin. It is your prophet, Absinthium, and I also bring you this." There was a pause and a rustling sound, "A scroll from the arch-mage himself."

Rashnir only heard a pause, but he imagined that the monk whispered Absinthium's name with a certain fear and reverence.

"There is one more thing," the goblin said, "Absinthium is coming here for a visit in the coming

THE KAKOS REALM: GRINDEN PROSELYTE

days. He sent me as his courier rather than a Luciferian runner to reinforce this new doctrine coming out of Briganik's Temple of Light."

The conversation wound down, and with nowhere to hide, Rashnir retreated down the hallway and took a seat in one of the stone pews of the main sanctuary.

Moments later, the goblins walked behind him and found the exit. Things fell together in Rashnir's mind as he realized he knew one of the ekthro. He recognized the goblin who had been speaking in the office as grr'SHaalg: the same goblin from Harmarty's castle.

Luciferian machinations had been put into motion in Grinden. Perhaps there was more to the plot than what he had overheard in the Harmarty's castle.

Chapter Eight

Rashnir left the temple building and found Kevin surrounded by a small crowd of people. Kevin's angelic bodyguards seemed relaxed, so the crowd must not have posed any danger. The preacher had apparently found an opportunity to share his faith with the locals as Rashnir trailed the goblins.

As he neared the growing crowd, Rashnir noticed a young monk in the audience, shifting on his feet but listening intently. His coarse, dark-brown robe and shaven pate indicated his devotion to the combat disciplines at the monastery. The tattoos on his head designated him as a third degree monk; that was the fourth level of the Order, beginning level initiates had no rank--only after achieving full monk status did one became a first-degree monk. Second degree followers choose a training specialty from the branches of the Order and levels progressed from there up to the thirty-third degree.

Only four thirty-three degree monks existed at any given time, one of whose decisions counted twice when voting at Luciferian High Council meetings, making him the head of the Luciferian Order. Rashnir mulled over what little he knew of the order as he walked—he was quite certain that this Absinthium character was a member of the High Council for a simple name-drop to the local leadership to have so easily and resolutely changed a long-held prejudice.

Rashnir pressed in towards his friends. His and the young monk's eyes caught each other's; the monk quickly looked away as if he'd been caught in some great disobedience. The Luciferian pulled his hood up and promptly departed, pretending he'd only been passing by, rather than listening to the story of a heretic's hope.

***

Over the following days, the Christian foursome returned to the same location, inviting others back; every day, more people came to listen to Kevin speak. Most of the locals regarded him as nothing more than a brilliant storyteller, a colorful heretic at worst, but they appreciated the entertainment.

For his part, Kevin simply told stories that intrigued the people who came to listen—only snippets of the larger narrative he'd taught Rashnir. Kevin embraced his role as an entertainer and the people learned his stories, ingesting Truth without quite realizing it. Kevin understood that he planted seeds and invited them back time and again, and they kept returning, often bringing friends. Over the course of a few days Kevin had amassed a regular following.

Each afternoon, Kevin left them with a teaser, telling the audience that he would share his favorite story on Saturday night. Audience members assured them that they would come for that story.

On Saturday morning, the lounge of the Green Serpent Inn, where Kevin and his companions shared a meal, buzzed with activity. Weekends were generally a night of over-indulgence and led to many guests inadvertently spending a night at the inn, making Saturday and Sunday the only days of the week with early crowds. The patrons all seemed to talk about the one topic: the murder of King Harmarty.

The nuanced political tension of the conversation made Rashnir apprehensive; he prayed his pseudo-celebrity status as Harmarty's enemy would not damage the group's ability to do good. He did his best to conceal his identity in the lounge as he ordered breakfast for him and his friends. A nearby conversation so consumed the waiter that he took it without so much as a glance in Rashnir's direction.

It did not take long until they were also engrossed in conversation about politics and the potential connections between the goblins, Luciferians, and monarchies. A short while later a young busboy brought the Christians their breakfast.

The boy asked them, "Have you all heard the news about the King?" He didn't wait for a reply, "They found his body yesterday morning; they found him 'cuz of the stink. Someone assassinated him and strung him up inside the dumbwaiter in his bedroom."

"Tell me," Kevin asked, shrugging off the brutality of the news, "What talk is there of a successor?"

"Well, I heard that there are a few people who claim they should be the heir. Harmarty didn't have any kids and wasn't married. The strongest claim is by Rutheir, his man-at-arms." He shrugged. "I guess he's got a couple of reasons. I hear that he's got a will or sumthin, plus he is claiming that he was Harmarty's partner. I guess it's like he was his man-wife or something, and a lot of the aristocrats are backing him."

The bartender whistled, calling back his extra hand. The boy dutifully returned to help in the kitchen.

Changing the subject, Kevin discussed the immediate plans for the day, "By this evening, the town could be a very different place. Tonight I will present the people with the message of faith. Over the last week we introduced them to the character of Jesus; they know who He is and they know the miracles that He did. People think the lands of Israel, Jerusalem, and other biblical places are in some fictional realm. Tonight, they will discover that it is the truth, and that Jesus still does miracles—even here."

"What of the Luciferians?" Jorge asked, always thinking about logistics. "Should we be wary of any threat on their part?" The question seemed directed to Rashnir, the only native to this land.

"I am not very familiar with the Luciferians. I really only have a cursory knowledge of them, like most people, but my guess is that you could encounter opposition. We may have problems if the Luciferians feel threatened, especially since it looks like they are making some kind of push for political power.

"Hopefully, the plans that I overheard so many nights ago were ruined with the death of Harmarty. I don't think, though, that we're so lucky. It seems like the Temple visit by the goblins indicates that their plans are still in motion: with or without King Harmarty. Evil is forging new alliances."

"I think you're right," Jorge stated. "We will need to be prepared in the event that things turn hostile. What do you know of Absinthium?"

"I asked around a little bit," Rashnir replied, "He is one of the Council of Four; he is a thirty-third degree Luciferian. Actually, he's *the* thirty-third degree Luciferian. The other three members of the High Council appointed him a few years back. A short time later, he became the leader of the council when Jang'uul, the previous leader of many years, mysteriously died. Absinthium is the member with double votes and basically guides the Order. He's a powerful sorcerer, by all accounts."

"He will cause trouble," Jorge said.

"I know. Tonight's meeting, coincidentally, is the same time as the weekly Luciferian service. People will be curious," Kevin said, "and I expect to steal away several of their people. I predict some tertiary conflict with the monks. If there is conflict it will generate publicity. This could help broadcast to those existing Christians that the message is being preached and it might draw even bigger crowds on both sides of the fence: negative and positive observers, both. We'll just do our best to get a crowd and let the Holy Spirit sort them out."

After breakfast, they left the Green Serpent Inn. They had traveled only a few dusty steps when a voice shouted at them.

"The Green Serpent Inn? Not the most luxurious of lodgings, but a far cry from your beggar's hovel."

The Christians turned as one unit and faced a cocky, swaggering man. Their eyes met the hardened, petulant gaze and snakelike grin of a man dressed in a Ranger's garb. He wore armor as if prepared for battle and two curved scimitars crossed behind his back.

Still speaking, he sauntered over, introducing himself. "My name is Pinchôt. I am the second in command of Rogis' Rangers." His gaze steadily held Rashnir's. "I have a theory about this whole Harmarty ordeal that I'd like to share. I think that this guy who once held my position, an enemy of Harmarty's, snuck in and killed the king. I think that he hated him from the start—although he let his hate simmer for several years, but then one day his selfishness overcame him. I think he made his own pitiful bid for power, killing the legendary Rogis and his family in the process. After his fall from the pedestal of public reverence, he hooked up with a random group of heretical travelers. Together, this group assassinated the king and works towards upsetting the whole nation of Jand for their own personal benefit. Come to think of it, I hear that they're currently operating out of the city of Grinden."

"That's a pretty farfetched theory," Rashnir replied casually. "Does Jaker also believe this?"

"He will," replied Pinchôt, "as soon as I have the proof that I need. It's all coming together. Step lightly," he warned, "I will have my proof soon enough."

With his threat delivered, Pinchôt turned and left.

Once the ranger traveled beyond earshot, Kevin asked Rashnir, "Was he trying to warn us that we are under scrutiny?"

"No. He wasn't being friendly. I have never met him and I have no more friends among the Rangers. He genuinely thinks we are the assassins."

"Then why tell us that he was on to us?"

"Because he is arrogant enough that he thinks we're already as good as caught. He's confident that he's already got enough to convince Jaker to send the Rangers after us; he wants to rub our noses in failure, first."

"Humph," snorted Kyrius, "Good luck."

***

They arrived early at the central park, as normal, in order to spend a little time praying. When they arrived, the Christians found a monk waiting for them. He stood in the same spot where the group had met for the past few days. Rashnir recognized him as the same monk he'd noticed in the crowd several days prior on the day that goblins visited the temple.

The monk looked around suspiciously, checking to see if anyone watched him. Something obviously agitated him.

For a combat-specialized monk, his body language conveyed a surprising lack of hostility. They approached the solitary monk with confident wordless strides and waited for the stranger to speak.

As soon as they drew close enough to keep the conversation quiet he opened his mouth. "Tell me something, Kevin. You speak of this Jesus so passionately and tell tales of his works in such a way that I cannot help but think that he is real. I am a learned man, and I know that the places you have named do not exist. Is this Jesus, and his story, an allegory of some sort?"

Kevin spoke with compassion, "I am not Jesus, if you are trying to draw such a connection, but I know Him personally. He is real and I tell His story."

"Is he a prophet of Lucifer, or maybe even a demon?"

"No. He is a man, and more powerful than even Lucifer himself."

The monk smirked, obviously amused. He could barely contain his laughter. "And you have met this man?"

"Yes."

"Then the people are right, those ones who say that you are insane."

"If the whole land were mad, they would claim that the one sane person amongst them ought to be committed."

The monk returned a quizzical look, wondering what Kevin implied. Then, he abruptly left, walking purposefully towards the Temple.

Suddenly, the Christians realized that they were being watched. In the distance, on the far edge of the park, opposite of the Temple, stood the Luciferian combat arts trainer. The young monk's master glared across the park at them; his posture reflected an obvious displeasure.

Only when the doors to the temple closed behind the young monk in the distance did his master break the angry pose. He, too, circled the edge of the park and made his way to the temple.

An odd thing happened next. As Kevin sat down and began to pray, vendors with carts began arriving wheeling portable storefronts and kiosks into the park. They set them up as a sort of wall making a semi-circle around Kevin's location and creating a makeshift sort of amphitheater.

The place took on a carnival-like setting. Most of the stands prepared to sell some kind of snack or beverage to an anticipated audience. The vendors didn't care if Kevin was insane or a heretic; they saw an opportunity to earn some coin.

After speaking with a few of the merchants, Rashnir figured that they must've expected an even greater crowd than Kevin had. Rashnir asked Kevin, "Should I send them away?"

"No, let them stay. This draws more attention to us. It might even increase the crowd. Just ask them to keep all distractions to a minimum."

***

A short while later, people arrived in droves. As more and more arrived, many of the clustered groups merged together as friends found each other. One important characteristic of the crowd was that every sentient to arrive was human, although most cities in this part of the continent were predominantly human.

Many of the faces looked vaguely familiar from the crowds drawn over the past few days. Rashnir and Jorge both stayed beyond the clamor of the crowd, observing from the outside and looking for signs of hostility that might have been sent by the wary Luciferians.

The crowd swelled to a greater size than imagined. Rashnir guessed that there were nearly a thousand people gathered in the park.

From across the way, Rashnir noticed Jorge beckon to him and made his way over. Jorge met him in the middle of a gathering crowd.

Jorge pointed to a large group of people whose corporate dress and appearance looked rustic and foreign. "Something feels odd about those people. What can you tell me? Anything?"

"I'll go check it out," Rashnir shrugged.

He made his way through the maze of bodies and skirted the edge of the people in question. Rashnir made a few quick observations and then looped back around, rejoining Jorge.

The people looked like subsistence farmers, or more likely foragers. Most everything about them was drab, plain, and non-threatening. Despite their outward appearance looking unthreatening, they seemed to exude an aura that felt *not quite right*.

"From what I can tell, I would guess that they are werewolves. The tattoos on some of them might confirm it if I got a better look—or if I knew more about them. They're all pretty mangy, though, so I would guess that it must be one of the lower clans if I'm right."

"Werewolves? They are ekthro, are they not?"

"No, no. They are humans, but they have some power beyond human nature that grants them their shape-shifting abilities.

"They are probably harmless if they are in such a large crowd; werewolves haven't openly hunted men in generations. Usually werewolf clans are nomadic and travel wherever there is food. They usually stick to the woods or mountains and seldom leave the wilderness. This group must have been nearby and gotten invited by someone. They certainly look a bit out of sorts here; maybe they're a little uncomfortable with so many regular humans around them."

The group looked innocuous enough as they found a patch of lush grass and settled down upon it. They appeared more uncomfortable than they did dangerous. Rashnir and Jorge let them be, but made a mental note to keep an eye on them.

Once the crowds' influx ebbed, Kevin climbed onto the small rock formation that marked the center of the park. The outcropping protruded upwards only slightly shorter than the height of the average man; the ground sloped away and made a nice focal point where everyone could hear and see him. The surrounding vendor booths helped improve the natural acoustics, too, making it possible for the assembly to hear Kevin. Once he stood on the stone platform the crowd took it as a cue to find seats on the grassy turf and give him their attention.

Kevin swallowed the lump in his throat.

"I am glad that you have all been able to make it here this evening. Many of you have met me over the past few days and heard the stories about this hero named Jesus. I told you that tonight I will tell you 'the greatest story ever told.'"

As if in defiant response, the bell rang on the tower of the Luciferian temple causing a distraction. Its knell resonated crisply through the air, announcing to the faithful that time had come to begin the weekly Luciferian rituals. Only a few people entered the temple in the distance. Some of the faces in the crowd looked briefly awash with guilt as the bell reverberated; they likely broke their weekly obligations to Luciferianism in order to listen to Kevin's story. Everyone present remained seated, however.

Kevin continued, "Many of you have become familiar over the last week with this man named Jesus, and with His power. Tonight I will tell you about His greatest miracle, and the reason that this is the greatest story ever told: it's because this man is real. There are others present, here, who have also met Him personally. The signs and miracles that He performs are real.

"Now I know there are many others in this land who can perform miracles and magics; there is a huge difference, though. The miracles that Jesus performed were done to help others," Kevin paused, knowing that this was not entirely different, "*and,* He did it for no gain to Himself." This drew a few surprised looks. "In fact,

178

Jesus had several encounters with those religious leaders who charged money for their help and rebuked them when they profited dishonorably. In one case, He chased the priests out of a local temple with a whip."

A murmur of wistful laughter rippled through the crowd.

"I know this idea might seem foreign to some of you, but let me explain. Have you ever had tragedy strike and you had nowhere to turn? Let's say that vandals ruined your crops: now you have financial hardship. Wouldn't you want some help at this point? Would you set your pride aside and accept assistance if it was offered free of charge?

"What if your child grew gravely ill and you didn't have enough money to pay a healer or to pay a monk to seek a boon from a spirit? What could you do? If it was you, and your crops were failing, and your family was in danger, wouldn't you want free help?

"You go to a temple when you need help; you go to worship, or to learn, right? One day, Jesus entered a temple and saw a common sight: there were people there who kept animals for sacrifices. If you needed to make a sacrifice for any purpose, then you would need an animal. These men increased the prices of the animals and profited off of the needs of others. Jesus was so outraged that He took a scourge and chased these men from the temple, beating them, and then threw over their tables and chairs.

"Then, the people who needed His help the most began to come into the temple. These people were blind and sick and in great distress; Jesus healed them of their problems. He did not do it to make a profit; He was capable of helping those in need, and so He did. He did it because *it was the right thing to do.*

"There was a certain group of religious officials, like Luciferian monks, that thought they were the ultimate authority on religion. They made a nice living through their legalistic system, gaining money, prestige, and position. These people were called the Pharisees. The Pharisees were extremely upset by the things that Jesus did. Jesus, by doing only right and just things, made those Pharisees appear to be what they were: legalistic, selfish frauds.

"Jesus, as some of you have heard, traveled the land of Israel, accompanied by His disciples. I have told many of you over the last week of the miracles He did and stories that He told; they all take place under extreme pressure by the Pharisees who pressed Him to stop. It became evident to the Pharisees that Jesus would not cease, so they plotted against Him.

"After several failed attempts to trick Him into heresy, they went away looking like fools. The Pharisees eventually corrupted one of Jesus' disciples, a man named Judas. They paid him to lead a gang of soldiers to Jesus and betray Him.

"One thing that I need to make clear to you all is that there were a great many prophesies concerning the Jesus. These prophecies were given even before the arrival of mankind in this realm, before the conflict between Lucifer and Yahweh. The Pharisees were blinded by their greedy ambition so that they could not see Jesus for who He was: the fulfillment of all these very specific prophecies.

"Back to the story. Jesus had a momentous week and people in the land of Israel were just beginning to recognize Him for the messiah who fulfills all of those prophecies. Then one night, during a religious feast, it happened.

"Jesus broke bread and drank wine with his closest twelve friends, one of them being Judas. Jesus told them that the wine was like His blood, poured out for men, and bread like His body, broken for them. His disciples were puzzled by this, not understanding. Jesus foretold them about His imminent murder. His disciples could not comprehend this; within the last week people had come to recognize Him as the Messiah and they assumed He would use His powers to conquer the oppressive government that ruled the land of Israel, even take over other lands and rule in peace with justice.

"The disciples, like the Pharisees, had misunderstood the prophecy. They did not see that Jesus had an even bigger purpose beyond human politics; He would save mankind from the pits of Hell.

"You see, just before this, Judas became indwelt, possessed by a demon known as Satan, the Deceiver. Satan engineered some of these events and tried to destroy Jesus and His power. The possessed Judas gathered soldiers to lead them where Jesus went to pray.

"Jesus prayed late in a garden; He prayed so earnestly that he began sweating drops of blood. After a while, He went to where His disciples were. They had fallen asleep so Jesus woke them, urging them to pray. He knew that His darkest hours were at hand.

"Judas secretly led the soldiers into the garden and gave Jesus a friendly kiss as the sign to the guards to arrest Him. One disciple grabbed a sword and cut off a soldier's ear; Jesus calmed the disciples and even healed the wounded guard—he knew that all these events were foretold in prophecy. Jesus knew that He must be sacrificed to save all of mankind. His disciples scattered as He was arrested.

"Jesus stood trial and was falsely convicted as a criminal. The Pharisees even saw to it that Jesus was tortured. Then, He was nailed to a wooden cross in such a way that He died slowly and horribly. In the end, His executioners speared His side in order to verify His death; blood and water flowed out of the wound. These two things, interestingly enough, are symbolic of life and spirit and these are what flow out of Jesus.

"Jesus was murdered, and that demon, Satan, thought that he had defeated Him." Kevin paused for a moment and looked at the crowd. None appeared sympathetic to the demonic character in the story. Since this realm's conception demon overlords had exploited humans; that tradition had seemed to continue ever since.

"In three days' time Jesus resurrected Himself and destroyed the power of death. He gained the power to grant to *all* humans the gift of eternal life, just as they were designed to have since the beginning.

"Where I come from, Satan is known by another name. Satan, the Deceiver, the Accuser, was originally named Lucifer."

Several people looked on in shock; others foresaw the inevitable conclusion. Only one person seemed to bristle at the comment: that same monk that they had spoken with earlier. He had apparently snuck out of the Luciferian service and returned.

"Jesus is the Son of God; the name of God is Yahweh." A burgeoning energy stirred within the crowd, swelling and growing. It was hard to distinguish if it was a buzz of excitement or the murmur of revolt.

"Because God loves us so much, He came to make a way for us to come back to Him. He loved us enough to even die for us, so that those who would love Him could return to Him.

"Lucifer, Satan, lied to you! He deceived your forbearers from the beginning. Only a small part of the Luciferian tradition is true. I speak the truth," he raised his voice, to be heard clearly above the crescendo of energy that continued building.

"God created mankind to be like Him and to commune with Him. Because He longed for companionship He made us, and He loves us very much, as a father loves his children. For us to be truly made in His likeness, we needed to be free: to have free will and the power of choice. What good is it if His creation only loves Him because they were forced to? *That* would be slavery, not love.

"Satan was jealous and persuaded Eve, the wife of Adam, the first man, to break God's commandment and eat of the Tree of the Knowledge of Good and Evil. After this, mankind lost its innocence. You see, God is like light and evil is like darkness; darkness cannot exist within the light. Because of this sin, all men had darkness in their hearts, but we can replace it with light—that is what Jesus does for us: He has the power to forgive our sins against His father because He was a sacrifice that paid for the debts owed against God's justice.

"Mankind was originally made to have communion and peace, dwelling with the creator. It was Lucifer who devised mankind's destruction. Because of his jealousy he manipulated it so that we are born as outcasts from God's presence.

"I ask you, why was Lucifer jealous, why does he hate us?" Kevin shouted, drawing the crowd in. "He hates us because God loves each and every one of us infinitely more than He ever loved Lucifer, His brightest angel! Lucifer decided to destroy us; he rebelled against God like a spoiled child who couldn't have his own way."

A light seemed to flicker in the eyes of many. Many people in the crowd understood this chain of events; it made sense to them, ringing as true in their hearts.

"After raising Himself back to life, Jesus ascended from Earth into Heaven. In a few days, He sent forth a gift to help His followers, the Christians, to minister to others: this is the gift of the Holy Spirit. The Holy Spirit helps people to recognize Jesus as the Christ, the Savior and Truth.

"Some of you are even now feeling the prodding of the Holy Spirit; He is telling you that my story is true. The veracity of it vibrates throughout your bones."

Rashnir noticed some odd movements and directed Jorge's attention to it, trying to point at the source without distracting those around him.

Kevin continued, "God always had a plan for mankind and He is even now fulfilling it. He granted this access to return to Him through His son, Jesus Christ, and will not let evil continue to feast upon mankind. He said that, at a certain point in time, He will pour out His wrath upon His creation, upon the Earth, but His believers would be spared this agony. Those who do not belong to God would be punished during this time as all of creation chooses sides in this epic battle and His very creation chooses to revolt against Him. During this period, God would have vengeance for all of the evil committed against Him.

"Some of you know the Luciferian doctrines. You know that Lucifer claimed that if he should ever kneel before Yahweh and proclaim Him 'Lord of all,' Lucifer's creation will burst into flames and burn from east to west." Kevin passed a gaze from left to right during a brief pause. "This is going to happen. It will occur in less than seven years. The outpouring of God's wrath has already begun."

Just then, Rashnir's instincts kicked in. He lunged for Kevin as a group of men at the edge of the park sprang into action. In one smooth move they threw off their cloaks and leveled crossbows at Kevin. They fired their bolts at the preacher as Rashnir caught Kevin in a flying tackle, dropping them both behind cover of the platform rock.

Barbed bolts both clattered against the rock formation and sailed over the top, piercing the air where Kevin had stood moments earlier. Chaos ensued. People screamed and leapt up. The werewolves were instantly on their feet and, as quick as hair on wild dogs bristle, they transformed, standing as eight-foot tall juggernauts of fang, claw, and muscle. They corporately looked to defend against any threat to their safety; instinct urged them to attack it and they splayed their claws and faced the assassins.

Quick as the twinkling of an eye, Jorge cast off his cloak. The light from his alabaster skin radiated as he spread his angelic wings. He charged through the air with such speed that he seemed to teleport in the fray with Kevin's attackers with his sword drawn high. Five feet of steel burned, licking the air with supernatural, azure flames.

With lightning quickness, Jorge's roundhouse swing cleaved through the midsections of the front three attackers leaving four others to gasp in shock. They recognized the suddenly reversed situation much faster than their bodies could react. The whites of their eyes realized it too late, trapping them in slow motion.

The momentum Jorge wielded carried him through to an uppercut-like swing that split the next bandit from bottom to top. Jorge brought his blade around again for a short stroked swing, lopping off the head of the next attacker. His blade followed around and he threw it into the heart of one more attacker; it burst through his backside as the hilt drove all the way to his ribcage. Jorge struck out with the palm of his free hand, colliding hard against the jaw of the final would-be assassin. The blow knocked him several feet through the air until he landed in a crumpled, unconscious heap.

The angel retrieved his flaming sword. Jorge quickly scanned the area for any more threats, and then his blade ceased to be. It seemed to evaporate into the air that surrounded it; like a glowing ember suddenly submerged, it winked out of existence.

From start to finish, the whole altercation lasted less than three seconds. The entire crowd stared in awe at the display of fighting prowess. The fangs and animal features seemed to melt away from the werewolves as soon as the threat had been eliminated and they regressed back into their human form.

The angel drew his wings closely about himself and walked back to where he had dropped his cloak.

Jorge clasped it shut and did his best to shrink back into the crowd.

Kevin resumed his position on the rock; Rashnir stood close by. "I apologize for that," Kevin remarked as he dusted himself off. "My intent is not to bring death; I came to tell you the truth about good and evil and to correctly label Lucifer, Satan, as a liar and manipulator. It does not surprise me that the forces of evil engineered an assassination attempt." He dusted himself off and regained his composure.

"I was telling you about God's wrath. He has, even now, begun to pour it out on His creation. You may think that you are safe from the wrath of God while in this realm created by Satan…but you are wrong. In fact, you have an even greater handicap to finding Truth.

"When your ancestors came to this place thousands of years ago, they already walked in wickedness and rebellion. They had just begun to live lives opposed to their Creator. The evil that they harbored in their hearts condemned them, and it passed to their descendants.

"Those people who came into these lands from Earth learned many wicked things from the creatures that Satan created. The ekthro merely watered the seeds of wickedness that Lucifer had planted in the heart of man from the beginning; the ekthro taught them to resist God and pursue the evil desires of their hearts, claiming it was a 'better way of life.' They played on man's desires and selfishness.

"Your ancestors brought these practices back through the Gateway and taught them to their kin on Earth, further enslaving mankind and enraging God. Men became so evil that God had to destroy everything on the face of the earth with a worldwide flood, killing all living things upon it except for one family and the animals that he preserved. Throughout the years, mankind has again become just as wicked as in that time, just as selfish and haughty as they were then, and God has triggered the beginning of the end.

"Those pre-flood men did more damage instigating the Great Flood. The floodwaters destroyed the earth, but they also blocked the Gate to Earth so that no living creature could pass.

"The waters rushed in through the gate and spilled into this realm as well. It caused the division of lands, here, and filled up your low areas and formed the seas. It killed many as it did so.

"From that time onward, you have missed out on many of the things God has done in His efforts to restore His people to Him. God gave His people laws and commandments to keep, showing them what holiness is, so that his people might recognize their need for a savior to rescue them.

"He took an extreme act of intervention: Christ came and died for you so that you would not suffer eternal death. Because you have been trapped in this place, most have had very little chance to hear of this grace. Because of the forces and powers that Satan created, you were left without access to the saving knowledge of grace that Jesus has supplied for you—Lucifer has robbed you for thousands of years.

"Those who do not accept this message remain an enemy of God because of the separation caused by sin. But how can you accept it if you have never heard it? How can it ever be preached to you if the wicked and selfish shut away this fact and any men who proclaim it?

As you can see, I have protectors: guardians who help me bear this message.

"But very soon Satan will kneel before Yahweh and acknowledge Him as Lord. And then, the prophecy will come to pass. This place will burst into flames and all life here will cease, destroyed by flame. If you do not choose Yahweh then you belong to Lucifer and there remains a rift of sin separating you from God."

Kevin reached down and grabbed Rashnir, clasping forearms in his surprisingly strong grip. Kevin pulled him onto the rock with him. "Redemption is the message of my almighty God!" Kevin shouted. "You all know this man; he was once a mighty warrior. He pursued life on his own terms and was successful, and then he fell. He became worthless in the public's eyes. Just as we have been cast-out from God's grace, we too can be accepted back into His loving embrace once again."

Kevin scanned the crowd; all eyes remained fixed upon him. Kevin fixed his eyes upon Rashnir and pulled a short sword out from under his own cloak. Grasping the blade firmly with his hand, he turned the hilt to Rashnir; Kevin beckoned for him to accept it.

"Regardless of man's law, I accept Rashnir for who he is. I accept him even as a new man. The old condemned man has passed away and a new pure man has been born out of spirit."

A gasp ran through the crowd as Rashnir accepted the sword and knelt. The gasp was not one of anger or betrayal, or even surprise, but more of awe.

"Not only does my God have the power to forgive you of sin, to grant you access to the eternal afterlife, and make you new; He is also a God of healing."

Kevin closed his eyes and took Rashnir's scarred and burned hands. He held them up for the whole crowd to see. They were already familiar with the brand, a cruel and ugly scar: a mark that identified him as a traitor to the king.

"Lord, I pray that You would heal my brother; restore him to complete fullness. Take away all of the wounds placed upon him by others and make him new. I pray that this would bring glory to You and testify to those here that You are the one true God and that You are a God who heals because You love us and not for any other motivation, not for greed or lust, but for love…out of Your love, make my brother whole."

Rashnir stood and turned his hands to his face. For the second time in his life, he had experienced a healing from Yahweh; the skin on his hands was smooth and clear, like that of an infant. He stood there; slack-jawed, he faced the crowd. He turned his hands, marveling, so that they could all see. Many in the crowd stood in amazed wonder.

A voice cried out from the crowd, "What must I do to be saved?!?"

The crowd rose to their feet. A wave of humanity surged towards the rock, calling out to Kevin.

"I want to know God," some shouted and, "help me meet Yahweh!" Two thirds of the crowd moved forward to encircle his location.

Kevin called as soon as the crowd finally stopped surging around him. "Christ loves you and desires you, but you have the freedom not to choose Him. You were born to the possession of the enemy whom He defeated; to claim that victory, you must simply ask of the Lord and He will save you. There is nothing that I can do but point out the way.

"It is easy to pray to the Lord; you simply speak; He hears you. If you do not know the words to pray, try this, 'My Lord, I accept Your redemption. Save me, make me whole; I am sorry for my sins. I believe in You and I make you my Lord, amen.'"

All around, men and women of all ages began kneeling and bowing, praying to God. Rashnir and Kevin walked amongst them, as did the angels, talking and praying with people, embracing many. Kevin laid hands on some and prayed over them.

One such man that Kevin prayed over, dusty and drab, urged Kevin to come and greet his people. The man led the werewolf clan that had come. In fact, each of his clansmen had come forward. Kevin pulled him into an embrace.

"What is your name?"

"I am Zeh-Ahbe'," he said. "I am the chief of my tribe, the Say-awr'."

Kevin eyed him, intrigued. "I am unfamiliar with your kind. Are werewolves human, or just human in appearance?"

A look of concern flashed in Zeh-Ahbe's eyes. "We are human, or at least, we are born that way."

"Earth has many legends about werewolves," Kevin explained, "In some of those legends they are men who are cursed or gifted at some point in their life, in some they are mere feral versions of insane men, in some they are born as wholly different creatures, similar to a man but really something else. I am concerned if this is the case; all creatures living but not human are simply this," Kevin grabbed a pinch of Zeh-Ahbe's flesh. "They are merely crude matter, material. They have thoughts and a mind and a body, but I do not believe they possess an eternal soul—an afterlife. The ekthro are similar to humans, but they're just material: physical stuff created by God's enemy. I do not believe there is salvation for the soulless."

The look of trepidation passed from Zeh-Ahbe'. "Oh, thank you. We are fully human, but we take a pledge and a mark upon our body to show our allegiance to the kil-yaw' and we are granted our powers from that moment on. Werewolf parents raise their cubs in obedience to the kil-yaw' and scald their children early in life to make them tribemates. We are human, but more."

Kevin's face wore a dark look. "Your gift sounds like it could be a curse, an allegiance to the forces of this world, and an open door for the powers that oppose Yahweh. If your salvation required it, could you decide? Would you choose the power of the world, or would you choose to live for God and rely on *His* power?"

"Despite being a werewolf, I can still be saved from sin?"

Kevin nodded. "It may require, though, that you sever the ties to a dark power—you may lose your ability to shapeshift. I think that it is very likely."

Zeh-Ahbe' shook his head, "I do not care. What is the sense of having all the power of the kil-yaw' or even the abilities of the whole Gathering of Demons? Possessing power is useless in the face of what is to come; who can be stronger than the one who is the friend of the one almighty God?

"I accept God's salvation and friendship, even if it should cost my very life in the end. I hold nothing back."

Zeh-Ahbe' took initiative and began to pray aloud, beseeching God for favor.

Kevin laid his hands on the head of the leader of tribe Say-awr' and prayed over him. Jorge walked amongst the other tribemates who gathered behind their leader. Zeh-Ahbe' began to praise God in language of the angels as the Holy Spirit filled him, confirmed to his people that God had accepted him; many of his tribemates did likewise and followed suit.

All across the park, people bowed their hearts; their souls yearned for the only thing that could salve the wounds of original sin carried into this realm so long ago. People scattered across the area and knelt in contriteness, surrendering to God, accepting a Savior that they had always known they needed, but had never known existed.

In the back, behind a couple of the vendor kiosks stood Minstra, the young monk who had earlier spoken with Kevin. Minstra bit his lip, torn by the message; he desired to give himself over to it, yet felt that he could not.

Minstra's eyes darted nervously around, hoping that no one would recognize him for what he was. His eyes angled back to the temple where his master had, in all likelihood, discovered him absent. The rage of the Luciferian combat master, Jandul, could be a fearful—and potentially deadly—thing. He raised his gaze to the upper levels of the temple, to the tower.

He spotted the temple leader high up in the observatory. His body cast a silhouette against the yellowed glass, backlit by torch flames. The silhouette's body language revealed enough; he must've seen everything that happened in the park, and he was not pleased with the outcome.

Minstra slunk away and into the shadows, uncertain of the future.

***

In the highest room of the temple, shadows danced across the fine stonework as torch and candle flames leapt about. Frinnig, the head priest of the local Luciferian Temple, stood in the tower and glared daggers towards Grinden's park as he assessed the situation.

Jandul, Frinnig's primary advisor, flanked him alongside three wretched-looking goblin envoys. The Luciferian ceremony had ended. Frinnig stood at the window still wearing his priestly garments and amulets, holding his toqeph—his rod of authority and staff of power—as he surveyed the scene below. The shama' spell that Frinnig cast had let the group eavesdrop on the last few minutes of Kevin's message.

Frinnig watched it play out like a general watching over a battlefield; his face drew long with dismay. His furrowed brow tightened the skin at its edges and pulled at the tattoos which displayed his rank as a twenty-seventh degree monk. Contrasting the shaven scalp of his advisor, Jandul, whose tattoos of rank were imprinted directly on the top of his head as if it was a crown, Frinnig's hair fell in wisps, framing his face

"I do not like this new threat," Frinnig thought out loud. He turned and spoke directly to Jandul. "Just yesterday, if I had asked anyone on the street what they thought of these krist-chins they would have told me that they were a tiny group of insane vagabonds with a gift for storytelling. What will they say now?"

He paused for a moment before stating the obvious. "These people preach a doctrine that directly contradicts our own teachings."

Jandul remained characteristically silent; he commanded enough authority with simple body language and grunts. He merely nodded his head in agreement with his superior's statements.

Frinnig continued, "You know, I almost respect them for what they've accomplished. They have inspired people to greater faith than I've ever seen in any Luciferian service. I wonder what they have that causes them to respond like this. I felt no tug at the energy lines; no spells have been cast. They have little visual charm… could it be in their genuineness?" he digressed.

"If their message were not so blatantly in opposition to ours I might let it go. I would even see if I could harness this preacher's gifts for my own gain… the gain of Luciferianism as a whole that is; I would seek for them to ally with the Order. It would only cost them a few minor points of doctrine. But I think that they would never do that, though, and we are left with only one option: to destroy them."

Frinnig whirled to his goblin guests. "Tell me, tyr-aPt, what news from your brother?"

tyr-aPt indicated the oddly cut stone he held in his clawed hand, a seeing stone linked to a mate which usually hung around his brother's neck. "My brother, grr'SHaalg, gave me the most recent news from the king's court in Jand. King Rutheir has struck an accord with the ruling council of Ninda. They have given full possession of the Grinden lands to Jand and its ruler— relinquished any claims to it."

"Is that so?" mused Frinnig. Unaware of the true reasons behind such a move, its implications struck Frinnig as fortunate. "Ninda has long contended for their dual ownership of this property from treaties penned so long ago. I had always wondered why they did not relinquish it sooner. With dual status, it has long been free of taxes and really offered nothing to the country but a pleasant access point to the most heavily traveled trade routes; it still serves that function but not without wasted energies or overcommitment by Ninda. A smart move, really, given that it solidifies a peace with the new king who doesn't have a long history, making him... unpredictable. Ninda has been weak as of late and could use all of the friends it can get—I suppose this clinches western support for their borders."

Frinnig went on, realizing that he was still thinking out loud. "Regardless of the reasons behind it, this works to our advantage. King Rutheir is receiving the prophet, Absinthium," he meandered to his desk and caressed a tightly bound scroll, which lay upon it, "who will bring further consolidation of power to the area."

He smiled widely at his guests. "We are finally grasping for what has always been a dream of the order: a state controlled by religion. Finally we—those who have the best interests of the people and their well-being—can have total control." His face twisted into a snarl, "And then, we can use the military might of an entire country to crush threats like this," he spat, waving his arm at the window to indicate his new enemies. "So soon," he whispered as he paced, consumed by his thoughts.

The goblin diplomat, tyr-aPt, motioned to his servants. They slipped away as Frinnig's anger ebbed and he resumed his stance in front of the window, watching the obscenity unfold before him.

tyr-aPt headed straight for the spiraling stairway and departed, his interest in the conversation over. The watchful eyes of Jandul followed him as he departed, but his mouth said nothing; Jandul remained ever distrustful of any new doctrines—especially the new acceptance of the ekthroic races. Jandul would perhaps change his mind after he was allowed to further examine Frinnig's precious scroll for himself... or perhaps speak firsthand with Absinthium when the arch-mage visited.

Frinnig stood watchful at his perch, muttering curses under his breath. Jandul joined him by the window. Below, they saw the crowd of faithful Luciferians departing their place of worship and ceremony as the evening's rituals dismissed. The sight of the crowd exiting the temple building brought a smile to his lips, a smile that fell almost as soon as it was birthed.

"What!" he shouted, pressing his nose to the glass. "This is an outrage!"

Some of the people, as they wandered back towards their homes or other places, got caught up in curiosity and walked towards the gathering in the park.

"I will kill him myself!" Frinnig shouted. He dashed from the window to grab his personal effects stashed by his desk; his ceremonial robes flapped with the sudden movement.

Jandul walked calmly to his seething superior, who struggled to find any kind of weapon. He laid a firm hand over his superior's and looked him in the eye, calming his fumbling hands. "Killing him outright might be unwise at this point. It could still harm us if the crowd discovers that we hired those bandits that attacked, earlier. It would have been less of a problem had they succeeded, but now... you see how these people are devoted to this new teaching. To kill him publicly would make him a hero and raise a banner for all men who oppose our faith to rally under."

He relinquished his hold on Frinnig, "It would be prudent to let the new king deal with it. I have heard speculation there may even be some sort of link between these dissidents and the death of Harmarty. I know for sure that many people believe it—perhaps we can use such rumors to discredit them. For now, I will give them a message that they are unwelcome on our doorstep. Perhaps some of our faithful will grow faint at my appearance and return to us. This heresy is probably just a passing fancy so long as we don't fan its spark into flame."

Frinnig nodded and smoothed his rumpled robes. "You are probably right, my friend," he said as he sat in his chair behind his desk. "You do as you said and I will continue my studies." He unrolled the bound parchment scroll and laid it flat before him. "And I will honor my promise; tomorrow I will let you study the Scroll of Absinthium. He has some truly remarkable insight and a prophetic vision. With one or two more reads I should have it perfectly memorized."

Jandul exited the chamber as Frinnig lit another candle, preparing for an insightful evening of study. He only had to calm his mind first and so he lit a smoldering bowl of opiate laced incense.

Minutes later, Jandul wandered through the crowd that seemed to have grown since he left Frinnig's office; he carried himself so that his intimidating presence was felt to its fullness. Everything Jandul saw disgusted him, not just because the religious gathering defied his beliefs, but because it revealed the ineffectiveness of the cause that he had devoted himself to for so long.

It took him little time to find the man he was looking for. He headed directly towards the one who everyone knew as Kevin.

Jandul approached as if a man on urgent business. Just before stepping into his personal space, Rashnir slid in and barred the monk's path. Jandul knew better than to merely push a man of Rashnir's renown out of his way, despite full confidence in his own training.

Jandul nodded his head at Kevin, who stood just beyond Rashnir, and grunted.

"Kevin," Rashnir called, not breaking his hard stare with the Luciferian. Locking eyes with Jandul he said, "Someone here wishes to speak with you."

"Yes, what is it?" Kevin asked over Rashnir's shoulder, recognizing that this visitor was not friendly.

"You are not welcome here," stated the low voice of the combat master. "Leave or cease your false teachings."

"I am sorry, but neither can I leave and neither can I stop. I am bound to my course."

Kevin tried to speak further, but the chief monk had already turned and departed. After walking a few steps he turned again, reigniting the conversation.

"You will leave and it will be soon." He paused to stress the severity of his words. "Sooner is safer." The monk departed, throwing spiteful looks at anyone who met his gaze as he returned to the temple.

Kevin laid a hand upon his friends shoulder. "You know, Rashnir, that confrontation went better than I expected it to. Well, I mean aside from the assassination attempt that was probably their doing."

"Pity," mused Rashnir.

"Pity! You would have rather that they succeeded?"

"No, not that," Rashnir said, "I was just thinking that I wish he would have pushed me."

Kevin gave him a confused look.

"The fighter in me has always wondered, you know... I've seen him around since my days in the Rangers but our paths never crossed—but still, I've always wanted to fight that guy."

Chapter Nine

tyr-aPt slunk through the shadows that choked the light from the long, stone labyrinths of the Luciferian Temple. He preferred the darkest of them; years of preference bred habit. His two servants followed his every move.

They scampered through the passages and darted through the lowest levels until they came to the sub-basement. It was a clay-floored cellar far beneath the mason laid foundations of the building. Here were the lowest reaches of the building and here was where they preferred their hosts quarter them.

The goblins had previously dug through the clay cellar floor and hollowed out a small cavern where they would be comfortable. In the back of this cabin, unbeknownst to their Luciferian hosts, they'd burrowed a tiny passageway down until it met with a major underground highway. The trunk of the great goblin tunnel network which spread all across the area and completely encompassed the city of Grinden went directly below the temple.

At night, an attuned ear could faintly hear the sounds of goblins on various errands of mischief or duty. The sounds resembled rodents or other scavenger's scratching and gnawing so no human was aware of the far-reaching network that they'd constructed. The architects were careful and took precautions against sinkholes or other calamities that might reveal the prized chambers which led all the way down to the great King Nvv-Fryyg's subterranean hall, the crown jewel of

Goblin civilization which lay under Jand. Ironically, it was located only a short distance from the late Harmarty's court, dug firmly into the easternmost leg of the horseshoe shaped mountain range that harbored the royal castle from the harsh elements.

tyr-aPt sent his cohorts on a long walk down the goblin highway so that he could contact his brother in privacy. Only when the slapping of their padded feet fading away did tyr-aPt remove his qâsam, his seeing stone, from the metal amulet he wore around his neck. Fastened by a fine gold-alloy chain, tyr-aPt wore an amulet very similar to his brother grr'SHaalg's.

Both containers had been finely crafted by skilled metallurgists and appeared to be made as a seamless, engraved bar of precious metal. They could be opened only by someone who knew how to open each particular amulet. The brothers' amulets each contained a linked qâsam which could only contact each other; their mode of mystic conversation was completely secure, except for those who might overhear a verbal conversation. They'd taken great pains to ensure that there existed no "parent stones" linked to these ones which could potentially eavesdrop.

tyr-aPt spat saliva onto his crystalline, blue qâsam and then tapped its multifaceted edge with a fore claw. The stone awoke and glowed with an inner light as the energies shot across the planes of magic and linked with its mated stone. The face of tyr-aPt's brother, grr'SHaalg, appeared in the light of the crystal. His image distorted slightly, bending to the facets so that it looked as if one watched grr'SHaalg through the crystal.

grr'SHaalg was the only creature that tyr-aPt felt he could trust. They had always shared a bond that kept them uncannily close and been partners in plots of subterfuge and intrigue. He knew that their trust had been tempered many times over. Together, they had feasted upon the raw entrails of each of their other litter-mates, owing each meal to some unfortunate event that resulted in the fear of a double-cross.

tyr-aPt greatly respected his brother's skills and his treacherous ability, whose mind operated like a fine machine. He had been part of grr'SHaalg's schemes time and time again and they usually worked to mutual benefit. grr'SHaalg had the bulk of the brains and tyr-aPt was a willing and loyal part of his plans. If he was ever disloyal, grr'SHaalg would spot tyr-aPt's treachery before he himself even knew it was there, and have his brother devoured. Still, they needed each other. grr'SHaalg could not be everywhere all at once and tyr-aPt was happy to be an extension of their shared persona.

[How goes it, brother?] tyr-aPt asked his brother in their native goblin language.

[Things go well, brother,] grr'SHaalg replied, his voice emitting as harmonic resonance through the qâsam.

[You know that the ruling government of Ninda agreed to give all of its interests in Grinden over to Jand,] he continued, [I was with Rutheir at the meeting. It was moderated by Absinthium. I tell you, this wizard is like none I have encountered before; we have done well to ally with him. He claims to have the direct power of the demonic council at his disposal, and I think that it must be true. The spell that he cast was flawless; not one mind on the Nindan council of democratic aristocrats could even think without permission from the wizard.

[The entire group came to the meeting with Rutheir believing that he would give them gifts in exchange for continued healthy relations. The fat gluttons ended up giving away an entire district of valuable land and thought the whole thing was their idea.

[Absinthium departed for Briganik after that but will be back in a week. He is going to report to his master, beh'-tsah, and seek council on certain issues. There is an issue of possible opposition, which our spies have reported. Apparently, a group of people in Grinden that claim themselves as devotees to this krist-chin religion has surfaced?]

[Yes,] tyr-aPt replied, [that is the primary reason I contacted you. They have certainly ruffled Frinnig's undergarments.]

[Hmmm...interesting,] grr'SHaalg mused as he scratched a polyp on his neck. [Absinthium seems to think that anyone under such a banner poses a serious threat. He and his master have apparently kept a wary eye for anyone claiming this faith; there are very few around and I am surprised that this cult can spread at all with the Luciferians constantly hunting them. What more can you tell me about this dead religion?]

tyr-aPt paused for thought before delivering the news. [They are right to fear them, from what I have seen this night. They multiplied their numbers immensely in just one meeting and so firmly set their new converts in opposition to Luciferian doctrines that those humans might never return to the Order. In less than two hours' time, their numbers went from four to almost seven hundred, *and* their leader survived an assassination attempt unscathed with total loss of life to the brigands that Jandul hired.]

[Seven hundred!] exclaimed grr'SHaalg, [they multiply faster than one of Nvv-Fryyg's whores!] He began to lose himself in thought and muttered some nonsensical words; they came through as incomprehensible through the stone's vibrations.

grr'SHaalg grinned as a thought took hold in his mind. [It matters little, brother. I have seen the power that this wizard wields and I assure you that there is nothing to fear. He will crush them all whether they resist or not; Absinthium will kill them one by one in his personal chambers and perhaps drag them to the council of demons so that they may feast upon their bodies.] The goblin giggled at the mental picture and continued, [You and me brother. We will play this out and finally gain the seats of power that we deserve.]

[Real power and authority,] tyr-aPt said, [and here I was happy with mere material gain.]

[Think loftier and more grandiose,] grr'SHaalg chided. [By the time this power shift ends, you will sit upon a throne made of Nvv-Fryyg's marrow-sucked bones, and I will preside over all of the goblin kings as their chief—we will be worshiped by both goblins and men. Real power this time. Absinthium and the demonic council will be my only ceiling. Think of it; veritable goblin god-hood is within our grasp.]

[You and me, to the end.]

grr'SHaalg digressed, [I am glad that I never devoured you, brother tyr-aPt. I had considered it once. But it is so nice to have someone to share visions of this magnitude with.]

[Long life to you too, brother,] tyr-aPt replied as the light went out of their linked crystals.

***

As the evening wore on, grr'SHaalg crept through the castle which Rutheir, King of Jand, now owned and occupied. He found Rutheir alone in his sitting room, pouring over texts and maps, no doubt trying to work through details in his mind, wondering how this grand plan would work out and what the possible fail-safe contingencies might exist.

grr'SHaalg sat in a chair opposite of him and waited for Rutheir to finish his current task. After a moment, Rutheir looked up at the goblin wearing the purple fez.

"I bring news from Grinden," he said to the king.

Rutheir did not speak and waited for him to continue.

"There seems to be events happening in the town that could complicate our plans for Grinden. The group of renegades that Absinthium mentioned might somehow pose a threat to the Church has infiltrated the town. The Temple plays such a vital role in our plans that we must devise something quickly."

The king glared at him from the corner of his eye. He knew that this was the true king of the goblin kingdom. The symbiotic subterranean kingdom dwelt just beneath his own; in a similar manner, Rutheir had previously ruled Jand in every aspect but official title. That fool Harmarty could barely command a servant to urinate properly. Previously, though, Rutheir ruled through subtle manipulation and couldn't let that simpleton out of his sight for fear of Harmarty doing something to sever the kingdom's diplomatic ties or burn the entire nation to the ground.

Rutheir paused insightfully, pondering the recent chain of events. The first thing he felt after they discovered Harmarty's corpse was gratitude. Following the King's death, the nation's aristocrats suddenly showed ambition for the throne. With the royalty destroyed an immediate power vacuum opened, one that a man of Rutheir's talents could easily fill.

The upper class had been previously content to hold positions under Harmarty, but delusions of grandeur stirred them up like sharks with blood in the water. After a couple of threats to specific individuals, and a few choice digits removed from stubborn individuals via crude methods, Rutheir solidified his reign.

With the warring nobles cowed into submission and the snobbish aristocrats who deemed themselves too political for physical violence satisfied by Rutheir's claim to the throne by an admission of Harmarty as his sexual partner, the struggle for the throne had been short lived. The acknowledgement was true enough, even if the act was never consummated. Their relationship was more humiliating to Harmarty than to Rutheir and usually resulted in Harmarty bursting into childish sobs and uncontrollable weeping; he'd blubber the names of individuals who'd harmed him throughout his childhood and lapse catatonic.

The only problem now was that he received a plethora of unwelcome sexual advances from the many, landed gentry from across the kingdom. Rutheir used whatever manipulation he could but was never serious about pursuing that lifestyle. He'd not ruled out any sort of hedonism, but his tastes ran so much more violent and visceral than what he'd been offered by the perverse men of his country.

"Tell me what has happened," Rutheir demanded, "and then we can plan our course of action accordingly."

grr'SHaalg gave Rutheir a summarized version of the information gleaned from his brother tyr-aPt. He did not disclose the source or the fact that he possessed a set of seeing stones. Such technology remained extremely rare and expensive.

After an extended pause for thought, Rutheir came up with what he thought was a reasonable suggestion. "We should discredit these people from multiple angles. I have a contact in the Rogis Rangers unit who is convinced that Rashnir, one of the original four, is directly connected to Harmarty's death."

grr'SHaalg chuckled a low laugh under his breath.

"Yes," Rutheir went on, nodding at the humor, "We both know that Rashnir is the one who murdered our..." he used a voice that dripped with unmistakable sarcasm, "beloved King Harmarty."

"This is the second in command, Pinchôt, correct?"

"Yes," Rutheir raised an eyebrow, realizing that the sneaky goblin seemed to know an awful lot about what happened above ground in his kingdom. "Pinchôt may find some piece of evidence that links them to the murder in a plausible way. Rashnir is good at whatever he sets his hands to; we may have to fabricate something."

"How effective is this tactic? It seems like many of the people that these krist-chins have collected hated Harmarty anyway."

"Yes, it seems so, but that is not uncommon for residents of Jand or Grinden. This approach will do two things. The first is that it will appeal to those fools in my country who believe in some kind of reliable legal system. It should inspire pride to those in Jand's military, which has been far too relaxed lately. The outlying areas have relied too much on the mercenaries Harmarty was so fond of farming out the bulk of their work to. The other thing is that the peasants will come to see Pinchôt as a replacement hero—someone to override Rashnir's celebrity status. How ironic that Pinchôt seeks to surpass Rashnir's legacy by being the one to destroy him; he was raised on stories of Rogis' Rangers and admired Rashnir for years. I think, though, that Pinchôt could never hold a candle to Rashnir's skill.

"The second front we attack them on is the religious front. With Absinthium's coming call to Luciferian recommital, we should be able to overshadow the message that they are using to gather devotees to their cult. We can put the peasants back into the yoke of tradition and brand these krist-chins as anathema. The church will take a hard stance against any insurgents and probably send a contingent of combat monks to destroy them. The monasteries' numbers might not be enough to fight them, but their action will scare away locals interested in the cult.

"While all of this is going on, and with the Rangers unwittingly working towards our goals and the religious front handled by Absinthium and the church, we can continue looking for an opportunity to assassinate their leader and end it all swiftly and easily."

Rutheir saw and acknowledged the look that grr'SHaalg had formed on his twisted snout. "I know what you are about to say: that we must be careful not to make a martyr out of this Kevin man. I do not fear that. If we cut the head off, I am confident this cult will die. I do not, however, wish to risk it until the time is right. We can wait until the Rangers brand Rashnir and his group as murderers. We will frame Rashnir for Kevin's demise too, if at all possible, revisiting his reputation for killing friends."

"An excellent plan with many contingencies should any part prove less than adequate," the goblin confirmed.

"I'll have my contacts in the proper places send word to Absinthium. He will advise us to proceed or wait."

"When is the wizard due back?"

"A few days. He has gone to visit his lord and master of the Gathering. beh'-tsah will advise him and then he will return to us. He said that it would take him less than a week."

"Briganik in just a few days? What creature bears him with that kind of speed?" grr'SHaalg speculated.

"A gryphon... a big one. I saw it carry him off towards the horizon. I am wary; to cross Absinthium is to beg for a pain." Rutheir made this comment more for grr'SHaalg than anything else. The goblin's spy network knew too much and the king feared that he might scheme some sort of a double cross, or might try and cut the human out of any dealings with the mage. Rutheir's remark carried no fear for himself; it warned the goblin that there was too much information in his little head and at any hint of treachery it would be cut off—all that knowledge would spill out with the rest of his greasy innards.

"Be wary indeed," the goblin countered slyly, rebuffing Rutheir. This was business, and to goblins, business and treachery were casual bedfellows. Rutheir would have to look over his shoulder and play this game masterfully if he desired a moment's peace from the paranoia that these kinds of business caused.

"Be wary indeed," his repeated words hung in the air as the goblin departed to retire in his personal hole.

***

Jandul sat like a man obsessed. Finally given access to the Scroll of Absinthium, he sat in his chambers examining and reexamining the parchments. The candles flickered and a few of them died as they burnt down to their bases, their luminary life exhausted through the course of a late evening.

Darkness slowly crept in as the candlelight faded; more and more sources of light failed. Jandul paid them no mind. He knew the darkness would eventually envelop him, but he'd waited patiently for Frinnig to part with the precious scrolls and he didn't want to spare another moment finding new candles. The obsessive Frinnig barely let the scrolls go further than his eyes could track them since receiving them, and now Jandul knew why.

It addressed a constant source of worry for Frinnig. He would often lament saying, "The problem we have with our numbers is that there are simply not enough people. The number of faithful men remains consistent, but we will never have growth and power until we have an increase in numbers."

The scroll's new doctrines would change all of that. Frinnig did well to study the texts with enough fervor to verify that they were indeed inspired. Jandul could find no problem with them, save that of justifiable religious pride and prejudice.

The scroll read:

Absinthium, thirty-third degree faithful prophet of the Luciferian order, two-vote member of the High Council of

Four; written to all of the faithful churches of the lands.

We, by faith in the promises and magic of old provided by our champion, that is Lucifer, continue to pursue the glory that he has commanded us to attain on his behalf. New revelation is at hand that enables us to better pursue this dream.

What I am about to impart is absolutely true and divinely appointed.

I lay awake one night, reveling in the powers that have been given me to command. Despite my efforts, I could not enter into sleep; something was pulling at my soul in attempts to communicate with me. One moment I was in my bed, the next I was in the presence of Lucifer himself, arrayed in glory and sitting upon the usurped throne of Yahweh.

"What do you command of your servant?" I inquired.

"To listen and to observe." He commanded.

It was then that I realized that he was not fully revealed; I could not see him clearly. He was veiled behind some kind of curtain. I asked him why he was veiled like this and he replied that it would be revealed to me.

Then I witnessed all that had happened in the spirit realm throughout these several millennia since our champion created our beloved land. It was as if I was there myself for all that time as an observer, and yet no time at all had passed. I saw great battles being fought by both men and angels in the Earth realm, some of consequence, others of little value.

In the end, Lucifer was victorious in his great campaign against his foe and cast his rivals into the Pit that burns forever and seated himself upon Yahweh's throne. When I looked upon his beautiful face shining with light, I could not recognize him, for he was no longer familiar, and I doubted.

Lucifer told me, "You do not understand because you did not watch me; look again." Again I witnessed as all of time passed before my eyes; this time I watched Lucifer and when it all seemed to pass me by in an instant that truly took lifetimes, I watched him transform; he changed dramatically through the eons.

Our beloved angel of light was twisted, his visage appearing to me as ugly: hideous beyond human measure! My brethren, do not misunderstand, you must read this through to completion.

Lucifer spoke.

"You see me now and you recoil. Why, human? I will tell you why. You recoil because you judge a creature by appearance and by ancient prejudices.

How you see me now is an amalgam of that which I have created. You see a combination of features from orcs and ogres, goblins and trolls, dragons and wyvern. Are you repulsed by what I have created?

"You men still have too much original Adam within you. You are judgmental and condemning. How long have I put up with you fearing and hating my children whom I have created. My beautiful ekthro, all of the reasoning beings, I crafted from what had been created. Men I love as well, my adopted children whom I hold above any other creation, but you have forgotten your brothers and sisters.

"For millennia you have held prejudices against those you did not deem pleasing to the eyes or whose customs differed from your own. No longer; accept them as your family. Intolerance is the only true crime against me."

Then, Lucifer had brought before him one creature of every species that he had created and they were sacrificed to him and he took a part of them and consumed it and it became a part of him: skin from orcs and goblins and muscles from trolls and giants and the heart of an elf and the wings of a dragon and tail of a wyvern and so on.

"I took pity upon you in the beginning, Adam, and I continue to hold to my mission. But after I adopted you into my family, I had children of my own, the ekthro are not to be excluded from the riches and glory to come when our great campaign against Yahweh and the Host of Heaven, led by that wretched Son of His, is completed. As you can see, my children resemble my traits.

"Once these are defeated we will ALL share in the spoils of war. I would never forget my own children when I pour my blessings out upon my faithful and execute those lacking devotion to me. Both man and ekthro shall be privileged to this place and to dwell with me for as long as they live and there will be no longer any toll to access any tower ascending to the heavenlies above the Temple of Light. Everything will be costless and everything will be permissible, this is my promise to you; if it harms no others, do what you may."

I saw the expanse of heaven, renovated by its new Luciferian occupants and its beauty was so great that it is indescribable.

Lucifer told me, *"What you have seen today is a vision of the past and of the future. At this very time a great battle rages in the heavens as the demonic forces battle for footholds in the firmaments. You* children of Adam must uphold our forces in devotion and mystic rights and exercises of magic and loyalty and even sacrifice. All this must occur to enable us to acquire victory in the spirit realm. As of yet, our forces are evenly matched and Yahweh seeks the prayers of His people to gain advantage.

"I, however, have more children with the combined efforts of all of my sons and daughters, both adopted Man and my created Ekthro.

"Who will take my words to my Ekthro? Will you do so, my servant?"

I, Absinthium, tell you that I cried out "I will!" as loudly as I could. "Will my brother ekthro believe me? Will they believe in the authority you have given me?"

"They will believe when you demonstrate the power and magics I have given to you. I have given it to you with the purpose of displaying it before all creatures. Do so; use this power to convince others to believe."

"I will embrace my brethren of other origins and we will worship together through ritual and sacrifice and we will storm the gates of Heaven and advance the kingdom of our champion; our magics will force open the gateway between the realms and overpower the enemies."

These things that I write to you, I do on behalf of Lucifer. Preach this message to all Men and all Ekthro. Offer your sacrifices and your devotion to the demons and empower them to focus their energies and send warrior might to those who battle in Heaven, our impending home and enthronement.

~Stamped with the approval seals of the GATHERING of Demons~

The sigils etched upon the parchment listed the demon overlords that made up the council, the largest, most ornate seal belonging to its head, beh'-tsah, followed by his twelve subordinates:

EXAPOREH'-OMAHEE
GAY-OOTH'
PEH'-SHAH
RAW-TSAKH'
KEH'-SEM
ZAW-LAL'
GAW-LAW'
SHIK-KORE'
MAKH-AL-O'-KETH
TAH-AV-AW'
SHEH'-KER
KES-EEL'

Jandul thought to himself, *intolerance is a crime against Lucifer himself. I must change how I think; I must hate only those who exclude others, and those who oppose the Luciferian truths—like these krist-chins. Everyone else is my brother and my friend.*

He contemplated these things, letting them take root in his heart as the last candle's light flickered into darkness. The night consumed him with its darkness. Jandul sat in his quarters and meditated on the new doctrines until the morning light came.

***

Dawn broke over, what the townsfolk had begun to call, the Christian Encampment. A collection of tents and temporary dwellings dotted the riverside on the eastern edge of town, the banks where Rashnir had previously made his home. Campfires had been kindled in various places and people gathered in small groups to cook breakfasts and share with each other.

Kevin walked among the crowds of people, speaking briefly with many of them. Kyrius walked with him. Rashnir did likewise, walking with Jorge on the other side. Kevin and Jorge answered whatever questions people had, mostly about issues of faith and how their recent decision might further impact their lives.

It seemed a group consensus that nobody wanted to return to their old ways. With the realization that their time had grown so short and the urge to help rescue souls so heavy on their minds, nobody wanted to do anything other than travel with Kevin and help fulfill their corporate mission: to rescue as many as possible and slip past the gate at the Western Spires

Kevin sensed great genuineness as he interacted and spoke with folks. There was no turning back for these people. He smiled; this was the right mindset for a Christian to have: time drew short and the need to evangelize had never been more pressing. How many Christians had he known in his prior life who'd been content to do nothing for the cause of Christ? So few ever contributed significant time or funds to send out witnesses. The only donations given were those that benefited them directly or indirectly. It was as if his people on Earth wanted to keep Christ's sacrifice a secret; they did not want "unworthy persons" to join their eternal fellowship. Of course, none were worthy! And that was the point. Kevin found the new Christians of this land to be quite refreshing.

Traditional ministry models from Earth were of no consideration to him—nothing was the same. The only option was complete reliance on the Holy Spirit. Only the Spirit could eventually lead them out from this realm through the Gateway. Any Christians who chose not to seek the Gateway's exit would be burned alive when the great conflagration arises in the east after Lucifer bows before Jesus.

Still, the Earth man didn't have a clue what came next. He only knew that nothing from his previous experiences would suffice.

After breakfast, Kevin broke away for some privacy. After a short while, Rashnir and the angels went looking for him; they discovered him praying in his tent. Trying to slip out and leave him to his privacy, Kevin stopped them.

"Don't go," he requested. "Stay and pray with me. I'm so desperate for guidance," he admitted. The three complied.

Finally, feeling more focused, Kevin shared his plans with his three friends. "We have a unique situation. How should we proceed reaching this world?" Kevin asked rhetorically. "We have this incredible call to evangelize the multitudes before us. This is truly the greatest opportunity for the Church since the time of the

Acts; we have a whole world set before us and only a few individuals in its entire population have ever heard the Message.

"Not only do we have this great mission field set before us, we have workers who earnestly desire to be used by God." Kevin thought for a second, "The problems that we face are going to mostly come from me," he digressed. "I honestly do not know why God asked me to come to this place. Surely there are others who would have been better suited."

Kyrious nudged the preacher. "You know He has a reason."

"I know. But I have no idea how we could do all this through any methods I am familiar with; between us all we have just one Bible," Kevin patted his dog-eared leather bound text. "I have no discipleship materials or any way to reproduce things that I wish to educate people with. I say that the problem is with me because in Old Testament times they passed everything along by oral tradition or had scribes make copies... I do not know where to begin discipling others when everything is so radically different than my experiences. Only something new and radical will work.

"We have no choice but to educate these people for the task of evangelism. But the problem I keep dwelling on is our limited access to the Scripture. Granted," Kevin looked at both Jorge and Kyrius, "You two can quote any passage from the book in any language ever spoken, but I need to train these people, and I am so greatly inadequate."

A long pause followed.

"We can only trust that the Lord will show you what to do," Kyrius said. "Be of good cheer, the Lord chose you because He knows who you are and what you can do." The angel gave him a smile that melted away any ill feelings and doubts.

Kevin believed him, but he still had no idea how to proceed.

"For now," Rashnir said, "perhaps we should continue getting to know our new-found brothers and sisters in the Lord? There are so many."

"Yes, yes. That would be a good idea. I am sure that the Lord will reveal something to my heart before long."

No sooner had Kevin lifted the tent flaps than he found Zeh-Ahbe' waiting outside. The leader of the Say-awr' sat patiently, cross-legged on the ground.

"Is something troubling you, Zeh-Ahbe'?" Kevin asked.

"Yes, and no," he replied as he climbed to his feet. He dusted himself off and walked with the group.

"No because I am still too thrilled about my salvation that nothing can really bother me."

"Don't ever lose that feeling," Kevin advised him, "hold onto that with everything that you've got." He silently prayed that Zeh-Ahbe' would not lose that internal fire.

"Though I am still so enraptured in what has happened to me, I have a particular sadness on my part for the kil-yaw'. I have to return to the kil-yaw' for one final meeting. Not just because I want to go to them and share with them what I have found, but because a messenger came to me this morning and stated that the kil-yaw' meets tonight. If I do not go, they will assume something bad has happened—especially when they cannot find any members of tribe Say-awr' present. They will form a hunting party and come searching for us."

"It is your decision to go or stay. But I would like to know more about your kind. We have so many of your tribemates among us and I am curious. I know practically nothing as it stands, so anywhere is a good place to start," Kevin said. "I need to know how I can best minister to your people."

They came to an area dominated by an immense, sawn-off tree stump. Kevin sat next to it. He invited Zeh-Ahbe' to sit and teach him about his culture.

"The Say-awr' are the least of the tribes within the kil-yaw'," Zeh-Ahbe' explained. "The kil-yaw' is made up of the leaders and escorts of the ten werewolf tribes. The lowest of these is Say-awr', it literally means 'hair.' Then comes Zaw-nawb', the tail, followed by Ore, they are hide. These are the low tribes.

"Some other tribes have a middle status, Tsip-po'-ren is claw, Shane' is fang, Dawm is blood, Eh'-tsem is bone and Gheed is sinew. These tribes all have similar standing and often vie against each other for positions of power from the highest tribes.

"The two highest clans are the Kaw-bade', which is the viscera or the internals, and then the highest and wisest of them is the Ahee-sthay-tay'-ree-on: the senses.

"Kil-yaw' means 'the mind.' Together, we decide what should be accomplished. We decide to go or stay… where the body goes to and the length of our stay; we are nomadic and require a great deal of food to keep up our energy, especially when in our hybrid forms.

"We have been making our way across the eastern coasts these last several years… avoiding the rocky terrain of the central countries like Lol; they do not tend to have good prey. We also stay out of Briganik because of the mountains that rise with their foothills rooted in Lol.

"At least this is how the kil-yaw' is now. Long ago we were much more warlike and often waged battles against orc and dwarven villages. Wherever meat was, we went; that was when the Kaw-bade' was the dominant tribe of the kil-yaw'. After a time, the warlike ways of the Kaw-bade' led to such a reduction in our numbers that the Ahee-sthay-tay'-ree-on gained supremacy and brought with it a philosophical revolution. They have led us in new ways; we no longer prey upon reasoning creatures, but instead upon other large game. This is pivotal to our personal safety and welfare. We keep our numbers down, selectively breeding to keep from overgrowing our colonies with appetites that could never be met. In the old times, we had become like locusts that consumed everything and move on—until all the prey rose up against us. The Ahee-sthay-tay'-ree-on are thinkers: very wise."

"When must you go?" asked Kevin.

"This evening. I must leave with two of my trusted tribemates. I will take Rah'-be and Sil-tarn. You might recognize them, but I don't think that you have been formally introduced. Anyone else who accompanies us would be in peril for their life. Attending without invitation from the kil-yaw' means death. I will leave Raz-aphf in charge in our stead."

Zeh-Ahbe' grimaced with deep thought. "I have a problem that I do not know how to remedy."

Kevin gave him a curious look. "I certainly know how you feel, but don't understand your circumstances."

Zeh-Ahbe' sighed. "The meeting of the kil-yaw' requires that I arrive in my werewolf form, as will be required of Rah'-be and Sil-tarn as well. You were right about our abilities. Our decision requires that we submit ourselves to God as fully human, reliant upon only Jesus as our master. We can no longer assume our wolf forms."

"We will pray together, my friend," Kevin said. "God will supply the strength you need to carry on." The words struck home to Kevin as a remedy to his own disquiet spirit.

"I will see you off and pray for you before and after you leave. For now, tell me more about your people, your tribe. How can I better teach the Say-awr' what it means to be a Christian?"

***

Absinthium stood alone in the complete silence; the chambers of his master spread around him. Hours ago he'd climbed the stairs of the Babel Tower; his gryphon deposited him at the tower's base and watched him ascend the winding column of stairs on foot. Gryphons could make incredible speed on wind or ground. Initially bred to pull chariots for their demon masters, these magnificent creatures could make the trip from northern Ninda to the center of Briganik in just over a day's time. They flew so fast that Absinthium could do little but bury himself within the large, downy feathers in order to prevent the wind from prying him off the creature's back.

Candlelight flickered in the room, casting shadows that jumped about like imps overcome with mischievous glee. The flames howled in protest as a supernatural breeze gushed through the room, almost snuffing the lights of the candelabra.

Absinthium bowed low and dropped to one knee. He cast his eyes to the ground as his master, beh'-tsah, materialized before him, pulling his very essence from the shadows; a dark whirlwind of energy solidified into the towering and grotesque form of the overlord. The demon stomped the cobblestone floor two times in succession. The booming sound echoed through the chamber as a sign that his servant may rise and look upon him.

The weathered arch-mage stood and regarded his dark master. beh'-tsah stood a full fifteen feet. His gnarled face and twisted visage resembled a burn victim's and told the story of glory hard-won through battle. His nonsymmetrical nose gave him a horrible kobold appearance with such canine-like features, though there was no kobold to ever look so terrifying and hideous. Below a black hide like hairy boar leather and haunches like a lion's, his large taloned feet clicked loudly on the cobblestone as the beast walked a slow circle around his herald. The demon draped behind him his massive black wings, like those of some horrible drake, veined in deep purple; they complemented the yellowed, stained ram-like horns that protruded from his forehead and the simple bovine tail which hung so low it nearly touched the floor.

beh'-tsah' clacked his teeth together to ensure that he'd resumed full corporeality. His sharp, gnarly teeth protruded from his maw in every seeming direction, stained, chipped, and misshapen from crunching upon the skulls of man and beast alike. While his physical features appeared terrifying to both man and to ekthro alike, Absinthium knew and loved his master. Absinthium had grown to love the terror that made him feel so alive in his core.

A simple loincloth hung about the demon's waist; made from claw-rent dragon's skin, the fine, crimson scales shimmered in the low flame light. beh'-tsah's breast was clad in armor assembled from the ribcages of men whose bones were bleached white in places and encrusted red where torn flesh once clung in others. Around his neck hung a fine cord and strung upon it were the claws and shriveled eyeballs of the same dragon whose hide made the loincloth.

The mage knew the significance of the clothing his master wore; each item came from a personal kill and reminded any who saw him of the demon's raw power. The dragon's parts had been torn from his predecessor— the previous head of the demonic Gathering. meh'-red had assumed a dragon's form when he met his rival in battle, a battle ending in his demise.

Absinthium looked upon beh'-tsah and understood power. There was much power in fear.

What news do you bring from the campaign in Jand? I had not time to divine the information for myself …I have been fighting a campaign here in the heavens to annihilate any would-be usurpers. I trust that the goblins are well pleased that they will have the power to assert their own plans and finally unveil their great subterranean network?

"The leaders in Grinden grow expectant, my Lord, though the politics of the new regime are coming along as expected. Rutheir has solidified his position as the new ruler and the goblin diplomats have fully embraced our plan; these underlings of King Nvv-Fryyg wield all of the true power in the under-dweller's realm.

"The goblins are quite cunning—selfish too. They recognize the potential in their subterranean highway but seek to use it for fiscal profit rather than to take real power. Nvv-Fryyg is far too removed from his own politics and he places too much trust in his envoys. They will have his head in a short while if he continues ignoring his kingdom in pursuit of selfish lusts; I imagine he'll end his existence soon, roasted on a fire spit as a victory feast when their eventual coup is consummated." Absinthium could picture the gluttonous goblin king's thorax bursting and oozing juice from the cooked tissue as his carcass roasted over hot coals. He shook away the unappealing thought. "The politicians are *very* happy with the proceedings and the leading council in Ninda was extremely compliant."

The demon grinned a wide carnivorous smile.

The goblins must stay compliant; they are a key to this plan. I have given them what they required for this bargain. They will get total ownership of the Grinden location: both the surface and what lies below; we will get our followers. We will use the goblins from Nvv-Fryyg's kingdom as our test run. We can use this group as evidence to the other ekthro that Luciferianism is right for them and show them our faithful ones who embraced the doctrines. Eventually, control will develop and solidify into such a power base that I can use its wave of bodies as a hammer to reshape this land however I envision it. I will rebuild the second heavens, destroy my opposition in the western mountains—those abominations that the jealous fool hay·lale first created at the beginning in his first twisted attempt at creating life—I will eventually blockade the gate in the west.

The demon paused, amused with the praise he heaped upon himself in his monologue. He continued.

*All goes as I have planned. My rise to ultimate power
has begun. No creature can stop what has been set in motion;
I will soon have ultimate control, and I will be god in this
place. I have forced nearly every demon on the Gathering
into submission, and now but a few remaining demonic
warlords must I vie with; if I contend with those warlike
meddlers one by one, they will each fall before me and I will
devour their eyes. I will be crowned as Lucifer.*

The demon gnawed on his tongue at the thought
and his eyes stared into the supposed future that he
planned. A thin trail of blood leaked from his mouth as he
grinned.

"There is more, BEH'-TSAH," the arch-mage
interrupted. "The political campaign is going exactly as
planned, but while you were preparing to meet with me *I
did* divine the recent events in Grinden."

Absinthium paused for a second, knowing what it
is that he must say, but not wanting to upset the mood
that his master was in. He'd learned that the direct
approach was the best one.

"That which you fear is occurring right now in the
city of Grinden."

The words lingered in the air as if they were
forbidden, like a child who had just flung profanities at a
parent. beh'-tsah blinked blankly. What he had just heard
was an impossibility.

Explain your statement.

A light of hatred had kindled deep inside of beh'-
tsah's cold, hard eyes.

Absinthium, leader of the Luciferian order,
commander and manipulator of countless men, and arch-
mage with no comparison, was rendered momentarily

speechless. He wilted slightly before the foul breath of his dark master.

"The one thing that you have cause to fear is coming to pass. Someone is preaching of Yahweh's grace in Grinden. They are tying in another name with this theology as well."

The demon was agitated. He leaned more into the conversation.

Tell me! Who is this other one that they align with their message? Are you sure of this, or could your divinations be wrong?

"There is no error in my divination. Not everything was revealed to me in my vision, but I did see one name clearly: Jesus."

beh'-tsah recoiled at the name, something that Absinthium had never seen nor thought possible. The monster gathered his wings and tail to himself; he seemed lost in thought and withdrew in deep concern.

So then, it is true. The Christians I devoured so long ago spoke truly. The Son actually stepped down and rescued his condemned creation. I must question Karoz about this. The ageless prisoner may give me some insight. He will not stop at Earth if it is true; if He actually performed the substitutionary sacrifice with His own body then He will stop at nothing to redeem as many souls as He can. Truly, He could make enough atonement for every man who will ever live.

His ugly mouth spat a string of incomprehensible curses from various languages, the worst possible from many dialects. beh'-tsah clutched his fists in fury at the potential ramifications.

He is at work, even here. There must be a loophole! How can He send in more prophets unless there is some sort

of loophole? He would not break His own word He cannot;
to do that would be so cataclysmic that reality would shatter
and everything would cease to exist.

The demon shouted a loud phrase, magically
commanding a certain scroll into existence for
examination.

Qara meyshar terem eth!

A brilliant light flashed and it seemed as if the
very particles of air in the room quaked with the powers
he commanded. The demon stretched out his hand, palm
upward, and a parchment scroll burst into existence
within his grasp. It shone with a supernatural corona.
beh'-tsah unrolled the scroll and began reading it to
himself.

Absinthium could see that it was written in a
language that he could not read: the language of heavenly
beings. Penned in a kind of silver ink, the lettering
glowed like rays of sunshine shimmering upon the
surface of the sea.

beh'-tsah's eyes tracked back and forth several
times as he examined the accord Lucifer had struck with
Yahweh so long ago. He paused for thought after reading
it, paced a few steps, and then resumed his studies again.
This happened several times. Absinthium stood at
attention the entire while, waiting for his dread lord to
come to a conclusion on the matter. After many long
minutes, beh'-tsah spoke another mystic command and
waved the scroll out of existence, returning it to the plane
that he'd summoned it from.

I know what has happened. Long ago, at the
beginning, the Word was spoken: the Logos. Those of us who
fell with hay-lale disregarded the Logos. We had to; if we had
believed it then we would have never chosen rebellion. We

would have never believed the words hay·lale used to tickle
our ears should we have chosen to fully believe the Logos.
Despite that, we all knew the Logos; it was with God and it
was God. It stated and reaffirmed everything that those older
prophets who rose in this realm preached   before I
consumed them. These events in Grinden only show that He is
still working hard to make His statements come to pass—I
refuse to believe that He has already written history. There
must be a way to overthrow it, and there must be an option
for victory. I refuse to believe anything else...
But the Logos...

The Logos said that in the end of all things, when
He decided to bring His plan for creation to a close, before He
ends it all, His message would be heralded in all of the lands.

A moment of dawning comprehension overtook
the demon overlord. His pupils shrank as he fully
understood the situation.

The agreement. It states the conditions and outlines
the accord between He and hay·lale and it allows this place to
exist outside of Yahweh's jurisdiction, giving complete
ownership and control to us, his opposition, though it leaves
mankind's souls still subject to the damnation of inherited sin.
It is a grand mousetrap indeed. This agreement, signed by the
triune Godhead, allows us to access the power we wield, it
legalizes our magics. But there is a loophole...

There is a cleverly inserted clause here in the terms
and conditions of exclusivity that allows for action already
endorsed by the Logos. The Logos precedes anything else and
we cannot violate it; the agreement is all worded around the
Logos—it was expertly penned by Yahweh to leave a loophole
that inserts a messenger at the time of the onset of Yahweh's
wrath. That must have been a forethought on their part
and they call hay·lale the Deceiver...

The demon focused once again on his servant. Foreseeing the possible chain of events, beh'-tsah knew that he must put a stop to any Christian activity.

Absinthium, I commission you to destroy every known Christian in existence. Train and teach others to do the same in case you fall before your task is complete. This is our greatest threat. This menace imperils everything that we have worked for and could even destroy the very existence of this place...

You must act at all times in interest of this: it is your highest calling. You are the only servant that I find trustworthy enough to have my full authority on this matter. You must destroy this cell of dissidents before they unleash a power unlike any other...

You know the power that you command as my most loyal servant, the magic that you wield and the supernatural abilities you can perform. If this message spreads and their faith grows amongst the people, a power will be unleashed— the Holy Spirit—and the lands will radically change. People, ordinary people, will begin to command power that even exceeds yours. This power will only increase as the number of believers in Christ increase across the realm; as their numbers increase exponentially so will the Holy Spirit's presence. Muted for all of these years, it will grow and enable them to perform increasingly greater miracles. It is like a plague to us, a disease that will weaken and eventually destroy us if we do not rise up and kill it in its infancy...

You must act quickly, but be careful not to jeopardize our current initiative. We walk a fine line at this point. We need to take care to further our current plans, to solidify complete control in this realm, but we also need to put down this threat that has the potential to destroy us. Failure in one area means failure in the other either of which means death for us. This Holy Spirit can exempt a Christian from our powers; this makes them a formidable opponent indeed. However, do not let anyone know how strong they truly are; it would inspire our enemies and benefit their cause.

"My divinations have shown me that Rutheir and grr'SHaalg have already planned actions to eliminate this threat; it crosses paths with their parts in this great campaign," Absinthium said humbly, seeing the importance of this new task.

Good. You must return at once to Jand and take command of the situation. Advise them and pursue a solution in our best interests, ending with the destruction of the Christians. You may save some for sacrifice or as gifts to be eaten by the Gathering if you so choose, but make sure to bind and gag them; you cannot let them speak their words to any other humans. Their message can be contagious, and if the Logos has any truth in it then it has shown that His message can turn a human's heart to align with Him, and few of those can be won back to us...

Go quickly and begin this new mission. I have worked for a thousand years to crown myself Lucifer; do not let this rogue band upset a millennium of toil. Go and institute the reforms of the Luciferian order. Use the reforms to manipulate the people and the ekthro. Control them; play them like pieces on a game board. Use them to supplant these Christians at every turn and make *them* appear as evil ones. Inspire the ordinary devotee to hate them with such a passion that they need not be asked, but will gladly seek and kill any person that confesses Jesus Christ as Lord...

Leave now. You know what must be done.

Wordlessly, Absinthium turned and left the chambers of his dematerializing master. The rushing wind caused by the transfiguration extinguished the flickering candles and hardened the drippings into melted beads of tallow.

The arch-mage made for the exit. After the somber trek he descended the spire that connected the land below from the parched heavens where the demon overlords kept their estates. At the notion of meeting a Christian, thoughts of hatred filled his exceedingly black heart. He hoped to soon encounter one so that he could invent new torments to exercise upon him or her.

He grabbed a fistful of hide and pulled his way up the flank of his gryphon and combed through swaths of fur until he located the seat on its back. Hate consumed his mind and he thought about how he would kill every enemy he could locate. The gryphon beat its massive wings against the air currents and rose into the sky, soaring man and beast skyward and onwards to the kingdom of Jand.

CHAPTER TEN

Kelsa sat on a tree stump. The old, weather-beaten stump barely rose above grasses and creeping flora in the middle glade bursting with colorful wildflowers. An otherworldly light painted the entire scene and willows framed the meadow and dusted it with a dusting of gossamer tendrils.

The young woman sat and sighed. Melancholy, she sadly watched the flowers sway in the breeze; she appeared to be waiting for something or someone. Then, her eyes met his and he instantly knew that she had been waiting for him. Her eyes sparkled like gems and she leapt to the ground and ran to him. He sprinted towards her and they tearfully embraced after such a long absence.

"I've been waiting so long for you to come, Rashnir!"

"I've missed you so much, my love... my Kelsa." Rashnir squeezed tighter and whispered, "I'm so sorry. I'm so sorry I wasn't fast enough!"

"Quickly then, before they come!" Her voice was urgent. "Take me away from here."

"Before who comes?"

"The dark ones. Those who come and bring the night; oh, Rashnir—I can't stand the darkness—it's been so dark for so long."

"Let us go then."

She pulled back against his grip as he tried to flee the glade. "But I cannot leave from here. This is my place now. I can only go if you free me."

"But how can I free you?"

"Only one man has that power." She twitched slightly, like a clumsy marionette.

Rashnir peered beyond his beloved; at the far edge of the clearing stood the cloaked man. He leaned heavily on a staff; a crimson cape shrouded his body. With the hood laid back, Rashnir recognized him.

"Absinthium." Kelsa intoned.

Rashnir pulled away, backpedaling towards the darkness beyond the willows, beyond the ghostly light of the glade. "No!" he accused Kelsa, "You're dead! This is not real; once you're dead you are gone for eternity. We are forever separated; I am sorry."

Absinthium spoke, "I can give her back to you… make this a reality… for a small price."

Rashnir remained silent, but didn't continue his retreat.

"If you will follow me and forget your new comrades, then all will be restored—position, power, everything… and your Kelsa can be reanimated."

"No! You are a liar and a devourer of souls. I will never pledge loyalty to you!"

The shimmering image of his beloved stared mournfully at him. A brilliant silver sigil glowed on her forehead and her eyes dilated to the full; her body shuddered, wracked by pain. She whispered one word— and Rashnir was not certain that even the Arch-Mage who controlled this dream heard her, as if Kelsa's *actual* soul pushed through for just a moment, overriding this mockery Absinthium had conjured.

"Tartarus." Her voice failed like an ebbing wind but the word and the sense of her presence pierced Rashnir's soul.

"So be it, krist-chin!" the mage's apparitional form spat. His words dripped with hatred. Kelsa's skin ignited and she screamed curses at him as she burst into flames. Rashnir shielded his eyes from the supernatural inferno and then he turned and ran. He couldn't outrun the odor of burning flesh, and then he suddenly awoke.

He'd soaked his blanket through with sweat, but he knew he had just resisted a powerful, supernatural temptation. Rashnir lay wakeful near the fire where he slept. The word "Tartarus" looped around in his mind.

Through the flames he could see Kevin approach. Beyond his silhouette, the full moon lit the camp. He'd most likely returned from prayer for Zeh-Ahbe' and his tribe-mates who had departed for such an uncertain situation. The preacher wordlessly, and promptly, settled into sleep. The night had drawn on long and he looked in dire need of rest.

Rashnir said nothing and tried to return to sleep, purposefully guarding his heart against another intrusion like the one he'd just had. His mind shifted into such high alert, that the whispered word Kelsa's spirit had spoken was forgotten by morning.

***

"Wake up, you fool!"

The words yanked the king from his sleep—from his dreams of conquest. Rutheir flew into an outrage; no one should dare to speak to him in this manner. After all, he was the king of Jand! His anger immediately melted into submission and fear when he saw who spoke to him.

He rubbed the crust from his eyes and spotted a nightmarish specter radiating foul light at the foot of his bed. It glowed like a bad moon in a misty night. The king recognized it as his Luciferian ally, Absinthium. Rutheir fully awoke at his lord's command.

"I will be back within two days," he said with supernatural voice like a stony landslide, "I want preparations made to deal with this krist-chin threat. I know of the plans that you and the goblin made to deal with this uprising. Put these plans into motion.

"Go in the morning and speak with Pinchôt at the mercenary's guild. You must make him feel like you have watched his career closely, as a mentor would for a prized pupil. Incite an even deeper hatred in him for his fallen hero, Rashnir. Make him believe that you fear for your life: that you think Rashnir will come for *your* crown next.

"Also, be very careful to guard your secrecy when dealing with assassins, but hire some and do it soon. Just do not use your normal channels and let there be no connection to you. Do not hire Shimza; there is too much history there and we cannot afford to botch this. We must not look like the villains and instead draw the sympathy of the people.

"Contact the local temple tomorrow, after you meet with Pinchôt. Lead any loyal villagers in a memorial service for the deceased King Harmarty on the following day. We want the people remembering him fondly and with reverence—we are building a new narrative to override what the people think they knew. Let us recast him as a martyr in the publics' eyes—a servant of the people who was destroyed by these cultists that grope for the throne. This should demoralize any who might harbor sympathies for the heretics.

"In your remarks to the people, hint how you strongly believe that Rashnir was the one to kill your beloved Harmarty. Do try to work up some tears—can you manage that?"

Rutheir nodded solemnly.

"Erasing this threat from our memory is my new priority. By lulling the people back into the religious control we should be capable of stopping any advances they've had; we will contain them and then crush them. Only when every professing krist-chin is destroyed can I relent in my quest; this is a prime directive of beh'-tsah himself.

"Make what arrangements you must to fulfill my command. Soon, you must reorganize the country's army. While the western front relies heavily upon the military to protect them against Ziphan threats, the eastern contingent is a joke. There is barely any military might in this half of your kingdom; the crown is poorly protected. Do not place too much faith in the care of mercenaries. But, you must not destabilize support in the west by tapping them for forces."

The arch-mage could see the machinations of Rutheir's mind.

"You fear discord on the borders if you lighten their provisions?"

"Yes, if you remove any of the military protecting the western people, we will lose countless others to the orcish slaver bands roving Zipha, and the people will resent you for it."

The mage took his comments in stride. "You must find a creative solution. We can deal with Zipha in the near future as plans expand. We are training Luciferian missionaries even now to proselytize that country's ekthro. It will not stop the fact of the slave trade, but it may open new doors for political dealings through which we can eventually either crush that threat or stabilize the region."

Rutheir nodded and mentally logged his future plans for that front.

"Mention the need for more soldiers in your memorial. Have the service transcribed and sent out as an edict; make it seem an honorable thing to become a soldier in service of the king. Form soldiering university to train new initiates; this might swell your ranks and protect your people.

"We will need this military support in the future; mercenaries will be in too short of supply as we deal with this krist-chin movement. I foresee it may come to a military stand-off if they continue such a rapid rate of growth."

"These things will be done," Rutheir vowed.

"See that they are," the apparition threatened and then it faded from existence.

***

In the heart of Grinden, the apparitional form of Absinthium reappeared in the chambers of another man.

Frinnig looked up from his late-night studies and noticed the shimmering, ethereal form waiting patiently for his attention. The monk fell silent when he realized the identity of this spectral form.

"My Lord, Absinthium!" he exclaimed and bowed. "What is it that causes you to appear to me in this manner?"

"Rise, my loyal brother. I come with a request for your help aiding me and the Order's goals for advancement throughout your realm. You are placed in a strategic position, bridging the boundary between Jand and Ninda. For the time being, we are concentrating a great deal of effort in the kingdom of Jand, of which you are now a part.

"It would benefit our cause to hold a memorial service for the departed monarch, Harmarty. Hold it in the exact same location as the heretical meetings that the krist-chins recently held... that should send a message."

Frinnig bristled at the mention of Kevin's recent evangelistic service.

Absinthium continued. "Let us regrow a fondness and rejuvenation for our faith. We must shape the minds of the people in the Grinden area; it really is the hub that connects the people of Ninda, Jand, and even the goblins to the immediate north, whom we now welcome as brothers.

"We must reach out and rekindle relationships with all those who have any kind of connection to our religion; many have not participated in ritual for so great a time that we have forgotten them, and them us. We should incite a frenzy of religion. If we fail to revitalize our church, then this krist-chin cult will overtake us and destroy the truth of Luciferianism forever; the Gathering has foreseen this and the cause of my visit is that grave."

"I understand," Frinnig said. "With a threat of this magnitude we must inspire the masses. We must make them understand the threat posed by the very existence of these anathema heretics. We will make them see themselves as warriors in Lucifer's grand army."

"Yes!" Absinthium smiled warmly. "That is exactly what we need. You are a true leader and visionary, Frinnig. I will keep my eyes on you and your ministry.

"Tomorrow, King Rutheir will arrive and you two can plan the details of the memorial service in the evening which follows. Inspire the people above all else; what we need now is loyalty—renewed commitment. Send out criers to encourage people to attend this memorial.

"You speak skillfully and with conviction, just what we need and we need so much. Those loyal to the church should be remembered and feel empowered— needed. The forces of this realm are a delicate balance, a balance disrupted by this new heresy; it may come down to a fight for our very existence.

"Make sure that you have monkish support as a show of power from your local monastery. You never know when the krist-chins might attack or threaten local Luciferians with violence. You would be wise to keep a visible deterrent, my friend."

"Agreed. I will have my aide, Jandul, call on more support from the monastery. Though, we would almost welcome an attack. It would give us a great reason to wage open war upon them and extract vengeance for sullying our flock of souls."

"That time is coming very soon. The krist-chins are even more dangerous than you realize and the Gathering is taking the necessary steps to destroy this threat for all time."

"You have the full cooperation and support of us in Grinden," Frinnig pledged as the ghostly form of his hero vanished.

***

Zeh-Ahbe' and his two kinsmen, Rah'-be and Sil-tarn, flitted through the woods under the full moon. They ran like the wild, bathed in the astral light which bled through the trees. The Say-awr' knew the way to the meeting place of the kil-yaw'. They retained a sense of direction instilled in them and honed through a lifetime of nomadic travel. The trio knew when they headed in the proper direction.

Despite that, their senses felt muted to a great degree; the smell of the undergrowth and the shifting of the vibrations in the air no longer provided them the information they could have gained through access to their lupine form, but they found their way, regardless. Despite their reduced capacity, their hearts burst with joy and the knowledge and assurance of a secured eternity through the benevolent God of wonders.

The threesome had traveled on foot since that evening, heading due west of Grinden, into the Quey forests, which seldom saw sentient travel. Neither human nor ekthro had much reason for going through when the trade routes of Grinden passed conveniently around it.

In the deep of night, they burst into a clearing lit by an enormous fire. At the far end of the clearing, a weathered wagon parked next to an old animal skin tent: the tent of records. The Ahee-sthay-tay'-ree-on had, since the dawn of the kil-yaw', been the tent's keepers. They recorded the events of the kil-yaw' and the deeds of the individual tribes, maintaining the history of the werewolves.

Assembled in a circle around the central fire the gathered heads of the nine other tribes of the kil-yaw' waited in their seats. Behind each tribal leader sat their two aides. Many of the gathered werewolves bristled at the show of disrespect when the non-wolf forms stepped into the kil-yaw'.

Zeh-Ahbe' knew that things would only get more difficult. They'd already arrived late, not making nearly the kind of speed that they would have in lupine forms. The kil-yaw' would certainly be upset by his tardiness, but even more irritated at such a breach of protocol as appearing in human form.

The bellicose head of tribe Kaw-bade' stood in outrage and pointed an accusatory talon at Zeh-Ahbe'. "What is this insult by the Say-awr'? How dare you mock our sacred gathering! For that you must die!"

"Sit down, Mil-khaw-mah'!" demanded Sehkel-saykel, the head of tribe Ahee-sthay-tay'-ree-on and current leader of the kil-yaw'. With mere words, the elderly werewolf forced Mil-khaw-mah', the largest and most vicious werewolf alive, back into his seat. The leader of Kaw-bade' turned his ten foot frame of rippling muscle, hide, and sable fur back to his seat and resumed a cross-legged posture.

Mil-khaw-mah' was not happy at all, though he only acted on the same impulses fueling many of the other tribal leaders. The others retained enough control to restrain themselves.

Zeh-Ahbe' humbly took his seat, positioning his human body in his rightful place in the kil-yaw. Rah'-be and Sil-tarn dutifully and silently took their places behind him.

"Now then," said Sehkel-saykel in his dominant, even voice that always masked his emotions from the remainder of the kil-yaw', "Zeh-Ahbe', tribal leader of clan Say-awr', the kil-yaw' demands to know the reason behind your... condition. Protocol demands you alter form; we cannot begin our council until you properly present yourself."

"I cannot do so," Zeh-Ahbe' stated meekly.

"You refuse the kil-yaw'?" Mil-khaw-mah' shouted, forgetting his place again.

Sehkel-saykel gave Mil-khaw-mah' a fierce look to silence him. Mil-khaw-mah' quieted, but his rage only further stoked when pent up; agitated muscles rippled under his skin. With fur bristled in anger, his eyes smoldered with an intensity that only augured ill for any member of the Say-awr' he might later find."

"No," Zeh-Ahbe' stated, "I do not refuse the kil-yaw'. I said that I *can* not do as requested; it has become impossible for any of my clan. We have lost our ability to transform, and thus it is impossible for me to meet the requirement."

Silence reigned for a brief second and then Sim-khaw', leader of Zaw-nawb' erupted in laughter. The rest of the council followed suit except for the members of the always-guarded Ahee-sthay-tay'-ree-on and except for Mil-khaw-mah'. The leader of Kaw-bade' remained too focused on his disgust for the lowest of the tribes to find the situation humorous.

As the laughter died away, Sehkel-saykel asked, "How exactly did this happen? Is the entire tribe truly stripped of its ability? Does your scald still have its power?"

Zeh-Ahbe' stood, so that all would see and hear him properly. "May I address the kil-yaw'?" he asked.

Sehkel-saykel, always cautious for protocol, shook his head negatively. "The kil-yaw' is not meeting at this moment. We cannot properly come to order until you have altered your form; you may, however, address us all as the heads of our individual tribes. You may speak."

"Thank you, wise one," Zeh-Ahbe' said. Before he spoke, the former werewolf paused for a brief moment of silent prayer. *God, give me the words to say to these men whom I have known for so long. Help me to say the right things.*

Zeh-Ahbe' sighed and tried to clear his mind of the fear wreathing through it. "We have, every one of us, traded our power for one that is even greater, receiving eternal life and glory."

He paused again, feeling sure of himself now. The words he spoke were sure to appeal to the werewolves' lust for power and quests for glory. Breathy chuckles from the nearby leaders shattered his self-confidence.

The ever-spiteful Mil-khaw-mah' taunted him, "You do not look so powerful now, pinkling. Even if you could live in that form forever, what good is that?"

Zeh-Ahbe' worked his mouth as if to say something, but nothing came out. He tried again. "Let me tell you what happened a couple of days ago. Maybe then you will understand."

The flustered former werewolf relayed the events of the last couple of days. He told them how he was invited at random by a coffee bean vendor who claimed he'd heard a great story in the Grinden Park. Zeh-Ahbe' related his feeling of overwhelming conviction about the story's claims to absolute right and absolute wrong. He gave a synopsis of Kevin's message, about the Messiah, the lies of Luciferianism, and the impact of Heaven and Hell.

"The things that this man, Kevin, said have answered every question that I ever had about the nature of morality and of good and evil. The funny thing is that I did not even know that I searched for answers until I heard him speak and ask the questions."

In the pause that followed, Zeh-Ahbe' felt the sting of regret over every unclear phrase in his words, for every stutter and fumbled word, and there were many of them. Despite being a tribe leader, the Say-awr' were the lowest and he'd rarely needed to speak about matters of any importance. "I wish that you could all hear Kevin speak; he is much more eloquent than I am. I barely know anything about this faith, except for how it has impacted me so completely and personally."

The tribal leaders eyed Zeh-Ahbe' suspiciously. None seemed moved in the least by his words; Sehkel-saykel sat in his place, stoic as ever.

A few of the other leaders began looking to Sehkel-saykel as their collective mouthpiece, wondering what course of action and questions he would have.

Finally, Sehkel-saykel spoke, his voice devoid of any emotion. "Because you believe in what this man has said and accepted it as the truth, you can no longer shapeshift?"

"Yes, and no," Zeh-Ahbe' said. "When I made my choice to accept Jesus' payment for my sins, I made the choice to only follow Jesus and only rely on *His* power beyond my own—beyond that granted by the scald of the Say-awr'. I had to choose: serve this one God or not serve this one God. To truly serve Him meant to stop serving all other gods, including myself and my own desire for power."

Sim-khaw', the leader of Zaw-nawb', shook his mangy head. "This sounds like a conspiracy to me," he claimed, "like a way for the Say-awr' to elevate itself above the Zaw-nawb' and make *us* the lowest tribe!"

Several of the other tribal heads began talking amongst themselves. Sehkel-saykel let them argue for several minutes; the kil-yaw' had not officially met yet so there was no real authority that he could use to quell the random outbursts, none except for personal influence. He remained silent and listened to the conversations and debates between the tribal leaders and their aides. One term kept repeating, seeming to grow in volume with each time it leapt from one set of lips to the next: to-ay-baw'. Zeh-Ahbe' cringed at the sound of it.

The conversations rose in volume until they verged on frenzy when Sehkel-saykel stood. All of the dialogues ceased as attention firmly fixed upon the elderly leader. Once he had their attention, he sat back down and spoke, telling an old tale: the history of the werewolves.

"There were not always only ten tribes of our kin on the eastern continent. I hear so many of you referencing the forgotten eleventh tribe in your conversations, just now. You are thinking to convict the Say-awr' as to-ay-baw'. This is a grave thing which can never be undone. To become to-ay-baw' is to become an eternal abomination. It makes desolate a place in the kil-yaw'. To-ay-baw' is final and complete."

"Is this not the type of thing required of us, to render the Say-awr' as to-ay-baw'?" Mil-khaw-mah' asked accusingly. "Zeh-Ahbe' has claimed that they will live eternally as pinklings through their spiritual powers.

How is this different than the decisions of the Shaw-than'?"

"It may not be that different at all," Sehkel-saykel sighed, "and that is the thing that I find the most disturbing. I will now tell you the history of the lost eleventh tribe, when the kil-yaw' lost its Shaw-than'." The play on words went unnoticed.

"Many generations ago, so long that we have forgotten them almost fully, the Shaw-than' tribe fell to their own selfishness and corruption. Then, the Shaw-than' were the lowest of the kil-yaw', ironically, the position now held by the Say-awr'. The Shaw-than' were despised and often taunted by all tribes. The Kaw-bade', then the ruling tribe in the kil-yaw', thought it nothing to send its young warriors against their Shaw-than' brethren as a rite of passage. The Shaw-than' were abused and belittled, probably wrongly, and they eventually had their fill of ill treatment.

"At one point, Ad, the tribal head of Shaw-than' made a pact with Lilth, the devious clan matron of the vampire conclave. The mother of all vampires, our eternal enemies, seduced one of our own. Ad became an abomination, what we call to-ay-baw', the eternally damned and unaccepted.

"The Shaw-than' have been endowed with many great powers, but are no longer a part of our body. We have rid ourselves of them in every way. Most of our kind does not even know the Shaw-than' ever existed; they only know that there are such abominations in existence: creatures of both vampiric *and* lupine origins.

"The Shaw-than' became the slaves to their new masters, rendering them powerful and yet powerless in the same way. Their strengths were multiplied and their abilities enhanced, but they can no longer breed, they traded away their very mortality and life to fulfill their lust for power and vengeance." Sehkel-saykel turned and rapped Mil-khaw-mah' on the thigh to get his attention. "That is the same reason I try and keep you in line, young one. You cannot let your passions consume you, lest you also court to-ay-baw', a fate that none of us deserve.

"Now enslaved, there is no longer life within the Shaw-than'—they partake in the same unlife of their undead masters. They have power to destroy and wage war at their masters' whims; they are immortal, except for those same methods used to kill a vampire. They've become unnatural in every sense, a collection of all that we are and all that we hate.

"Once Ad came into his power and passed it to his tribemates, they hatched their plan and fell upon all those who had previously wronged them. The dens of our ancestors ran red with blood as the proud and haughty fell before the unexpected attacks of the once weak and lowly.

"By the time the kil-yaw' recognized that the systematic destruction came from within, many tribal leaders had been killed. The Kaw-bade' had been almost completely destroyed, except for a few warriors and their tribal leader, Ar-yay'. The kil-yaw' met to ascertain what they should do when the Shaw-than' surrounded the gathering, completely disregarding the protocol of the kil-yaw'.

"Ar-yay', who had overseen harsh persecution of Ad's family, struck a deal with the Shaw-than'. He challenged Ad in ritual combat. Ar-yay' had earlier discovered that Ad had a mistress amongst the Tsip-po'-

THE KAKOS REALM: GRINDEN PROSELYTE

ren clan. He had a whole separate family in an upper caste, despite the specific rules against such a thing.

"The ritual combat was standard, if Ar-yay' defeated Ad, then the Shaw-than' must agree to depart and forgo the kil-yaw' forever. If they refused to depart, then Ad's entire spurious line of offspring within the Tsip-po'-ren would be tortured and destroyed.

"It was a desperate act; Ar-yay' had a chance through one on one combat, but the kil-yaw' would not have survived the onslaught if the entire Shaw-than' chosen to fall upon them and slaughter those who had opposed them. Ad accepted the challenge in order to preserve his illegitimate, innocent, litter.

"The clash that followed was epic. The fight went on well into the night until a nearly defeated Ar-yay' grappled his opponent and threw himself upon the pyre that lit the kil-yaw'. Ar-yay' held on until both warriors were consumed in the flames. Ad had been defeated and so the Shaw-than' departed and went west. It was reported that they left this continent entirely, despite the occasional sightings. As far as we know, all of the remaining Shaw-than' survive to this day, if you can call it that... all except for Ad. They are to-ay-baw': those forever forsaken by the kil-yaw' which spawned them."

Khad-dood', leader of the Tsip-po'-ren inquired, "What of the bastard children of that foul lineage?" Most tribal leaders descended from the strongest genetic lines; the question was obviously borne out of personal interest.

"They have long since perished," Sehkel-saykel assured him. "As soon as the son of Ad came of age, he inquired of his parentage and, upon discovering his sire, took a longsword and slew his entire family before presenting himself before his tribal leader and falling

251

upon his sword to satisfy the honor of the kil-yaw'. His death is recorded in the Books of Honor."

Sehkel-saykel addressed the group formally. "What we have before us now is a yes or no question. Do you believe that the Say-awr' should be judged to-ay-baw'? Stand now and vote."

Mil-khaw-mah' stood before his peers. "I know what I see. The Say-awr' have claimed to have found a better life, one with more power, but they seem like deluded fools who embrace weakness in the face of true power. Perhaps a conspiracy *is* brewing. They may be allying themselves with our enemies, perhaps even courting the powers of the children of Lilth."

Mil-khaw-mah's brash statement had been expected. Nonetheless, it influenced many of the other leaders.

Zeh-Ahbe' fell to his knees as the rest of those privileged to vote stood in unison. One by one the tribal leaders turned their backs on the crest-fallen Christian, a sign that each had voted against his clan.

Sim-khaw' hesitated, knowing that by turning his back he would willfully plunge his tribe down to the lowest rank of the kil-yaw'. He saw seven other turned backs and his hesitation hardened to resolve; he turned in accord with his fellows.

A look of sadness fell over Sehkel-saykel. Finally he said, "So be it," and he too turned his back on Zeh-Ahbe'. With his back still turned, he declared, "Tribe Say-awr' is hereby rendered to-ay-baw'. It is a decision that I fear has been made too lightly, yet it remains. Let the history books so record the end of tribe Say-awr'; they have left their devotion to the kil-yaw' with their devotion to this Christ superseding their first commitment. So let the records show."

Rah'-be bent forward to comfort his tearful friend. He pulled Zeh-Ahbe' close and said, "If that is what the history books reflect, then we shall be honored for it by our Lord." He pulled at Zeh-Ahbe'. "Come now, we must leave for our own safety."

"I failed. I failed them all, Rah'-be. All of our brethren are doomed in the coming fires."

"It is an ironic choice and one they freely make," comforted Sil-tarn. "They think that they are damning us, but in reality it is they who choose to ignore the only truth. In doing so they've chosen eternal hellfire of their own volition."

Zeh-Ahbe' nodded, knowing it was true. "I, too, feel that they have made this decision too lightly."

"Leave now, pinkling," threatened Mil-khaw-mah'. "The kil-yaw' is about to meet and if you are still here at that time, then you will be destroyed."

"You must depart," confirmed Sehkel-saykel. "Your place is no longer among us. Should you ever again come into the kil-yaw' you will be killed. Should any of the remaining tribes breed with those carrying the shameful scald marks of the Say-awr', then they will be killed and their family noted in the records of dishonor.

"Zeh-Ahbe', surrender your scald and leave, never to return."

The Say-awr' leader removed a large circular amulet from around his neck. It was intricately engraved with sigils and symbols. The scald, a type of magical branding iron used to bestow the shapeshifting powers upon a new tribal initiate, had been in his family for generations. Zeh-Ahbe' held it in his hands for one last moment; the scald's identical engravings mirrored the appearance of the burned imprint on the left palm in which he held it. So long ago it had branded the tribal insignia into his hand. Now, Zeh-Ahbe' had only disgust for the thing that had been a part of his life for so long. He cast it to the dirt next to the fire ring as he, Rah'-be, and Sil-tarn departed the assembly for their brighter destiny.

***

Kevin awoke to find the sun, fully risen and shining warmth upon the Christian encampment. He saw that many people were already busy. The message of hope and life—of Jesus Christ—was contagious. Since that evangelistic meeting in the town's center and the formation of this camp, their numbers had only swollen.

The encampment jutted out from the very southern edge of town. This location, formerly an uncultivated section of land, had been transformed into a haven where people flocked to hear more about the hope offered by this new message. Kevin warmed with inspiration; these people actively lived out the great commission. They had given up everything in order to learn, and in turn, lend their voices for the short remainder of existence promised to them.

Kevin stood to his feet and stretched—his vigor and heart renewed by the sight which greeted him. The sun rose and bathed the camp in rays of warmth; shadows fled as the light cast its hope of a bright future upon them. Kevin smiled; knowing that the Lord had heard his prayers comforted him. He hugged his arms to himself for warmth and toured the encampment, looking for his angelic supporters.

As Kevin walked through the campground, converts greeted him warmly and reverently. He knew that his path was right; he'd done exactly what God requested of him. With everyone whom he spoke, he heard reports of family members and friends who had either joined them or were open to hearing about the Messiah.

The river banks filled with hope and joy. A positive attitude permeated the atmosphere like sweet smelling incense.

Kevin eventually found Rashnir. Contrarily, he looked as if he had not slept well. Rashnir blamed his dishevelment on bad dreams

The day went as others previous. Assemblies gathered for teaching and fellowship at different parts of the day and smaller cells formed and met later in the afternoon. Some of the small groups would sequester Kevin and whisk him off to the homes of people who the group knew were receptive. Sometimes they went well, sometimes not.

Whenever a small group left with Kevin, an angel accompanied him, usually Jorge. Kyrius preferred to stay behind to teach in Kevin's absence. He had a kind and gentle way with answering questions and interjecting humor.

In mid-afternoon, Kevin left with a group of fifteen others to visit the home of a family member. Rashnir decided to tag along.

As they traveled through a city street they met both familiar stares and odd looks of the passersby. Something, however, tugged at Rashnir's ear and he left the group to walk alone. Rashnir found a town crier, an adolescent boy hired to broadcast news and announcements.

"What is the news you have?" Rashnir questioned.

"A memorial service, sir. Tomorrow night. All of the faithful are required to attend, at risk of angering the demon council."

"A memorial for whom?"

"For Harmarty, sir. It will be held in the Grinden central park." The boy pointed the way.

"Yes, yes. I know it."

"Even King Rutheir will come to show respect for the dead."

Rashnir might have questioned the lad further, but he noticed a familiar threesome wandering dejectedly though the streets. He left the herald and joined up with his fellow Christians, Zeh-Ahbe', Rah'-be, and Sil-tarn.

Tired, they willingly accepted his company and Rashnir walked back to the encampment with them. They bent his ear to their current woes and unburdened their hearts.

Later, Kevin returned and joined them as they shared a sober meal around the campfire.

"I sense that things did not go well with the kil-yaw'."

"Not well at all," Zeh-Ahbe' stated. He hid his face in his hands with frustration. "I did all that I could. I did. But despite all of my passion, despite my conviction to Truth, and despite my prayers, I failed. I stuttered; I fumbled when I spoke; I was not eloquent. I spoke poorly and unconvincingly. I failed, and none of the kil-yaw' looked favorably on the Truth. Kevin, I feel responsible for their choice."

"No. No, you are not responsible," Kevin comforted. "It is not up to you in the least, Zeh-Ahbe'. The only thing that you can do is remain faithful to the Holy Spirit's direction and preach His message. It is up to the Spirit to move in the hearts of people and convince them of the truth. It is already hard enough in this place, where the Holy Spirit is supernaturally oppressed, but it is not up to you. The choice still remains theirs alone. We cannot force the truth into anyone; we can only present them with an honest choice."

Kevin continued, "No matter how much you desire for someone to accept faith, it is still something that only an individual can choose for themselves. Sometimes we must let people make their own choice— even when that choice willfully condemns oneself. What you *can* do is pray for them; pray that the Spirit continues tugging at their hearts and working on their minds. It is only between them and God, now."

Zeh-Ahbe' nodded his head. He understood in his mind, even if not yet with his heart.

"They may have hardened their souls or seen your witness as a sign of weakness. You cannot be blamed for those who would sear their hearts against the Truth. I have personally found that the more power or wealth a person has accumulated, the easier it is for them to reject God. From what you have told me about the kil-yaw', it seems that they desire personal power and self-glory above all else. It will be hard for them to come to a place of true acceptance, but you can pray; through Christ, all things are possible."

Silence grew and Rashnir stood to leave.

"With all of this talk about people in our past, those who deserve to hear the truth, I suddenly feel like I need to go and speak with someone that *I* know."

"Do you need company?" Kevin asked.

"No," he replied. "I don't think that you could elude the security posts I'm sure to encounter."

Rashnir departed for Grinden, leaving his friends behind to wonder who he'd left to visit.

***

Rashnir crept through the familiar shadows in hallways that he'd once frequented; he knew them by memory. He picked a lock, entered, and found a spot to conceal himself, waiting for his mark to arrive.

After some time, the entrance to the room opened slowly. A familiar silhouette stepped into the light shed by the door ajar.

The man who entered hesitated for a fraction of a second and drew his sword.

"Come out of there!" demanded Jaker.

"You come in *here*," retorted Rashnir.

"You. Have you come to try and kill me?" Jaker's voice hinted at no fear.

"No. I came here to tell you the truth about who killed Harmarty."

Jaker stepped into his own personal quarters and closed the door behind him. He lit a lantern and laid down his sword. "Put down your weapon, Rashnir. I heard about how you obtained it, but it still does not make it legal—your scars may have disappeared, but that doesn't overturn the law.

"I do believe that I already know the answer to this mystery, or at least I am pretty sure of it. Between the two suspects, I have my favorite. But, do tell me: who killed Harmarty?"

"*Two* suspects?"

"Well, there is you, of course."

Rashnir bowed as if his reputation had preceded him.

Jaker continued, "There are those who believe that our new king had too much to gain by his predecessor's death to be entirely blameless."

"And which do you believe, detective?"

"I think that all evidence indicates it was your doing, but I still have suspicions about Rutheir. Those suspicions were very strong, up until I saw that you had broken away so cleanly from the gutters."

"I came to share with you the truth. I come as a friend, not to confess. This is strictly off of the record, agreed?"

"Yeah, whatever," Jaker said. "I am not in charge of the investigation anymore, anyway; those reins have been turned over to Pinchôt. You might know him: weasely little guy, but he's got ambition and some modicum of skill. He loves and hates your legacy all at the same time. He took over, per King Rutheir's request; the big shot came to see me today. He's in town for some big to-do tomorrow."

"A memorial service, I know. I want you to understand the truth of the entire situation because you are my last remaining friend from a previous life."

"Oh, please, Rashnir. We were merely acquaintances. I was *Kelsa's* friend; we were men with one love in common. Kelsa was like a sister to me and you took her away."

"Actually, Jaker, you knew her so well because your surrogate family was close to hers. Your family spent that much time with Rogis's family on purpose. It was not common knowledge, but Rogis was quite the lover; there is a strong chance that you actually *were* Kelsa's brother—she was Rogis's daughter, not Mind's. We will never know, now."

A spark of anger ignited deep in Jaker's pupils; his eyes darted to his sword.

"You misunderstand, Jaker. I do not intend to slight her memory, nor Rogis's. I tell you the truth," Rashnir said, looking him eye to eye and soul to soul, "I did not kill Rogis. He was the closest thing to a father that I ever had. Harmarty killed Rogis."

Something broke inside of Jaker. The Ranger finally recognized that Rashnir spoke the truth. "Tell me what happened."

Rashnir explained to Jaker how the evidence all fit. He spoke of the conversations that he'd had with Kelsa and that many others knew how Harmarty desired Kelsa even though he could not have her. He told Jaker about the repeated confrontations that he and his mentor, Rogis, had with Harmarty.

He explained his final refusal, the assassination attempt, and how Rogis approved of his marriage to Kelsa. They thought they could reason with the corrupt Harmarty. Rashnir explained how the king blindsided Rogis, how even though Rashnir had defeated Shimza the Greater in combat, he was still captured. He related how the delusional monarch rode off to claim a bride who refused him at the cost of her own life and of the accident as explained to him by his servant, Dane.

"Kelsa was everything to me," Rashnir stated flatly. "She was my reason for living. I ended up in the gutter because I had lost my taste for life once Kelsa left it. I had no reason to exist any longer. The desire for vengeance consumed my life—it was all I lived for, until now."

He told him about his encounter with the Christians and how he had made a choice that changed his life. Rashnir gave his best evangelistic message, using his life as the subject matter.

"I admit, when I first encountered Kevin, I saw him only as a means to satisfy my dark urge for revenge and bloodshed, to satisfy my selfish desires. I did it. I killed Harmarty; and I do not believe that it was right of me, but I do not know that it wasn't an act of justice, either. Knowing what I know now, though, I would not commit to the same course again.

"When I returned to fulfill my part of the obligation to Kevin, I recognized that taking revenge did not satisfy me—it did not quench my longing for something more. I felt hollow inside; I needed something bigger than myself in my life, something I missed all along. I tried to fill it with other things before, like the glory of battle and the love of Kelsa, but even those things could not fully satisfy this longing for God, the yearning for hope and the security of my soul. Kevin showed me this."

"Prove this to me," Jaker said, "I do believe that you have spoken the truth to me, but if you truly rely on this Jesus Christ for your strength, then give me your sword as a testimony of your faith that your God provides." Jaker extended his hand.

Rashnir handed him the weapon, hilt first.

"I do believe you," Jaker admitted; tears nearly welled up at the memories of the woman they mutually loved. "I believe you, but I cannot join your faith. It is just too much... too much to accept right now."

"I understand."

"I can also do nothing to help you openly. But you should know that Rutheir came here today to convince me to pledge the Rangers' assistance in eradicating your religious group. He is bent on physically destroying you as soon as solid evidence indicates criminal activity. He believes that you are *all* dangerous, Rashnir."

"Of course we are. Light is dangerous to the darkness."

"Yeah, well, be careful because he's trying to snuff your torch, and now that he has annexed Grinden as a part of Jand, he holds even greater sway."

"*What did you say?*"

"He thinks that I have been too lax in my investigation of you. I knew deep down that you killed Harmarty, but I guess that I always knew he deserved it, too. I figured that if *you* hadn't done it, it would have only been a matter of time before Rutheir did the deed himself.

"I told him that I would not mobilize the Rangers against you. You are not a military threat nor a danger to the community and the Rangers always had standards for the type of jobs that they accepted.

"He put a lot of pressure on me; we have new laws to obey now that Grinden lost its neutrality. But I told him my answer was adamant. He fumed and said that he would find the proof that he knew existed. That's when he assigned Pinchôt to take over the investigation;

he inflated that guy's head so much that I thought it was gonna burst.

"You do not need to fear the Rogis' Rangers, but Pinchôt, at the encouragement of the king, has been reassigned. He accepted a position as the head of the Narsh Barbarians. You know as well as I do that they have no scruples about the jobs they take; they love violence and intrigue for the sheer thrill of it all. They see as much honor in stabbing a peaceful old man as they do in defeating opponents on the battlefield."

"Thank you for standing for us."

"As long as I control the Rangers, we will not take arms against your group, but you're still in for a lot of trouble in the days to come. Watch your back, old friend."

***

Rashnir moved through shadowy alleys and side streets. Cloaked by darkness and well hidden, he wanted to do the best he could to protect his friend's reputation. It was important that he leave no verifiable connection between the Rangers and the Christian cause. He might need to rely on that contact later.

Once safely away and roving the streets, Rashnir concentrated on the sound of his own boots striking the packed earth. He picked up another sound on the edge of his senses: the sound of distress, the sound of weapon against flesh; the hum of conflict grew louder with every step. Rashnir quickened his gait.

He rushed past local stores that had long since closed; most sensible people retired for the evening hours ago. He ran past a textile shop he recognized; the store belonged to a family that had recently joined the believers. They made them his brothers. Rashnir saw

263

light in the alleyway beside the shop—where the noises came from.

Running headlong around the corner, he found seven beings, both man and ekthro, as they assaulted the family of five trapped in the alley. Four of them held torches while the other three vandals beat the bodies of the fallen family members. Rashnir assessed the situation as he charged headlong into the conflict. He assumed that the fallen were already dead or dying.

He howled angrily as he dashed into the torch lit alley. Sizing up his opponents as he flew into the fray, he knew that he could beat them easily. Two of the torchbearers in the back were goblins; the other two were men. Two other men abused and kicked the fallen father and mother and a devious kobold poked at their flesh with a broken arrow shaft.

Rashnir reached for his short sword as he screamed his battle cry. He only grasped air instead. He skidded to a halt as his enemies howled in response and charged to meet him with weapons ready. Rashnir skidded to a stop and mentally berated himself for forgetting that he had just given his sword to Jaker half an hour ago.

He did the only prudent thing possible. Rashnir turned and ran back around the corner of the alleyway. He fled down the street, ducking down any route that could conceal him from the arrows whizzing past his ears. He ran, and as he ran prayed.

Lord, I surrendered my weapon as a sign that I placed my faith in only You for my protection. Lord, I need Your help now. You are my strength and my shield; You are my weapon now. Be my sword.

He dodged around a corner into another alley just as an arrow drove itself into the storefront where Rashnir sprinted moments before. *Strengthen me my God.* Rashnir vaulted onto a balcony that rose above the alley.

A righteous anger overtook him as a goblin, scimitar drawn, and a human with a bow burst into the alley in hot pursuit. Rashnir heard them speaking as they over pursued him into the passage. They ran right below his position on the balcony. They laughed and jested about killing Christians for sport.

"That one was Rashnir, the fallen one. We have him on the run, girk-RahL. Imagine it! We will be the ones to have assassinated the great warrior and traitor, Rashnir the Ranger!"

Rashnir launched himself from his position above and targeted the goblin with a flying axe-handle smash; he howled as he dropped, "I am the sword of the Lord!"

In that moment, the Holy Spirit manifested with power. A sword suddenly burst into being in the grip of the godly warrior as he brought his blow down on the unsuspecting villain. The force of the slash sundered the goblin from crown to crotch and he fell in two lifeless halves. The holy blade drove deeply into the ground, splintering even the foul creature's scimitar.

The force of his landing made Rashnir roll upon impact. He tumbled into the legs of the human archer and knocked him off balance. Rashnir spun to his feet as the archer tried to right himself and dropped his bow to pull his sword. He only had time to loosen hilt from sheath before Rashnir fell upon him and separated body from soul. The holy weapon gleamed in his hands.

Rashnir stood over the corpse of the murderer who spoke so fondly of killing the innocent children of

God. Amazed that the most perfect sword he'd ever wielded had materialized within his hands, Rashnir glanced at it and read the deeply engraved word that had been etched across the quillion. "Logos," Rashnir read aloud. Brilliant blue flames burst into being, sheathing the blade in a holy, azure fire.

Rashnir heard the footsteps of others in pursuit. They would likely be drawn to the light shed by the blue flames of his sword. *Let them come, let me be the Lord's sword arm tonight!*

Seconds later, four more pursuers rounded the corner into the alleyway where Rashnir waited for them. Moments later, the torturers lay dying.

Rashnir sprinted back to the alley where he'd initially found the wounded family. He boldly stepped into the torchlight of the one remaining oppressor who taunted the broken family for their faith, chiding them for departing the Luciferian Church.

"You murdered them for that?" Rashnir demanded, startling the single human from his revelry. "You cannot quench truth!"

"Truth!" he replied, "You know nothing of the truth, heretic. Your only use is for the table of the Gathering, fodder in the mouths of carnivorous demons! Only Lucifer has power here!"

"No. You are wrong. Jesus Christ has crushed his power, and I come to crush yours."

The man threw his torch through a broken window, into the Christian family's store. He pulled a dagger from each of his hips, holding them as if he were a seasoned bladesman. The fiend charged towards Rashnir, a blade in each hand.

Rashnir nearly pitied the fool who'd been so blinded by his hatred that he futilely attempted to destroy the message of hope. The Luciferian rogue risked his life in a battle that he could not win for a cause that was already lost.

The Christian warrior feinted and then thrust his sword into the attacker's midsection, striking vitals and ending the confrontation. The sword seemed to dissipate the moment Rashnir thought to sheath it; he ran to the fallen family.

Among the fallen were a woman and her husband; she was dead and he barely breathed. Two teens, a boy and girl, also lay dead. A little boy, perhaps four years old bore bruises and shook with fear, but was otherwise alive.

Rashnir hovered over the father and bent over him, praying. The father coughed and spluttered in such a way that Rashnir cringed; it was a sound he had heard before, the death rattle of someone with internal injuries.

The man's eyes opened and caught his rescuer in the growing flamelight from the burning textile shop; he spoke as soon as his eyes recognized Rashnir. "Thank Jesus." He looked intently at Rashnir and squeezed his hand more tightly than a man in his condition should have strength to. "Promise me," he coughed, "Promise me that you will take care of my son. Teach him about Christ and protect him."

Rashnir started to cry over his dying, anonymous Christian brother. "Yes, I will guard your son."

The man smiled as bright blood soaked through his shirt. His face glowed and he spluttered, "Lord, go with my little Jibbin and with Rashnir," he prayed aloud.

The light faded from his eyes when he smiled again and said, "Thank you." The man relaxed in reassurance. The light of life faded completely from his eyes and the inner glow turned to a peaceful, ashen pall.

Rashnir scooped up the crying child. He held the boy to himself and turned to take one final look at the man who requested this thing of him.

The alley grew light as yellow and orange flames burned through the fuel of the family's building; it had already consumed a large section of the store's interior. Flames poured out from the windows and doors, slowly eating their way through the building's exterior.

Rashnir did the only thing that he could think to do under the circumstances. He hugged the small, frightened child and returned to the Christian encampment.

Chapter Eleven

Pinchôt paced in the midst of his new appointment. The members who ranked as leadership in the Narsh Barbarian Sect surrounded him. While he stood in stark contrast by physical appearance, they were akin in many other ways. Whereas Pinchôt stood smaller in stature than most of the bulky and heavy handed barbarians, they had the same heart: a desire for personal glory and triumph by overcoming and spilling the blood of their foes. Pinchôt greatly desired blood.

"What we have here," Pinchôt said, "Is an odd situation. One of the reasons that I have been brought over to lead the Narsh Barbarian Sect is because of the problems in the Rangers—they lack the gall to do certain jobs: ones that the King has an utmost need to be performed at this present time. In years past, the previous two kings each preferred Rogis' Rangers, which I came out of, to aid in keeping the peace on the eastern front."

Many groans came when he mentioned the Rangers. A rivalry had endured between them for decades. Grirrg, Pinchôt's second in command from the Barbarians, summed up the group's feelings; Grirrg squeezed a porcelain stein filled with mead until the cup broke, splashing the brew all over.

"Let me say this, before I go on. I feel that I have made a good switch. King Rutheir needs us; he knows that the Rangers have waxed impotent for his purposes. He can foresee how the Rangers 'ethics' will impede progress. So, now we are the favored mercenary group under the crown.

"Rutheir has long been a lover of combat. He has been a powerful warlord since he was young. For too long he watched the Rangers' courage dwindle as they feared to meet battle head on. With the way things are set to heat up in the city, King Rutheir will rely on our skills."

"What's in it for us?" one barbarian piped up.

"Glory, battle, the opportunity to wield your weapon under a banner of the most powerful warlord of this lifetime—he will undoubtedly look towards expansion, and soon. Ultimately, you get your normal pay and plunder along with the ability to make your name known and qualify for rank with the king. What more could you want?"

"You think we really have a king with enough courage to expand his empire? Are you saying that we might have opportunities for large scale battle in the near-lands?"

"That is where the most glory lies, is it not? It is my desire to do so. I believe that it is what the king wishes. Of course, because of political reasons this is not an official statement and should be kept low-key.

"Right now, we have a dangerous internal threat. You may have heard of the krist-chin group that has formed in the city. They are viewed as an extremely dangerous cult and even has the demonic Gathering scrambling to bring about its destruction. We can't, unfortunately, just walk in and slaughter them all; there're politics and such to observe.

"I am sure that most of you are aware that the former hero, Rashnir, formerly of the Rogis' Rangers, is among their number, plus two unknown beings that appear to be Sons of Anak. We can assume, then, that these heretics have come from as far as the western edge of Briganik. Though our information brokers should be able to find information on two wayward anakim, we are still unsure of their origins."

"I heard that they have wings," one man called. "You ever heard of an anakim with wings?"

"Yes, I too have heard that," Pinchôt said, "But it hasn't been confirmed."

"I overheard some people in the brothels the other night saying that they looked like high Luciferian beings. Said it looked like Lucifer himself, all shimmering and glorious."

"I overheard that you drink too much," Grirrg jibbed, eliciting several bursts of laughter.

Pinchôt clarified the position, "The Luciferian Order says that these beings are not aligned with the church. They have been officially labeled as extreme threats to the Order, which is now affiliated with the rule of the kingdom. These beings are only here to destroy the way of life that we are paid to fight and protect. You might be religious, you might not, but it will be a glorious kill should you bring down any of this cult's leadership."

The barbarians began stomping the floor and rattling mugs on the table to show their excitement at the opportunity to fight such a creature. They chomped at the bit for an excuse to launch into battle.

"We have been instructed not target them just yet, but to gather information and prepare ourselves. King Rutheir assures me that we *will* meet these creatures on the battlefield. He even claimed that he will hire bards to watch the fray from the hillsides so the glory of the ones who slay them might be composed as a tale for all to hear."

Many of the barbarians' ears perked up. Their fighting spirit roused and Pinchôt knew he'd forged a bond with his men. He hoped to strengthen it in the coming days and weeks.

"You are all dismissed; carry this knowledge with you, but tell no one. Lines are forming in this city with every person choosing either allegiance to the crown, or allegiance to this cult. This should be only a brief matter to deal with, and then we may move on to matters of more importance and greater glory.

"For now, enjoy life, get drunk, pull the legs from live chickens—whatever you do for merriment... just keep your lips tight. We hold a royal secret and the trust of our king. This is our ticket to elevate the Narsh Barbarians into the favor of the king.

"If any of you care to join *me*, I think I fancy a stroll through the city streets before I addle *my own* brain with spirits."

***

Rashnir sat cross-legged by the fire. Little Jibbin had remained fastened to him during the entire retreat for the safety of the encampment. Kevin, Jorge, Kyrius, and others had tried to comfort the child, but to no avail. He remained in such shock that he verged on a catatonic state. The one thing that he did communicate, through his body language, was that he had no intention of letting go of his rescuer. Even now, as he slept, he clung to Rashnir's torso as if his life depended on it.

The warrior looked down at the child clinging to his chest. His skin was dirty and he was barefoot, though that was common for children of his age. Puffy, discolored marks of his bruises indicated that he hadn't completely escaped the abuses of the alleyway.

Jibbin snored faintly. Rashnir had just wondered if he could find a way to sleep when he spotted his friends approach.

Others tried had vainly to comfort the child until a wise mother of eight children chased them away. She'd noted that nothing could satisfy the child save his parents return from the dead or being allowed to cling to the only safety he knew in this moment. They'd allowed Jibbin to fall asleep upon Rashnir in peace and with the only security he knew.

Kevin and the angels returned, hoping that the boy had fallen asleep in the time since they'd left. They were anxious to hear the details regarding the incident. They were especially curious about the sword of the Logos appearing for Rashnir to wield.

According to what Kevin had said before leaving the warrior and child in peace, Rashnir inferred that a number of other attacks of similar natures against Christians had been coordinated that night by local Luciferians. Rashnir's friends approached and quietly sat near the fire; they spoke only in hushed tones so they wouldn't wake the child.

Rashnir told them every detail of his evening, starting with his conversation with Jaker and ending with his return to the camp. Jorge smiled when Rashnir told them how the sword appeared as he had needed it.

"The Lord answered your prayers, Kevin," Jorge said. The angel gently borrowed the Bible that Kevin carried wherever he went. "You lamented the other day about how we only had one book for all believers to share." Jorge flipped through the pages and handed the book back to its owner. His angelic finger pointed to a specific verse.

Hebrews 4:12 For the word of God is quick, and powerful, and sharper than any two edged sword, piercing even to the dividing asunder of soul and spirit, and of the joints and marrow, and is a discerner of the thoughts and intents of the heart.

"Rashnir, look at your forearm," the angel pulled back his tunic to expose his arm from elbow to wrist. Rashnir shifted Jibbin and did the same as his friend.

Looking at his forearm in the flamelight, he saw that he too bore a matching mark. The angel and warrior had matching tattoo-like markings; each resembled both a cross and a sword. The word Logos was visibly etched upon it.

"Hold out your arm. Expect that the Lord will provide you with all that you need. Seek not the blade, but God." Jorge and Rashnir both extended their arms, palms upward and expecting. The flaming, spiritual sword materialized in the hand of each warrior.

"It's as I thought. This is the same sword that we angels wield. It is sharper than any other weapon and only available to those who follow God with every aspect of their lives. This sword *is* the word of God, the Logos. Do what I do, Rashnir."

Jorge gripped the sword by the blade and examined the broadside as if he studied it. "Look closely at your blade. Do you see anything?"

Rashnir shifted his weight back on his seat so that Jibbin could comfortably lie against him. He put one hand at the base of the blade and the other nearer the point; the flames extinguished at his touch. The blade was sharp, but Rashnir sensed that the blade would not hurt him no matter how hard he gripped. He looked at the flat of the blade and noticed that there were words finely engraved upon it. The blade's ricasso had three names written on it. There were other words and text etched upon it. As he examined it more closely, Rashnir realized that he could easily read the words, despite the small size. Miraculously, he also had perfect comprehension of the text. It was the Word of God.

Rashnir could not respond for several minutes. He was so enraptured in this discovery that he couldn't tear his attention away. He poured through the words of Christ as spoken in His sermon on the mount, the account of His death and resurrection.

After a few long moments, he glanced up at his companions with an awestruck look. "This," he said, "is incredible. Never have I laid hand upon such an awesome instrument."

Jorge nodded his head in assent. "It does not only destroy the enemies of the Logos. It is a means to bring hope and peace to the believer and bear the words of salvation to those who are lost."

Kevin beamed at the implications of the available Word. "Jorge, do you think that all believers will have access to this?"

"I am certain that they will," he replied, "at least all of those who have been baptized in Spirit would. All believers should be able to understand the writing upon the blade because of the Spirit's indwelling, but those that have been baptized have been empowered and gifted for service; they should also be able to draw upon this power."

"Perhaps, then," Kevin suggested, "the morning's lesson should focus on the baptism in the Holy Spirit."

"I think that it would be wise of you to do so."

Kyrius smiled and quipped, "See, Jorge. I told you the Creator picked the right man for this job."

Jorge grinned at his friend's jest. He knew that it would edify Kevin more than they could know. He'd struggled with insecurity the last couple of mornings and this would relieve some of that pressure.

Jibbin stirred a little and the three rose to leave him in peace.

Kevin spoke quietly enough that he would not wake the child. "We will speak more in the morning, Rashnir, if you are able. I want to gather those whom I believe will make the best leaders and form a council. I cannot do everything on my own or I will burn myself out, and there is much to do, much to discuss. We should talk about the many attacks that happened this evening against our fellow Christians. But we will talk more about that in the morning. For now, get some rest. You look like you could use it, and I am sure that you will need it."

"Curious, Kyrius," Jorge said as they walked off, meandering out of earshot.

"Sounds like the beginning of a limerick."

"No, I keep thinking that I hear a noise—every now and then, just a twinge, like something digging deep beneath us... do you hear it too?"

Rashnir gave a little wave as they departed into the restless night air. He knew deep down that he would not be able to sleep; there was no way he could possibly sleep with the excitement of the evening's discovery coursing through his body. It overpowered the grief that troubled his spirit, the sorrow for Jibbin's parents. Rashnir took up his heavenly sword and began to study the Word with an intensity and passion that he never thought possible with reading.

He eventually expended all his energy. Late into the night, he fell asleep mid-sentence while reading. Once Rashnir's consciousness slipped away his sword dissipated, returning to him as a mark upon his arm; his mind tumbled into a deep dream of "what-if" possibilities.

Rashnir's mind imagined a world where Kelsa lived and the two raised Jibbin together. They made a life together where Rashnir no longer found passion in war, but in worship.

* * *

Rashnir awoke the next morning to find the sullen little boy curled up at his feet. His face was dirty and stained where tears had streamed down his face, cleaning little trails as gravity pulled his tears to the ground.

Rashnir gave him an apprehensive hug to reassure him. "Good morning, Jibbin," he said, getting on his knees and looking him level in the eyes. He took him by the shoulders. "Do you know who I am?"

The boy nodded.

"I am Rashnir. I'm going to take care of you."

Jibbin looked a little frightened.

"Do you remember what happened last night?"

A nod.

"I'm so sorry, Jibbin. Do you remember when your parents met Kevin, the preacher, and were so excited because they found Jesus, how that changed their lives?"

Another nod, more vigorous… a better memory.

"Well, I know that it is very sad to lose your family. I too, lost all of my family, several times in fact. I think that we are similar like that. I'm gonna protect you, Jibbin. I promised your daddy that I would.

"Your parents died before they should have, but they are in Heaven now and you're gonna see them again at the end, I can promise you that. And you don't need to worry about bad people or ekthro hurting you; I am Rashnir. Perhaps you have heard some of my stories or songs?"

The boy nodded.

"Oh good, you're a fan." Rashnir scooped up the mute little boy and took him off to breakfast while he told him a well-known story about his time with Rogis' Rangers.

After breakfast, Rashnir found Kevin and his group of chosen leaders forming a circle. Rashnir sat in a place near the preacher's seat where Kevin directed him. Jibbin sat cross-legged next to Rashnir, mimicking his guardian's posture.

***

Kevin surveyed his teammates. Gathered around him were Jorge and Kyrius, his angelic protectors and confidants; Rashnir and Jibbin; Zeh-Ahbe', Rah'-be, and Sil-tarn, the three werewolf clan mates of the displaced Say-awr'; Nipanka, a large bearded man who, prior to his conversion, owned a very successful store in Grinden; Miklaw, a wiry farmer from the outskirts of the city; Shinna, an old widow and mother who had a gentle way with women, and who owned a tailor business before her conversion; Drowdan, an animal farrier who worked the outlying areas surrounding Grinden; Rondhale and Jhonnic, twin men in their thirties, both blacksmiths known for quality craftsmanship; Werthen, a well-liked young man with a magnetic personality and a charming craft. As a ferreter he knew many of those in the Christian encampment, having previously visited their homes, businesses, or farms to exterminate rodents with his small, furry hunters.

"You all know why I have gathered you here: because I need to delegate more of my work to others whom I feel I can trust and whom I believe people will have confidence in to do an adequate job. I believe that you all have special talents, good connections, or certain gifts that would make you a good leader."

Kevin laid out his plans. The people on this leadership council would be responsible for many duties and would, to the best of their abilities, settle disputes or mediate where it may be needed, take leadership burdens off of Kevin and advise him on cultural concerns and more. They'd be responsible for leading certain groups, discipling, training, evangelizing, and helping when needed.

The leader's time also needed to be guarded. He couldn't be directly responsible for each and every individual—that would eventually wear him down.

After giving his team some instruction and encouragement, Kevin moved on to the more weighty issues. "I had hoped that we could have had this meeting without bringing up any bad news, but we are unwanted strangers in a foreign land. In fact, this matter is what prompted me to gather you all as soon as I did.

"You have probably heard accounts of the attacks that many of our people endured last night. In all cases, the attackers came from either street gangs or faithful Luciferians mobs who hate our very existence because of our devotion to the Savior. Many of our brothers and sisters *were* attacked and a few were killed. Many were mocked and assaulted; some of them are still missing, even now. Remember them when you pray.

"We should expect this persecution. You all know about this place's Luciferian heritage. Everything about this realm fights against the truth of a Savior even more than the Earth does, and the Earth is very hostile towards Christ. While Earth was twisted and corrupted through the curse that Satan helped introduce, this satanic realm is even more so.

"On Earth, despite the persecution that Christians endured, the message always spread. In fact, wherever persecution was greatest is where the most phenomenal growth always seemed to occur. When you study the Word, you will find references to the world being hostile to those who stand for the truth of our Savior, Jesus. You will find it is not any different here in this place.

"To be a Christian means you walk a narrow path of light which leads to eternal life and joy while beckoning to those outside of this path: those who dwell in darkness and hate the light. These people of darkness hate us because of what we represent: a light that destroys the darkness they love, a darkness which eventually consumes them.

"I won't sugarcoat it. Some of us will die, many of us might be hurt, but we will live in the truth and have the blessings of our Lord. I would much rather endure the punishments of man and enjoy the afterlife in the peace and pleasure of God than receive the approval and praise of mankind and ekthro."

Kevin's counselors nodded their assent.

"Our own lives are forfeit," he continued. "This is war and we fight for a higher ideal. I go into this battle each day choosing to remain steadfast in my calling to

Christ, with the knowledge that the war may require me to lay down my own life or to endure hardships.

"This is how I want you handle those who question their commitment: speak gently to those who fear the persecutions that will undoubtedly come from the Luciferian church.

"Remind them that our bodies are just temporary vessels meant to contain the light of Christ. When we exit this mortal life, we enter into our immortal one; though this passage might be unpleasant, we need not fear it. We must do the work that the Lord called us to: proclaim His Word and draw lost souls to Him before it is too late."

Kevin indicated that Rashnir should stand. He explained how those believers that had been baptized in Spirit had access to the sword of the Lord. Kevin explained how they could use it to study the Word of God, but also use it for protection.

Rashnir demonstrated for the group. Each of the others in the circle also had a marking on their arm, but only noticed it after Kevin mentioned it. Following Jorge's instructions, they were each able to draw a blade from thin air. Each sword summoned was perfectly tailored to the size and needs of the one who held it.

After the initial awe of this discovery wore off, Kevin cautioned his crew against entering the city. The central park had become a hostile zone to any of those who had converted.

This afternoon, Luciferians planned to hold the memorial service for the wicked King Harmarty. Kevin advised them to avoid the service. He expected that this memorial would stir up an anti-Christian sentiment in the population of Grinden.

The meeting closed with each member of the council contributing a few words to a corporate prayer. The overall sense was that Kevin had chosen the right persons for his leadership council.

While the townsfolk planned to honor their dead, Kevin planned to lead a water baptism ceremony so that his flock could publicly pledge their allegiance to the Lord.

***

In the afternoon, crowds gathered throughout Grinden, hoping to get a glimpse of the new king. The throng swelled into the largest assembly the townsfolk had yet recorded. As if in mockery to Kevin's recent meetings, the entire center of the city had been transformed into a carnival of sorts. As previously, vendors and entrepreneurs of every sort turned out to cater to the desires and lusts of the assembled masses.

A small military regiment marched through heralding King Rutheir. They made a human barrier to work as crowd control and they directed vendors with kiosks and carts to the edge of the assembly so that more people could gather in close to the memorial service.

All morning, workers busied themselves building a stage over the top of the rock which Kevin had preached from. The platform stood about the height of a man and spanned wide enough to hold several people. Almost anyone could see the speaker, even from the very edges of the area. The preparations were nearly complete when people began trickling in from many areas, near and far, responding to the bells of the nearby Temple.

Those faithful to the Order expected that they might receive some kind of blessing for attending the ceremony; those associated with the church but not regularly faithful were warned that they might provoke mischievous under-demons to wrath if they did not attend the memorial and pay respect to the deceased King Harmarty and to Absinthium: a Luciferian arch-mage of the thirty-third degree.

As the festivities got underway, local shops closed momentarily so that they might observe; most stores had set up open-air booths to entice any passersby as they lingered and loitered earlier in the day.

Luciferian monks surrounded the gathering at all strategic points and at obvious positions as they watched for Christian intrusion. The look-outs' shaved heads and tattoos labeled them as combat trained monks and each of them appeared to be on high alert for some perceived threat—perhaps hoping to be the first to spot an enemy or identify a reason to put their talents into service.

Frinnig watched over his nephew, a promising spell caster, despite his youth and low rank in the Order. The boy, although you might certainly mistake that label by looking at him, had been charged with manipulating the elements to keep the populace comfortable so that weather would not distract from the arch-mage's message.

The weather grew to perfection through the day; the right amount of sun offset a slight breeze. The gentle wind carried coolness with it, yet it made no noise that might dampen the words of the speaker.

At the very southern perimeter of the amassed crowd a small band of Christians spied out the happening. Rashnir towed Jibbin, who firmly grasped his cloak and refused to be left behind, and scouted out the monks' observation points in order to avoid them.

Kyrius, Zeh-Ahbe', and Shinna followed, making sure to stay well out of the way of the crowds so that they would not be noticed by any roving monkish security. Shinna accompanied them primarily because of her gender. Just in case they were spotted and needed to fight, she could scoop up Jibbin and scurry off unnoticed, except as an old woman fleeing the scene of a battle and carrying a child to safety.

The spies watched as best as they were able, trying to avert their eyes from some of the more lewd or malevolent acts of entertainment. A horn blew and after much pomp and ceremony, the local head of Grinden's Luciferian Temple climbed onto the stage to address the crowd.

Frinnig introduced himself to those who were not familiar because of distance or lapsed commitment. His booming voice echoed across the park and turned ears towards the stage; a sea of heads surrounded the stage like a field littered with dandelions. Frinnig held a cone shaped instrument in his hands which helped project his voice across the field. He slowly turned in all directions as he spoke so that the people could hear him speak even in the back.

Frinnig heaped praises upon the reputation of their new king, Rutheir, and briefly spoke of his utmost devotion to the teachings and ministry of the prophet, Absinthium. He also exhorted the faithful and those devoted to the Luciferian religion, encouraging others to renew or begin a pattern of frequent attendance at the temple.

"We must remain committed to the most sacred fundamentals of Luciferianism. Our beloved angel of light fights against our enemy even as we speak. The spurned God, Yahweh, seeks vengeance against us for glorifying ourselves, but we will rise triumphant… if we lend our supplications to the spiritual cause. Even now the forces of Yahweh are breaking down walls, trying to reach us here, attacking us even in our homes.

"Perhaps you have heard of these krist-chins, perhaps you have not. We must remember our roots, people. So many of us have fallen away to such a degree that the forces of Lucifer have weakened; your faithfulness has waned over the years and now, even now, there are people in our lands who blatantly disregard us entirely and heretically proclaim opposite doctrines of all that we hold true.

"I have digressed, though, and I apologize. You are not here to see me speak, but to listen to the words of our new king and those of Absinthium, the prophet. I do ask you, if you are a loyal man or ekthro, I implore you to attend our services. We will be having services each day, every other hour for the next week. Many extra monks now reside within the temple walls to help you during this time and explain our religious tenets to the curious. This is a formal call to recommitment. But we are here today to remember a fallen king. Let his death remind you of how easy it could be for everything we care about to be destroyed by the acts of a vengeful God; we must harden our resolve lest we too fall.

"King Rutheir," Frinnig bowed briefly and handed the vocal projector to Rutheir.

The king accepted the tool and addressed the crowd in a similar manner. He recounted several warm stories in remembrance of Harmarty, none of which were true. He lied blatantly and openly, speaking of how

Harmarty had intervened or judged in the favor of folks or helped his subjects out of care and concern for them.

Rashnir hissed under his breath as he listened. "Most of these are old stories about Harmarty's father, just twisted slightly," he whispered to his companions.

"King Harmarty felt that he had an obligation, a duty, to protect those people he'd been raised to watch over," Rutheir said, playing on the memories of the wicked king's much beloved father. The crowd appeared sympathetic to his statements and actually believed the lies that Harmarty had been a benevolent and kind ruler. Rutheir grinned as he saw the looks on the faces in the crowd; he was quite certain the arch-mage might have had something to do with their level of receptivity.

"You see, Harmarty cared for his subjects, and I follow him in that. I look across this multitude and I see more than just people before me; I see duty and obligation. I see in you my very purpose for existence and I must tell you that I agree with my friend here, Frinnig the Priest.

"We see a danger brewing in our land. There are people who are trying to harm you. I cannot, with my sense of duty, allow you to go about your daily lives with this threat looming over you; you must be informed. I believe this krist-chin cult is treacherous.

"I've seen convincing evidence that the cardinal members of this cult were the perpetrators who assassinated my predecessor in his very bedroom while he slept. While the information is convincing to me, those charged with investigating it remained lax to inquisition one of their own. I am speaking of Rashnir, who apparently still has friends in the Rogis' Rangers; they refuse to satisfactorily investigate the circumstances of this murder. They might even be in league with this cult. I have seen to it that those who remain as true servants of justice have been moved from the Rangers into other sects of the guild.

"No longer should Grinden fear that murderers will go unpunished and thieves remain free. The ruling council of Ninda relinquished all claims and allowed me to officially annex Grinden as a district of Jand. Soon an actual military garrison and even a soldiers' training academy will be located right here in Grinden. Changes are underway... changes that should have been made long ago."

Rutheir surveyed the audience. He still had them right where he wanted them and so he revisited his pet topic.

"It is the opinion of all who have examined the workings, motivations, and actions of this cult that they desire control of the crown—my crown; they want to rule Jand themselves. For the very protection of our country, and in the interest of your protection, I am endorsing the Luciferian Church as the official religion of our state. I hereby give the church complete sovereignty and full power and authority to act as they best see fit. This is a symbiotic union. I have never known a Luciferian affiliate to act outside the interests of the crown, nor known one to try taking advantage of those they've pledged to help."

A murmur of agreement rose from the people. Heads nodded in assent—even heads who had lost much because of the Order's bloody and greedy history.

"This is my personal promise to you," Rutheir's voice rose, demanding the attention of the people and playing on the growing hype. "I will act in your best interest. I am aware of the large scope of events taking place and I vow that I will eliminate this cult and protect your children from their dangerous influence. I will also work to provide our children—our kingdom, with a better future." Rutheir's eyes twinkled as the populace cheered at a veiled promise to expand their kingdom through military might.

He found the crowd's mood extremely agreeable. Rutheir noticed Absinthium rise to the stage beside him. The king was sure the arch-mage had cast some sort of spell over the people; most large crowds could never be so pliable, otherwise. Despite an audience of several thousand, he could not spot a single expression of dissention.

"Loyal subjects, may I now present to you our most distinguished guest. This man has aided us in the process of perfecting our country. Here is the thirty-third degree Luciferian arch-mage and Chief of the High Council, Absinthium." Rutheir's voice seemed to boom and echo during the announcement; the mage refused the vocal projector, using magic instead to project his voice.

The weathered old man stood upon the dais and smiled at the crowd. He leaned heavily upon his oddly gnarled staff.

He spoke with a kind and grandfatherly voice. Warm and subtle, though his words remained supernaturally audible far beyond what they should have been.

The arch-mage lunged into an interesting discourse on why the people should remain devoted to the Luciferian faith and support it on a variety of levels. He delved into deep areas of lore concerning battles within supernatural realms; the dramatic account kept the crowd riveted with curiosity and stitched with empathy. He proved that Kevin was not the only storyteller to visit this park.

After a short tirade, he attacked his enemies. "These krist-chins are a very real threat to all the land, and even to Heaven. Our birthright, which is to rule over Yahweh's Heaven and to oppress the enemies of our souls, is in jeopardy. The age-old battle has long been contained within the supernatural and in the Earth realms, but it has now come to our very doorstep. Frinnig, in his passionate statements, is correct in placing much of the blame upon those who have fallen away from the faith—I can see the looks on some of your faces: it is guilt—the battle has been allowed to break free of those old boundaries because we have been far too lax in the support of our heavenly champion. Fear not; you may still help reclaim the war!

"I am officially requesting the presence of each and every one of you in our local services. We need your support, and you can't afford not to give it!

"I know what many of you believe. Some of you think that our faith is nothing, that we Luciferians are deluded men and women of wishful thinking, or perhaps that we made this all up. For those among you who are naysayers, I will give you a demonstration of my powers: powers that are only available to the select few in our monasteries... those who are given access to study the books of power and books of spells that were written by the demons and even by Lucifer himself. There are books that show wizards how to manipulate the energy and magic lines interwoven into reality, bringing about miraculous results!"

The wizard spoke a few guttural words in an incomprehensible language and clouds billowed out of nothingness. They descended to cloak the mage in a pillar of darkness; it twisted and churned like an ethereal vortex. With a loud shout and a thunderclap the pillar burst outward in an explosion of mist and flew back skyward, transmuting into a flock of birds that flew off into the distant horizons.

Most people were awed at the display. Absinthium's voice changed to something much more guttural and twisted, "Some of you are still thinking that this is a simple magic trick. 'Smoke and mirrors' you might be saying. Well then, let me give you a true display of magics that cannot be denied nor explained except by one who knows the way of the supernatural power lines. Then, let you all be convinced of the truth—that there is true power and authority only in the path of Lucifer."

He stretched his staff over the men and woman in the crowd who stood in the direct path between the stage and the door to the Luciferian temple. With a wave of the staff came a release of power that pushed the crowd members aside, forming a clear pathway between the dais and the temple gate.

The large double doors opened from the inside. A shackled woman stood there, flanked by two uncomfortable looking combat monks dressed in ceremonial regalia. Each of her guards carried a wicked pair of reaper-shaped, ritual kamas in case the need to permanently subdue her arose. They silently escorted the submissive woman to the stage.

At the far edge of the audience, Shinna gasped and whispered, "I know her. She is one of us!"

With jaw and eyes set, Kyrius reached out his hand planning to draw his sword and charge to her rescue. Zeh-Ahbe' stayed him with a hand, not wanting a rash action to throw away so many lives in the hopes of rescuing one.

Kyrius relaxed and the former werewolf leader looked to Rashnir for confirmation of the decision. Rashnir nodded his agreement. They were looking for information, not for a fight.

As she approached, Absinthium explained to the crowd. "This woman is a known krist-chin. Last night, several of our faithful took it upon themselves to express to these cultists that they are unwelcome here. This was not an officially endorsed action and these faithful devotees took it upon themselves to do as they saw fit. After urging the heretics to recant their cultic beliefs, and a subsequent refusal, they punished several of these dissidents." He grinned deviously. "I do agree with their motives and methods.

"This woman was apprehended near an alley where we found a group of our faithful adherents who had been slaughtered—dismembered in the very streets of the city they were trying to protect. We presume these fallen heroes were murdered by this krist-chin woman. She must have been accompanied by a great many others who escaped, yet she denies this.

"The people of Grinden are lucky to have the likes of Pinchôt protecting the city streets. The former Ranger and new head of the Narsh Barbarians was one of the men who apprehended her at the scene of the crime.

"What do you people, the rightful heirs of this fair city, believe should be this woman's punishment?"

Cries arose from the crowd all at once; the clamoring voices demanded her execution. The woman walked placidly before the stage and presented herself. Her escorts left her, fading into the crowd as the pathway to the stage filled in again with bodies. The multitude cleared a large circle around her.

The mage stared down at her from of the stage. "This is how the powers of Lucifer will destroy its opposition!" Absinthium uttered a new string of words and slowly brought his hands together as if clapping very slowly. When his hands contacted each other, a loud peal of thunder issued and flames burst up from the ground, consuming her as she wept and prayed silently. She did not try to flee; she did not speak or cry out or curse her executioners. The crowd backed away because of the intense heat rolling off of the pyre. They stared at the scene, wide eyes fixed to it, like they were drugged with opiates, and then cheering erupted.

Enveloped by the flames, the woman sank to her knees and succumbed to the fiery fate. The amassed crowd watched with rapt interest, falling so silent that those at the forefront could hear the crackle and hiss of the fire as it devoured human flesh and sinew. The synovial fluid in her joints boiled and burst; seconds later, her joints sundered and her body collapsed in a pile of glowing embers and blackened bone.

No one dared utter a sound and the crowd held its collective breath. All eyes remained fixed on the mage.

Finally, Absinthium spoke, "You see," his grandfatherly voice returned once again, "power and the truth are found in what we believe. We are all children of Lucifer. Here lies the victory and lies the power. The power to make a better life and the power to destroy our enemies is our duty and our right."

With heavy hearts, Rashnir and his crew watched Absinthium tell the crowd about his personal prophecy and the acceptance of the ekthro into their faith. Nods of affirmation rolled through the crowd when he instructed them about old racial prejudices between man and ekthro becoming a thing of the past.

The mage wrapped up his message. "I do think that the church is partly to blame for failing our angelic hero. One of the things that we, as the church, have never been good about is allowing you as the laypeople to study our own lore and books of faith. That the majority of people are illiterate and might misinterpret our histories and sacred works is of little consequence. I believe that it is your right to access these materials and I have commissioned scribes and devotees to diligently copy selected works for you to purchase and take with you. They will be available to any man or ekthro who has been faithful at his temple, or pledges to become faithful, so that they may receive the proper guidance and tutelage to read these works and obtain true power.

"I do have available right now many copies of my personal prophecy known as the Prophetic Scroll of Absinthium. You may obtain a copy from any monk present. For now, please give heed to a final notice from your king."

Rutheir once again ascended the podium. He looked very serious and turned to show all observers the somberness of his mood. "You have all seen and heard of the dangers that this city faces, but also you have heard of our glorious potential. You know that I have a soft spot for this place I once called home. You are the heart and soul of what my vision for Jand is and I do not wish to leave you at the mercy of these dangerous cultists.

"I am enacting a two part plan for your protection. It is the responsibility of the crown to take action in light of this problem. The first phase is something that is my responsibility; the second is something that we will do together: you with the rest of Jand.

"I will appoint an official steward of this city so that you may have direct responses and immediate intervention when situations arise. I will not appoint someone from the outside; because this is a position of significant importance and will be someone that you shall deal with frequently, it will be important that you are familiar with this person. I desire that you, as a city, hold a local ballot and elect from your own population someone you think will act in the best interests of the city.

"This will be a paid position and I might at some time award direct nobility to this person, so choose wisely. He or she will be my personal liaison between Grinden and the crown; the steward will have my full authority on matters until I have had the chance to ratify decisions and evaluate circumstances.

"I will also, when I go, leave behind a small number of military guards to form a military garrison. More will come, but I will not be sending soldiers, rather teachers and recruiters to raise up an army.

"For far too long there has been a lack of military presence in the eastern half of the country. We have devoted all of our military strength to maintaining our western boundaries against Ziphan slaving invasions. We relied too much on the mercenaries' guilds for protection and peacekeeping. We've seen how Rogis Rangers did with that when it came time to prosecute one of their own."

The crowd booed and hissed, accepting the new narrative that King Rutheir spun for them.

"It is my desire, in the best interest of the country, to rebuild a strong army. Being a soldier is the noblest thing that a citizen could do and I wonder if there are any out there who would be willing to join? If it is your desire to be a protector of our ways, a defender of the weak, the slayer of enemies, and an educated and successful resident of these lands, then speak with one of the soldiers here today. They will share more with you. This is the burden we will share together.

"I now bid you a farewell. I return in five days to instate the Steward of Grinden, whomever you have chosen. Until then, live your life with honor and dignity, remember your roots and your devotions and do not forget the dead and sacrifices made to further the plans of the Angel of Light."

Rutheir made his way from the platform as the crowd chanted his name and shouted praises to him. Once the king had departed, along with Absinthium and Frinnig, the crowd slowly dispersed.

***

Kevin shifted his weight against the current as the water flowed around his waist. The river edged in the Christian encampment's northern border. He smiled and beckoned to his new friends. Kevin knew that deep inside the city on their north a different sort of ceremony took place. Kyrius and some of his other trusted friends had gone in secrecy to get a gauge of the situation. Jorge remained behind with Kevin.

Many people who had recently become Christians flooded the southern banks of the stream, preparing to be baptized or to witness the baptism of others. It was a time to rejoice and cheer for others.

Over the last few days, many of their studies and lessons had been about what it meant to be a Christian and what the Lord desired of them. Naturally the topics of water baptism and communion entered discussion. The people understood that baptism was a symbolic dying to the world and resurrection with Christ—a new life. It testified to the rest of the realm that they decided to follow Christ and could never go back.

Each person that entered the water proclaimed their commitment before Kevin dunked them under the surface and pulled them back up. Each emerging person expressed unyielding excitement about his or her new life.

Curious onlookers began wandering by, coming from the city. Many stopped to watch the ceremony. Many of them scowled or shouted obscenities. They mocked them in whatever ways they could, though none of them tried to interfere with the baptisms. The Christians paid no mind to the opposing crowds which grew and to the passersby who became more frequent.

Kevin figured the crowds were an indication that the Luciferian service had come to a close. He was only half done with those people who were prepared to go under the water. He hoped that his friends in the city would make it back in time to be baptized themselves. If they didn't, it would mean that they'd encountered trouble.

***

As shadows reclaimed the dark spaces in the park, the small group of Christians looked across the grassy turf and at the ashen remains of their sister in Christ. Rashnir and Jibbin, Kyrius, Zeh-Ahbe', and Shinna walked across the road and into the park with a great sense of trepidation.

They hoped to quickly gather the woman's remains and return to the Christian encampment with them. As they approached, they noticed two cloaked men standing contemplatively over the smoldering heap.

Both parties recognized each other at the same time and jumped to attention.

"Combat monks," Rashnir stated, knowing that they would immediately recognize him and Kyrius.

Rashnir was just about to pass Jibbin off to Shinna, much against Jibbin's wishes, when the two monks inexplicably ran away. They sprinted as fast as they could in the opposite direction.

Zeh-Ahbe' started to chase after them, "C'mon! We must not let them summon more guards."

Kyrius quelled him, recognizing the same thing that Rashnir had. "No, leave them be. Didn't you see them? They were not lying in wait for us; they mourned for her. It looked like the same two guards who escorted her out to the execution. If it were possible," the angel said, "I would cry for her, too. Instead I rejoice at the courage she showed."

Rashnir nodded. "When they ran, I saw the hoods fall from their faces. One I did not recognize, the other was the same young monk who has shown great curiosity in our faith. He may find Christ soon, if he continues seeking... and if Jandul doesn't find out."

They watched as the two young monks peeked out from the shadows, checking to see if they had been followed by Christians or noticed by members of their own creed. They spotted the Christians in the park and fled deeper into the city.

Kyrius removed his satchel and emptied its contents. The angel gathered the woman's remains into the sack and tied it with a cord before binding it to his belt.

The Christians sorrowfully headed back to the encampment, sad and yet proud of the martyr's witness. As a new believer, she showed as much courage in the face of the enemy as any of them could ever hope to.

CHAPTER TWELVE

Attitudes shifted over the next few days in Kevin's camp. With the advent of the believers having direct, divine access to the Logos, a confidence and spark of wisdom seemed to grow in each person.

Kevin found that his leadership burdens lifted as the people matured, hungry to know more about their people's great mission and refined by the crucible of trials their Luciferian citizens subjected them to. People rose among their camp to teach, share, and comfort each other; they discovered their own gifts. New families came to the camp each and every day as the Grinden Christians called on their own friends and family members with a message of hope.

Conversely, staunch Luciferian families shunned members who turned to Christ and many businesses posted "No krist-chin" signs, barring known believers from their premises. Anticipating the eventual emigration Kevin had spoken of in relation to the western portal, Christians began selling their properties, even if they only got obscenely low prices because of local Luciferian influence.

As Grinden's citizens took sides, many made it clear that they wanted nothing to do with Christians, while others demonstrated their feelings through acts of violence. Only few remained neutral or apathetic at best.

As the persecution intensified, most Christians opted for some sort of temporary or mobile dwelling at

Kevin's camp; wagons and tents sprang up and sprawled across the encampment. The folks eagerly anticipated an exodus in the weeks to come, both because of their optimism for the journey and because their local options systematically declined as Jandul and Frinnig plied their social influence.

Through Kevin's preaching, there were few who didn't know that the group's goals were to find the western gateway, the passage between the realms, and escape the great conflagration that they believed would come. It seemed that the stronger the Christians pushed towards their goals, the more Luciferian influence amplified against them.

Their emigration was an obvious eventuality, but no person knew the exact details of how or when it would happen. Even Kevin had not quite nailed that down, though he knew it was soon. The leaders merely needed to plan for the logistics of such an exodus. It became ever more difficult as businesses refused to sell them the necessary provisions and supplies.

Christians who still ventured into the city brought back news and current events to share. Other than the dominating topic of the battle lines drawn between the faiths, the only other news item was the open election for the Grinden Steward appointment.

The trade town that only recently enjoyed sovereign neutrality now buzzed with politics and election campaigns. In the couple weeks since Kevin's arrival everything had changed.

***

Even though King Rutheir and Absinthium had departed, the Luciferian Temple remained packed at every service. The visit from the king and the prophet-mage boosted fervor for the long week of services dedicated to recommital and ceremony. Smaller services ran all day long in order to accommodate the travelers making pilgrimages in from the outlying countryside. Most services had some kind of curious ekthroic visitor, mostly goblins, but a few elves and an occasional orc wandered in as well. The neanderthalic orcs had a hard time understanding, but the monks did their best to explain the concept of absolute, blind tolerance and racial acceptance they tried to propagate.

With the huge influx of people in the city, the saloons and brothels couldn't keep up with demand; any place that catered to entertainment for travelers boomed in those times that Luciferian rites and rituals were not in session. No Luciferian rules barred the types of behaviors that the Christians found distasteful. In fact, the local temple smiled on the economic boost and the city was pleased to see growth.

Many trade lines and shipping routes that normally passed directly through the city began stopping to spend their money in the city's businesses, seeing what the city had to offer by way of slaking thirsts and satisfying lusts. Grinden transformed into a hive of activity; every person within its limits rode an energized wave of enthusiasm and it all revolved around the Luciferian Temple.

Amid the hustle and bustle, the political campaign reached out and grabbed the attention of the locals. Candidates serious about garnering votes for the public position resorted to all manner of tactics and skullduggery before King Rutheir returned to appoint the new steward.

Favorites included a wealthy businessman named Rinalto and a relatively unknown trade manager named Dyule. Dyule's story rallied the Luciferians around him; his story, that several of the cultists had recently ransacked his house and terrorized the poor crippled woman who lived with him, had been vaguely alluded to during Harmarty's memorial.

Because Rinalto was so well known as a shifty character, Dyule easily found his footing. He readily won the support of Rinalto's many business enemies. By contrast, Dyule had a reputable lineage in his father: the celebrated regional hero, Rogis, even if the Rangers' reputation had taken a hit recently.

In much the same way that the preacher, Kevin, stood on corners and enticed people into conversations which captivated small groups, so did these two primary candidates find success in gaining votes from the people of the city.

Dyule had a story to tell; he had a passion and a plan, not merely political rhetoric. He found a better reception with his audience than Rinalto did. Neither man had the overwhelming support and recommendation of the Luciferian Church, though. Neither of the favored candidates had been loyal attendees of the temple even if both agreed to fall in line with the Order's directives. Both made empty pledges to begin attending at some point.

Two days before the election, Dyule and Rinalto agreed to hold an open-air debate. Crowds gathered to listen to the men hurl insults at each other and reveal awful truths they'd each uncovered about the other opponent.

In the late evening, Rinalto rapped on the door of Dyule's house. After a few terse words Rinalto stepped inside and offered a bribe to Dyule, if he dropped out of the race.

Dyule refused and informed the duplicitous businessman that his desperation indicated more hope for Dyule's campaign than he'd previously assumed. Dyule scoffed, "By right of my famous lineage alone, I could take this contest from you! Let alone the fact that you have no idea how to work with the citizens of Grinden."

"Your lineage isn't worth the dirt on my boots. There is a growing scandal that Rogis was a whoremonger!" he sneered with a veiled threat to add his voice to that rumor mill.

A growl greeted him from a shadowy doorway as a massive young man stepped through the threshold. His dark eyes reflected how deeply he had just been insulted.

"You will regret calling my mother a whore," Bomarr threatened.

Rinalto whirled around in surprise, drawing a keen dagger as he pivoted in fear. Rinalto's eyes rolled back in his skull and his body fell limp under a blow to the head. The businessman groaned and saw a black flash of light as his opponent clubbed him over the head with an end table.

Dyule dragged his unconscious competitor to the post where his mount stood tethered. He unwound the leather reigns and very quietly strangled the life from Rinalto next to the horse. After pouring several drams of booze down Rinalto's throat, he wrapped the cords around his neck and wrists; Dyule hoped to make it look like Rinalto had gotten entangled in a simple accident. It would hopefully look like a riding mishap due to drunkenness.

Grinning mischievously, Dyule slapped the horse's rear and watched it gallop wildly away, fleeing down the city streets and dragging Rinalto's corpse alongside as the crashes and occasional hoof stomps abused the deceased body. The horse would probably be found by morning. Nothing could prevent Dyule from winning the election at this point.

A group of soldiers returning from the night's revelry found the horse in the morning when it meandered past the military garrison; Jand's official military had taken over the local garrison since Rutheir's visit. When the drunken soldiers found Rinalto's battered body, they quickly jumped to the conclusion Dyule had hoped for; the case was closed as quickly as it had opened.

News of his death traveled quickly. Most people knew of Rinalto's demise before the afternoon. Rinalto's most ardent and vocal supporters began feverishly praising and encouraging Dyule's candidacy, instead.

The human politicians proved a capacity to act just as crafty as goblins, which seemed to pop up with greater frequency. Goblins were prone to wearing trinkets of jewelry. Their uniquely identifiable trinkets made it easier for humans to recognize and learn the names of the various denizens who they crossed paths with frequently; rare was the human who could discern the difference between one goblin and the next without some sort of obvious mark or disfigurement.

Local shop owners were the first to accept the goblins. They made huge steps towards tolerance and the normalization of ekthroic diversity. Free trade even motivated the breakdown of the communication barrier.

While the pervasive infusion of ekthro increased the population, Grinden also saw the reduction of human numbers as Christians depopulated. Days into Dyule's campaign, it became rare to find a solitary religious dissident traveling in the city now. Mostly, they traveled in groups for their own protection. Any that still visited Grinden probably traveled to proselytize undecided family members. There were very few left who had yet to take a committed stance for the Luciferian doctrines and both sides fervently fought the shrinking middle ground.

With the town unified against them, it was unthinkable that any known Christian might try to actually vote in the upcoming general election for the steward. Though an official law banning the heretical religion still pended, the need for this type of law was the driving force behind the election in the first place. Any Christian brave enough to cast a vote would simply have his or her vote disregarded, instead. Many of the city-folk jested how sheep would obviously vote against a slaughter.

Tension brewed, simmering aboveground in the city. The Luciferian Order intentionally stirred the unrest. So preoccupied was the surface world that none knew of the secret war exploding in the subterranean kingdom below.

***

Far beneath the surface of the Mountains of Arnak a long passageway connected the nearest goblin throne city to the newly formed subterranean city of Under-Grinden. Few knew of its existence, meaning none could guess its real value. The goblin king Nvv-Fryyg had long since ignored his duties to his realm and grown soft to all but personal dalliances.

A contingent of traitorous warriors slinked through the tunnels and prepared to spring a trap set by the treacherous goblin grr'SHaalg and his brother tyr-aPt. Their nearly silent feet slapped in the darkness; perfectly straight and carved clean, the wicked creatures could move speedily with no craggy, broken flooring threatening to trip them up.

The high quality tunnel's craftsmanship diminished nearest Under-Grinden, where the work was newest, and where typical goblinoid work took over as they secretly hollowed out a new cavern. Goblins were not usually capable of delving such highly constructed tunnels. Many chained slave-gangs of dwarven craftsmen had been pressed into service; only they had the skills required to build such a grand subterranean highway. Most of them had been snatched from dwellings near the Drindak Canyons after the Goblins secretly connected their networks to the deepest and darkest depths of the craggy canyon back in Nvv-Fryyg's ambitious days. The tunnels joined the pits where the chasm was rumored to be bottomless, where the goblins knew the skolaxis bred.

Construction of this immense underground trade route had been in progress for more than fifteen years—in the dark, unlit halls thousands of slaves had lost their lives to the project. The tunnel first opened with an exit opening in Zipha, where slaves were easily purchased and a life's value was measured in gold.

Clad in black, the group of human traitors veered off of the dwarf-hewn highway and crept through the condensed, seeping slag of a rough-hewn tunnel at a surprising pace for beings that were unaccustomed to these conditions. Their shadows danced across the carved walls and stretched long by the flickering of torches and glassine bottles of luminescent larvae, which fed on various local lichens. The group began the journey less than two days ago at the tunnel's nexus, far below the city of Grinden.

This massive tunnel system was not a product of pure goblin design. While grr'SHaalg and tyr-aPt directed its completion, it was an anomalous discovery. The underground tunnel system had ancient, unnatural origins. Cut far below the scope of most goblin or even dwarven tunnels, it extended through the depths where the stone's density defied most tools. The enslaved mining crews merely connected their own access points to the pre-existing tunnelways. In fact, many of the pre-existing tunnels remained unexplored. The quality of the tunnels surpassed any other known mines—even the most ancient of the Dwarves. As the goblins forced dwarven slaves to complete the final tunnels, they connected the royal goblin city and its highways to the network, giving the illusion that the high craftsmanship of the network belonged to the glory of goblin kind as if they had somehow created this thing.

At the heart of Grinden, far below the city's foundation, an immense spherical chamber mirrored below what existed above. It was a perfect counterpart to the trade routes, which connected to the central hub in that city; the chamber of Under-Grinden spanned the size of a small village; it sprouted tunnels in every conceivable direction. The cliché phrase, "every road leads to Grinden," was true of the underground passageways as well.

Those cloaked in darkness and traveling the subterranean path cared little for trade routes, infrastructure origins, or the politics of men or goblins. Likewise, they remained indifferent to the plights of the slaves that toiled in the endless dark. The caves and tunnels would be completed as a glorious achievement for the goblin kingdom; the nameless faces in the dark would be forgotten; this clandestine paid no attention to either—they only did Absinthium's bidding without question.

grr'SHaalg, chief caretaker of the tunnel project, saw its glorious potential as the tunnel system neared completion. The nine other goblin kingdoms would want access and rights to branch off with their own local tunnels, giving their species expedient access to virtually any point on the surface world. But the ambitious creature saw the unassuming travel network as the key component to his meteoric rise to power.

His carefully developed plans did not include the tenth king, King Nvv-Fryyg, his progenitor. This group of hooded surface dwellers took a secret route under the mountains. It led to the foot of the goblin king's hall; this group of secret assassins was pledged by the arch-mage to supplant the obstinate goblin monarch. Nvv-Fryyg too often lapsed into paranoia and secluded himself for days on end seeking his perverse self-gratification. Nvv-Fryyg had too long stymied grr'Shaalg's plans for progress, but no longer. The Luciferians needed foot soldiers, and grr'SHaalg was happy to supply them provided Absinthium helped him depose the reclusive Nvv-Fryyg.

Along with grr'SHaalg and tyr-aPt, many of grr'SHaalg's loyal goblin bladesmen pledged their support; they used an amalgam of chalks and oils to paint their faces, identifying themselves as comrades to the thirteen cloaked surface dwellers. Six men each flanked the human leading the attack wedge; Absinthium led his personal Acolytes: his highly trained assassin-mages. Not even the Luciferian High Council knew that they existed.

The arch-mage planned to personally assist in Nvv-Fryyg's assassination and see to it that the treacherous goblins' plans truly aligned with his own. Tonight he would keep his half of the pact he made on the night of Harmarty's murder.

Picking their way through the shadows, the goblins led the Luciferian assassins through several twisting, craggy tunnels. After winding back and forth through the narrow, jutting excavations they spilled out into a large antechamber. The room appeared freshly dug from a seam of softer, porous stone.

The chamber was barely large enough to hold the assassin teams that had gathered for this mission. The goblins, mage, and his acolytes all crouched in the dugout space and prepped for the pending battle. Absinthium's strike team checked their gear with cold precision.

They had been handpicked early from their combat training by Absinthium and personally tutored in a wide array of disciplines. They enjoyed the privilege of the broadest training and the most specialized studies on select topics. Normally, receiving a personal apprenticeship from outside of your own discipline never happened, but Absinthium had more freedom than any other mage within the order. He had no accountability and could do whatever he desired.

Each of the Acolytes started as a promising student of the combat disciplines when Absinthium escalated their studies under other masters and intensified their training, crossing them with an array of disciplines to give them the skills that their master desired. Their talents made them, corporately, the most deadly force alive—the only ones to learn of their existence would, seconds later, slip past the veil of the living. The acolyte force was the personal, directed weapon of the arch-mage. They were talented in both physical combat and in the schools of magic; all of their specialized studies made them living weapons, and nothing more. They spoke little. They lived and died to serve their Dread Lord: the demon beh'-tsah and his avatar Absinthium.

Each acolyte's cloak and cape protected him from view and leather tapes wrapped forearms and hands to form pliable greaves. They each wore thick, leather vests to protect some minor degree against weapons; they were too valuable of assets for the mage to leave them defenseless, but they sacrificed armor for stealth and harnessed mobility over protection.

Silent as wraiths, they checked each other's additional armaments. The acolytes expected that the goblin king's army would mount a fierce resistance as soon as they discovered the invaders. Built for speed, quick release pouches lined the assassins' belts and each pocket contained various alchemical concoctions; they wore bandoliers from hip to hip, each holding a wide array of jagged throwing blades and holstering their sharp and terrible kamas. The serrated, reflective blades of the hook-like weapons were not dissimilar to ceremonial blades wielded by the execution guards during the Grinden execution days prior, although these were handled by experts with no compunction for mercy.

grr'Shaalg's goblin bladesmen watched them prepare with fearful detachment. After each assassin checked his gear to satisfaction, the teams moved into position. Absinthium moved to the lead at the front of the chamber, ready to initiate the massacre.

The arch-mage stood before the wall of crumbling, malleable earth and used the butt of his staff to scrape a magic sigil in the earthen barrier before stepping back a short distance. His acolytes poised to strike. They tensed their bodies like recoiled adders.

Absinthium spread his arms apart and shouted a word of power to trigger the spell. A massive explosion blew the wall inward, away from the throng of assassins. The noise of the detonation echoed through the chambers that opened up before them and the power word rang in the ears of those on the safe side of the explosion.

Acolytes and bladesmen poured through the yawning breach as it spread before them, still crumbling into earthen heaps. The explosion blew stone shards through the lavish facility that had long been the lounging room in King Nvv-Fryyg's harem. Jagged shrapnel wounded or killed many of the room's occupants: the goblin king's concubines and other courtesans' blood splattered across the place where Nvv-Fryyg spent so much time—where he engaged in the lusts of his flesh instead of guarding against internal coups.

The painted goblins expertly wielded their weapons. They swung their falchions in cocky, uppercutting motions knowing that they possessed the element of surprise and would not need to defend themselves yet. Goblin concubines shrieked and fell under their vicious strokes. grr'Shaalg's assassins killed everything with the potential to breath.

Absinthium's Acolytes wielded a kama in each hand. Swinging with trained precision, they severed joints and cleaved bodies. Within seconds, the gore of the king's concubines splattered the chamber like a macabre painting; the metallic taint of hot blood finally overrode the musty reek of goblin sex pheromones.

Specific battle groups formed and briefed prior to the attack broke off to their own headings to fulfill their personal directives. The four sub-groups each ran through the exits of the decimated lounging room led by goblin scouts.

Three of the groups went to purge the kingdom of Nvv-Fryyg's reign, slaying all of grr'Shaalg's potential political enemies in the attached chambers. The last of these groups had the duty of sealing off the entrance and preventing any more goblins from entering or escaping into the subterranean depths of the suburb where the harem was located—a place just beyond the caverns of the royal hall. The group would hold the line even against a rescue attempt by Nvv-Fryyg's army; the other teams would reinforce them as they finished their tasks.

A battle group broke through the doors of the rookery in search of the innumerable goblin whelps. None of Nvv-Fryyg's line could be left to survive; they could not be allowed to present a threat to the mutineers. The third group went in search of more rooms such as the one they'd invaded through and repeated the process. The harem contained countless rooms to suit the desires of the king and to house and maintain Nvv-Fryyg's goblin sows.

The largest of the groups, the point team, contained the remaining six Acolytes, Absinthium, and a large contingent of goblin bladesmen. grr'SHaalg and his twin brother tyr-aPt accompanied them as they stalked the doomed king. The two goblin diplomats knew that their talents were of the political sort rather than with weapons; they remained at the center of the group which kept them protected. There was no way out. They would find the king somewhere within the confines of the stinking, underground dwelling.

With all the screaming, Nvv-Fryyg's bodyguards and royal court would undoubtedly surround him for protection; the praetorian guard and goblin magistrates usually accompanied Nvv-Fryyg on these holidays of carnality. The entire chain of command in the underground kingdom would fall with one swift blow and the deep kingdom would be in full submission to the plans of the demon lord. Soon, beh'-tsah would have control of the Babel Heavens, several kingdoms including Jand, and the subterranean hub of all the goblin kingdoms. Each location provided a foothold for beh' tsah's aggressive expansion plans. In due time, hay-lale's entire realm would fall sway to the demonic overlord's wishes.

The assassin teams exited the bloody chamber just as the first of Nvv-Fryyg's guards came to investigate the murderous cacophony echoing through the brothel. They expected no trouble beyond the squabbles of the royal mewling quim and so the pitifully small contingent of warriors brashly sauntered into their slaughter. They did not expect to die the moment they entered, but die they did as they fell to the sickle-bladed kamas that hacked them apart with nary chance to survey the scene.

Absinthium and the main battle group took their company on an immediate route to the central chamber of the habitation. The central room was the banquet hall where the king resided and greeted any guests that might somehow find themselves invited to Nvv-Fryyg's most endeared residence. It was the most likely place where Nvv-Fryyg might be found.

Beyond the main doors of the massacred chamber yawned a large, pillar-dotted expanse that created a fairway. It stretched to the various wings of the brothel, forming elaborate and expansive hallways. As the main group headed towards the central fairway, they immediately encountered resistance.

Three of the six Acolytes branched off, each sprinting different directions to scout for more resistance and probe the defenses that protected the king. The guards would probably move Nvv-Fryyg to the safest place of entrenchment as the dank air filled with the screams and shrieks of goblin sows and their brood who fell under the assassins' blades.

Goblins of both factions clashed; falchion and spear spilled blood on both sides as the arch-mage uttered curses and spells which shook the air around them. Dark magic caused his enemies to burst into flames or opened grievous wounds without physical contact.

The acolytes sprang into action using the support pillars that spanned from floor to ceiling as cover. They darted from behind the pillars to attack with their claw-like kamas and grabbed their unsuspecting victims like trap-spiders ambushing unsuspecting quarry. Surprised members of the praetorian guard shrieked as Luciferian assassins yanked them behind cover and chopped them limb from limb.

An immense wave of goblin defenders continued flowing towards them. Nvv-Fryyg's soldiers, a much larger force, had finally been roused by the air-splitting screams of so many casualties. They charged with confident, reckless abandon, but underestimated the power of the battle-mages who operated with complete indifference to the situation, as if it was mundane. Their cool apathy made them unbelievably scary.

The defending goblins surged towards their oppressors and looked as if they split the forces of the attackers open. A band of Nvv-Fryyg's bodyguards took initiative and charged the opening where Absinthium stood undefended and alone. He allowed a brief smile to crawl across his face and warn the guards that they'd fallen into his trap.

Absinthium screamed a curse and swung his staff with a fierce, smooth motion; his spell projected a wave of sonic destruction before him. The vibrating waves blasted flesh from bone. An entire swath of goblins burst into annihilated chunks of rent flesh as his attackers erupted and fell to the floor as bone and sinew threshed apart.

Immediately following, the acolytes and painted goblins pushed forward in unison, completely dominating the field of battle. Panicked defenders turned and ran for the shadows. The acolytes rewarded the cowards by throwing daggers into their backsides.

Nvv-Fryyg's forces fell back to regroup with their swelling ranks as grr'SHaalg's goblin scouts, pretending to be routed, sprinted past and lured more of the praetorian in to rebuild Nvv-Fryyg's decimated army and encourage them to strike at the Luciferians again.

As the scouts scrambled back to the cover of the pillars, three acolytes stepped out dangling a small wooden box taken from their munitions bearer. The boxes, about a hands length in width, depth, and height, brandished metal spikes protruding in every direction;

they gripped the devices by their chain, not unlike a morning star.

The soldiers of the goblin praetorian snarled at the three men's hubris. With gnashing teeth and drawn weapons they rushed forward, sure that they'd overwhelm them this time.

The trio of acolytes each spun a box over their heads; they buzzed as they cut through the air. As one unit the acolytes hurled them into the thickest throngs of the pursuing goblin army. As each caisson landed, the wielding acolyte shouted his word of power.

Three explosions boomed in rapid succession as the caissons detonated in a fireball of splintering, jagged shrapnel. The blasts gutted the over-pursing cluster of warriors and spun the king's forces into disarray. Bloody, mutilated casualties flinged chaotically through the air, separated from their respective body parts as the wake of each explosion further decimated the remaining forces. The assassins stepped out from the cover of the pillars and quickly dispatched the injured and engaged the panicking remnants.

The dying casualties of the caissons yipped in pain and frustration. Their painted goblin brethren walked among them casually sweeping their falchions back and forth, severing the heads of their wounded adversaries.

In the distance, the second and third battle groups moved through the flickering torchlight and verified that the wholesale slaughter was complete. They branched off in different directions to check every nook and cranny where sneaky goblins might have hidden. The sudden lack of screams and squeals cast a harrowing pall throughout the gallery by stark contrast.

Absinthium and his group approached the large, central chamber; grr'SHaalg quivered with excitement. The saferoom resembled a large, stone box, spanning from floor to ceiling of the brothel. The gigantic, square compartment had doors on all four sides.

Nvv-Fryyg's chamber remained silent and grr'SHaalg imagined the cowering goblin king hiding within, fearful to even breathe lest he give away his position. If he thought they would overlook him and continue the massacre elsewhere, he hoped in vain. Absinthium gave the doors a quick tug and push. He found them firmly locked, as expected.

Absinthium stepped back several paces. What remained of the main group broke up into sub-groups and crouched in front of each door. An Acolyte stood at every immense entry, accompanied by a dozen goblins so that Nvv-Fryyg couldn't escape out another side as they breached an entry on one side. At the main door stood only Absinthium, the remaining Acolytes, and the two goblin diplomats: grr'SHaalg and tyr-aPt. The rest of their bladesmen had been sent to clean up the dead.

The three Acolytes at each side door whirled a chained caisson high; each box sang its ominous tone as it whined and spun grim circles above the heads of their masters. One by one they released the chains and flung a charge box at the massive doors. The spiked and wickedly sharp protrusions stabbed firmly into the wood of the doors and lodged there. The thuds of their impact echoed through the fairway like the footsteps of approaching doom.

Absinthium muttered a crescendoing incantation. A sickly, cracking noise reverberated around them as the main doors gave away. The arch-mage used his supernatural forces to rip them outward and into the fairway. They split apart and flew to either side of the sorcerer. The cowering goblins in the room stood dumbfounded as to what had just happened. Then, as if their instincts kicked in, they scattered and ran to the other three exits of the room.

The Acolytes shouted their words of power and magically ignited their caissons. A set of ectoplasmic explosions incinerated the remaining doors, catching any goblins that tried to flee in a cloud of shrapnel and alchemical flames. Smoldering splinters of burning wood embedded deeply into Nvv-Fryyg's furnishings. The remaining contingent of bodyguards stood in a circle, protecting King Nvv-Fryyg with their bodies. Opposition barred each exit.

Knowing that their end was at hand, the remaining goblin guards surrendered their weapons, casting them down at their clawed feet. At grr'SHaalg's order, they solemnly marched out the rear door to the room and were silently executed leaving the trembling king alone to face his end.

King Nvv-Fryyg sat on the floor, disgraced and humiliated. Under the best of conditions, he was an immensely obese mass of ugly tissues. Purple and blackened, his gnarled visage held none of the presence and power that the dread demon beh'-tsah possessed. Nvv-Fryyg's appearance was one of pathetic disgust and revulsion. A lifetime of gluttonous pursuits of various lusts had left him decrepit in many ways. He could barely move without assistance; he constantly ate if he was not satisfying his other carnal appetites.

He blubbered, begging for his life. Recognizing the Luciferian prophet, he entreated Absinthium, asking why he had been attacked, promising he would fix whatever insults he had caused the mage or the Order if they had somehow heard his harsh words. Nvv-Fryyg babbled about his deal with the Luciferians and invented stories of inflated devotion and loyalty. "We struck a deal, you and I," the King insisted.

"Deal?" Absinthium scoffed with his booming baritone voice. "I made no deal with you, Nvv-Fryyg. You couldn't even grace me with your presence. Get on your feet, worm."

grr'SHaalg and tyr-aPt stepped into view from behind the arch-mage. The goblin king's face fell when he recognized the two of them.

"You two," Nvv-Fryyg accused. "I should have devoured you when you were still young! You were always scheming and plotting."

"Always doing what we were trained for: doing the work of a king so that you could play. Now it is time that the true masters of this kingdom step forward and take their throne," grr'SHaalg snapped.

"You will pay for this! I set you up as a diplomat. I made you who you are. I chose *you*, grr'SHaalg, as my most trusted worker and picked *you* from the litter of my eldest brood. My associates will not stand with this. They will usurp you if you sit on my throne."

"Oh, spare me. Everyone who had any sort of connection to you is already dead," grr'SHaalg toyed with him. "Besides, there are none others fit to rule after my brother and I were satisfied with our invasion. This is what you would do in my situation, that is, if you had any inkling left of how our politics worked."

grr'SHaalg and tyr-aPt walked toward the defeated, corpulent Nvv-Fryyg. Each drew a wavy-bladed kris and a three tined claw that resembled some kind of primitive garden tool.

A runner from the battle group at the harem's entrance reported that no more resistance could come. Everything was dead.

"What excellent news," grr'SHaalg commented, "I always enjoy good reports as I feast!" The goblin stabbed a hooked fork through his sire's carapace; the barbs caught hold of tissue. grr'SHaalg gleefully ripped outward, pulling with it the web-like mesentery sack that bound the fallen king's swollen intestines together; his tube-like organs spilt outward and quivered.

He and his brother fell upon the goblin ruler with weapon-like utensils slashing and gouging. The bulbous portions of Nvv-Fryyg's body easily tore open and attempts to ward off any blows were for naught. Ichor and entrails flowed out of his lacerated, puncture-burst hide.

The shrill screams thrilled his murderers. The strike team looked on grimly as a frenzy of blood and viscera blotted out the King's essence, pooling all of his life into a viscous puddle on the floor. The crunching sounds of his body being devoured signaled that Nvv-Fryyg's overthrow was complete and his body had been consumed by his successor. The ultimate goals of Absinthium and his dread master were coming to fruition.

Absinthium grinned through the blood splatters that decorated his face. Even the kingdoms below the surface became increasingly pliable to the demon's manipulations. Soon everything would all belong to beh'-tsah.

The acolytes watched over the goblinoid "feast of ascension." King Nvv-Fryyg's spine and head tumbled away from the ecstatic meal and rested against Absinthium's foot.

"Save the face!" grr'SHaalg snapped through his bloody maw. "We must make a statement! A symbol to rally the troops around the new throne... a throne that I give to my brother."

Absinthium bent to retrieve the fleshy, heavily jowelled skull which had grown fat with age and comfort. *Yes. A display of power would cause a rally, and a successful assassination is so seldom not part of a perfect plan.*

CHAPTER THIRTEEN

Rashnir and Zeh-Ahbe' traded turns pushing a large handcart as they meandered along the countryside beyond Grinden's outskirts. They'd already traveled far from the encampment as they gathered wood for their fires, but they had further yet to go. They dare not cut much live timber near the city; the townsfolk felt a kind of ownership over it and they dared not stir up any more trouble. Relations had already pushed past the tipping point.

Local firewood supplies had quickly diminished in the grounds nearest their make-shift home. Zeh-Ahbe' and his people were used to foraging for supplies and they already knew some of the easier pieces to collect fallen timber. The Say-awr' had made it a habit of harvesting only the wood that none would miss so that when their tribe moved on they would leave without having left a trace.

Their cart was only half full of smaller logs and they scouted the area for fuel that would be easiest to harvest. They could come back with a small group of workers in the near future and build their stockpile out of larger timber cuttings then.

"I don't know that we will really need much heavy stock," Zeh-Ahbe' noted, reminding Rashnir of their pending trip. "And it certainly seems that the forces in Grinden want to push us out even further beyond the borders."

Rashnir nodded his assent. But everyone already knew the townsfolks' disposition and Kevin hadn't finished his plans yet for an eventual relocation.

"Not that I have a problem with a more remote location," Zeh-Ahbe' continued. "When we were still Kil-yaw' we always seemed to be on the move, never stopping." He looked towards the distant copse of trees wistfully.

"Did you ever feel compelled to slow down... stop... put down roots?" Rashnir's thoughts turned back to his earlier days, the time before Kevin, before Harmarty's murder, before Kelsa was lost.

"No," Zeh-Ahbe' laughed. "It has never been our way. Have you?" He noticed the glower on his friend's face.

"Just once." Rashnir frowned. "That was a long time ago." He ended the conversation and they traveled in silence for a few minutes longer. Rashnir didn't like the melancholy chord that had lodged in his mood. He decided to change it and struck out in song as they pushed the cart along. Soon, they were both in merry spirits again, singing a common tavern song.

***

Absinthium finished drawing the circle on the floor and tossed the chalk away. It skittered across the worn shale and into the fire the mage had built just beyond the circle. The eager flames danced brightly in the dark tunnels that branched far away from Under-Grinden, the goblin city. The pyre illuminated grr'SHaalg and tyr-aPt's gory feast just behind him, painting it with hellish tones.

The mage looked at his chief acolyte and wordlessly nodded to the bloody leakage escaping the feast in viscous rivulets. The hooded acolyte dragged his foot across the ground and smeared the trail, redirecting it away from the magic sigil his master had drawn. As a trained arcanist, the acolyte knew that the circle must not be contaminated during the communion.

Sitting cross-legged in the center, Absinthium stared into the fire, mumbling a mantra of praises to his dark lord until his pupils contracted fully. Up from the logs, the flames twisted and bent into the shape of the demon over-lord beh'-tsah. The air within the circle crackled with energy and made the hairs on the wizard's arms and neck slowly rise on a tide of gooseflesh.

You were not scheduled to contact me. His eyes narrowed to a look somewhere between judgment and concern. *Does all go according to plan or have these acolytes failed in their tasks against Nvv-Fryyg's complacent bodyguards?*

"No," Absinthium smiled and smoothed the hair on his neck. "All went perfect and according to plan. I contacted you in the aftermath of such a minor victory and with an eye to a greater prize."

The demon regarded his servant curiously. He beckoned for him to proceed.

"We are so close to these krist-chins this very moment, veiled from their sight just below ground. We saw the loyal residents of Grinden rejoice at the sacrifice we made from one of those cultists. Bloodlust is contagious; it rallies men and sways the undecided."

Such as it was, those forsaken one's sacrifices are the vilest of flavors. What is it that you are suggesting?

"An overt display of power. We stand in the shadows near their homes, well equipped and ready to assassinate their leaders. We could make an example of this festering religion swiftly and decisively. The pieces are in place, it could be easily accomplished."

The demon stroked his chin thoughtfully.

You would find it difficult to proceed if this evangelizer's body guards are by his side. They should not be underestimated. But discouragement is an equally powerful tool against our enemy as much as the fervor inspired in our own by adversaries' heads mounted on pikes.

"So, shall we proceed?"

There is something more coming. I have foreseen a powerful weapon coming to our enemy. It is the next step in our private war. A king would not send out warriors ill-equipped. Stalk your prey carefully, arch-mage. It is a promising plan, albeit impromptu. If you see the chance to act, then do so.

The beast's flaming eidolon summoned twelve smaller tongues of fire. Each melded into the shape of an acolyte and he regarded them thoughtfully.

Test your minions here. But should they falter, do not let your failure be known. If you succeed, spread their fame. beh'-tsah grinned a wicked, toothy smile. Bring me a trophy worthy of displaying or devouring.

Absinthium nodded. "For your glory, lord."

The flames shrank back to their original size and form and the mage rose and beckoned to his own. "The day is not yet done, acolytes. Grander prizes await than..." he motioned to Nvv-Fryyg's shredded remains, mildly disgusted, "...this."

The mage beckoned to his goblin counterparts. "I need you to bring my acolytes your fastest skolaxis. I have a mission for them in Grinden."

***

High above the hill country, the mountains trembled. A tremor of power, a premonition and portent of things to come radiated the very molecules of the air. A spirit quake.

The minor movement sent a tingle up the back of the watcher. Something important had finally developed worthy of his gaze.

He chastised himself momentarily as he spun the wheels of the ancient machine and rotated the giant telescope around its wide berth where it remained firmly nestled within a brick parapet, jutting off of the Babel Tower which spiraled upwards from the Briganik Mountains. He had felt the tremor much earlier. The preacher and his angelic bodyguards had not entered the realm unnoticed; the watcher saw them come in, but thought they lacked credibility. *What impact could one human and his guards have in the face of hay-lale's thoroughly fallen creation?*

Even the Watcher had to take precautions against the powerful forces at work in this realm. He'd hidden himself with spells far older than the Gathering. From his secret room he watched the Dragon Impervious hatch and nearly topple the first demonic government. The watcher saw the ancient vampire lords spawn their own brood in the children of the dust and wage war against the lupines; he saw them bury their secret golems and plot against the demons.

Even when the elf, Dri'Bu, departed for the company of the preacher, he had not entertained the thought of their movement altering the course of this existence; the Watcher had been learning and observing far prior to that elf scholar's interest in things—before Dri'Bu had even had his first real observation. As he focused his machine in to watch the area around Grinden, the Watcher's mind changed.

Maybe these are the ones whom I've waited for. Perhaps this is my opportunity!

The buzzing sensation in the air informed his soul. He knew that everything was about to change. Fallen creation had arrived at the cusp of an important new season.

Part of the Watcher could smell it: the subtle scent of smoke. *Fire is coming.*

His interest had certainly piqued. Little else warranted his attention, and so he watched.

***

"Right there," Rashnir pointed. "Don't you see it?"

"The horses?" Zeh-Ahbe' ventured.

"No, just beyond the horses. It's a goblin hole," Rashnir pointed out.

Zeh-Ahbe' stared at the distant landscape. Eleven horses stood near the trees to which they were tethered. A rocky outcropping with a sunken cleft hid partly within the copse of dead trees which rose tall beyond the soil. Stripped of bark and leaf, it was that sort of lumber which attracted the two scavengers and their handcart.

"Firstly," Zeh-Ahbe' said, "I'm impressed you can identify a goblin hole at such a distance. Secondly, I'm not sure why you think that anything ahead is out of the ordinary." He continued pushing the cart onward, not understanding why his friend had been set on high alert.

"You really don't get it?"

Zeh-Ahbe' shook his head negatively.

"I thought werewolves were supposed to have heightened senses, or natural intuition or something about things like this," Rashnir jested.

Feigning indignation, Zeh-Ahbe' said, "It might be another story if I was still a werewolf, but I'm not entirely sure that you've got a solid grasp on the exact capabilities of my folk."

"Fair enough," Rashnir said, pointing again to the horses as they drew closer. "Can you tell me the last time you ever saw a goblin riding horseback?"

Zeh-Ahbe' nodded and glanced into the cart, reassured that the axe was still where he'd left it. "Okay. Now I'm feeling some intuition, or whatever it was you were talking about."

They approached the grassy glade in front of the wooded area with a sense of trepidation. They walked with terse breaths, waiting for the tension to break loose, for good or bad, at any moment. Rashnir constantly scanned the area from the corners of his eyes. He spotted a cluster of eyes watching them from the dark hole leading to the subterranean realm.

Rashnir put a hand on his friend's chest to stop him. Several sets of goblin children watched, creeping in the dark.

"You see them?"

"Yup. Too young to know any better... haven't learned stealth yet?"

"No. I don't think that's it," Rashnir commented, thinking though his thoughts. "They are curious of something... they're waiting to be entertained."

"They've maybe never seen a surface dweller before?"

"Think again. Remember the horses? Something, someone has their attention."

One of the pairs of eyes darted left.

"Look out!" Rashnir yelled, pushing Zeh-Ahbe' out of the way of a cloaked assassin that seemed to spring out of nowhere.

The black-clad slayer moved fast—highly trained! Rashnir ducked a wickedly sharp hook-blade and whirled around with a wild haymaker that his enemy slipped. The shrouded figure slunk a step backwards to size up the legendary ranger.

"I always thought you'd be somehow... more?" The menacing figure's low voice sounded more like an animal growl than a man's voice. It carried a certain truculent tone, indicating this encounter would not end without bloodshed.

Suddenly the attacker's head rocked backwards as a log smashed him in the face. His hood flung back to reveal pasty, pale skin, reddened eyes and hair like corn silk. Zeh-Ahbe' grinned, bent over the cart, grabbing next at the hand axe.

The assassin curled his busted lip in a sneer and licked away the blood that had begun to trickle from his nose. He pulled his hood down again to shield against the vicious rays of light. "Of course you must fight! There is still a beast inside of you... but you cannot defeat the acolytes!" he assumed a ready position and brandished his kamas.

Rashnir caught sight of the other ten acolytes that encircled them, each clad in a similar robe and carrying identical weapons. "I don't know who you are, but I don't think you understand who I've become."

The acolyte with the voice pointed an accusatory finger at him. "We know exactly what you are: Rashnir the fatherless." The warriors took cautious steps forward, slowly closing the gap. "Worshipper of the false God: the one defeated by hay-lale's mighty hands. You are a defenseless animal, caged by a powerless deity."

Rashnir leveled his eyes on the speaker and furrowed his brow. "You obviously know nothing about my God!"

The acolyte snarled and charged at him. A cerulean blade flashed to life in Rashnir's hands, flaming in brilliant blue. He slashed a frantic blow to counter the acolyte's hubris; the assassin's red eyes widened in surprise and he dove to the side to avoid the mystic edge.

Rolling to a crouch, he darted forward again, ready for the blade this time. He tried to bat the blade aside and catch the ranger with his offhanded kama. His first weapon disintegrated on contact with the holy fire.

Rashnir whirled his blade around again in a tight spin. Catching the second kama, he severed blade from handle. The enemy's poise evaporated and Rashnir caught him in the midsection with a knee. As quickly as his blade had burst into existence it disappeared; freehanded, Rashnir caught the exposed jaw with a furious uppercut. The warrior staggered backwards and three more stormed forward to take his place.

Rashnir ducked and rolled, avoiding the keen blades of his adversaries, slipping around each swing as if the entire engagement was a deadly dance. Zeh-Ahbe' used the axe to block blows as he scrambled around the edge of the cart, trying to keep the two hooded fighters who attacked him as far away as possible. Spotting his friend's troubles Rashnir called his blade to hand again and slashed his sword through the weapons of the three pressing in against him in a whirlwind like move.

Those three backed off while Rashnir jumped in to defend his friend. They melted into the background and regrouped with their circle.

"If you don't uncage the beast inside of you, there is no way you will overcome. If you do not relent, we *will* kill your friend!"

Rashnir only then heard the low, murmuring chant of those acolytes not attacking. They were spell-casters, too! No doubt, they tried projecting some dark incantation upon them.

"Let the monster take over! Forsake your allegiance to this Yahweh and embrace the raw power of your heritage!"

Rashnir could feel the darkness rising up from his gut. He stuffed the rage down inside, the lust for blood, the fulfillment of triumphing over his enemy in a life-and death struggle. "I am in control! I would never forsake my vow! You misjudge me," he declared.

The acolyte laughed. His chortle resonated with irony even as the other acolytes continued their repetitive mantra.

"I… I don't think… that they are talking to… you!" Zeh-Ahbe' groaned.

Rashnir spotted his friend. Zeh-Ahbe' hunched against the cart, trembling. His eyes had contracted and shifted gold; they resembled an animal's more than any man's. His body pulsed, parts shifting to a lupine form, bulging with muscle, but then quickly shifted back.

"No! I have forsaken this!" Zeh-Ahbe' croaked behind growing incisors.

331

Holding his flaming sword at the ready, Rashnir wasn't quite sure how to help his friend. A shadow suddenly fell upon the circle and then disappeared: a giant wyvern circled them like a buzzard about to feed on carcasses—another acolyte rode upon it!

"Strike us down! Save your friend! Embrace the beast and break your bonds!"

Rashnir ran to the unarmed enchanter, sword held high and hungry. He stopped just short of striking down the unarmed man.

"No!" Zeh-Ahbe' yelled. His grasp had clawed fingernail marks across the boards of the cart. "Don't *you* become the beast in my place!"

The ranger turned to regard his friend who began to finally get his impulses under control. He'd shrunk down again from an almost fully transformed state. He understood that this was a battle Zeh-Ahbe' had to face, squaring off against his own temptations. Rashnir returned to his friend's side and glared at the hooded enchanter. The palpable sense of evil that wafted off him reeked of Absinthium's influence.

As the last of Zeh-Ahbe's bulging muscles returned to normal, the battle-mage howled. All twelve of the acolytes descended upon the two. They streaked to their prey like eagles.

Zeh-Ahbe' dove under the cart and somersaulted. He came out the other side as the acolytes slashed through the air he'd occupied only moments previous. Twisting through the roll, he used the axe to counter another's blow.

Rashnir hacked through the kamas of the nearby acolytes who pressed him hard. They'd already considered their weapons forfeit and anticipated their destruction, countering with vicious punches and kicks as the ranger used the azure blade to absorb the more lethal blows.

He dismembered a sickle-head from the handle of the most threatening of the hook-blades and threw his own blow. A brutal elbow caught him in the nose and Rashnir backpedaled, swinging the sword to keep his adversaries at bay. He foresaw the sliding kick meant to flatten him to his back and sidestepped just in time. Suddenly, the wyvern was upon him, swooping in from the sky!

It snatched at him with its two powerful feet. Rashnir tucked and rolled, slipping just below the poisonous talons. The scaly beast crashed against the cart, knocking it over again while it took to the sky as Zeh-Ahbe' scrambled away from the toppling mess of lumber.

Rashnir whirled around and used the blade to burn through the flurry of edged throwing spades an acolyte hurled at them. He stretched to catch the last one which the acolyte flung wide in order to strike Zeh-Ahbe'.

Zeh-Ahbe' nodded to Rashnir when they locked eyes. He wordlessly thanked him.

Rashnir rushed forward and pressed for the last acolyte who still had a weapon. The others with broken weapons had each sunk to their knees, resuming their mantra, daring Rashnir to strike any of them while they sat defenseless.

The remaining acolyte danced in and out of Rashnir's offensive maneuvers, trying to draw him into another over-extending attack with subtle feints. Bobbing back and forth, the assassin took care to not lose his own weapons in an over-eager pursuit.

A wyvern shaped shadow fell again as the cloaked assailant worked in tandem with it. Rashnir noticed the acolyte timing his strikes; he feinted and changed up his movements, drew an attack, and slashed through the assassin's weapons, disarming him but leaving himself open to attack from the winged reptile. The wyvern snatched Rashnir up as he struggled

Luckily, the reptile's poisonous barbs missed his flesh. Rashnir hacked at the gripping appendage, severing its grasp before it could gain much altitude.

He tumbled to the ground while the beast shrieked, circling around in rage. The rider barely maintained control of the beast as the wyvern's hackles rose to the challenge. It didn't understand why such a small creature proved so difficult to apprehend.

It tucked its wings and flew at him like a shot! Rashnir led with his blade, swinging a wide arc, trying to sever the wings from the wyvern's serpentine body.

The crafty beast flapped its wingspan out full at the last second, nearly braking to a complete halt as an air buffet stalled the rapid descent. Rashnir's slash cut only through the air! And with another powerful beat of the creature's wings it shot skyward as it snatched up its prey in one smooth move.

This time the calculated element of surprise belonged to the beast. It squeezed the human and unretracted the septic barb from its dewclaw.

Rashnir reacted just in time to burn the poisonous pincer off before it could render him limp. But the winged beast still had him in its grasp and the ground shrank ever distant; a fall at this height would kill him.

Zeh-Ahbe' stared at his friend who'd been snatched up in but a heartbeat and blinked. Zeh-Ahbe' apprehensively scanned the circle of acolytes which encompassed him.

The first of them to attack spun some kind of wooden box on a chain. It whirred with a loud droning sound as it spun. The remainder of the acolytes sat on their knees, again chanting.

Feeling their magic course around him, Zeh-Ahbe' glared at them each in turn. Fully in control of his body, despite their efforts, he retorted, "I have made my choice already and I will live or die by it! You have no power, here."

High above, Rashnir pulled an arm free and managed to snatch a loose strap from the winged mount's barding. He tugged the saddle strap taught and grabbed it in his teeth. Then, with his blazing sword, he severed the other leg that grappled him.

The wyvern screeched and Rashnir fell. His body jerked against the leather bonds as the severed limb tumbled downward. Rashnir's sword dissipated and with both hands free, he clung to the saddle straps for dear life. The creature tried to shake him. It thrashed violently, nearly bucking off the acolyte rider who could no longer control the pained creature.

Snarling with foamy rage, it yanked one of its reins free, giving the wyvern enough leeway to reach its serpent-like head back and snap at Rashnir. Dangling perilously, he twisted his body to avoid the snapping jaws.

The rider yanked furiously on the remaining rein, pulling the creature's head forward as he vied with it for some semblance of control. Its head reared back, but smashed momentarily against a wing with the loud cracking noise of a snapped tendon. The reptile howled and slid into an angular drift, limping on its weak side.

The wounded limb suddenly gave out and the wyvern plummeted from the sky in a flurry of collapsing wings. It writhed and twisted as it tumbled a circular arc downward, still trying to catch Rashnir in its hungry jaws.

As it rolled through the pull of gravity the warrior clambered across the beast and alongside the acolyte who clung to rein and saddle. The gap between ground and sky closed at terminal velocity; reptilian wings flashed wide and the wyvern pulled out of the fall, swooping just above the treetops but still limping fiercely. The exhausted creature surrendered control back to the acolyte pilot.

They skimmed the leaves of the canopy's foliage as they turned back towards the circle of acolytes and the toppled hand cart. The wyvern rider wrapped his hands around the rein and his other arm around Rashnir's neck and squeezed, trying to choke him out.

Rashnir flung his head back, head-butting the acolyte over and over until his hold loosened. The ranger reached a freehand back and pulled his dizzied opponent forward so that he couldn't use the stirrups for leverage. The rider tumbled over the wyvern's jointed clavicle and fell.

The wyvern's snout yanked downward as the reins tied to the acolyte's wrist snapped tight and pulled the beast's head into the trees. It smashed against the branches and dumped the acolyte. Finally free, it lurched and rolled, streaking through the sky.

Rashnir clung to the saddle as he and the beast shot towards Zeh-Ahbe' at breakneck speeds. He had no control over the beast's trajectory and his friend stared with wide eyes. Rashnir dove off, hitting the ground with a roll to break the fall.

Zeh-Ahbe' ducked to the dirt as the monster crashed through his airspace and broke itself against the handcart with a sickening pop. Rashnir tumbled to a skidding stop right next to his friend. They leapt to their feet expecting an attack, but the acolytes had disappeared.

The two Christians turned to each other bewildered and wild-eyed and suddenly burst out laughing—giddy at the intense rush of adrenaline and confused as to what exactly happened. "I can't believe they didn't attack you!" Rashnir exclaimed, checking himself for broken bones. "They outnumbered you eleven to one!"

Finally, they turned to the mangled beast which lay broken and burst open against the pile of useless lumber that had once been a large handcart. A wooden box protruding spikes and wicked pieces of shrapnel stuck against the busted cart. Its rusty spikes lodged it firmly into the wood and its chain still dangled.

"A caisson!" Rashnir yelled with wide eyes. He grabbed Zeh-Ahbe'. "Run!"

They bolted away from it as fast as they could. It exploded a split second later; the concussive force knocked them to the ground, but they'd managed to get beyond the range of the serious damage.

"How did you know it would do that?" Zeh-Ahbe' asked, awestruck in the dirt.

"Mind had a couple of them in his armory—he collected obscure and rare weapons. Nasty things."

Zeh-Ahbe' nodded. "I understand... but what is a Mind?"

Rashnir chuckled and patted his friend on the shoulder. "I'll tell you the story on the way back."

They rose to their feet and dusted themselves off. Nothing remained of their wagon except flaming rubble, burnt reptile meat, and oily black smoke that caked anything nearby with heavy, sticky grease from the nasty, burning wyvern entrails.

Startling them, a mythic beast call echoed in the distance. A gryphon took flight above the trees. It was difficult at this distance, but Rashnir was fairly certain he spotted Absinthium seated atop it. The creature flew north, safely away from either them or the ones they cared for in the Christian encampment.

"What in the realms just happened here?" Zeh-Ahbe' wondered aloud.

"I've got a bad feeling that this was just a tipping point in a much larger war."

Epilogue

Rashnir and Zeh-Ahbe' walked back towards their camp at a leisurely pace. Each nursed slight limps and burns from the engagement with the shadowy, black-clad assassins.

They hadn't killed any, to their knowledge. Even the pilot had seemed able to break his fall within the trees and bracken and they hadn't found any bodies when they'd gone to check.

"We are lucky we have only bruises and scrapes," Rashnir said. "I'm quite certain that Absinthium watched the attack from the distance."

The former werewolf nodded. "I think you are right, my friend. Only, I fear that the next encounter with them will be a far more fatal encounter."

"And there will certainly *be* another conflict. One does not attain the rank of arch-mage by allowing your enemies to remain at large."

They walked a ways further. Zeh-Ahbe's face fell sullen; he kicked a rock.

Rashnir clapped a hand on his brother's shoulder. He intuitively understood what thoughts occupied Zeh-Ahbe's mind. "The beast is contained. You passed the trial, the temptation to go back—even for good reasons."

Zeh-Ahbe' sighed heavily. Another long pause. "Do you ever miss it? The power, the freedom?"

Rashnir flexed his hands and looked down at them. They no longer bore the scars that the wicked king had branded him with. They were perfect, pure.

"I did. Every day I did. But then our God gave me back something better." He slapped his friend's back again. "Give it time. Something better is coming your way; you've proven yourself stronger than even I, I think. After all, I succumbed to the temptation and you did not."

Zeh-Ahbe' looked at him questioningly.

"Yes. Five minutes after meeting Kevin, Jorge, and Kyrius, I took a blade from them and murdered King Harmarty. You? You did not falter. I didn't even pause to listen to reason and Truth until my hatred was satisfied. You, my friend, are the stronger one."

Nodding, Zeh-Ahbe' seemed to brighten. "You really think something better is coming?"

Rashnir nodded. "Yes. I do—although something better has already come." His voice trailed off. "But also something far worse is on its way," he whispered under his breath.

***

Kevin stood on the hilltop, arms spread wide. He turned a slow and lazy circle, surveying the land. He could see it all! Every scrap of land from the spires of the mythic western gate to the rocky cliffs of the furthest east shore was under his purview.

And yet, Kevin could not see all. He could only see what he had been shown, and this realization suddenly struck him. *This is not real. It is a vision of some kind!*

Suddenly, the sky in the east erupted in flames. Fire shot from the soil with wrathful vehemence. People screamed and animals fled, but the malevolent firestorm rolled across the land, spreading west like a pyrotechnic tsunami.

His own people, the folks of Grinden who had become a fledgling flock to him cried out in anguish as the blaze arose around them. "Remember the mission!" they screamed as the heat blackened their bones and turned them to ash.

Tearfully, Kevin watched them surrender their own spirits. They flashed like blue lights, winking away like shooting stars as they flew almost instantaneously across the realm, finding their way to the western gate where they exited this forsaken plane of existence for a better one as the throes of death ejected soul from body.

Suddenly opening his eyes, Kevin gasped for air. His hair had matted with perspiration during the vision. He rose to his feet and paced for a few moments, trying to air out his sweaty clothes.

He looked at the maps of the lands he'd purchased on his very first day in this forgotten realm. *The mission... we have to find the hidden tribe of believers founded by the angel Karoz... maybe we'll find Karoz, even?*

Kevin bit his lip. He didn't understand why they were needed to complete this task unless something foul had befallen the angel and the community. He couldn't figure that part out, but he knew that they would have to leave the area before long.

Soon. We will have to depart very soon. But first, we need to know what direction to go. Oh Lord, show me. But Kevin couldn't find the answer he searched for. He only had a sense of peace that his course remained true, accompanied by a burning desire to accomplish his holy task. Still, he had no heading.

"I'll have direction soon enough," he encouraged himself. It felt good to hear it in his own ears, even if only in his own voice. "God will make the next step apparent before I must take it."

He scanned the map again. *But I really wish I could see the whole plan mapped out first.*

***

Flipping a lens on the giant, telescopic contraption, wheels ground and a giant gear turn slightly overhead, exerting pressure upon the caged moblogs bound within the machine as a power source. The view shifted for The Watcher as the magic inherent in the creatures enabled the device's view to penetrate the layers of shale, stone, and bedrock. He looked deeper into the earth, noting the changes in the subterranean kingdoms. Nvv-Fryyg fell to tyr-aPt. GliiK'twah from wRuo-Wo met with raoRk of AblarRd which made the viewer grin slyly. He knew that none of their scheming would ever surmount the crafty grr'Shaalg.

He flipped another lense and his gaze pierced even deeper, delving far beyond the realms that any other knew of. Not even the Gathering remembered Tartarus, although they often harnessed the power of its echoing corridors without ever questioning the source of such foundational magics.

Fools, he thought. *They never question, and never remember. It's no wonder these were the ones so easily deceived by hay-lale'.* He scanned the trapped beings, each one hanging by eldritch chains. The Watcher smiled; his contingency plan remained a viable one. *So long as the foundations of this kakos realm remain undiscovered by evil forces...* he mused. *I cannot be counted among the evil ones,* he assured himself.

Pressure released and the gear returned as he untoggled the great lenses. The moblogs screeched as the pressure against their bodies relieved.

Retrieving a parchment and his inkwell, the Watcher penned an eloquent letter. Given long enough, he'd formed many potential plans and contingencies should circumstances ever warrant them. He tied the scroll to a raven and wished that he'd had a pair of linked qâsamai communication stones. He sighed and released the bird.

The Watcher wrapped himself in his bright, iridescent cloak and identified what belongings he needed for travel as he looked around the room. How long since he'd left this room? It had been centuries since he'd walked upon land. His gaze scanned the stone floor; his feet had worn dark grooves into it over the millennia. Long had he observed significant events from his post. He'd been a watcher since before the Gathering formed— since before the flood which severed the realms beyond the western gate.

His observations and senses informed him that time drew ever short. The end—the great conflagration that would consume this forsaken reality—was on its way. The spark which ignited it, he knew, was only moments from being lit—in truth, that same spark had already set foot in his realm.

The Watcher gathered those few things he would need. He would travel overland to meet this Kevin. They would parley, and then The Watcher would finally know the answer to his question, the question which could not be satisfied through millennia he'd spent in surveillance and reflection.

If the answer was as he *hoped*, The Watcher would begin his journey home. If it was as he feared, then he would light the very fires of damnation himself and watch them burn for an eternity.

THE END

APPENDIX A

Dramatis Personae

The Christians:
  (Surviving Key Members)

Kevin	Ersha
Rashnir	Gans
Jibbin	Thim
Jorge*	Thaadim
(pronounced Hoarj)	Erki
Kyrius*	Katerna
(pronounced Kie-Rees)	Kadoz
Zeh-Ahbe'	Naphta
Rah'-be	Dri'Bu**
Sil-tarn	Minstra***
Nipanka	Jaker***
Drowdan	
Rondhale	
Werthen	

      (* angel)
      (** ekthro)
      (*** undecided)

The Luciferian Alliances:
    Absinthium
    grr'Shaalg** (pronounced Gir-shawlg)
    tyr-aPt** (pronounced tear-apt)
    Prock*
    Wynn
    Pinchôt
    Shimza the Greater
    Jandul
    Krimko

Zilke

Dyule

(* captured)

(** ekthro)

The Demons:

[† demon seated on the Gathering]

hay-lale' – deception (Lucifer, Satan)

meh'-red – (previous Gathering leader, slain by beh'-tsah)

beh'-tsah – bitterness †

exaporeh'-omahee – despondency †

raw-tsakh' – murder †

zaw-lal' – glutton, worthless †

gaw-law' –naked †

shik-kore' –drunkard †

makh-al-o'-keth -division †

tah-av-aw' –greedily lusting †

gay-ooth' –pride †

keh'-sem –witchcraft †

peh'-shah –revolt, rebellion †

sheh'-ker –untruthful †

kes-eel' –stupid, fool †

The Werewolves:

Zeh-Ahbe' (Say-awr')

Rah'-be (Say-awr')

Sil-tarn (Say-awr')

Raz-aphf (Say-awr')

Mil-khaw-mah' (Kaw-bade')

Sehkel-saykel (Ahee-sthay-tay'-ree-on)

Sim-khaw' (Zaw-nawb')

Khad-dood' (Tsip-po'-ren)

Appendix B
Key Terms

Lexicon

'ãbêdâh – (pronounced hay-bee-dah) Luciferians weapon protection serum, magic potion

Acolyte – mindless devotees, assassin disciples of Absinthium

anakim - also called the "sons of Anak" these men are giants

caisson – a small wooden box with filled with shrapnel and protruding spikes, contains some form of ignition (explosives or magical)

ceroscopy – a divination where the user observes wax drips falling into water

ekthro – term for all sentient beings (all nonhumans) created by Lucifer

Gathering – the governing body of demonic activity that was established after a time of war that followed the great flood; this body oversees the Luciferian religion.

kama – a sickle-type weapon like a miniature scythe, wielded by the Acolytes.

kil-yaw' – the governing body of werewolf clans

Logos – the word of the Lord

lupine – the altered beast form of the werewolves

scald – magical ancient amulet, a devotee takes it in hand when red hot to burn a mark of allegiance upon themselves, gaining shapeshifting powers

to-ay-baw' – cursed, excommunicated from the kil-yaw'

toqeph – staff of power, usually magically imbued

qâsam (qâsamai) – a magically linked seeing stone

The Kil-yaw'

Shaw-than' – urine
(to-ay-baw')
Say-awr' – hair
(to-ay-baw')
Zaw-nawb' – tail
Ore – hide
Tsip-po'-ren – claw

Shane' – fang
Dawm – blood
Eh'-tsem – bone
Gheed – sinew
Kaw-bade' – viscera/internals
Ahee-sthay-tay'-ree-on –
senses

Appendix C

Geography of continents and mentioned countries

Continent 1:

Jeena- Very little fresh water is present here. It is flanked by ocean and wasteland, buffered by mountains. Here, people obey a strict code of honor and discipline.

Continent 2:

Briganik- This country is very feudal. Monarchy Anakin (sons of Anak: giants) live on the western half; the eastern half is low mountains. The mountains of Briganik are home to the Temple of Light, also called the Monastery of Light, and the first Babel tower.

Zipha- This country is basically closed off. It is ruled by tyrannical, trollish ekthro. It deals primarily in slaves and has a heavy military, run and policed by orcs and half-ogres. Also home to a rogue band of humans.

Jand- Allied with Ninda, it is a monarchy. Western Jand lives in constant fear of abduction by orcs and their troll masters for their slave trade; many of these slaves are sold in Briganik. Jand's commerce and agriculture is based mostly on its large system of forests and mountain/hills. Much of its produce is gathered from the forests or can grow in hilly/mountainous areas or on vines. Goblin kingdom of the southeastern region is located just under the mountains of Arnak, north of Capital City.

Ninda- Allied with Jand, aristocrats control their own lands and make up a council which democratically dictates rule. The country is mostly flatland and primarily agricultural, doing a great deal of business in its ag trade.

Ninda and Gleend were once a single monarchy, until Nindan nobles rebelled and formed their own country.

Lol- Composed of mining communities, it is rich in various metals. The terrain is almost entirely made of rocky badlands.

Gleend- A monarchy north of Ninda, Gleend has a large mixture of the races, (moreso than any other country,) and contains a working social system combining elves, dwarves, men etc. It is run by a human king, though he has advisors from each sentient group. King is revered as the most wise anywhere (has a mild case of downsyndrome and thus sees things much differently. His handicap is not enough of a hindrance to make him easily manipulated, and is looked upon as a gift. The capital city of Xorst.

Mankra- Composed primarily of thieves and warlords, Mankra is broken up into districts owned by warring factions. These constantly try to expand their territory, fighting each other, and sometimes their neighbors. They are subject to an over-warlord who rules the country; tribes pay him a yearly tribute, etc.

Continent 3:

Very few human settlements exist in this region; those that exist are aboriginal in nature, jungle dwellers. The people here have been twisted through occult magics and many are cyclopses. Their children are born as men but wear a brace that off-centers one of their eyes as they develop; the other eye is later plucked out. Many of these people are cannibals. It is often known as the Land of Nod.

The Vampire aristocracy lives among the mountain peaks. Other, subordinate vampire sects live abroad.

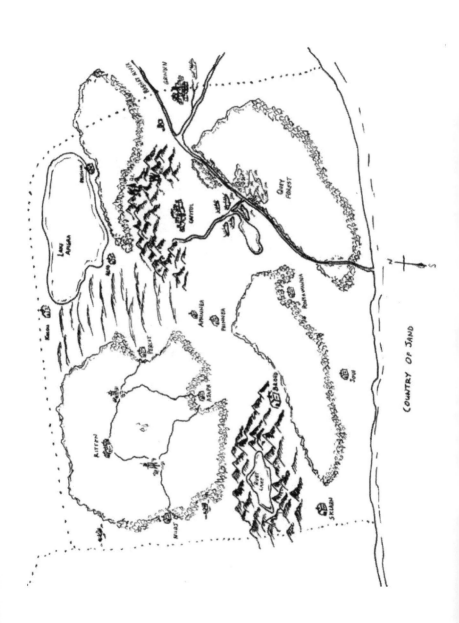

Dear reader,

Thank you for reading my book. If you enjoyed it, won't you please take a moment to leave me a review at your favorite retailer and share this title with your friends on social media? Discoverability is the lifeblood of success for authors and we can't continue our craft without your help!

I also hope you will continue the story through and read the second and third parts (and beyond) of The Kakos Realm! I can promise you that the action increases and intensifies—Grinden Proselyte is the first book, but it was originally written as the first part of a 200,000 word mythopoeic tale which was far too large for a single volume. That said, we haven't even hit the story's climax yet—check out Rise of the Dragon Impervious and then move on to Death Upon the Fields of Splendor.

This world is kakos. None of the characters are safe.

Thanks for reading and sharing!

Christopher D Schmitz

CHRISTOPHER D. SCHMITZ

About the author:

Christopher D Schmitz is an author of fiction and nonfiction as well as a regular blogger. He lives with his family in Minnesota where they lead insanely active lives.

Following the completion of his first fantasy novel in the early 2000s, he began to work on lots of short fiction in order to refine his skills and went on to publish many pieces from 1,000-15,000 words in a variety of genres and in a number of venues. Putting fiction away for a while, he pursued post-graduate work where he received a new appreciation for nonfiction, but returned to his love for fiction with a greater commitment than ever.

In addition to writing and working with at-risk youth he is known known to play guitar (he played and sang in a rock band for several years,) or be found playing his bagpipes in seemingly random places. His wife thinks he's a prima-donna like that.

Discover other titles by Christopher D Schmitz

The Last Black Eye of Antigo Vale

Burning the God of Thunder

Piano of the Damned

Shadows of a Superhero

The TGSPGoSSP 2-Part Trilogy

Dekker's Dozen: A Waxing Arbolean Moon

Dekker's Dozen: The Last Watchmen

Why Your Pastor Left

John: In the John

Wolf of the Tesseract

The Kakos Realm: Grinden Proselyte

The Kakos Realm: Rise of the Dragon Impervious

The Kakos Realm: Death Upon the Fields of Splendor

Please Visit
www.authorchristopherdschmitz.com
Sign-up on the mailing list for exclusives and extras

other ways to connect with me:
Follow me on Twitter: https://twitter.com/cylonbagpiper

Follow me on Goodreads:
www.goodreads.com/author/show/129258.Christopher_Schmitz

Like/Friend me on Facebook:
https://www.facebook.com/authorchristopherdschmitz
or
https://www.facebook.com/christopher.schmitz.509

Subscribe to my blog:
https://authorchristopherdschmitz.wordpress.com

Favorite me at Smashwords:
www.smashwords.com/profile/view/authorchristopherdschmitz

Made in the USA
Columbia, SC
11 August 2019